Justin "Matts" Matthews is good at a lot of things: Rubik's Cubes, playing guitar, herding cattle, and most importantly for his career in the NHL, hockey. He's not good at human interactions or social cues, especially when it comes to women. This deficiency is an annoyance rather than a problem, right up until he meets Sydney Warren. If it's not love at first sight, it's sure something close.

Sydney Warren, frontwoman for up-and-coming rock band Right Red Hand, is fierce, driven, and she doesn't do relationships. Being an out trans woman in the music industry is more than enough pressure—a romantic entanglement would be added stress she doesn't need. A romantic entanglement with a professional hockey player who, to all accounts, is only just learning to be an ally is definitely not what she needs. And yet.

After a chance encounter, Matts and Sydney become unlikely friends. However, in the stolen moments of their busy schedules—late-night phone calls between NHL games and concert tour dates—they start to question if maybe "friendship" isn't so apt a description for whatever this is between them.

But can they overcome the outside pressures from family and media that would rather their relationship end before it has a chance to start?

FREE FROM FALLING

THE BREAKAWAY SERIES, BOOK FOUR

E.L. MASSEY

A NineStar Press Publication
www.ninestarpress.com

Free from Falling

© 2024 E.L. Massey
Cover Art © 2024 JICK (@jickdraws)
Editor: Elizabetta McKay

First Edition, December 2024

ISBN: 978-1-64890-823-1

Also available in eBook, ISBN: 978-1-64890-824-8

CONTENT WARNING:
This book contains fade-to-black sexual content, which may only be suitable for mature readers. Depictions of transphobia and homophobia.

For my dad, who wishes I would just write a nice Western.
This is as close as I get to a Western, Dad. Look! Horses.

Chapter One

"HEY, MATTY. ARE you petting a dog in some back room at a party again?"

He almost hangs up the phone. Because, yes, Justin Edward Matthews—Matts to anyone who matters and Matty to his asshole stepbrother—is hiding in a back room at a party petting a dog. Again.

"I hate you," Matts says.

"You don't. What's the dog's name?"

"It's Hawk, Eli's dog."

"Give her a kiss for me."

He does. He's sitting on a fancy bench thing at the base of an equally fancy bed in one of the dozen bedrooms at the house where the party is taking place. He doesn't know if Hawk is allowed on the furniture or not, but he figures if she's mostly in his lap, they're good either way. He leans into Hawk's warm bulk and briefly buries his face in her neck.

"So," his stepbrother says, "the gay kid talked you into going out and socializing, huh?"

"Don't say it like that," Matts says, straightening.

"I'm not saying it like anything. I'm stating a fact. He's a kid. He's gay."

"He's twenty-one, and he's married to my captain. He's not a kid. And he's one of my best fucking friends. Use his name."

"Fine. Whatever."

Matts is regretting calling Aaron already. They used to do it all the time—calling each other whenever they got drunk. It was the way they bonded as teenagers when their families were recklessly combined. Matts was off at boarding school, so lonely it was hard to breathe sometimes, and Aaron was unceremoniously uprooted from the only town he ever knew, suddenly expected to call a stranger "Dad." Their relationship was easier then, born out of isolation and a shared resentment for the people they called parents. But in recent years, their conversations have gotten more and more stilted. Exhibit A: this conversation.

"Hey," Aaron says, like he can hear what Matts is thinking. "I'm trying. You know I'm trying."

"Try harder."

"Okay," he says quietly. An extremely awkward pause follows. "Well. Why are you hanging out with Hawk and not a less furry lady?"

Aaron has a point. The only good thing about going to parties is that sometimes girls will recognize him, and he can get laid without having to stumble his way through a conversation first.

"I came upstairs to use the bathroom. And it's time for Eli to check in anyway. I'll go back downstairs when he does."

Hawk is Eli's service dog. Eli doesn't go to parties much, but when he does, he brings her with him and keeps her somewhere quiet where he can have her sniff him or whatever she does to predict his seizures every so often. And he always has someone with him as human backup too. Tonight, Matts is the human backup. Because he's still doing PT for another week and isn't cleared to travel with the team yet. He made the mistake of having dinner with Eli, and afterward, Eli *looked* at him with his big stupid sad eyes and asked him to *please* go with him, and Matts is a pushover.

He doesn't like parties in general, but he especially doesn't like them when he keeps having to explain that, no, he's not Eli's professional-hockey-playing-husband. He's Eli's professional-hockey-playing-husband's injured alternate captain. Which is weird. Not because people are assuming he's gay. That's fine. That's whatever. But people are assuming he's *married*. Twenty-one-year-olds should not be married. Even if it seems to be working for Eli and Alex.

"The drinks are all colorful and sparkly," Matts says. Making fun of rich people's alcohol preferences is always a safe topic with his family.

"No," Aaron gasps with faux outrage. "*Sparkly*?"

"No beer cans in sight."

"The horror. Not even a bougie IPA?"

"There's a tended bar, and the menu is all cocktails."

"Gross. What color did you go with?"

Matts sighs in the direction of his drink on the nightstand. "Green. And then purple. And the worst thing is that I'm drunk after two of them."

He regularly goes shot-for-shot with Russian NHL players. A neon drink should not be laying him out. He tries to look at his tongue to see if it's changed color and is unsuccessful.

"Are you still on meds?"

"No, *Mom*, I'm off everything as of two days ago. Healing great. Should be playing again in another week. And I can't even celebrate with a beer."

"What a brave little soldier you are," Aaron says. "Hey, speaking of moms. Are you coming home for Christmas or not?"

"I don't know. Maybe. Is my dad…" He flips Hawk's ears inside out. One will stay that way. The other won't. He boops her nose, and she sneezes.

"You're gonna need to finish the question if you want me to answer it."

Matts sighs. "I don't know. Just…you think he'll ever apologize?"

"I think those would be hell-freezes-over type odds."

"Yeah."

"Come home anyway."

"I'll think about it."

The door opens, and Eli slips inside, music from downstairs bleeding through before he shuts it again.

"Hey," Matts says, "I gotta go. I'll call you Friday, and we'll talk about Christmas, okay?"

"Sure. Hey, uh, say hi to Eli for me."

"Yeah," Matts says, "I will." The word "thanks"

gets a little stuck in his throat, but he mumbles it out and follows it with "bye."

He slides his phone back into his pocket as Eli slides onto the bench beside him.

"You okay?" Eli asks. He's a perceptive little shit.

"Fine." Matts gestures toward the door. "It's just a lot. Do you always have to be so damn good at social shit? You're making me look bad."

"Oh, no," Eli says, "you do that on your own." He gives him a second look and gentles his tone. "You do look a little rough though. You want to go outside? Or we can call it early."

"Outside works."

They sit with Hawk for a few more minutes, and when she remains calm and sleepy, they bid her good-bye and head downstairs toward the backyard.

But halfway through the living room, Matts stops.

Because there's a girl in the kitchen.

Well, there are a lot of girls in the kitchen. But this girl is wearing black ripped skinny jeans, and her equally black ripped shirt—advertising some incomprehensible metal band on the front—has no sleeves or collar. The shirt's sides have been cut from arm to hem and reattached with long lines of glittering safety pins. Her lips are full. Her hair is a wild riot of brown curls.

She looks like the unholy offspring of '80s hair-metal-era Bon Jovi and '70s Joan Jett, and her whole vibe is…unexpectedly but thoroughly doing it for him.

"Who," he asks, "is *she*?"

"Absolutely not," Eli answers. "You are not ready for Sydney."

"Sydney," he repeats.

"No," Eli says again, forcefully steering them toward the back porch. For someone so lean, he's surprisingly strong. Sydney also looks lean and strong. Her glutes and thighs are particularly nice. She could probably squat him. He'd be happy to let her try.

"I thought the whole point of me coming tonight was that I needed to…expand my social realm or whatever."

"Social *repertoire* is the phrase I used." Eli is still pushing him. Matts is still resisting.

"Repertoire. Right." He cranes his neck to keep Sydney in sight. She's completely flat-chested, but her ass is something else. He wonders if she plays hockey.

"And, yes, it was," Eli agrees. "But I know that look, Matthew."

"Not my name."

"I know that look, *Justin Edward Matthews*."

That is, admittedly, his name.

"You don't want to meet her," Eli says. "You want to hook up with her."

"And that's...bad?"

"Have you ever even *spoken* with a trans woman before?"

"Trans...as in transgender?"

"No, as in transformer. Yes, transgender, *idiota*. And clearly, your taste in music is worse than I thought if you don't already know who she is."

"Wait, she's a boy? Or—used to be a boy?" She doesn't look like a boy. Though that might explain the boob thing. Is that bad to think? Eli would probably hit him if he said it out loud.

"And this is why you're not allowed to talk to Sydney," Eli says. "She would eat you alive."

Sydney catches him staring, and Matts waves as Eli finally, successfully, shoves him around the corner and through the sliding doors to the porch.

Sydney appears again, moments later, from the opposite side of the open-concept kitchen, and purposefully makes her way toward them.

"Oh, fuck me," Eli mutters.

"No thanks."

"Eli," Sydney says, stepping over the threshold to join them. "Who's your friend?"

"Hi," Matts says. "I'm Matts. I play hockey with Eli's husband. Eli says I'm not allowed to talk to you because you'll eat me alive."

She gives him a considering once-over. "Eli is likely correct, but I'm sure we'd both enjoy the experience."

Eli throws up his hands.

"Don't let him fool you though," she says conspiratorially, bowing with a flourish that somehow doesn't spill her drink. "I am but a humble bard, at your service."

"Bard, sure," Eli mutters. "*Humble* though—"

"You look like you need alcohol, Eli," Sydney interrupts.

He sighs. "I do. Syd, behave. Matts, good luck."

"Wait," Matts says, "aren't I supposed to be…monitoring you?"

"Monitor me with your eyes while I go acquire a beverage. I promise to swoon obviously if I need your attention." Eli throws one wrist against his forehead and falls briefly to one side before straightening and making his way back inside.

"So you're Hawk's understudy tonight?" Sydney asks.

She has dimples. It takes him a beat longer than it should to respond because of them.

"That's me. Temporary service human. Not as cute as the A-team upstairs, I know."

She gives him another leisurely assessment, and he suddenly wishes he was wearing something more edgy than khakis and boat shoes.

"I wouldn't say that," she murmurs over the rim of her glass.

He watches her drink; he watches the light from the hanging lanterns on the porch glint off the rings on her hand; he watches her tongue slide over her drink-stained lips. He realizes he's staring.

"So how do you know Eli?" Matts asks, only a little desperately.

She tips her head, expression suddenly assessing. It's an oddly predatory look for someone whose curl-augmented height barely comes up to his chin.

"You have no idea who I am, do you?" Sydney says.

"I—no." He squints at her, remembering Eli's assertion about his taste in music. "Should I?"

She reaches out to flick the collar of his button-down. "I guess not. Though one of our songs *is* on syndicated radio currently."

"You're a musician?" That makes sense. That makes a lot of sense. "What's your band called?"

"Red Right Hand." She looks like she's braced for

something as she says it, but the name means nothing to him.

"Is that, like, a Twister reference?"

She coughs on a laugh, then hides her smile with the back of her wrist, her long fingers—guitarist fingers?—splayed over the mouth of her cup.

"It's a *Paradise Lost* reference," she says:

> *"What if the breath that kindled those grim fires,*
> *Awaked, should blow them into sevenfold rage,*
> *And plunge us in the flames; or from above*
> *Should intermitted vengeance arm again*
> *His red right hand to plague us?"*

The cadence of her voice, the tone, is almost unbearably musical. She's not a guitarist, he thinks with sudden certainty. She's a *singer*.

"Math was more my thing than English," he says. "You're going to need to explain that."

She kicks one of his shoes with the toe of her boot, like they're sharing a secret. "See, that's the fun part. There's no easy explanation. Because the red right hand is meant to be a kind of divine vengeance against the rebellious demons. But the *form* that vengeance will take is uncertain. Maybe the red right hand is God himself.

Maybe it's Jesus since he sits at the right hand of God. But also, the mark of the beast is supposed to be on the right hand. So maybe it's the antichrist."

Matts thinks this is the most interesting conversation involving God he's ever had. If sermons were more like this, his mother wouldn't have had to poke him awake with her Bible highlighter so often during Sunday services growing up.

"So…you wanted to imply that you're a divine tool, but no one knows if you're good or evil? That's why you chose the name?"

"Mostly, we just thought it sounded badass. But it makes me look cooler if I say I appreciate the complexity of its literary origins."

It startles a laugh out of him, and she looks pleased.

Her whole face changes when she smiles. Though she quickly ducks to hide her smile behind the curtain of her hair. It's an odd, habitual gesture. Shy in a way that seems at odds with the rest of her.

"You met Eli through YouTube stuff then?" he asks.

Eli is a popular vlogger who started with videos about cooking but now talks about skincare and skating and service dog stuff too.

"Yeah." She considers him for a long moment and then seems to make a decision. "I'm a singer."

He *knew* it.

"And I'm trans. I started a vlog when I was fourteen to document the process of going off blockers and starting hormones. But I ended up posting a lot of videos of me singing covers, too, just for fun. By the time I was sixteen, I had a solid following and decided to share some original songs. And then I started doing short-form stuff. A couple went viral. Got the band noticed. We signed a record deal last year, and now we're touring and making a living doing it. So—living the dream."

She pauses for a beat. He tries to look attentive and supportive and not like he's wondering what exactly the whole gender changing process entailed. He doesn't need Eli to tell him that'd be a wildly offensive thing to ask. He probably shouldn't even be thinking it.

She narrows her eyes at him, and for a brief, drunken moment, he's afraid she can read his mind.

Pink Elephant, he thinks quickly. *Pink Elephant Pink Elephant Pink*—

"Anyway," she says. "There was this Texas influencer meetup thing downtown last year, and Eli and I ended up hiding on the roof together for an hour. We've been friends ever since."

"Eli is pretty great. Though he did try to keep us from meeting."

"Point deduction, for sure." She studies him over her cup, taking a leisurely sip. "You handled that better than I expected," she says finally.

"Handled what?"

"Realizing you were hitting on a trans girl. Worst case, guys like you, they get angry. Best case, they fall into a mental spiral about the Schrödinger's dick situation. You at least made an effort not to immediately look at my crotch."

He redoubles that effort now.

"Schrödinger's—wait. 'Guys like me'? What does that mean? And what does 'angry' mean? Have people *hurt* you?"

"Clearly, I can handle myself. And I just mean that most straight dudes typically need an adjustment period to be comfortable with the idea of sleeping with a trans girl. Or even the idea that they *want* to sleep with a trans girl."

"I guess," Matts allows. "But at least dicks are straightforward. I'd for sure know how to get a girl off if she had a dick. That's, you know, not always the case the other way around."

He can't believe he's saying this out loud. He's never drinking again. Or talking to another human. This is why he doesn't go to parties.

She's full-on grinning at him now, wide and completely unobstructed by her hair.

"Full disclosure—if you *are* looking for a hookup tonight, I am not your girl. I'm just flirting."

He can't decide if he's relieved by that or not. "Ouch. Am I not your type?"

Someone pushes past them, and she shifts to stand beside Matts rather than in front of him. She nudges him in the ribs with a pointy elbow.

"Consenting humans are my type," she says. "But I don't do one-night stands. Which I'm guessing is what you're angling for. If you're angling for anything."

He considers being insulted by that.

"No judgment," she adds. "If I was a twenty-something professional athlete, I probably wouldn't want to settle down yet either. Well…" She glances across the room at Eli. "Unless I was Alexander Price and found my soulmate at nineteen."

"Do you do friends?" Matts asks. "Or— Shit, not— I didn't mean—"

He tries to find a different way to say it other than "do you want to be my friend" like a five-year-old. Fuck, maybe that's his best option. "Do you want to be my friend?"

She studies him, bottom lip tucked between her

teeth. "You know, weirdly, I think I do."

"Cool."

"I also *do* my friends sometimes, too, just FYI."

Matts chokes a little.

"But only the really good ones. They have to have tenure."

"Something to aspire to," he manages.

"Something to which to aspire," she corrects, "if you want to be grammatically correct."

"I've never wanted to be grammatically correct in my life."

She laughs and gestures to the room at large, rings glinting. "Since *I'm* not an option, do you want me to introduce you to some cute ladies with absolutely no interest in marriage, kids, and a white picket fence?"

"Do they have legs like yours?"

She nods contemplatively as if she's taking the question seriously. "How do you feel about horses?"

"Uh. Generally positive?"

"Good enough. Let me introduce you to our resident rodeo queen. I have personal hands-on experience with her legs, and they're not *quite* as nice as mine, but few are. Hey now. Don't bluescreen on me. You okay, bud?"

"Sorry. You two have, uh... Are you—?"

"I told you; I sleep with my friends sometimes."

She did say that.

"So she…has tenure."

"That she does."

"Would she be interested in *me*?"

She looks at him like he's an idiot. "A six-foot-three professional athlete? Yeah, I think so."

"Okay. But I don't look anything like you. So if she's attracted to you—"

"Her type is also consenting human."

"Oh, good."

"Though, fair warning, she will want to talk about horses before, after, and possibly during sex."

"Weird, but not a deal-breaker."

He grew up on a ranch. His first vaguely sexual experience was under the bleachers during a rodeo. Horse girls are familiar territory, at least.

"I need to keep an eye on Eli though," he realizes.

She pats him on the back. "Well, they're currently both in the kitchen, which makes that easy. Let's go."

They go.

*

IN THE FOLLOWING week, Matts doesn't think much about Sydney.

He doesn't.

She's just a person he met while inebriated. And he was weirdly into her. And he completely embarrassed himself in front of her. And he *hasn't been thinking about her*.

Except.

The following weekend, the Hell Hounds are traveling again, and Matts is spending the night with Eli so he doesn't have to exist in his apartment alone. His roommate, Asher, is traveling with the team, and Matts just can't sleep in an empty house. Having slumber parties with his captain's husband is probably weird, but after the first two nights home alone with zero sleep, he stopped being proud, and Eli graciously allowed him to call the guest bedroom his own.

Tonight, though, Matts is sequestered in the guest room because Eli is filming a video in the kitchen before dinner.

Matts is poking around aimlessly on his laptop, and without really meaning to, he googles Red Right Hand. The first video in the results is just lyrics and sound, but the second is from a live concert, and he clicks into it, sliding on his headphones.

A drummer sits to the right back, and a bass guitarist stands to the left. Sydney is front and center in another pair of destroyed jeans, another cropped black shirt. Only, this time, she's wearing a patch-spangled denim vest, and she's got an electric guitar resting on one thigh. Her hair obscures her face as she picks out a starting riff that wouldn't be out of place in a Metallica song. The tension builds, the bass guitarist joins her, the drummer enters with a clash of cymbals and it's—compelling. Objectively. It gets a whole lot more compelling when Sydney looks up, grinning and fierce, finds the microphone on the stand in front of her and leans into it, bared teeth pressed against the grill as she starts to sing.

Matts's father raised him not to take the Lord's name in vain, but his father isn't here. And Sydney is singing.

Jesus Christ.

She's good. Really good.

Her fingers are still flying on the fret, her eyes closed, face tipped toward the stage lights, and it's—

He glances at his own acoustic guitar on the bed beside him—a guitar he's been playing nearly daily for more than a decade—and has to admit he wouldn't be able to keep up with her.

That probably shouldn't be as hot as it is.

Matts tries to focus on the lyrics as Sydney

approaches the chorus the second time, turning up the volume on his headphones.

> *Won't bow to you*
> *Or your test of litmus*
> *Try me and see*
> *If you doubt my fitness*
>
> *I'll swear to your god*
> *And mine as my witness*
> *If you're asking for proof*
> *I'll provide it with quickness*
>
> *Are you asking for it?*
> *Are you asking for it?*
> *I'll burn your house down*
> *With the match that you've lit*

And then she's stomping across the stage to play, hip to hip, with the bassist who is also incredibly talented, and Matts has to start the song over. Too much is happening at once. He's sure he's missing things.

He plays it three more times, all the way through, before watching the next video.

And the next.

And then Eli is knocking on the door asking if he wants to wash up for dinner, and Matts realizes he's been glued to his laptop for over an hour. He almost says no to *Eli's cooking* because he wants to keep watching. He isn't prepared to handle Eli's rightful concern if he does, though, so he pauses the video he's on and goes to eat.

After dinner, Matts forces himself to work on some sponsor and social media stuff he's been putting off. If he procrastinates much longer, his publicist will call him and use her disappointed voice, which is never fun. However, it occurs to him, as he's sending off the approval for the final shots of the most recent ad campaign he was part of, that he hasn't posted his weekly short-form content yet. He made an agreement with the team's management that he would post something Hell Hounds related once a week. It's part of the marketing team's initiative to have the players be a united, positive, visible force on social media. He typically fulfills his duties by hastily editing together highlights or putting trick shots or stickhandling drill videos to music.

But now, Matts has an idea.

He finds the first Red Right Hand song he listened to and chooses a thirty-second segment of it that ends with the kickass chorus. He spends a solid hour splicing together a series of his most impressive goals (and a couple fights) to accompany it. Matts even throws some filters on the footage and slows a few clips down so the action in the shots is synched with the bassline. He's proud of it when he's finished. The lyrics, the building tension belied by Sydney's nearly whispered soprano crooning just before the blatant alto aggression of the chorus—it's perfect. It's the perfect song for showcasing an athlete's talents in a "fuck anyone for ever doubting me" way.

The song reminds Matts of being sixteen, of driving his uncle's truck with the windows down, summer air in his face, Black Sabbath throbbing through the speakers, and a hunger for something he couldn't describe gnawing at his gut.

He thinks other people will empathize.

He posts the video and goes to cuddle with Hawk on the living room floor and do Sudoku puzzles while Eli finishes his homework.

Matts needs to chill out if he's planning to sleep tonight, and watching more of Red Right Hand's videos is not conducive to chilling.

He leaves his phone, face down, charging on the nightstand.

He doesn't think to look at it again until morning.

Chapter Two

SYDNEY MARIE WARREN rarely remembers her dreams. But when her brother inhospitably awakens her, banging on her bedroom door early on a Sunday morning, Sydney imagines she was dreaming about being an only child.

"*What*?" she snarls.

"I'm coming in," he says.

Sydney throws the first thing she can reach at him—her jeans from the night before with the belt still threaded through the belt loops.

Contact.

"Ow, fuck."

The belt buckle nearly hits her face when he throws them back at her.

"Swear to God, Devo," she hisses, shoving away the denim and pulling the quilt over her head. "I will end you."

"You say that a lot for someone who struggles to open heavy doors sometimes."

"I got back at 4:00 a.m. Go *away*."

"Okay, fine. But have you been checking your socials?"

Her jaw pops with a yawn. "You know we didn't bring our phones with us."

Sydney, Rex, and Sky—Red Right Hand's bassist and drummer—had been holed up working on their next album for the past three days. It had been a productive seventy-two hours but terrible for her sleep hygiene.

"You might want to find your phone."

She deigns to peek out of her blanket burrito at him. "What? Why?"

"Do you know a Matthews underscore 72?"

"A who?"

"On TikTok. And IG. Matthews underscore 72."

Sydney blinks blearily at him.

"A bunch of professional athletes are using one of

your songs. It started with NHL players and then soccer and football players picked it up, then rugby folks…" Devo waves a hand. "Now it's trending as a sound. Your Spotify hits are *way* up. And Rex just texted me a mostly incomprehensible paragraph, but it had a bunch of dollar sign emojis in it."

"Well, shit. What song?"

"'A Prayer for Arson.'" He proffers his phone's screen like that will mean anything to her before she puts her contacts in. "Looks like this Matthews underscore 72 guy was the first to use it. He plays for the Hell Hounds."

"Matts," she realizes.

"Hm?"

"I…might know who that is."

"Why are you making that face?"

"I'm not making a face."

"I've had the displeasure of looking at you daily for two decades. I've seen you more than *you've* seen you, and I promise; you're making a face."

"Fuck off." Sydney reaches for the jeans again, and he holds up a placating hand.

"Easy, Syd Vicious. So how do you know this Matthews guy?"

"I don't." She army-crawls to the side of the bed. "I

talked to him for ten minutes at a party a week ago."

"Well." He wiggles the phone at her. "Clearly you made an impression."

"Give me that."

She nearly pulls the drawer out of her nightstand searching for her glasses, jams them on her face, and snags the phone out of Devo's hand.

It *is* Matts.

Sydney doesn't recognize him at first. Because there's nothing of the awkward, if endearing, man she met at the party to recognize. The man in the video wearing the number 72 on his back is brash and fast and elegant and undeniably, confidently, physical—throwing himself after the puck and into fights, screaming for his victories and shouting obscenities at his opponents as refs push him toward the box. But in the close-up footage of him licking his blood-smeared lips, grinning, it's undeniably Matts. Just a very different Matts than the one Sydney met.

The way he's synched up the video footage of his goals and fights to her music, to her *voice*, is… It makes the song feel as if it's something bigger than it is. Like something more than just words and sound.

"Good, huh?" Devo says.

She plays it again.

Matts is sort of beautiful in his element. Even with his sweaty too-close-to-a-mullet-for-comfort hair in his face; even with blood in his teeth.

"It is."

Devo sits on the bed, and Sydney's too preoccupied playing the video a third time to hit him about it.

"The football and basketball players' versions are getting the most traction, but Matthews is the one who started it. And frankly, his is the best I've seen. I take it you didn't ask him for some free publicity?"

"No. I mentioned the band's name, but he hadn't heard of us before."

"You have his number?"

"No."

"Might want to get it and thank him. Posting that was a small thing for him, but shit like this makes a difference for us."

"You know you're not actually our manager," Sydney mutters, starting it over again.

"Until you hire a real one, I'm the best you've got. Speaking of, we need to talk about the spring tour set list."

"No. Please. Just let me sleep for a few more hours. I can't be a person yet. *Please.*"

"All right, fine. You're gonna need to stop watching

that if you're planning to sleep though."

He has a point. She drops the phone into his waiting hands.

He pockets it and stands, then cups the back of her head so he can press an obnoxious, wet kiss to her forehead before she can lean away.

"Sleep well, baby rock star."

"End you," she mutters, flopping over. "And shut the damn door!"

*

SYDNEY WAKES UP four hours later feeling vaguely human again.

She locates her dead phone in the tangle of her duvet, nearly falls off the bed reaching for the cord to plug it in, and then lays there waiting until it revives. She finds Matthews's IG profile and watches the video a few times, volume low. Sydney follows him before she can overthink it. She texts Eli.

> *You free later? I want to talk about Justin Matthews.*

Her phone rings.

"What did he do?" Eli asks in lieu of saying hello. "He's a work in progress, but I swear he's decent underneath the two decades of unchecked patriarchal nonsense."

"No—" Sydney clears her throat, voice raspy from disuse, and tries again. "No, he didn't do anything bad. He used one of our songs in his short-form posts, and it's blown up."

"Oh. Yeah. You know, he put real effort into that video. You should feel honored."

"I kind of am. What's his deal?"

Eli is suspiciously silent.

"What do you mean?" he hedges.

"Just—he's a weird one."

"You have no idea," Eli mutters. "He's basically living with me right now while the team is on their road trip. And I thought Alex was bad, but this boy's dietary habits are—"

There's a muffled shout in the background.

"Yes, I'm talking about you," Eli yells back. "No, that's not— Honey, I'm from Alabama; I won't judge you for ketchup on scrambled eggs, but what you do to *toast* is a war crime."

"Oh," Syd says. "He's there?"

"Mm. Constantly, these days. It's nice to have company, though, with Alex gone." Eli raises his voice again. "Except when said company rearranges your spice cabinet!"

The muffled voice—apparently Matthews—tries to argue, but Eli cuts him off.

"No, all spices should *not* be organized alphabetically. Go back to your puzzle, and let me talk to Syd."

Matts's voice suddenly goes quiet. He's still speaking, but Sydney can barely hear him.

"Yes, Sydney from the party," Eli says. "Well, I don't know. Do *you* want to talk to her? Uh-huh." His tone shifts, speaking to Syd again. "Sorry about that. Matts says hi, I think."

"You think?"

"It was implied. Anyway, what did you want to talk about?"

"Well, I wanted to talk about him, but that seems rude if he's right there. I guess I just wanted to see if he's good people."

"He is. Or trying to be, at least."

"Aren't we all. Okay. Can you send me his number? Provided he's okay with that."

"I...can..." It sounds like Eli wants to say a lot more.

"Stop thinking whatever you're thinking. The band wants to invite him to the cookout this weekend. To say thanks."

They probably do; it's not like she's outright lying.

"You're still planning to come, right?"

"As if I would deny Hawk a chance to see her beloved."

Hawk is absolutely infatuated with their livestock dog, Boogie. Boogie tolerates Hawk, which is apparently all she requires to feed said infatuation.

"You think Matts will come?" Syd asks.

Eli sighs. "He's been playing your album nonstop for the last three days straight. He'll be there if you invite him."

Matts's muffled voice in the background interrupts her response.

"Oh, I'm sorry," Eli answers him brightly. "Was that supposed to be a secret? Well, how was I supposed to know that your music preferences were suddenly confidential information? Listen, Syd wants me to send her your number so you can be friends, is that—? Lovely."

Sydney laughs into her pillow.

"All right, Syd," Eli says. "I'm texting it to you now. See you Saturday."

"Mm. Thanks."

Syd knows if she doesn't do it now, she'll take twenty minutes to rewrite it a dozen times later. So as soon as Eli sends Matts's number, she opens a new conversation:

> *Hey this is Sydney. Are you in town this weekend?*

> *Hi. This is Matts.* He answers immediately.

And then:

> *You already knew that.*

And again:

> *Yes, I'm in town.*

> Syd sends her address. *The band wants to thank you in person for the free publicity. Come to the cookout at my folks' place on Saturday.*

> *Is that an invitation or a command?*

> Sydney thinks it over, then: *11am start, but food is served at 12:30. Don't be late.*

> *What's late? After 11 or after 12:30?*

Sydney considers answering and then decides against it because that's funnier. If he really needs to know, Eli can tell him.

She tosses her phone to the side and rolls onto her

back, stretching.

It's always strange to come back to her bedroom at her parents' house after time away—like stepping into a time capsule that was never buried, all the different eras of her childhood mingled together. The glow-in-the-dark stars have been on the ceiling since she was eleven. The rock and metal posters papering the walls were accumulated over a decade of preteen and teenage angst. Her first and second guitars hang in a place of honor over the desk where she wrote her first song. Tickets and receipts and postcards cover her door: memories, good and bad.

The first memento Sydney taped to the door at ten years old is still there, front and center: a receipt from a gas station in Mississippi for a bag of candy and chocolate milk. The bravest, stupidest decision she ever made.

Her eyes linger on the sticker-covered lamp. On the milk crate full of sports medals and 4H ribbons. Lying in a childhood bedroom, still uncertain about what adulthood means, provokes a strange sort of nostalgia. Sydney doesn't want to go back, exactly, but the glow-in-the-dark stars and the ticket stubs remind her that those parts of her never left. She's twenty now, but she still houses her sixteen- and twelve- and six-year-old selves.

There's probably a song in that somewhere.

Sydney doesn't have a chance to feel out the possibility, though, because the distinct sound of Rex's motorcycle clatters into the yard and stops to idle, likely on purpose right in front of her window. She resigns herself to not going back to sleep.

"Syd," Rex yells from the hall a minute later, the front door slamming behind him. "If we're awake, you can be awake. Team meeting in five."

She goes in search of pants.

The landline is ringing when she squints her way into the kitchen five and a half minutes later, but none of the occupants—Devo at the stove, Rex standing in the open refrigerator sniffing something, Sky face down on the table—appear interested in answering it.

She snags the phone from the cradle on her way to collapse in a chair next to Sky.

"Ninth circle of hell, Judas speaking."

"What, Satan's busy?" her mom asks.

Sydney glances at Devo. "He's making eggs. Can I take a message?"

"Be nice to your brother," her mom says, more habit than anything. "And tell him to move fixing the back pasture fence up on his to-do list. The section by the creek is going to fall over the next time a cow so much as sneezes on it."

"I shall tell him to ready his post hole digger with *haste*."

"You do that. Save some eggs for me."

Syd disconnects and lobs the phone at the counter; Rex helpfully returns it to the cradle.

"Devo, Mom says save her some eggs and fix the back fence," Sydney relays, pushing hair out of her face. "Skyler. Rexler. I thought we agreed we needed at least twenty-four hours before we saw each other's faces again."

"Rex was having a moment about 'A Prayer for Arson' going viral and wanted to talk about capitalizing on it," Sky says. "Also, we're out of food."

Rex looks up guiltily from the open container in his hand.

Rex and Sky live together in a tiny studio in the city. Even though they swear there's nothing going on between them, they share a wardrobe, a bed, and often, it seems, a single brain cell. Sydney has known them for six years and has been playing with them for just as long, and she has never met a more codependent pair of human beings. Luckily, that translates well musically.

"I invited Justin Matthews to the cookout this weekend," Syd says, standing to go investigate the refrigerator's offerings herself.

"Pay up," Devo says.

Rex sets down his food and grudgingly gets out his phone.

"What was the bet?" Sydney asks. "That I'd invite him?"

"Nah, we knew you'd invite him," Rex says. "You can't resist a pretty face. The bet was whether you'd do it now or later. I figured you'd wait until after one of us suggested it. So you could pretend it wasn't your idea."

"Whereas, I know you have no shame," Devo finishes, "and said you'd do it before you even left your bedroom."

"A plague on both your houses," she grouses, fishing a container of blueberries from the crisper drawer.

"You live in the same house as me so that's weirdly self-sabotaging," Devo says.

"It's a *metaphor*."

"Oh," Rex says. "Is it time for another lecture from Professor Sydney? What are we discussing today? Austen? Milton?"

"No, I bet it's the… Who was the wizard guy?" Devo snaps his fingers. "Tolkien."

"It's Shakespeare, you heathens."

"Thank God you decided against going to college,"

Rex says. "The pretention would be unbearable."

"Pretentiousness," Sydney corrects.

"I think we're there already," Devo mutters.

She closes the refrigerator door. "You're both fired."

"Yeah?" Devo crosses his arms and leans back against the counter. "What's your blood type and your social security number?"

"...Devo is unfired," Sydney allows.

"In all seriousness," Rex says, returning to his leftovers. "How much do you know about this guy?"

Sydney pulls the protein powder out of the cabinet. "Eli says he's good people."

"He's still a professional hockey player."

"Guys. I just invited him to the stupid barbeque. To say thanks. I'm not *interested* in him."

"We also have a bet about that," Rex tells her.

Sydney doesn't dignify that statement with a response and assembles her shake with as much pride as she can muster. She might run the blender a little longer than is necessary if only to prevent further conversation.

"Hey," Devo says softly, knocking shoulders with her as she returns the milk to the refrigerator. "We just want you to be careful."

"I know."

"Speaking of being careful. I saw the new bike in the garage. Please tell me it's not yours."

"It's not mine," she answers dutifully.

"Syd."

"It was a good deal. And 250ccs was *not* cutting it anymore. I'm finally making real money; let me enjoy it a little."

He sighs. "Please remember that if you die, all of us lose our primary source of income."

"Noted."

"Hey."

She pauses because that's his serious voice.

"Hey," she answers, meeting his eyes.

I worry about you, his face says. *Because I love you. But I'm not going to say it out loud.*

I appreciate it, she tells him back. *And I love you too. But I'm also not going to say it out loud.*

"Okay," he says.

"Okay," she agrees.

Chapter Three

ON SATURDAY MORNING, Matts puts the address Sydney sent him into maps on his phone. When the route loads, under "places at this address," there's a business listed. Black Bull Ranch.

That can't be right.

"Eli," he yells over the music Eli's playing in the living room. Alex and the team get back that night, and Eli has been hit by a sudden need to clean everything as if Alex is going to be looking at the *counters* after two weeks away from his husband.

Matts will not be spending the night. His bag and guitar are already packed up and by the door.

"What?" Eli yells back.

"What's Sydney's address?"

"Didn't she send it to you? I don't remember; just put in Black Bull Ranch."

Huh.

Matts toggles to a new screen and googles it. "Black Bull Ranch," he reads, "dedicated to producing top quality Wagyu, Black Angus, F1, and F2 cross beef." He skims the rest of the website and can't help but be impressed. It looks like a small but well-run operation. Commercial and direct-to-consumer sales. And their stock is good-looking, even if he's used to Red Angus.

Thumbing through the pictures under the "Our Family" tab, he pauses.

Because there's a picture of Sydney.

She's on a dark quarter horse with a white blaze, grinning beneath a gambler hat, wearing black jeans, a brown canvas jacket and beat-to-shit work boots. Her reins are loose in one hand. The other shades her eyes as she laughs at the photographer.

The cognitive dissonance of Sydney on a horse is a little overwhelming.

Matts knows he shouldn't make assumptions about people, but after their brief meeting and his not-so-brief time spent Spotify-stalking her, he's put Sydney into a tidy little "rock star/city girl" mental box.

A box which is currently shattered.

"She grew up on a fucking *cattle ranch*?" Matts yells. "Why did no one tell me this?"

Eli just laughs.

Asshole.

Matts tells Eli he'll meet him there and drives back to his apartment to change. No way in hell he's showing up to a *ranch* in boat shoes.

But by the time he's tried on the only two pairs of jeans that are cut right to fit the *one* pair of boots he has with him in Houston, he's already running behind, and it takes another five minutes to get the sleeves of his white button-down rolled in a way that isn't going to drive him crazy for the next several hours. Matts chooses a plain brown belt to match the boots and decides against one of his belt buckles. He doesn't want to look like he's trying too hard. And then he messes with his hair for a few more minutes before giving up.

It's the longest he's ever spent getting ready for something that wasn't a date. Matts chooses not to interrogate that.

He only hits minor traffic heading down I-10 toward Katy. Just past the city limit, he turns off the highway and then turns off that street onto a one-lane, pothole-choked road. Staring out at a rolling sea of yellow grass on one side and corn fields on the other, the sun bright on the asphalt ahead, dust in his rearview mirror, Matts gives in to the impulse that's been sitting in the back of his head for the last week.

He rolls down the windows.

He puts on Black Sabbath.

He sings along.

When Matts arrives, the ranch gates are already open under an iron crossbar with BBR welded to it and the silhouette of a bull hanging beneath it. He quiets the music as he drives over the cattle guard and starts up the winding gravel road to the house, where several vehicles are already parked on the front lawn.

It looks a lot like the house he grew up in — a single-story stone structure sprawling a little awkwardly in the scrubby land where it sits. Not impressive, but well-kept. Not large. Not small. Not new. Not old. It's a ranch house. It serves its purpose.

When Matts slides out of the car, he can smell the cattle. Cattle and horses and heat and dirt. A tractor is parked off to one side of the house, a collection of trucks on the other, a horse trailer just visible around the corner. A barn sits farther down the hill, and a shop perches on the slope of the hill behind it. Hay bales and a slow-moving, content herd in loosely clustered groups spot the rolling open terrain. The familiarity is briefly overwhelming.

When he walks up the stone front steps, Matts finds a note taped by the bell that says, "Come in, we're out back." But he opens the screen door and knocks on the glass, just to be safe. When no one appears, Matts tentatively lets himself inside.

The long hallway off the entryway is dark and cool and cluttered with framed pictures. Matts gets distracted by a series of photographs that feature what appears to be Sydney and a boy who looks very similar to her, standing in a pothole in the middle of a country road. It's possibly one of the potholes he narrowly avoided on the way here. The pictures start with Sydney around the age of nine or ten (tiny, mostly hair, tongue out) and proceed with annual updates until what appears to be a present-day version of her (destroyed black jeans, vintage band shirt, still mostly hair, tongue out), arm slung around the waist of the now also adult boy.

"Dad says we'll take the picture every year until the city fixes the pothole or he dies. We're still not sure which will happen first."

The boy—now man—in the picture is standing next to Matts.

He's got Sydney's same dark eyes, mole-spotted skin, and wildly curling hair. But he's dressed more like a cowboy than a rocker, which makes sense, considering. It seems Sydney's style is the exception to the rule here.

"Hi," the guy says, extending a hand. "I'm Devo. Sydney's brother." He pronounces it "Dee-voh," and Matts is tempted to ask, but considering his own nickname and the story behind it, decides not to.

"Matts," he says, accepting the handshake.

"Yeah, I recognize you from the video. That was cool of you, by the way."

"I mean. It wasn't anything. I just liked the song."

The handshake seems a little tighter and goes a couple seconds longer than it should, but Matts has been over-analyzing the appropriate length and pressure of handshakes ever since he learned what a handshake was, so that's not a new concern.

"Where's Sydney?" he asks.

"Milk run. Literally. Though I think it was more an excuse for her to show off than anything else. Can't imagine who she's trying to impress though," Devo says pointedly.

Matts doesn't say anything, stymied.

"She just got a new bike," Devo clarifies. "Going to

the store is an excuse to arrive after the guests and park where everyone can see it."

"Bike. Meaning, motorcycle?"

"Unfortunately."

Matts needs a minute. He was just starting to get acclimated to the idea of Sydney on a horse. Adding a *motorcycle* to the mix just isn't fair.

"Eli's here," Devo says, nodding down the hall. "You know Eli, right?"

Matts manages a return nod, still trying to decide if he should be picturing Syd on a cruiser or a sport bike or maybe a little café racer— *It would have to be one of the latter. A cruiser would be too heavy, right?* He looks back toward the door, like maybe she's arrived in the last five seconds without them knowing. Beside him, Devo makes a noise that might be a suppressed laugh.

"Come on, kid. Let's go out back, and I'll introduce you around."

Matts isn't sure how he feels about being called "kid" by a guy who's maybe a year older and several inches shorter than him. But he goes.

The back porch is almost entirely devoted to rocking chairs that have seen better days and a selection of barbecue grills. Matts recognizes at least two from his father's similar configuration. There's a narrow in-ground pool and scattered lawn chairs around a fire pit beneath a few scrubby trees that provide a respectable amount of shade for their size.

The people are mostly located on the porch, though Eli is standing by the pool, shaking his head at Hawk, swimming happily in the wake of a handsome cattle dog with a tennis ball in its mouth.

Devo leads Matts to the group around the largest grill. "Everyone"—he claps Matts on the back—"this is the man who padded our paychecks this month. Justin Matthews. But he goes by Matts, right?"

"Right," Matts says faintly under the sudden scrutiny of all present.

"Matts, as in the plural of Matt?" a long-haired Asian guy with a full sleeve of tattoos asks. Matts recognizes him as the bass player in Red Right Hand.

"He contains multitudes," Eli says, stepping onto the porch. "Also, those are brave words from a man who calls himself 'Rex.'"

"We respect *everyone's* chosen names and pronouns in this household," an older woman says sternly. She has curly brown hair shot through with gray and a smile that makes Matts want to smile back at her.

"Tricia," she says, offering her hand. It's not a surprise when she follows it with "Sydney's mother."

Matts shakes it and then the hand of the man beside her who introduces himself as Sydney's father, Ben.

Sky is Red Right Hand's drummer, who seems to have carefully cultivated uncertainty about her gender from her undercut to androgynous clothing choices, but everyone else is using female pronouns to refer to her, so Matts figures that's safe.

And then, he's introduced to a growing collection of friends and neighbors, none of whom know who he is. It's refreshing. He talks to an elderly bow-legged cowboy with a dip cup in his hand about the upcoming rodeo. He talks to a pink-haired boy with more piercings than Matts can count about the new bar that just opened a block from Eli and Alex's apartment.

It's a strange, friendly amalgamation of people. But after half an hour, as Matts ends up shuffled back to the porch with the main group of Sydney's bandmates and parents, he's feeling a little winded.

"Don't let the band act like they're moochers," Sydney's mom says to Eli. "They used one of their first big paychecks to sort out a new roof for the house, even though we told them we didn't want any charity."

"It wasn't charity," Rex says. "It was five years of deferred rent and five years of future rent for our practice space."

"Please," Sydney's dad says, "you were doing us a favor. The horses are thunder proof now."

Sky nudges Matts with an elbow. "We turned a section of the shop into our practice space in high school. At this point, the animals are all pretty ambivalent about loud noises." She mimes playing the drums.

He can imagine.

Everyone pauses their conversation at the high whine of a motorcycle engine and crunch of gravel under tires.

"Oh, good," Tricia says. "She's still alive."

Sydney is, indeed, alive, appearing moments later around the corner of the house and stopping just beside the porch. She pulls off her helmet while still straddling the sleek black sport bike.

"Show-off," Devo mutters.

She shakes her hair out and somehow doesn't look like a cliché doing it. She smirks at Matts, eyebrows raised, rocking the bike between her thighs, and he realizes, yet again, that he's staring.

"Jesus take the wheel," Eli mutters beside him.

Matts forces himself to look at Eli. "What?"

"Nothing. You getting overwhelmed yet?"

"Little bit."

"Go sit by the pool and throw the ball for the dogs,"

Eli says charitably. "I'll send Syd over once she's done charming everyone."

He thinks that's probably a good idea.

However, only a few minutes after he's discarded his boots and rolled up his jeans to put his feet in the water, the dogs clamber out of the pool and flop in the shade, tongues out and panting hard from their exertions.

Matts relocates to a rust-spotted lounge chair near the dogs so he doesn't look like a total loser.

Twenty minutes later, he's half asleep.

The sun is bright behind his eyelids, and he's on the edge of being too warm, despite the December chill in the air, but still unwilling to move to a more heavily shaded spot.

He opens one eye just in time to see Sydney throw herself onto the ground next to him in a way that looks painful.

"So," she says as though they're already in the middle of a conversation. "Why 72?"

It takes Matts a moment to parse the question. "What?"

Sydney taps his bare ankle with the cool, condensation-beaded butt of her beer. "Your number. Seventy-two. I know hockey players are all superstitious weirdos. It has to mean something."

"I just liked it," he lies.

She gives him an unimpressed look.

Matts sighs and sits up on his elbows so he can see her better. "You know Rubik's Cubes?"

"The" —she mimes solving one—"puzzle thing?"

"Yeah. There's a certain number of total configuration options for a Rubik's Cube. And if you add the individual digits of that number together, it makes seventy-two."

Sydney sets her beer down in the grass. "Hold on. How many different configuration options are there for a Rubik's Cube?"

Matts sits up all the way, swinging his legs off to the side so he can face her. "It's a long number."

"I mean, I figured. What is it?"

"Forty-three quintillion, two hundred fifty-two quadrillion, three trillion, two hundred seventy-four billion, four hundred eighty-nine million, eight hundred fifty-six thousand."

"Holy shit, dude. How do you just *know* that?"

"I was into math when I was a kid. I even did a couple Rubik's Cube competitions before hockey took over my life."

"There's so much we need to unpack here," she

mutters. "Okay, you're saying that at twelve years old, someone asked what number you wanted on your back, and your *first* thought was adding all the individual digits of the number of Rubik's Cube configuration options together?"

"Nine," Matts says. "I was nine."

"How do you feel about Sudoku?"

He decides not to mention the app on his phone. "Um. Generally positive."

"So, you're good at math."

"I'm pretty good, yeah."

Sydney leans forward, drumming the fingers of one hand on his knee. "Okay, say that you and all your little hockey friends—"

"You mean my teammates? My professional, NHL teammates?"

"Sure, you and your professional, NHL teammates are all tied up at the end of a professional, NHL playoff game, and instead of going to a shootout, the deciding point goes to whomever can finish a Sudoku puzzle fastest. Each team can only nominate one person. Who would you nominate from your team?"

"...Me."

Sydney slaps his thigh like she's just won an argument. "Ha! So, you're fuckoff good at math, then."

"What does that even— Look, saying I'm the best at math out of everyone on the Hell Hounds roster isn't exactly a ringing endorsement of my abilities."

"Uh-huh. Those competitions you did as a kid. You win any of them?"

"Not *all* of them."

She grins and retrieves her beer. Her rings clink against the glass. "I knew there was more to you than just a pretty face."

That makes Matts pause. "You think my face is pretty?"

Sydney's mid-drink but still gives him a side-eye that rivals Eli's at his most judgmental.

"Objectively, yes," she says after swallowing and wiping her mouth on her wrist. "It's not a compliment. I'm only stating a fact."

"It feels like a compliment."

"Well. Far be it from me to try and police how you feel."

Matts has no idea how to respond to that, but says, "You have a pretty face too. Objectively."

She laughs like he's joking.

He isn't.

"I know I'm not entirely unfortunate-looking," Sydney says. "But your cheekbones are stupid. And I get the feeling your eyebrows probably just grow like that, am I right?"

Matts touches one eyebrow. "Like what?"

"I rest my case. I saw your face on a *building* last week. People aren't asking *me* to be in stoic black-and-white ads for fancy watches."

He knows exactly what ad she's talking about. It's a good picture of him. "Those ads are photoshopped." He feels he has to point it out.

Sydney rolls her eyes and then pauses, head tipped to study him before putting down her beer and wiping her hands on her thighs. She sits up, bracing one hand on his knee, the other reaching for his face, slow enough that he could stop her if he wanted to.

He doesn't.

Her first two fingers touch the skin under his ear, slowly tracing the edge of his jaw down to his chin, and for a moment, Matts feels like he can't breathe.

He has no idea what's happening, but he doesn't want it to stop.

It does, though, when Sydney suddenly jerks her hand back with a soft exclamation, shaking it as if she's been stung.

Matts reaches for her automatically, catching her wrist and pushing open her curled fingers to reveal—

nothing.

"What?" he says.

Sydney grins up at him. "Sorry, I thought I cut my-self on your jawline."

He exhales, thumb moving absently across her un-marred palm. "You're ridiculous."

"I am," she agrees.

Her fingers are long, slender, and capable-looking, with short nails and scarred knuckles. His attention lin-gers on her fingertips, on the calluses that thicken the pads.

"Guitar," Sydney says quietly.

Her smile has dimmed into something contempla-tive. The sun hitting the side of her face highlights the tiny little line tucked in her cheek that was, moments before, a dimple.

"I know." Matts lets go, but only to show her his matching calluses.

She takes his open hand as an invitation and simi-larly explores his fingertips.

"I play too," he clarifies.

"Mm. I'll be the judge of that."

Sydney's confidence is both slightly infuriating and terribly endearing.

"Will you?" he says.

"I have an acoustic guitar in my room."

"You're just assuming I don't play electric guitar?"

"*Do* you play electric guitar?"

"No," Matts admits.

"Right. So, you'll have to show me your acoustic skills later," Sydney says, voice low.

She's still holding his hand.

"Are we flirting?" he asks. "Is that what's happening? Because it's hard to tell."

"We are, but it doesn't mean anything. Keep your socks on."

"I'm not…wearing socks. You're confusing."

"You like it."

He does.

*

MATTS MANAGES NOT to embarrass himself or make any significant social faux pas through lunch, and by 3:30 p.m., he thinks he can leave without appearing rude. Most of the neighbors have already left, citing chores and early mornings. Eli and Hawk headed out at 3:00 to meet Alex. Matts is waiting for a break in the conversation with Sydney's bandmates to make his move when the phone rings inside the house.

Sydney's mom steps inside the propped open door

to answer it, and when she walks back outside a minute later, she's scrubbing an aggravated hand through her curls.

"Cows are out," she says.

All conversation immediately stops.

"Mary just called, said she'd seen at least thirty past the creek, so I'm guessing the fence is down at the culvert again."

Devo and Sydney both groan and roll to their feet in tandem with muttered curses.

Sydney's mom studies the remaining group on the porch, sighing. "And naturally, all the useful people have already gone home."

"*Hey,*" Rex says.

"No, no," Sky says, "that's fair."

Sydney's dad pushes himself to stand as well, and his wife immediately holds up a hand to stop him. "You're still grounded for another month. We are not setting back your very expensive recovery."

"I was just going to get some feed buckets and take the side-by-side over," he says innocently. "See if I can coax any back through that way. Stop others from leaving. Be waiting to help push them in once you bring 'em back. And I'll bring patch supplies."

She studies him with narrowed eyes. "Fine. Go

slowly."

"Yes, ma'am."

"Boogie!" she shouts to the cattle dog sleeping on the porch step. "Time to earn your keep." She lowers her voice as the dog stretches and ambles over. "Syd, can you call around to the neighbors and see if anyone is free to help?"

"Um," Matts says. "I can help."

"Appreciate the offer, city boy," Sydney says. "But there's not much you can do here unless you're secretly a practiced cowhand."

"Well, I haven't practiced *recently*, but…"

Arms up, Sydney pauses pulling her curls into a hurried knot at the back of her neck. "What?"

"I grew up on a ranch on the western slope, and I've helped move our herd to and from higher elevation grazing lands at least once a year every year since I was eleven. Point me toward a horse, and I'll help."

Sydney drops her arms. "Are you fucking with me?"

"Is that something people usually lie about?"

Sydney studies him a second longer and then shakes her head. "All right." She nods down the hill. "Let's go."

Thirty minutes later, wind in his face, sun on his

back, and the warm, familiar bulk of a horse beneath him, Matts has to admit his offer wasn't entirely altruistic.

He's *missed* this.

He's missed the push and pull of moving animals, applying enough pressure to shift but not spook. He's missed seeing a well-bred stock dog work, darting with ease where it's needed, tongue out, euphoric at a job well done. Matts has missed the feeling of being in the saddle, shifting his weight with his mount, stopping and starting, and occasionally breaking away to chase a wayward young thing with escape on its mind. His body knows what to do—his legs and core and back falling into patterns they remember, one hand working the reins, the other slapping his leg as he yells the cows forward. He was a little concerned his knee might act up, considering he'd just been cleared to resume normal activities the previous week, but it doesn't so much as twinge.

Matts feels good. Right. And he likes the way Sydney looks at him when she pulls back from the left flank of their little group and waits for him to draw even beside her.

She's wearing the gambler hat from the photo he'd found earlier that day, and it somehow doesn't look out of place with her jeans, combat boots, and cutoff band shirt plastered to the long, capable line of her sweaty torso.

Matts watches her bicep flex as she pulls on her reins.

"Well," Sydney says, "I guess you *do* know what you're doing."

"It'd be a stupid thing to lie about."

She considers him a moment longer, resisting as her horse fights for his head.

"Definitely not just a pretty face," she murmurs.

And then she loosens her hold, and they're jogging ahead again to push back on a few straying calves.

Matts finds himself smiling at nothing as they amble down into the culvert and across the rain-swollen creek, back onto the land where they started.

He offers to help Devo patch the fence because he knows from experience that playing with barbed wire alone, especially with night approaching, is a bitch. Devo tosses him a pair of gloves, and they work in silence through the sunset.

It's only after they've finished and they're loading up the side-by-side that Devo says, "So, can I ask about 'Matts'?"

"Sorry?" Matts says.

"Your name. It's fine if you don't want to talk about it; I'm just curious. Is it a hockey thing?"

"It's a 'my stepfather was also named Justin' thing. And my teammates were already calling me Matts when my mom married him, so."

Devo drops the pliers into the back of the side-by-side and turns to face him, hands on his hips. "How old were you?"

"Eleven."

"Kinda fucked you had to be the one to change your name."

"Well. It wasn't like they ever told me I *had* to change it or anything. It was just easier. And I prefer it now. My mom, uh, she passed a couple years back, and I haven't seen the man since, so I could have gone back to Justin, but I didn't. I chose to keep it."

Devo makes a noise Matts can't interpret.

"What about *your* name?" Matts asks. It feels fair.

"Ah, just a workaround for run-of-the-mill religious nonsense. The name on my birth certificate is Devotion."

"Jesus," Matts says.

"He was part of the problem, yes. Sydney's deadname is even worse."

Matts doesn't ask.

After a moment of silence, Devo nods approvingly.

Matts glances at Sydney's dad, who's fiddling with the solar lantern in the driver's seat. He wonders if he'll take offense, and Devo laughs suddenly, loudly, in the stillness.

"Oh, no," he says, "no, no, they weren't— I'm talking about our *biological* parents. Mom and Dad would never inflict those names on us."

"Truth," his dad says. He finally gets the lantern to shut off, and darkness closes in around them, only disrupted by the side-by-side's headlamps. "Looks like we're good here. I'll see you boys back at the house."

He puts the UTV in gear, and Matts hurries over to mount his waiting horse before he loses the only remaining source of light they have.

He's puzzled by the information that Ben and Tricia aren't Devo and Sydney's biological parents. Neither of the siblings favor stocky, fair Ben. But they're close to carbon-copies of lean, dark-haired Tricia. Matts wonders if they're still related. It doesn't seem possible three people can share a smile without some biological intervention. He considers asking but decides against it.

They ride back abreast at a sedate pace, and Matts wishes he could drag it out, swaying in a creaking saddle under the broad expanse of a star-spangled sky.

"You miss it?" Devo asks.

Matts doesn't ask for clarification. He doesn't need to. "I do."

"Well, any time you get the bug, I'd be happy to trade you a couple hours work for a couple hours horse lease."

"Careful," Matts says, "I might take you up on that."

"Eh. It'd be cheaper than paying a part-timer and less annoying than getting Sydney to help."

"Does she not pull her weight?"

"No," Devo sighs, "she does. She just won't shut the hell up. The only time she isn't talking or singing is when she's asleep. Or sick."

"That doesn't sound so bad."

It would be a relief to let someone else handle the bulk of the conversational burden.

"I imagine you're biased in her favor in ways I'm not," Devo mutters as they step into the circle of yellow light from the halogen bulb above the open barn doors.

Sydney is coming out of the tack room when they enter, yelling something about leather cleaner to her dad who's just inside the door. Ben stops Matts as he dismounts with a hand to his arm.

"Thanks for the help, son. I think you've earned at

least one more beer."

"I won't turn one down."

Ben pats Matts's shoulder and ambles out into the night.

"Gross," Sydney mutters.

"What?"

"My dad *likes* you."

"And that's bad?"

She purses her lips. "Yet to be determined. You still up for proving your musical prowess while you have that beer? Or do you need to get home?"

"No," Matts says. "I'd like to stay a while longer."

Chapter Four

SYDNEY HAS A problem.

The problem is approximately six feet three inches of professional hockey player who knows how to sit a horse and is currently playing Chet Atkins's "Mister Sandman" on her acoustic guitar *using a thumb pick*.

And he's good at math too.

And he's *pretty*.

If his face didn't look like that, the rest might be easier to deal with.

But it does.

She focuses on his hands instead.

That doesn't solve the problem.

The band is still there, clustered on the porch, eating second helpings of dinner and watching with interest as Matts shows an impressive level of guitar-playing skill. He's not as good as her, but music is her thing and supposedly hockey is Matts's. Or maybe math. Or looking good on horseback. The man is aggravatingly multifaceted.

When Matts finishes, he gets an encouraging round of applause.

"Finally, some sensible music," her dad says to the groans of the band members present. "Do you take requests? Maybe something that's been on the country charts in the last decade?"

Matts grins and immediately plays the recognizable G-riff of "Keep the Wolves Away" by Uncle Lucius. It's not an arrangement Sydney has heard before, but he's clearly practiced it. She wonders if he came up with it himself.

"You know," her mom says as Matts continues, "if you're going to play something with lyrics, I think you have to sing them."

The band murmurs in agreement.

Sydney thinks he's going to resist, but he doesn't, just smiles and starts over from the beginning.

He doesn't have a lot of range, but he seems to

know his limits. And his voice is well-suited to the song, something he also knows judging by his smirk when he glances up to meet her eyes.

She lets her hair fall in front of her face and goes to get another beer.

Sydney's mom gets up at the same time, headed back inside, and Sydney realizes she has about two minutes to prepare herself because, sure enough, when her mother steps back onto the porch, it's with her own guitar in hand.

"How do you feel about duets?" she asks Matts as he's finishing the song.

He looks surprised but gestures to the open chair next to him.

Sydney's mom nods, pleased, and turns to hand her guitar to Sydney. Sydney can't decide if it's dread or excitement tightening her stomach.

"Mother," she starts.

"Sydney Marie, you are responsible for every gray hair on my head. Playing a little country music will not kill you and *will* make me happy after a long day."

Sydney sighs and accepts the guitar.

She sits by Matts and tweaks the tuning of the guitar as her mom starts making suggestions. Sydney tries not to think too hard about the heat of Matts beside her.

About her guitar in his hands.

"Oh," Matts says. "Yeah, I know plenty of Little Big Town. How about 'Boondocks'?"

Sydney sighs again, purposely loudly, but her mom ignores her. Matts starts the first verse, and it's simple enough for her to accompany him.

It's not perfect, but they're skilled enough to play together without playing over each other. Sydney keeps her voice soft and high, smoothing out the edges she usually pushes to the forefront when singing her music. When they finish the song proper, Matts starts the harmony round, and Rex and Devo pick up the second verse like they've planned it. Sydney and her mom take the third, and they sing it through three times just because it sounds so damn good.

Matts transitions easily into "Wagon Wheel" by Darius Rucker, clearly delighted when they all keep singing with him—though Rex has to pull up the lyrics on his phone. And then after that, they do "Man of Constant Sorrow," which, unfortunately, everyone present knows because it's one of her mother's favorites. Sydney quickly adjusts to play the banjo part, grinning despite herself. By the end of *that* song, they're all singing, even her dad and Sky, neither of whom can carry a tune to save their lives. It's unwieldy and ridiculous and wonderful, and Sydney doesn't want it to end.

It has to though, which Matts makes clear after a final, laughing flourish. "Okay, I need to head out soon."

"One more," her dad says. "'Landslide,' if you know it."

The mood immediately sobers.

"Yessir," Matts says. "As long as Sydney will help me."

It's not really a two-guitar song, but it's absolutely a two-voice song.

"I'll take the first verse; you take the second?" Sydney says.

"Yeah," Matts murmurs, meeting her eyes, "end together."

"Landslide" is one of her dad's favorite songs. She's sung it at least a hundred times, but it feels different when her hands are idle and she's looking at Matts's fingers move with confident familiarity on the strings of her guitar.

Sydney closes her eyes.

It's clear he knows the song, that he isn't just BS-ing his way through it. And their harmony, when they join up together at the chorus, is perfect. It's just—perfect.

She forgets for a while that they have an audience.

It's not often that Sydney's feelings intercede when she's performing. She's usually too practiced for that, and it's not like the lyrics even particularly resonate with her. But by the end, with Matts's low, rich voice layered beneath hers, her throat feels hot and raw with an emotion she can't name. Want, maybe. Though what she wants, she isn't sure.

"Well, shit," Rex says as Syd opens her eyes again. "Maybe we should take you on tour with us."

Sydney's mom stands and moves toward the house. "Honey," she says, dropping a hand to squeeze Matts's shoulder as she passes him, "you are welcome back *any* time."

"Thanks. This has been nice. So. Thanks."

And then he goes bashful, as though he hadn't just fully impressed an actual, professional band. *And* her mother. Which is potentially more noteworthy.

"I'll walk you out," Sydney says.

He's quiet as he follows her through the house, lingering in the hallway, looking at pictures.

"So," Matts says as they step off the porch. "Do I pass muster?"

"Don't go digging for compliments. You know you're good. Though your clear preference for country music has you on thin ice."

"Well, luckily, I'm familiar with ice. Because of the...hockey."

"Yeah, I got that."

Matts turns to walk backward, hands in his pockets. "What do you have against country music, anyway?"

"You want the list of offenses in alphabetical order or by level of transgression? Because the genre's faults are numerous and *sundry*."

He doesn't respond for several seconds, and the crunch of gravel under their feet takes over, loud in the otherwise silence.

"I don't know anyone else who talks like you," Matts says finally.

"I'll take that as a compliment."

"It was one."

They linger by the driver's side door of his pretty little BMW coupe.

His eyes are dark and fathomless, and Sydney can't decide if she likes the way he's looking at her, one hand resting on the top of the car, the other on the door handle.

"Anyway, goodnight," she says as the silence gets awkward.

"Yeah. Goodnight."

She takes a step back. Then another. He's still not

getting in his car.

"Hey, do you think—" Matts moves toward her and then stops, almost as if he's making himself, rocking back on his heels. "Would you maybe want to play again sometime? I know it's not your style, and you're probably busy with your actual music, so it's fine if you can't, but it would be nice for me. If you're up for it."

"Well, we did decide to be friends. Friends have jam sessions."

"They do," he agrees solemnly.

"But you'll have to learn some electric guitar if you want me to do acoustic nonsense with you. For, you know, equality." Sydney holds out her hand. "Deal?"

It's weird. It's a weird thing to do.

But she wants to touch him, and the action affords her the pleasure.

Matts accepts the handshake: warm, tight, lingering.

"Deal," he agrees.

He gets in his car, and Sydney watches his taillights fade to black down the drive, and she doesn't flex her hand like some ridiculous character in a Regency era drama as she walks back up to the house.

She doesn't.

*

IN THE FOLLOWING week, Sydney doesn't think much about Matts.

She's too busy buying last-minute Christmas presents, exchanging said presents, arguing with Rex and Sky about their spring set list, ironing out their bus versus airline schedule for the summer tour, helping round up escaped cows *again*, and then helping with a complete back fence overhaul since, clearly, Devo's patch jobs are no longer working.

Sydney doesn't have time to think about Matts.

Except for, maybe, in the evenings when all the introverts she lives with have tucked themselves away in their rooms, and she finds herself going for a night ride with Boogie or slipping into their practice space to play some unfocused melodies. It's one of these nights, reclined on the mangled old couch against the wall beside Sky's drum kit, idly playing the same dozen notes over and over again, that Sydney gets a series of texts from Matts.

> *Tomorrow is my first game back.*
>
> *Theres 2 tix for you at willcall if you want them.*
>
> *Or Eli says you can join him in their box.*

No pressure tho.

We're playing the Stars so it should be good.

They're our biggest rival.

Clearly, Matts hasn't heard of the "no double-texting" rule, or more likely, he's elected to ignore it.

Sydney sits up, googles the time and arena location, and then sets aside her guitar, considering. It occurs to her that MJ—former childhood friend and current rodeo queen—is likely in town for Christmas and might be interested, considering she and Matts spent a solid half hour talking at the party a few weeks prior. And Sydney really needs to do something about her inadvisable crush. Seeing him make eyes at MJ would help in that pursuit.

Hey, she texts MJ. *You want a free ticket to the Hounds/Stars game tomorrow?*

By the time Sydney's forced herself off the couch, locked up, and headed back to the house, there's a response:

Is this a HHG thing?

HHG? Syd doesn't have a clue what she means.

Hot Hockey Guy.

We're not calling him that.

We absolutely are.

Syd sighs. *Is that a yes?*

Sure, why not.

Sydney's suddenly regretting extending the invitation.

Devo is in the kitchen when she slips through the back door, and he freezes, open milk carton inches from his face.

"You're disgusting," she says. "Any chance you want to go to a hockey game tomorrow?"

"Hard pass." He considers her, the milk in his hand, shrugs, and takes a drink. "Also, I thought Matts was injured."

"It's his first game back."

"Of course it is."

"He's just being nice because I invited him to the thing."

"Of course he is."

"God, you're infuriating."

"Of course I am."

"I'm going to bed."

"Of course you are."

She gives him the finger as she leaves the kitchen.

She texts Eli next: *Hey are you going to the game tomorrow?*

I am. You want to ride with me and Damien?

Is there room for one more? I invited my friend MJ.

As long as you don't mind Hawk encroaching on your space.

That's a feature not a bug.

She doesn't respond to Matts until she's in bed, staring at the glowing stars on the ceiling and wondering if she should respond at all.

I'll be there, cowboy. Make it worth my while.

Yes, ma'am, he answers.

*

MJ AND ELI get along like a house on fire. Once they

arrive at their box seats in the arena, Syd finds herself mostly tuning out their conversation to focus on the players warming up below. MJ is on one side of her and Damien, boyfriend of Rome—the second alternate captain—is on her other side. He's an exceptionally handsome man who, apparently, played hockey himself at the same boarding school Rome attended before electing to be a writer.

"All right, so," MJ says, nudging Syd with her elbow, "what number is HHG?"

"We're not calling him that."

"Calling who what?" Eli asks.

"HHG," MJ repeats. "Hot hockey guy. Justin Matthews."

Eli wrinkles his nose.

"You have to admit he's hot," MJ says. "Even people who don't like men would recognize he's hot."

"Truth," Damien agrees from the other side of her. "Though his hair is—"

"Distressingly close to a mullet?" Syd finishes for him.

"Yeah, that."

Even more distressing, Syd finds herself becoming endeared to the hairstyle. The jumbotron chooses that moment to focus on the man in question, tossing pucks to kids, grinning. His hair is thick and wavy, and the cut frames his face. Sort of. It's nice.

She looks down at Hawk; a safe action. Hawk looks back at her like she's fully aware of Sydney's avoidance tactics.

"He's number seventy-two," Sydney says.

"I always wonder why professional athletes choose their numbers," MJ muses. "I mean, they're all superstitious, right? So seventy-two has to mean something to him."

Sydney knows the answer, but divulging it feels like a small betrayal. Or maybe not a betrayal; Matts probably won't care. Maybe it feels more like a concession, allowing someone else access to privately shared knowledge that, until that moment, felt privileged. Intimate. Or maybe she's overthinking things. It wouldn't be the first time.

"Syd?" Eli says. "You're making a face."

She needs to get better about that. "He picked 72 because he likes Rubik's Cubes. And if you add all the digits in the number of Rubik's Cube configuration options, that's the number you get."

MJ turns fully in her seat to look at her. "What the fuck."

"*Really*?" Damien says.

"Huh," Eli adds. "I didn't know that."

"How do *you* know that?" MJ asks.

Sydney waves a dismissive hand. "Because I asked. He came to the cookout. You could have been part of the conversation if you'd deigned to grace us with your presence."

"And interrupt your geeky bonding? Perish the thought."

"I don't even like math."

"No, but with your powers combined, you'd probably get a perfect SAT score," Eli points out, not incorrectly.

"Sounds like you complete each other," MJ adds with zero subtlety.

The jumbotron returns to Matts again. He's leaning on his stick, talking around a mouth guard that's teetering precariously from between his teeth. He's doing nothing of note whatsoever. And yet.

"Please," Sydney says. "Do I look like the kind of person who ends up with…" She gestures to the jumbotron. "…that."

"I mean," Eli demurs, wiggling his wedding-banded finger, "I could say the same about me. And Alex put a ring on it."

"Faster than literally anyone found advisable,"

Damien adds. "And *I* don't fit the typical WAG profile either. Fantastic hair aside."

Eli points to him in agreement.

"Also," MJ says, "Matts could hardly take his eyes off you when he was supposed to be flirting with *me* at that party. So."

"Stop."

"Also, also," MJ continues, "I invited him to go home with me, and he turned me down, which, if I'm offering, people don't typically turn me down. Unless they're interested in someone else."

"And," Eli interjects, "when he laid eyes upon you for the first time, I believe he said something to the effect of 'who is *she?*' while—" Eli gasps theatrically and throws a hand to his chest, pretending to swoon.

Sydney is certain Eli is embellishing because she's certain Matts has never swooned in his life.

"Okay, enough," she says, maybe a little more honestly, a little more gravely, than the tenor of the conversation until that point would permit. "I'm not a masochist. Even if he was curious enough to start something with me, it would only end in disaster. I'm not fishing for compliments here; I'm being realistic."

MJ sighs at her.

Eli sobers. "Hey. We'll drop it if you want to drop

it. But also, saying *curiosity* is the only reason he'd be interested in you is selling yourself incredibly short."

"I want to drop it," Sydney grits out.

They drop it.

She's surprised to find that she enjoys the game for the game's sake. She's watched hockey a few times on TV, usually during the playoffs when it's on ESPN, but never an entire game from start to finish. Watching with the partners of two players on the ice makes it even more interesting, especially because Eli likes to shout at the refs, and Damien likes to mutter expletives and entreaties to deities—in a combination of English and French—under his breath. It's charming.

Sydney always considered hockey to be a brutal sport, with its checking and fights and the sheer size of the players. But it's also elegant, not despite but *because* of the physicality. Two-hundred-pound men balanced on precarious knife-edges, moving with speed and skill. And in addition to somehow hurtling themselves across the ice without dying, they're also displaying impressive hand-eye coordination and teamwork, and—

She winces as one particularly massive Hell Hounds defenseman slams an opposing player into the boards.

So, yes, it's violent, but it's also beautiful. Especially

when Rome intercepts the puck and passes to Matts, and Matts shoots it straight between the legs of the goalie. The puck hits the back of the net in the same instant that the goalkeeper's knees hit the ice, and Sydney is out of her seat screaming about it before the horn even sounds.

She's decided: Hockey is pretty great, actually.

The Hounds win, and the four of them wait for the stands to empty before taking the private elevator down to meet with Alex and Rome.

But Alex and Rome aren't the only ones in the hallway when they emerge from the elevator. There's the giant defenseman, and the goalie, and Rome's boyfriend, Damien, and—

Matts.

Who is grinning, bare-footed, and wet-haired. The shirt that he isn't wearing is rolled up in his hands, and he's using it as a whip to chase around the others, and they're all shrieking like they're middle school boys and not professional athletes with multi-million-dollar contracts.

They stop as the elevator empties.

Matts, who is the closest to them, slings his shirt around his neck, still laughing and *half naked* as he approaches.

Sydney realizes she's made a critical error.

He hugs Eli first, and then, as though it's natural, as though it's something that they do, he hugs her. Regrettably, Sydney knows she will be replaying this moment mentally later. Possibly several times. Because the heat of him is—and his *chest* is—

He smells like citrus, and one of his hands easily spans a good portion of her upper back, and his stubble-rough chin is pressed to her temple, and—

Sydney remembers, belatedly, that she's supposed to hug him back, which results in her returning the gesture just as he's starting to let go, ending in an awkward, backward-forward lurch before they break apart.

"Hey," she says.

Smooth.

She tries again. "Nice goal, cowboy. I'd say you held up your end of the bargain."

Better.

He scrubs a hand through his hair, looking away, and the aw-shucks gesture should feel contrived, but it doesn't.

"Yeah, well." He doesn't appear interested in finishing the sentence.

"Hey, Matts," MJ says brightly. He startles like he didn't even notice her. He doesn't hug her.

"Hey," Matts repeats. He doesn't have a chance to say anything else because the giant defenseman is stepping between them, attention unmistakably on MJ. This, at least, is familiar territory.

"Hi," he says, extending a hand. "I'm Dimitri."

"His name is Kuzy," Alex, Eli's husband, shouts from down the hall.

MJ takes Dimitri's hand and flips it. She makes a show of kissing his knuckles, to his absolute delight.

"Mary Jane," she says. "But you can call me MJ."

"Call you beautiful," Dimitri says.

The line shouldn't work, but between his low, Russian-accented voice and charming, self-assured smile, it clearly does.

"I'll answer to it," MJ allows.

"She's a rodeo queen," Matts adds helpfully. "Her horse's name is Mouse. You like horses, right, Kuzy?"

Sydney can't help but notice these are not the words of a man hoping to hook up with the girl he's talking about.

"Horses," Dimitri (Kuzy?) says, nodding wisely. "Good. Best animal." He glances guiltily at Hawk. "But dogs also best."

"Nice save." Eli laughs, leaning into Alex's side.

"You got dinner plans tonight?" MJ asks Dimitri.

"You," he says.

"Mm. See, that could be interpreted a number of ways, and I like all of them."

Dimitri's grin widens. He nods down the hall, giving her hand a tug. "I think, food first. Then we talk interpret. Okay?"

"Works for me. Bye Eli, bye Syd. Bye...everyone else I didn't meet."

They set off toward the garage together, and the men in the hallway all roll their eyes like this is standard behavior before greeting their significant others. Well, the goalie greets Hawk, who, as soon as her vest has been removed, goes charging into his arms and bowls him over.

With Hawk in the mix, Sydney realizes that everyone is paired off—Sydney and Matts left in a pocket of space that is just their own.

"How does he just *do* that," Matts mutters, eyes still on Kuzy and MJ's retreating backs.

"Oh, to be a certified Hot Person," Sydney agrees. "Where you can make eye contact and then ride off into the sunset."

"No," Matts disagrees. "I'm hotter than Kuzy, and that shit never happens to me."

She raises an eyebrow at him.

"What? I know what I look like. I'm just saying. Being hot isn't enough. You have to be able to talk to people. And I should probably be embarrassed that someone who's only been speaking English for, like, four years is way better at talking to girls than I am."

"You seem to do pretty okay talking to *me*." Sydney doesn't mean for it to sound loaded, but it does once the assertion has left her mouth.

"Yeah. But you're an outlier. Statistically."

"I'm a statistical outlier. Possibly the weirdest compliment I've ever been given."

"I doubt that. Don't celebrities constantly deal with creepy adoring fans?"

"Bold of you to call me a celebrity, but..." Sydney considers it. "There *was* one guy after a concert who said I had the most beautiful teeth he'd ever seen, and instead of an autograph, he wanted me to bite his wrist and leave a mark so he could go get it tattooed on him at a shop down the street."

"Did you?"

"No, gross."

Matts tips his head, studying her.

"What?"

"I'm wondering if it would be weird to ask you to smile. Because I can't remember any specifics about your teeth. But I'm also pretty sure that's rude to ask." Matts appears genuinely puzzled by this conundrum.

Jesus. How is it possible for a man to be so endearing?

Sydney helpfully bares her teeth.

He leans forward to consider them more closely, and after a moment's contemplation, Matts reaches out and uses his thumb to gently push up her top lip, exposing her canine. She lets him. His thumb drifts down to her bottom lip and presses. His fingers under her chin are warm and firm.

"Bad news," Matts says gravely. "Creepy guy was right."

Eli appears in Sydney's peripheral vision. "Hey quick question. What the fuck are you two doing?"

Matts straightens with a lurch, wrenching his hand back, and Sydney nearly sways forward to follow it.

"We were talking about Sydney's teeth," Matts explains, his neck flushing a mottled pink. Sydney wants to put her mouth on it.

"See, Matts," Alex says, slinging his arm around Eli's shoulders as he joins them. "This is why you're single."

Matts's eyes cut to the side, and the flush isn't just endearing, it's heartbreaking.

"Hey," Sydney says. "Leave him alone. He's being charming."

"I am?" Matts asks.

"You are," she insists. "Ten out of ten. Highly recommend. Would be flirted with again."

"Don't oversell it," Matts mutters, but he's smiling again, a small, bashful thing that makes her want to punch something.

Damien and Rome amble over to join their little group, and Sydney clears her throat, taking a conscious step back. "Well, this has been fun, but I've got an early morning so we should probably be going, right Eli?"

"Right," he agrees, his eyes narrowed.

"Oh," Matts says. "I thought— Can I text you later? About music stuff?"

Sydney's trying to stop herself from doing something stupid. Like telling him to put his fingers on her face again.

"Well," she says with a flourish that hopefully comes off as cocky and not hysterical, "if music be the food of love, play on, and all that."

"*Wow*, okay," Damien says.

"What?" Matts asks, looking first at Sydney and then Damien. "Doesn't that mean 'yes'?"

It occurs to Sydney with slowly dawning horror

that Damien is a private-school-educated professional writer, and he's probably aware of the opening lines from *Twelfth Night* and what they mean. She can't get away with honesty couched in expected misinterpretation here.

"Nothing," Sydney says, desperately meeting Damien's eyes before looking back at Matts. "Just, yes. That's— Texting is fine. Music is fine." She salutes him for some ungodly reason, but he salutes her back, so at least they both look like idiots.

Blessedly, Eli calls Hawk to him, links one elbow with Alex and one with Sydney, and pulls them down the hall, yelling goodbye to the others. Rome and Damien follow. When she glances over her shoulder, Matts has one hand up in a subdued wave, the goalie's arm over his shoulder.

Sydney exhales once they exit into the parking garage, but her relief is short-lived.

A few seconds later, Rome asks Damien, "So what did that thing she said mean?"

"It's from *Twelfth Night*," Damien answers. "This guy Orsino has a massive crush, and he says, 'If music be the food of love, play on' because music was considered an amplifier of love. So, he's calling for more, hoping that if he overdoses on music, it will stop his obsession in the same way that you stop having interest in food if you eat too much."

Sydney decides she will simply perish, effective immediately.

Damien continues, "The next line is 'give me excess of it, that, surfeiting, the appetite may sicken, and so die.'"

"Damn," Eli says. "Just lay your cards on the table, Syd."

"Well, no one was supposed to *know* that," she says. "It's one of the most misinterpreted Shakespeare quotes of all time. He was supposed to think it was an over-the-top flirty way of me saying 'yes.'"

"So, you're fine with flirting with him, but you don't want him to know you're *actually* interested in him?" Alex sounds deeply confused.

"Of course! What is difficult to understand about that?"

They're interrupted by the door slamming open behind them and Matts jogging out.

"Time to get in the car," Rome says, dragging a protesting Damien out of earshot.

"Yeah, let's get Hawk settled," Eli says to a similarly objecting Alex.

Since God has not seen fit to acquiesce her request

for a tidy death, Sydney remains where she is, making resigned eye contact with Matts, who is still shirtless and now has his hands jammed in his pockets. The gesture pulls his jeans down to show off the stupid *V* cut of the muscle on his hips. It's possible he's not wearing underwear. It's also possible he exists purely to vex her.

"So, hey," Matts says. "I feel like I made you uncomfortable. I should have asked before touching you. And I want to apologize." He sounds like he's reading from a script, but his expression is earnest.

"No," Syd says. "You didn't make me uncomfortable. You're just… As you pointed out earlier, you're attractive and shirtless, and then you were touching me, which was *fine*. I just got a little flustered. Dazed. Befuddled. Hot and bothered, if you will."

Matts glances down at himself as though he hasn't noticed his state of undress. And then scrambles to pull his shirt on.

"Sorry," he says from inside the fabric. It looks like he's trying to shove his head through one of the armholes. "You're usually so confident. It was weird to see you…uh, flustered."

"Yeah, well, okay, hold on. Come here." Sydney helps redirect his head so it pops through the collar. "I need you to understand that I am 90 percent bravado and 100 percent anxiety."

"That's not how percentages work," he says, raking disheveled hair out of his face.

"Matts."

"Sorry. Sorry, I understand. So. We're good?"

"We're good."

"And I can text you?"

"You can text me."

"Cool."

"Cool."

Neither of them moves.

Matts rocks back on his heels.

"I'm going to go get in the car now." Sydney says. She does not salute this time, which is only a small consolation.

Once she's climbed into the back seat, Syd folds over to bury her face in Hawk's neck.

"Well, *that* was certainly something," Alex says.

"Be nice," Eli hisses back. "She's having a crisis."

She is.

Chapter Five

MATTS IS ON his way to Eli and Alex's place for an early dinner on Sunday afternoon when Aaron calls him.

He presses the Accept button on his car's touch screen. "Please tell me you're not drunk at 4:00 p.m."

"I don't *only* call you when I'm drunk."

Matts doesn't respond to that. Aaron is quiet for a moment, clearly trying to think of a recent example he can use as evidence.

"Whatever. I'm not drunk *this* time."

"So, what's the occasion?"

"It's, uh… Shit, I'm not good at this."

"Not good at what?"

"Giving people bad news."

Matts's stomach sours. "Just fucking tell me."

Aaron sighs. "Your dad's been to the doctor a few times this last month. When he went in yesterday, they said it's cancer. They caught it early, I guess, so that's good. He didn't want anyone to tell you, but I figured you'd want to know."

Matts swallows. "What kind of cancer?"

"It's in his lungs."

"From the smoking."

"Yeah. He's most pissed about having to stop. And he hasn't yet, actually. Says he'll have one last good weekend and give it up on Monday."

"Of course."

"Anyway, it doesn't sound like it'll kill him any time soon, but since you skipped Christmas" —Matts ignores the judgment in his tone—"I figure he won't tell you until it's obvious that something is wrong. Which means late spring. You *are* still planning to come back for the spring drive, right?"

Every year in May or June, once the snow has melted, they move the cattle from their land in Gunnison up to Gothic. In the late fall, they move them back. Fall drives have been hit or miss since Matts was drafted, but he's never missed a spring drive. The snow doesn't start melting until playoffs are well underway.

"Yeah," he says, "I'll be there."

"Good."

Neither of them says anything for several seconds, and the silence stretches to the point of discomfort.

"In other news," Aaron says, "Bud got that drone you sent the kids stuck in the big pecan tree. We had to shoot it out. I'll send you a video."

"Shoot it out," Matts repeats.

"We weren't going to climb our asses up there, and that thing is worth too much to leave it."

"So you…"

"Shot the limb off where it was stuck. It's fine, by the way. The drone, I mean. The tree is missing a limb now."

"Yeah, I got that." He smiles despite himself. "Send me the video."

"I will."

He pulls into Alex and Eli's garage and rolls down his window to punch in the visitor code.

"Hey, I've got to go, but thanks. For telling me. Keep me posted about Dad. About how he's doing but also—"

"The bills," Aaron sighs.

"And don't—"

"Tell them," Aaron finishes. "I know."

"Right. Okay. Bye."

Matts parks but doesn't get out, hands on his knees, pulling at the fabric of his track shorts, music muted, engine running.

He's struggling to reconcile the force of a man that is his father with the reality of cancer. He's not a child anymore; Matts knows his father isn't the indomitable, all-knowing character he grew up idolizing. He knows, intimately, that his father is fallible. Human. But cancer is a development in that schema that he's not at all equipped to handle. Especially not in the next five minutes before he's supposed to go socialize with a good portion of his teammates and their partners. Matts decides he just won't deal with it now. He turns off the engine and collects the bags of grocery items Eli requested on autopilot. He spends the elevator ride refocusing, trying to go back to the mental state he was in ten minutes before.

When Matts gets to Alex and Eli's apartment, he opens the door without knocking, yells hello to the assortment of people already there, and makes his way to the kitchen to dump Eli's requests on the island. Where he pauses.

Because Rome is dipping a chip in some salsa. And Rome is holding a baby. A *baby* sits in the cup of his elbow, one hand fisted in the collar of his shirt. She's dressed in a green onesie, and she has a tiny, poofy, whale spout of a ponytail on the top of her head.

"That's a baby," Matts says dumbly.

"Excuse you, that's *the* baby," Eli says, moving forward to grab her ankle and smack a kiss on the bottom of her tiny bare foot.

Matts doesn't think that's hygienic, but the baby seems to find the foot kissing deeply amusing.

He realizes this must be Finley, the sister Rome's in the process of adopting. Rome talks about her all the time. But Matts doesn't like babies, so he typically avoids the conversations where photographs are shared and he might be expected to make commentary about how cute a drooling infant is. *This* baby is pretty cute though.

"We've got her for the next month," Rome explains. "It'll be the first longer visit in the transition process, and Damien is being very chill about it."

Damien has a diaper bag slung across his chest and holds his phone in one hand and a stuffed lobster in the other. He's staring at the baby as if Rome might yeet her across the room at any moment. Damien does not look particularly chill.

Eli kisses Finley's other foot, grins at her giggles, and then sighs, an overloud, dramatic thing. "Alex. I want one."

Alex pats Eli's back consolingly. "And you'll have one in approximately three to four years." He says it like it's something he repeats often. "Your parents still want to kill me over the elopement. We need to give them some time to acclimate to the idea of becoming grandparents. And you need to finish college first."

"Curse you and your logic."

"So, hey," Damien says, coming to stand next to Matts. "I brought you something." He digs out a book from the bag on his hip and hands it over.

No Fear Shakespeare: Twelfth Night

"Uh," Matts says. "Thank you?"

"It's what Syd was quoting from last night," Rome adds. "Maybe read the first few pages. See if it interests you."

"Or, literally, just the first page," Damien murmurs.

Matts is pretty sure they're both insane. "Sure, yeah. Thanks."

The baby lets out a shriek and reaches two sticky-looking hands toward him.

Rome proffers the shrieking, sticky child to Matts.

"You wanna hold her?"

"No, no," Matts says, taking a step back, gripping the book with both hands. "No, I'm good."

Finley shrieks again, and Rome bends to set her on the floor, where she promptly crawls to plop herself between Matts's feet.

Matts freezes as she gets a handful of his leg hair and tugs experimentally.

"Dude," Rome says. "She's a baby, not a bomb."

This is true. He'd know what to do with a bomb. Tossing a child out the nearest window is likely frowned upon though.

Blessedly, Hawk chooses this moment to amble in from the living area, and the baby abruptly loses interest in him in the face of a dog.

Within minutes, they're playing something like tag, in which Hawk follows Finley in an army crawl before switching places and letting Finley chase her. Damien follows them both, watchful.

Eli hoists himself up to sit on the counter next to Matts. "Hey, so, speaking of Syd," he says, even though they aren't anymore. "Are you planning to see her again any time soon?"

Matts takes a second to reorient himself. "Tonight, actually."

"Oh, *really*."

"Just for a jam session."

"Uh-huh."

Matts knows what Eli—more specifically Eli's eyebrows—are implying. "She's not interested in me."

This draws objections from several people present, including Jeff and Jeff's wife, Jo, who *weren't even there yesterday*.

"She isn't," Matts argues. "She straight up said to me that her flirting doesn't mean anything, and she wasn't interested in a hookup."

"Implying she's interested in more than a hookup?" Alex suggests.

"*No*."

"But if she was, would you be down?" Alex asks.

"If she was interested in a hookup? Yeah, probably."

"What about more than a hookup?"

"I mean. Also, probably."

If he's being honest, Matts is still not sure how he feels about the whole trans thing. But Sydney is—Sydney. There's something almost magnetic about her. And yeah, he always says he's only interested in hookups, but that's because a hookup is easier than dealing with the whole "mortifying ordeal of being known" thing. He thinks he might want to know Sydney though. And if that means being known in return, well, maybe the vulnerability would be worth it. Maybe it wouldn't be a disaster.

"But she's an actual rock star," Matts says, more a continuation of his internal thoughts than the external conversation.

"And?"

"And. Hypothetically. If I was going to try and shoot my shot, how would I...do that?"

"You're acting like you've never hit on a girl before," Alex says.

"I usually just hook up with whoever hits on *me*. And she's not some girl. Have you *met* her?"

Eli gives Alex the significant look that Matts has found married people often use with one another. He's not sure what it means though.

"You could compliment her teeth again," Eli says. "That seemed to work yesterday."

"Lean against something," Jo says wisely. "Everyone knows the sluttiest thing a man can do is lean against something."

"Preferably while wearing a button-down with the sleeves rolled up," Eli says.

"Oh, yeah, good," Jo agrees. "Work the forearms."

"French tuck your shirt," Eli suggests. "And something on your wrists—like those bracelets you have, the jade and tiger's-eye ones?"

"And do the swoopy thing with your hair," Jo says, reaching up to run her fingers through it, pushing it to one side rather than slicked back. A loose curl falls into his eyes.

"Better," Eli agrees. "And she always wears all those rings. You could use that."

"Ohhh," Jo says. "Nice. Like, ask her about a particular ring. Use it as an excuse to hold her hand. If she responds well, ask her out. Jeff did that with the scar on my knuckles the night we met. It was smooth as hell."

Matts thinks about the strangely fraught moment at the cookout when he was holding Sydney's hand in his, her rings cold, his palm hot. He thinks about the pads of her fingers pressed to his calluses. She has a ring that looks like a dragon on her right index finger, wings folded, neck lying alongside its own tail. It's noteworthy. Matts could point it out. Could reach for it.

He could do that.

"The important thing," Eli says brightly, "is to be yourself."

Except Matts knows that's not true. He learned

early and he learned well that his best options for socializing were silence or parroting something someone else had already said that received a positive reaction. But that only works up to a point. That works with acquaintances and business relationships and small-talk interactions. The necessary vulnerability of a relationship is a different, more terrifying monster than talking in the locker room or shaking hands with a sponsor. Because he doesn't have to imagine how devastating it would be to share all of himself with someone and them to find him lacking. It wouldn't be the first time someone preferred the edited, curated version of Justin Matthews to the messy, raw file.

The problem, of course, isn't that he thinks no one would date him. The problem is that he's sure people would, but they wouldn't be dating him for *him*. He's attractive and a professional athlete, and perhaps most importantly, he has money. He knows these things make the rest of him more palatable. But he doesn't want to be tolerated because he can afford an enviable lifestyle. He doesn't want to be a pretty prop in social media posts and otherwise ignored at home.

The question is if he can find someone who would love him for who he is rather than what he can provide.

The fear is that the answer is no.

That night, Matts puts on a button-down shirt and rolls it to his elbows. He wears the jade and tiger's eye bracelets. He swoops his hair. He has to google what a French tuck is, but in the end, he'll admit he looks pretty good.

When Matts gets to the ranch, a large, shiny tractor unit of a semitruck sits in the yard that was not there during his prior visit. He parks next to it, and when Matts gets out, he can hear the semi engine ticking as it cools down. Whoever it belongs to only preceded him by a few minutes.

Matts doesn't have to wait long to figure out who that someone is.

The front door opens before he's even up the porch steps, and Sydney ushers him inside while shouting something about blasphemy down the hall.

"Uh, hi?" Matts says.

"Sorry, sorry, come in," she says. "My uncle, Wade, just showed up unannounced, *as he is wont to do*, and he's already dispensing heretical takes. Come meet him and help me settle this."

Matts has no idea what *this* is, but he follows Sydney obligingly into the kitchen.

She's wearing an oversized, age-faded Judas Priest

tour shirt and either very short shorts or nothing underneath it. For his sanity, he decides there are shorts in play.

"Wade, Matts, Matts, Wade," Sydney says.

Wade is a sixty-something, six-foot-something Black man who bears no resemblance to Sydney or the rest of the family Matts has met.

"No biological relation," Wade says, perhaps accurately interpreting Matts's confusion. "Syd adopted me when she was ten."

"And he kept her from becoming a missing person. Or a dead person," Devo says from where he's sitting at the table reading. "So, we adopted him."

Matts has questions.

"And since he's incapable of settling down," Sydney continues, "we're currently his *only* family in the southern United States."

"I have a nomadic spirit," Wade says gravely.

"You have no game is what you have. And also shit taste in music."

"Young lady, I *provided* your musical education."

"And now the protégé has surpassed the master."

"Sounds like the protégé is getting too big for her britches."

"He thinks the new Edge Land single is *good*,"

Sydney tells Matts as if that's supposed to mean something to him.

Matts looks to Devo for help, and Devo shakes his head minutely.

"Is it?" Matts asks.

Sydney gives him a look of utter betrayal. "Ugh. I forgot you only like music by men who write about tractors and beer and girls in cut-off shorts sliding into the passenger seats of pickup trucks."

"Don't forget the songs by women about wives murdering abusive husbands," Devo says, eyes still on his book.

"Those are okay, actually," Syd says. "I rescind my complete disdain for the genre and redirect it to the aforementioned sort."

"I don't *only* listen to country music," Matts argues. "I was listening to Black Sabbath on the way over here. And obviously, I like your music."

"Respectable," Wade says.

"Suspicious," Syd mutters, eyes narrowed. "Are you trying to ensorcell me with good taste?"

Matts doesn't know what "ensorcell" means, but he can guess from context that it's a good thing. "Is it working?"

"Yet to be determined." Syd pulls herself up to

perch on the counter. "Anyway, Edge Land is a punk band. Their new single is terrible, but Wade says it's important cultural commentary or whatever and not just antiestablishment pandering sitting precariously on a couple barre chords."

It's probably bad that Matts finds her curled-lip disdain so endearing.

"So," he says, to make sure he understands, "you don't like Edge Land, or you don't like this particular song?"

"The former. I'm not a huge fan of punk in general—I prefer rock and metal—but I can respect the bands that are actually trying to be agents of social change and manage to do so with a modicum of musicality. Black Flag, Dead Kennedys, The Clash, Petrol Girls, Bad Breeding. But Edge Land is far from their ranks."

"Aren't rock, metal, and punk basically the same thing though?" Matts asks.

"Oh, kid," Wade says.

"Here we go," Devo mutters.

"Maybe don't say that in front of, literally, anyone ever again," Sydney says. "Who taught you about music?"

"No one with sense," Wade says.

Matts didn't realize music was a thing that was supposed to be taught. "No one, yeah. But…maybe you could? If you want."

Sydney's legs, kicking idly at the lower cabinets, go still. "Dangerous invitation, Matthews. Words like that will get you a syllabus of listening homework."

"Don't threaten me with a good time."

"I shall consider that gauntlet *thrown*, sir." She's grinning.

Matts is proud to be responsible for it.

"So," he says. "Am I allowed to ask how Wade prevented you from becoming a missing and-or dead person?"

Sydney meets Wade's eyes, shrugging.

"Well," Wade says. "It was ten years ago, and I was at a truck stop in Mississippi. Had just woken up, 5:00 a.m., and was about to get on the road. I was walking back from the showers when this wisp of a thing, not even yea high"—he holds a hand to his hip—"comes walking up, bold as you please, eating candy and asking where I'm headed. I says Nevada, and she asks if I'll pass through Texas. I says yes, by way of Dallas and Odessa. She says Dallas'll do and asks for a ride."

"She was ten," Matts clarifies.

"She was ten," Wade agrees. "Said she was twelve

when I asked, not that twelve would have been better."

"So, you took her?"

"Not at first. I said no way no how, she needed to get home to her family. She said her family was in Texas. I asked where she started from, and she said she'd taken a Greyhound bus from Georgia and then walked to the truck stop from the bus station. Said if I wouldn't take her, she'd keep asking around until she found someone who would."

"Georgia?"

"She was lying, of course, but I didn't know that."

"The truck stop was just over two miles away from my house," Sydney explains. "I figured if Wade thought I was already far from home, he'd be more likely to take me where I wanted."

"And she was right. As soon as she started walking to the next truck, I agreed. It was stupid and could have got me in a whole hell of a lot of trouble, but I didn't know what to do, and I knew she'd be safe with me until I could figure it out."

"He was playing Metallica in the cab," Sydney adds as if this is an important part of the story. Then again, for her, it probably is. "It was the first time I'd ever heard secular music, much less metal." She sighs, pretending to swoon. "It was life-changing."

"So, I plied her with beef jerky and good music and tried to figure out if she was a runaway or in some nasty custody battle situation, and she was extremely unhelpful."

"But he wore me down, and I gave him Mom and Dad's phone number," Sydney says. "I mean, not my biological parents. Mom and Dad are technically my aunt and uncle."

"I called," Wade says, "and they got in the car and met me in Fort Worth. Where I handed Sydney and most of my CD collection over and promised to visit the next time I was passing through the Houston area."

"Which he's done ever since," she says, pointing to him. "Exhibit A."

Matts has potentially more questions than he started with.

"Anyhow," Wade says. "I know you two had plans, and I'm running on fumes." He nods down the hall. "We can finish discussing your lapsed musical taste in the morning, Syd."

"Yeah, yeah. Clean towels are in the cabinet as usual. Sheets aren't fresh, but you're the one that slept on them last."

Syd shrugs on her jacket and grabs Matts's wrist to tug him toward the back door. "You ready?"

The katydids are shrieking as they make their way down the tire-pitted gravel road from the front house to the equipment barn. Matts has to watch his feet in the darkness. Clouds almost entirely blot out the moon, with only a few bright stars visible in the slashes of black sky, and they move quickly in a dizzying, dark-blue wave. Matts stumbles over his feet looking at them, and her hand reaches out, just for a second, to steady his elbow.

"So, you've got questions," Sydney says.

He takes that as tacit permission to ask them. "Why did you run away from home?"

He'd considered it a few times. Knew *his* reasons. But Matts figures hers are probably a little different.

Sydney exhales, long and slow. "My biological parents were—*are*—pretty hardcore religious. So you can imagine they didn't take it well when their five-year-old son started insisting he was a girl."

Matts can imagine. He doesn't like it.

"I learned I couldn't say anything out loud when they were around, but Devo called me his little sister when it was just the two of us. And he managed to steal some girl's clothes from the church's lost and found for me. Bought some nail polish from the dollar store, stole some makeup one time, though that was never my thing."

Sydney shoves her hands deeper into her pockets, kicking a stone to skitter farther down the road in front of them.

"When I was ten, Devo was twelve. And he was allowed to walk to the library by himself. He found some books about transgender kids, and he checked them out and smuggled them home to me. But my parents found them, and it—"

She kicks another rock. "Well. A lot of things happened. But they cut off my hair. It was long and pretty much the only thing I liked about my body. They buzzed it. Said they were going to send me to a place that would fix me. And I didn't want to be fixed. So I left."

"How did you know you'd be safe here?"

"I knew my biological parents hated my aunt and uncle. I didn't know why, just that they were a 'bad influence.' Enemy of my enemy and all that. And I didn't know where they were in Texas, but I had their phone number, and I figured I'd call once I was in the state. I didn't understand how big Texas was."

"Devo wasn't joking," Matts realizes. "Wade might have saved your life."

"Yeah. Ten-year-old kid trying to hitchhike across multiple states. Pretty stupid, right?"

"I don't know. I think it was brave."

Sydney's a few feet ahead of him, and she turns to face him, walking backward, hands still in her pockets. The wind tosses her hair in her face. "It's not bravery if you're incapable of being any other way."

Matts disagrees but says, "So they let you stay? Once you got here?"

Sydney makes an inelegant noise. "My biological parents were insultingly willing to get rid of me, and Mom and Dad were...weirdly willing to take on the shit show that was a surprise traumatized kid."

"What about Devo?"

"Devo—" Sydney pauses, starts again. "That took longer. He wanted to come immediately. But he was still their perfect son, so they fought a little harder for him. Until he realized that if he stopped being perfect, they stopped caring so much."

"Conditional love is really something."

"It was more than that." Sydney spins suddenly so her back is to him again. "He was pissed and thirteen, and he pushed them too far on purpose. Antagonized them. Worse than he should have. When CPS got involved, they finally agreed to let him come. I don't think even my biological parents liked the people they'd become at that point."

"Well. Shit." Matts isn't sure what else to say.

"Yeah."

Motion-activated lights flick on as they approach the barn, and Sydney pauses to type in a code on the door before pulling it open. She ushers him inside, turning on lights as they go.

The practice space is clearly differentiated from the rest of the shop, with black foam-paneled plywood walls wrapped around a drum kit, a selection of guitars on stands, a keyboard, mics and amps and pedals, and a sound mixing table. Black cords spill everywhere, and notebooks and loose sheets of paper lay stacked on the ground, beside the turntable, and on the ripped couch against the wall by the drum kit. A dozen boxes line the opposite wall, one on top of the stack half open and spilling out merch shirts. It smells like weed and sweat. He loves it.

Matts sets his guitar case on the couch and pauses to look at a series of Polaroids decorating the space between foam sound panels. One in particular catches his eye: Sydney, Rex, and Sky sit on bleachers together. They look young and different, while still recognizable as a unit.

"The band in its infancy," Sydney murmurs from his shoulder. She's close enough he can smell her hair.

He tries not to let on that he's taking advantage of that.

"How did the band happen?" Matts asks. "You were, what, sixteen?"

"Mm. Fifteen. And freaks flock together." Sydney pokes her own face in the picture. "Especially in rural schools. I showed up in a Megadeth shirt and skinny jeans first day of freshman year, with a trans Pride patch on my backpack. At lunch, there was only one table I figured I could sit at without potentially endangering my life, and there they were."

Matts gets a sudden, unwelcome sense of vertigo because there was a very similar table at his school cafeteria. And he was never kind to the people sitting at it.

"Rex started arguing with me about music before we even exchanged names," Sydney continues. "And I ended up going over to his house that night for a jam session. We talked Sky into learning drums later that week."

"Wow." Matts is still trying to imagine how he would have treated the kids in the picture when he was fifteen. He's not enjoying the exercise.

"We probably should have convinced some of the others to join us too." Sydney sighs. "Because now we desperately need a second guitarist, but finding one has been hell."

"I thought hell was your thing."

She punches him in the shoulder, but it's gentle, and she's smiling again. "You know what I mean, smart ass. Any chance you want to audition?"

"Pass." He steps to the side to look at a series of articles featuring the band. "Maybe if I retire early."

"I thought that word was off-limits for professional athletes. According to Eli, he can't even think it too loudly or Alex will get hives."

"Oh, I guess it's not the same for me."

Sydney falls backward onto the sofa and tucks herself against the arm, legs to her chest, chin in the valley between her knees. "What do you mean?"

"Only that"—he unfolds the bent edge of an article from *Rolling Stone*—"I probably don't love hockey the way most of the guys do. Alex *loves* hockey. For him and Rushy and Kuzy and Rome, hockey is part of them. It's not like that for me."

"So what is it like?"

"I...like being good at hockey. And when I was younger, I liked the attention it got me. The validation. And I like what hockey gives me now. Money and a team and friends. But I wouldn't be destroyed if my career ended sooner than expected, you know? It's something I do. Not something I am."

"That's shockingly healthy."

"I guess."

Matts pauses as he unfolds another wrinkled article because it's not an article; it's a photo spread.

Of Sydney.

She's reclining in an empty bathtub, wearing leather pants, a few strategically placed chain necklaces, and not much else. Kohl smears her eyes, and her hair looks like someone's run their damp fingers through it. Her head is tipped back, eyes barely open but staring directly at the camera. A cigarette dangles between two black-nailed fingers as a waft of smoke drifts from her bruised-looking mouth.

Half of him is turned on, which Matts thinks is fair. The other half is too focused on the cigarette to fully appreciate that, apparently, Sydney has even more tattoos hidden by her oversized shirt.

"You smoke?" he asks.

"Oh Jesus, don't look at those. I do *not* smoke. That was one of many artistic choices I wasn't super comfortable with that day. I don't typically wander around with my tits out either."

The relief Matts feels is palpable. "It's a good picture." He feels he can appreciate it more, knowing she doesn't have a pack of cigarettes in her back pocket.

"But it sets a bad precedent, right?" Sydney says. "Like, it glamorizes smoking. But also"—she waves a hand—"I do look...annoyingly badass. Which is probably me internalizing the idea they're wanting to perpetuate, but—"

"It's a good picture," he repeats.

"Yeah." Sydney sighs, then stands with a sudden lurch, picks up one of the guitars, and ducks to slip the strap over her hair. She nudges the amp with the toe of her boot. "You wanna tell me why you looked like I killed your dog for a second there? Did a smoker break your heart or something?"

Or something.

Matts turns to face her fully. "My dad smokes. Always has, as long as I can remember. And I just found out a few hours ago he's got lung cancer. And my mom was— Cancer killed her a few years back. So I guess that's...fresh." Saying it for the first time out loud makes it feel suddenly, viscerally real in a way it hadn't up until this point.

"Well shit," she says.

"Yeah. Sorry."

"What are you apologizing for?"

Matts shrugs. His mouth is dry and his eyes are wet and his throat suddenly feels hot. He turns to look at the wall of articles again. He hasn't cried in front of someone else in a decade, and he's not going to start today in front of Sydney Fucking Warren, of all people.

"What are your thoughts on hugging?" Sydney asks after a moment. "Because you look a little devastated right now, and I'm shit at talking about feelings, but I give excellent hugs. Like, top tier. I can provide references if you'd like."

"I…like hugs," he says, and it would feel embarrassingly childish if not for how she nods seriously, slinging the guitar around to her back, and steps into him.

She's right. She gives good hugs.

Sydney tucks her face in the space between his chest and chin, her hair brushing his jaw, and she smells like vanilla. Like leather cleaner. Her arms are tight around him without being too restrictive, palms pressed to his flank and shoulder, fingers splayed and firm.

Matts doesn't know what to do with his hands, so he mimics her, avoiding the guitar as best he can. But then, Sydney shifts even closer, tightening her hold, squeezing an exhale from him, and his hand on her shoulder blade moves of its own accord, sliding up beneath her hair to cup the back of her neck. It feels right; the curve of humid skin fits perfectly to the space between his thumb and index finger.

"Jeff says you have to hug for ten minutes for it to be effective," Matts murmurs, mostly for something to fill the silence.

"Ten *minutes*? How is Jeff an authority on hugging?"

"His wife has a PhD."

Sydney tips her head up to look at him incredulously. "A PhD in hugging?"

"Uh, bats."

"She has a PhD…in bats."

"She did her dissertation on bats. The degree was something biological."

"And this gives her credibility regarding the science of hugging how?"

"I'm just saying she's smart, so she probably knows stuff. Which means Jeff probably knows stuff."

Sydney narrows her eyes. This close, he realizes they're hazel, not brown. "Hey, Matts," she says. "What's sixty-seven times ninety-four?"

He thinks for a few seconds. "Six thousand two hundred and ninety-eight."

"Right. And what's the difference between active and passive voice?"

He looks at her blankly.

"You are, literally, the poster child for the concept that just because someone is smart in one aspect doesn't mean they're smart across the board."

"I can't tell if that's insulting or not. But also, what's the worst thing that could happen? You can't overdose on hugging."

Sydney looks like she wants to argue but can't seem to source a rebuttal. Matts is strangely pleased by that.

"Well, I'm not hugging you for ten minutes," she says. "Part of the appeal of my hugs is that they leave you wanting more, which would not be the case if we stood here for ten minutes."

He's pretty sure that's not true. Matts is also pretty sure he shouldn't tell her that.

"But," Sydney continues, "I can do a solid minute."

She rocks a little, and he rocks with her. She turns her face so her cheek is pressed to his chest again. The rocking turns more into a barely discernible sway, and Matts hazards moving his thumb, just a little, where it's resting on her neck. He can feel the downy whirl of baby hairs trying to curl beneath her ear.

It occurs to Matts that he's never been afforded the luxury of just enjoying another human so close to him before—not without the anxiety, the expectation of what's happening next. Hookups are such hurried things. He's never been allowed to linger. To touch. Sydney feels so alive against him, her lungs expanding with each breath under his hands and against his chest, and she's so warm and her skin is so soft and she smells *so fucking good*.

Matts walks his fingers down the terrain of her spine, knuckles bumping against the back of the guitar. He considers that she's the one who offered to hug him. That has to be greater than or equal to a positive hand-holding response. Maybe, at the end of the night, he'll ask her to get dinner next week. Maybe she'll say yes.

"So, we're leaving for the spring tour on Wednesday," Sydney says.

"Oh." His hand pauses its exploration. His fingers curl into the age-softened fabric of her shirt. "How long will you be gone?"

"Until May. But we'll be back for at least a week around Easter between the two legs."

May. That's four months. That's fine. He can be patient.

Sydney loosens her hold, hands sliding from his back to his sides to his belly, pushing just enough to create space between them. "Okay, I think that's enough."

It's not. But if the goal is to leave him wanting more, it's certainly effective.

"We should play," she says, stepping back, and it feels like a loss.

Matts lets go with a degree of reluctance he doesn't want to examine.

"We should," he agrees.

And they do.

Chapter Six

SOMETIMES SYDNEY FORGETS.

Sometimes, entrenched in the joy of doing what she loves with people she loves, of looking in the mirror and being content with what she sees, of calling home to proud parents and standing at the edge of a stage, eyes closed while people scream her lyrics back to her, sometimes Sydney forgets that she's not just some girl living her dream.

But she is always reminded, eventually.

Today, that reminder comes in the form of two drunk men at the bar where they're celebrating after yet another sold-out show.

It's 2:00 a.m., and Sydney's past her threshold of overstimulation, the adrenaline from the show faded to an uncomfortable alcohol-heightened buzz under her skin. She steps outside to breathe and post some pictures on Instagram, and as she's choosing which filter to use on the selfie she'd taken with the crowd that night, she's interrupted by a group of girls who recognize her—who had been at the concert earlier that night. Sydney signs their tour shirts, takes selfies with them and a few other people who are attracted by the group's attention. And then, leaning back against the warm brick of the club, she's just opened Instagram again when two men approach her. The casualness of their interruption, the ease with which they poison the well of contentment in her chest, is startling. There are people close enough that she doesn't feel physically in danger, but none of the people are so close they can hear the quiet, pointed words. The threats of what they'd do if they could get her alone. The favor they'd be doing the world if they did.

Sydney doesn't respond. What can she say to people whose purpose isn't to listen.

She backs her way inside. Points them out to security when they follow her. She orders an Uber to the hotel and texts the others she's leaving. She has the car pick her up at the back entrance.

Sydney cries, furious about crying, while she showers.

After, lying in the dark, she can't sleep. She unlocks her phone, stares at the still-unposted selfie from an hour before, and then swipes away. Sydney doesn't want to be alone. But her closest friends are rightfully celebrating their victory, and she knows if she calls them, they'd come back, but they'll also be drunk, and they spend too much of their time worrying about her as it is.

Her parents aren't an option. Her mom needs what rest she can get and her dad's blood pressure is already a mess.

Sydney tries Wade first on the off chance he's driving overnight. No answer.

MJ. No answer.

Eli. Straight to voicemail.

Matts answers immediately—before she can rethink the impulse and hang up.

"Hey," he says. "Hold on, let me put you on speaker."

"What are you doing?"

"Cooking. My internal clock is fucked, and I figured if I couldn't sleep, I'd do something useful. So. Meal prepping."

"How are you defining 'cooking'?"

Something clatters in the background. "Salmon, brussels sprouts with a balsamic reduction—Eli's recipe—and sweet potatoes. And I've got a crock pot with chili running and cornbread in the oven too. Should end up with a dozen meals between the two when I'm done."

"Shit. Is there anything you can't do?"

Matts thinks about it. "Navigate social situations without anxiety. Conceptualize the benefit of the switching strategy when faced with a Monty Hall problem. Laundry. There are probably others."

"Stop being funny, I'm trying to be grumpy, and you are distressingly close to making me smile."

"I'm sorry?"

"You're not forgiven."

"All right, well, fuck you, too, I guess."

"Much better, thank you."

"So," Matts says after a comfortable silence. "Why are you grumpy?"

"Because I want to be liked by everyone all the time, and that's objectively not a feasible goal."

Matts doesn't laugh like he's supposed to. "What happened?" His voice is low. His tone is uncomfortably perceptive.

"Nothing terrible. I wasn't in danger or anything," Sydney says. "Just assholes being assholes."

He doesn't say anything. It feels like he's waiting.

"And it's not even new. I get a dozen shitty comments a day on my social posts, but it— Our record label warned us that the bigger we get, the more notoriety we'll get. A band entirely made up of queer people is a target, and a queer band *fronted by a trans woman* is... I don't know. Something even more enticing than a normal target." She takes a breath. "Sorry. That was a lot to unload on you at 4:00 a.m."

"No, it's fine. It sucks you have to deal with that."

"It does," Sydney agrees.

"I saw a couple posts on IG from the concert," Matts says slowly. "It looks like that went well, at least?"

"It did." Sydney considers the hesitance in his voice. "I didn't post anything though. I don't think Rex or Sky did either."

"I follow your tag. The Red Right Hand tag. So, my dash has been flooded with video clips the last few hours."

She doesn't know how to respond to that.

"I also follow Devo, and he posted a picture of you two backstage. But he captioned it 'having fond thoughts of being an only child.' What's that about?"

"It would appear," Sydney says, "one cannot engage in a bit of innocent tomfoolery without being labeled a menace to society."

"Are you not?"

"I mean. I'm definitely a menace to *Devo*. I feel like 'society' is an unfair extrapolation. I was bored. He was there."

"Maybe the next time you're bored, you can work on my syllabus instead of tormenting your brother."

"Your syllabus."

"You said you'd provide me with a musical education."

"I did say that."

He's quiet. Sydney can hear him moving around in the background, can hear the sound of a pan sliding on the stovetop.

"Are you serious?" she asks. Just to be sure.

"Yeah, of course."

Sydney sits up. "Well, we're going to do this right, then. Let me get my laptop."

"I'm not going anywhere."

It takes her a few minutes to locate her glasses and get things set up on the little desk against the opposite wall.

"Okay," she says, blank document open, "we need to establish a bassline first. Now, I want you to answer honestly, and I promise I won't judge you...much. What music do you typically listen to?"

Matts makes a noise that feels like the verbal equivalent of a shrug. "I'm not picky. I have a couple genre playlists from Spotify. Rap. Country. Pop. Rock. Alternative. Just depends on my mood. Nothing I've curated."

Sydney can't fathom interacting with music that way, but Matts probably can't fathom having to use the calculator app to decide how much to tip at restaurants.

"Right. Okay. I'm going to name some artists, and I want you to tell me your thoughts about them. Positive. Negative. Ambivalent."

"Okay."

"Black Sabbath."

"Positive," he says confidently.

"Queen."

"Positive."

"Van Halen."

"I can't actually think of any Van Halen songs."

She sighs. "Guns N' Roses."

"Were they the ones that did 'Sweet Child of Mine'?"

"Yes."

"Then positive."

"Dio."

"Who?"

"Oh, Matthews. Rage Against the Machine."

"Uh...ambivalent."

"Metallica."

"Same answer."

"Judas Priest."

"Negative."

"Jesus."

"Is that a band?"

Sydney laughs despite herself. "That's an exclamation of dismay."

"You said you wouldn't judge me."

"I said I wouldn't judge you *much*. This is me judging you a very small amount."

"You wanted honesty," Matts says. "That's my honest opinion. They're just a little too screamy."

"Screamy," she repeats. "*They're too screamy*, says the professional hockey player. Hockey's default setting is screamy. *Your* default on the ice is screamy. Especially when they put you in the timeout box."

"Penalty box," he says, aggrieved.

"All right, all right. Fine. I did ask for honesty. Let's talk about more recent bands."

"I like Red Right Hand," Matts says promptly.

"Pandering will get you everywhere. How about Mastodon?"

"Don't know them."

"Fungi Grotto."

"I feel like you're making shit up, now."

"Edge Land?"

"Negative." And then, after a funny little pause: "Their music is 'antiestablishment pandering sitting on a couple barre chords.'"

"It *is*," Sydney agrees gleefully before pausing, fingers poised over her laptop keys. "Wait. That's almost word for word what I said about them in the kitchen the other day."

He is suspiciously silent.

"Matts."

"People like you more if they think you share their opinions," he says quietly.

Sydney settles her wrists on either side of the track pad. The heater is loud in the early-morning silence. She feels like she's suddenly lost control of the conversation, as though she has to tread carefully or a tenuous balance will be lost.

"Some people," Sydney says. "Some opinions. I'd prefer your actual thoughts though."

"Sorry," Matts says haltingly. "Habit. I've never listened to them, so no thoughts."

Sydney stands and paces over to the window. Behind the sprawl of glittering cityscape lights, the sky has a predawn blue cast. The exhaustion of the night is finally setting in, and the lights blur as she blinks gritty eyes. She closes them, leaning her forehead against the cool glass. "Do you...typically repeat things back to people because you know it will make them like you?"

"Not all the time." Matts takes an audible breath. "Sometimes, I feel like everyone else was given a manual for social interaction when they were born. But I wasn't. Cheating's always been the easiest way to even the score."

"How is repeating things others have said cheating?"

"It's like copying off someone's paper, right? Everyone else seems to come up with their own ideas just fine."

"Eh," she disagrees. "You clearly haven't seen the over-compressed political memes my grandparents post on social media."

There's a choking noise, followed by: "I just spit Gatorade all over my counter, so thanks for that."

"You're welcome."

"It doesn't always work, anyway," Matts says as if it's an admission. "Half the time, you think you know what people want to hear. But then you talk to a different person or—" He laughs in a way that feels like the opposite of a laugh. "Or you end up with a different team, and suddenly, what was normal to say in one locker room is making everyone really fucking mad at you in another." He sighs. "Anyway. I'll try not to do it again with you."

Sydney wishes she was talking on the phone at her great aunt's house. Because her great aunt has one of those ancient landlines attached to the wall in the kitchen and she's desperate for the tactile anchor of wrapping the coiled cord around her finger. Sydney opens her eyes. God, she's tired.

"So," she says. "Can I ask you a super invasive question? With the understanding that you are fully permitted to tell me to fuck off because it's none of my business."

"Yes."

"Are you autistic?"

Matts doesn't respond for several seconds.

"I don't know," he says. "And that's not a cop-out. It's just that my parents were told when I was a kid they should get me tested. I was held back in kindergarten because I was good at math but wasn't meeting any reading benchmarks and most of the time refused to speak. Had behavioral problems and struggled with social cues or whatever. But they never did. Mostly because I don't think they wanted to have to deal with what came next if they did."

"Well, shit," Sydney says, leaning back. Her forehead leaves an oily smudge on the window.

"What?"

"I have ADHD. Didn't find out until after I moved in with my parents, of course. I've always been good at socializing and reading and writing but had terrible issues focusing on things I didn't care about. Like math"—Matts makes an affronted noise—"or Texas fucking history."

"Remember the Alamo," he says somberly.

"I was just thinking," Sydney says around a laugh, "that with our powers combined, we might make one fully functioning human."

"That would be nice."

"Wouldn't it just," she agrees.

They fall into a companionable silence, and Sydney pulls her sleeve down over her palm to wipe off her forehead smudge. She makes her way back to the couch.

"Hey," Matts says. "Do you want to play a couple

shitty speakerphone duets before I let you go? Or do you need to rest your voice?"

"I do. But I've got my acoustic right here. You can be the lead singer. I'll accompany you."

"You sure?"

Sydney puts the phone on the table and pulls the guitar into her lap. "You're already on speakerphone. What do you want to play?"

"How about 'Wonderwall'?"

"Gross. Why?"

"Because."

"Because why?"

"Because *maybe*," he sings, "you're gonna be the one that *saves* me—"

"Oh, fuck off."

*

THE FOLLOWING EVENING, Sydney and Sky are procrastinating packing their bags, painting their toenails to the soundtrack of the Hell Hounds–Vegas game on the TV, when Rex barges into the hotel room, sunglasses still on.

"Afternoon," he calls. "What are you lovely ladies up to?"

"Passing the Bechdel Test," Sydney says. "Oh, no,

never mind, you've ruined it."

"Funny." He jumps over the back of the couch and settles between them. "Are you lusting after hockey men? That's not very Bechdel of you."

"Maybe we're talking about strategy."

"Can you name *one* hockey strategy?"

"Hit opponent," Sky says promptly.

"Score goal," Sydney adds.

"Yell about it," Sky finishes.

"Yeah," Rex says, "that's my fault. I should have put better parameters on that ask. *Why* are you watching hockey?"

"Because," Sydney says, "we needed a break from trying to decide if we're willing to be complicit in our own objectification if we're paid really well for it."

"Also," Sky clarifies, "Matts is playing."

"Minor detail," Sydney mutters.

"Ah." Rex pushes his sunglasses up into his hair. "Is this about the article?"

"Mm," they both agree.

They've been offered a print and digital feature for *Tone Dead* magazine. The print version includes the cover and a three-page article with four pictures. The pay is…nice. But they want to focus on Sky and Syd and that they're queer women who don't exactly fit within the more traditional concept of a gender binary. And Syd knows that publicity is publicity, and the magazine wouldn't be interviewing them at all if they didn't find their music somewhat praiseworthy on its own merit. But Sydney is tired of being used as a subversive carrot. Especially when, in at least one picture, they want her to be a mostly naked subversive carrot.

"It *is* a tidy sum," Rex says. "Are we leaning one way or the other? Money or morals?"

"Money," Sky says.

"Morals," Sydney says.

"Sounds like you need a tie breaker."

"Except, it's not your tits they're trying to monetize," Sydney grumbles.

"Which is offensive, frankly. I have great tits."

"You do," Sky says consolingly. She caps her polish, then leans forward to blow on her toes. "In all seriousness, if you don't want to do it, we won't do it. We all know the appeal is that taboo shit sells more—but that doesn't mean it wouldn't benefit others. I mean, they're still treating our bodies like they're worth admiration. That's not meaningless."

"Fair," Sydney admits. "But wouldn't it make you feel a little dirty?"

"If it did, I'd buy myself a very nice loofa with the

money they're throwing at us."

"Quick swerve," Rex says, pointing to the TV. "Syd, I believe your man just used all three of your strategies."

Sydney turns up the volume as the replay rolls, and sure enough, Matts slams another man into the boards, steals the puck from him, and near-simultaneously rockets the puck into the goal. His teammates crash into him, and yes, they all shout quite a bit about it.

"Forget music," Sky says seriously. "We should coach hockey."

"Is that allowed?" Rex asks. "Him shoving the other guy like that?"

"Mm," Sydney agrees. "As long as he had possession of the puck and Matts didn't hit him from behind. Totally legal."

But the man Matts checked is furious, regardless of the move's legality, and within seconds, there are people paired up all over the ice, and the refs are trying to separate Matts and the Vegas player, both of whom have lost their helmets and have their hands fisted in each other's jerseys. Matts is trying to shake off his remaining glove, grinning while ducking the other player's flailing arm. His sweaty hair clings to his exertion-flushed face, and he does this little shuffle with his feet that propels him just out of reach of the ref trying to grab him. And then all gloves are off, and they're both swinging, and the crowd is roaring. Sydney's biased, but she's pretty sure Matts is the winner by the time the refs drag them apart and banish them to their respective penalty boxes.

Matts licks his slightly bloodied lip, still grinning, face even more flushed as the other player shouts after him. He shoves his fingers through his hair as he steps into the box, and he yells something that clearly involves the word *fuck* back. Matts sits down and accepts the water bottle handed to him. He tongues the split in his lip, eyes on the ice.

"That's hot, right?" Sydney says. "Like, yes, violence is bad or whatever, but that was objectively hot, right?"

"Yes," Rex and Sky agree.

"Also," Sydney says belatedly. "Not my man."

"Sure," Sky says.

Someone knocks on the door, and they turn as a group to greet Devo, who looks perplexed by the scene in front of him.

"Are y'all watching *hockey*?"

"Matts just scored," Rex says. "It was hot."

"I'm sure. Are you all planning to pack at some point or…"

"We've got four minutes left in the third," Sydney says. "I'll finish when it's over."

"You say that like it means something to me."

Sydney flaps a hand at Devo. "I'll be ready to check out in an hour."

"Sky? Rex?"

They grumble but get up and head to their own room, leaving Sydney and Devo and the now too-loud TV.

Sydney turns the volume down, and Devo sits next to her. He pulls her open laptop from the coffee table onto his knees and enters her password like a habit. She doesn't think to stop him until it's too late.

"What is this?" he asks, scrolling through the open spreadsheet.

She has no way to answer that isn't damning.

"It's for Matts."

Devo waits.

"I'm…educating him. About music. That's just my planning document. I need to see what he's already familiar with and what he likes, and then I'll go from there."

Devo sighs.

"Yes, all right, I like him. Sue me," Syd says, eyes firmly on the TV screen. "I'm not trying to start anything. I'm not stupid. But he's a good person, and I've decided we're going to be friends. There's nothing wrong with that."

"I didn't say anything."

"It was implied."

"By my *breathing*?"

"Go away," Sydney says.

"Wait, what's this?" Devo clicks over to her Google Docs tab, and Sydney snatches the laptop away from him before he has a chance to find the even more damning content therein.

"Absolutely not," she says.

"Are you working on a new song?"

"No comment."

He studies her defensive position, then slaps his thighs as he stands. "Fine. But with all due respect—which is none, actually, so, with undue respect—I think you're setting yourself up for a broken heart."

"Maybe." Sydney's aiming for flippant but isn't sure how successful she is. "But I've never had my heart broken before. Worst case, the experience will be good for my creative process."

"Uh-huh. Just out of curiosity, what would be the *best*-case scenario, in your opinion?"

"No comment," she repeats and pointedly turns the

volume back up on the TV.

Devo makes a show of stretching and taking his time walking to the door. "Hey, for your planning spreadsheet, you're missing Queensrÿche and Pansy Division in your list of 1990s bands. Pro tip."

She makes a shooing motion, even though it is, technically, also his room.

He rolls his eyes and leaves.

Sydney waits a requisite, petty few minutes through the end of the game and the incredibly endearing line of players giving the goalie head pats before grudgingly updating the spreadsheet. And then she sits, laptop open, and considers the pile of clothes on her bed. The acoustic guitar is where she left it beside the nightstand in the early hours of the morning.

She looks at the laptop screen again. Sydney doesn't have to swipe to the other tab to remember the words on it. She doesn't have to pick up her guitar to feel out the beginning reverberating notes of the song segment that's been sitting between her ears for the last several hours. She can hear it in her head: a slow, wailing riff over a low, hard bass line.

> *The devil's in the details when you make*
> *deals with devils,*

but wisdom's no match for want
And I want, and I want, and I want
I want you to haunt me like a house you'll
abandon
I think I can stand it if you take me for
granted
I'm all doors, no locks, just come inside
Take what you find
Fuck shit up
Rob me blind

Chapter Seven

MATTS BUYS AN electric guitar.

He tries not to think too much about his motivation.

He buys a white-on-white Fender Stratocaster and a mini amp and gets new headphones while he's at it so he can have the best possible sound quality while practicing quietly. Matts has never been good at doing things in moderation.

Matts *has* always been good at playing songs by ear. His father discovered that talent a year or two into teaching him guitar. Matts had thought, at first, that he was going to get into trouble when his father found out he wasn't actually reading the music on the stand in front of him. Remembering what a song was supposed to sound like and just making his fingers do that was far easier than trying to translate what notes on a page meant. The problem was that he started to embellish as his technical skill improved. And that's when his father found him out, though he wasn't angry about it. Matts's ability to listen to a piece of music and then more or less recreate it from memory quickly became a party trick trotted out at family events and dinners with friends. Matts liked the attention, the approval. And much like the recognition he received for his hockey-related talents, it drove him to work harder and practice longer. Praise has always been his most compelling motivator.

Since signing his first NHL contract, Matts has mostly played for himself. As an established professional athlete, people tend to forget you're anything else. But Matts's guitar travels with him like some of his teammates travel with their favorite pillow. Playing redirects his focus and soothes the anxious chatter in his mind. His road roommates are used to him quietly practicing for half an hour or so before he goes to sleep. It's become a part of him; a skill crafted for the enjoyment of the action rather than preparation for a performance or in pursuit of validation.

So, it's strange to find himself targeting his

practices again when he's at home. He exchanges the acoustic for the Stratocaster, pulls up a song from one of Sydney's educational playlists, and tries to memorize and recreate it. Just in case.

Two months into Red Right Hand's tour, Matts can reliably play a dozen rock and metal and even a few punk songs from Dio to My Chemical Romance. He can also play most of Red Right Hand's first album because he's recently developed a potentially troubling habit. When he can't sleep at home, Matts uses both the MP3 jack and the headphone jack in his mini amp, pulls up a Red Right Hand song, and plays along with them, with Sydney's voice in his ears as if she's right there with him. Like, if Matts closes his eyes, he can almost imagine they're in the practice space at the ranch.

He knows this is probably not normal, which is why he doesn't tell anyone. So, six weeks later, Sydney still doesn't know that he's purchased the guitar. They text about other things—his musical education, the tour, his games. And sometimes, she'll call him after performances since she's always the first back to the hotel. They've had three over-the-phone acoustic jam sessions. But Matts can't seem to bring himself to mention the shiny new resident on her stand in the corner of his bedroom. And it's been long enough now that he feels like he can't. That it's become an embarrassing secret he shouldn't share. Or maybe he's overthinking things.

More likely than not, it's the latter because he's also been overthinking other things, such as if he should send the band tickets to the Hell Hounds versus Kings game since they'll be in LA, and it's the night before their performance. But is it weird that he knows that? That he checks their tour schedule to see what city they're in each night?

And then there's the Pride stuff. The Hell Hounds "hockey is for everyone" game and associated philanthropic events are in April. Matts already volunteered to be part of the media campaign, which isn't unusual as he was part of it the prior year as well. But last year, it felt more like penance to make up for his prior behavior toward Alex.

This year, Matts wants to participate because it's a cause worth supporting and because he's tired of the shit he sees on social media about Alex and Rome and now Sydney. The comments about Sydney are probably the worst. Or maybe they feel like the worst because… well, he doesn't know why. But Matts wants to be a little more vocal, a little more specific, with his support this year. He has a list of things he's considering but figures he'll start with the easiest one, which involves talking to

Rushy. Matts doesn't know if it'll make a difference, but if it will—

Two days before the Kings game, they're taking a breather between drills when Matts sees his opportunity; the coaches are setting up a new configuration of cones and stickhandling trainers, and Rushy is alone.

Matts loops around to the crease, waiting for Rushy to finish taking a drink and toss his water bottle onto the top of the net.

"Hey," Matts says.

"Hey," Rushy agrees.

"So you know how last year for Pride night, you used a different tape from everyone else? With the bi flag colors?"

Rushy gives him a critical look. "I do."

"Where did you get it?"

"Are you trying to tell me something?"

"*No.* I'm not—I mean, not that that's—no." Matts tries to rally. "Do they make tape in the trans flag colors? Because I looked online and couldn't find any, and I also don't know if I'd need special permission or…"

"Ah." Rushy's expression shifts, but Matts has no hope of interpreting it. "Probably. I just asked Jessica, and she made it happen."

He was afraid of that. But it's fine. Matts will brave

Jessica's office for Sydney. Not that it would be *for* her. Exclusively.

The trainers call for them to line up again.

"Hey, Matts," Rushy says. "Will it sound super condescending if I say I'm proud of you?"

"Uh, yeah. Probably."

"Okay." Rushy taps his stick against the side of Matts's skate. "I won't then."

Matts goes to get in line.

"What are you grinning about?" Rome asks, knocking shoulders with him.

"Nothing," he says.

Coach blows the whistle.

*

PRACTICE ENDS WITH a give-and-go drill that involves a lot of chirping from the guys watching, hands folded on sticks, chins resting on gloves. Matts typically keeps his chirps to "fuck you," "fucking try me," and variations therein. But he enjoys listening to the shit the other guys come up with, even if it's not particularly imaginative at times. Case in point, Asher's go-to is, "You suck at hockey." But Rushy is in top form, shouting along with the spectators as pucks ping off the goalposts and glance off the blade of his stick. Chirps like "Bro, how you gonna eat lunch with no hands?" and "You can pick up your participation trophy on the way out," and "Better luck next time, 10-ply."

When Alex is up, Rushy resets and salutes. "Whattaya got for me, oh captain, my captain?"

Alex ignores him. When he's fed the return pass, Alex crosses over, fakes left, and finally sinks a goal, top shelf, just over Rushy's right shoulder.

"Hey, tendy," Alex shouts through his exaggerated celly, "maybe if you switch to Geico, you'll save more."

The guys howl.

"Maybe if you hadn't used that chirp a hundred times already, it'd be funny," Rushy yells back.

"You admitting I've scored on you a hundred times, duster?"

And then they're playfully roughhousing, Rushy dramatically throwing off his gloves and squaring up to Alex while the others circle around them. They dissolve into a pretend fight as the coach gives up and calls an end to practice.

"So," Asher says to Kuzy as they're shuffling into the locker room, "who did you leave with last night?"

A couple of the guys went out to a bar the night before to celebrate Asher's birthday. Matts skipped it, but he's not surprised to hear Kuzy took someone home.

The man has some sort of magnetic pull when it comes to beautiful women.

"Pretty lady," Kuzy says predictably.

"What about that rodeo girl though. Aren't you seeing her?" Asher asks.

"MJ? Nah. She's not want serious. Just..." He considers. "Butt dial?"

"Booty call is for sex," Rome says. "Butt dial is when you call someone by accident."

Kuzy makes his familiar "English is ridiculous" noise. "Yeah, I'm her booty call." He shrugs. "It's hard." He pats his chest, feigning resignation. "But I survive."

"Yes," Rushy says dryly, "how sad for you."

"She's hot," one of the rookies says with standard, rookie-level tact.

"Mm," Kuzy agrees.

"Is she bossy?" the rookie asks. "She looks like she'd be bossy."

"I'm all kiss and no tell," Kuzy says.

"I think the phrase you're looking for is 'I don't kiss and tell,'" Jeff points out.

Kuzy considers this. "No."

"Fair enough."

"What about you, Matts," Alex says. "You asked out Sydney yet?"

"No. Maybe when they're back from their spring tour."

Rome sighs like Matts's inability to pull is a personal failure.

"When is that?" Jeff asks.

"May."

"Are you at least talking?" Rome asks.

Matts knows there are multiple different definitions for the word *talking*, and in this context, he has no idea which one Rome is referring to. He decides to pivot instead of answering.

"Actually, they're opening for Killer Sunday at the Crypto arena the day after we play the Kings. I was thinking about offering the band tickets to see us since they're supposed to get to LA on Friday morning. Do you think she'd want to come?"

"I don't know," Alex says. "But I do know an easy way to find out."

"How?"

"*Ask* her."

"Hey," Kuzy says, contemplative. "We've got break after Kings. Three days break."

"Oh," Rushy adds. "We should totally go to the concert."

Kuzy points to him. "*Yes*. Wingman for Matts."

"I don't need a wingman," Matts argues.

"No, you clearly need several," Rome says. "I'm down."

"Same," Jeff says. "Jo is in Mexico for another week anyway."

Matts strips out of his gear, trying to ignore the growing number of people committing to take him to a Red Right Hand concert while Jeff calls out seating options from the ticketing app on his phone.

His own phone lights up as he's about to head for the shower, and he only pauses, reaching for it, because he can see in the text preview that the message is from Sydney.

"Booty call?" Kuzy asks from his stall beside him.

"It's 11:00 a.m."

"So?"

Matts swipes to open the text from Sydney.

> *It looks like y'all play the Kings on Friday and then don't play again until Monday. Any chance you want a ticket to our show Saturday?*

He knows he could shower and then respond, but he doesn't. Instead, he stands there, naked, and tries to figure out a response that isn't too desperate sounding. He finally texts back.

I could stick around for another day. I could also get the band tickets to the Kings game on Friday if you want to go?

That'd be cool. You want to bring any of your teammates to the concert?

Matts looks up. "Sydney just invited us to their show."

Several of the guys whoop, including Alex and Rushy already in the shower.

"Well, that's good, seeing as I've already bought our tickets," Jeff says, holding up his phone. "Venmo me at your leisure, gentlemen."

Matts focuses on his screen. *Jeff already bought concert tickets for half the team. But I'll have will call hold 4 tickets to our game under your name.*

Send me your seat numbers, and I'll get you backstage passes for after.

You sure? I can't promise the guys will be on their best behavior.

That's fine. I'm never on my best behavior.

Matts can't decide if this is going to be brilliant or a disaster. On the one hand, he'll get to see Sydney twice in a forty-eight-hour period. That's good. And he's been playing well recently. Especially since they changed up the lines and put him on Rome's wing. Matts isn't ashamed to admit that he wants to show off.

On the other hand, that's two opportunities for him to do or say something embarrassing. And statistically speaking, he's more likely to do or say something embarrassing when he's tired, high on adrenaline, or both. Which doesn't bode well. Exhibit A: whatever the hell happened the last time Sydney saw him after a game.

Her teeth really are nice though.

Alex thwacks him on the thigh with a towel as he walks by, and Matts nearly drops his phone. "Stop pining and shower," he suggests.

Matts thinks that's probably good advice.

*

ON FRIDAY, THEY get to LA with just enough time to check into the hotel and nap for an hour before they have to bus to the game. Matts slept on the plane and better than he usually does in a hotel bed, and by the time they're doing their pregame rituals in the tunnel,

Matts feels good. Solid. Awake. *Ready*. He's not anxious—hasn't been anxious before a game since playoffs the year before. But he is something. Something more than excited. Hungry, maybe. He *wants*.

Matts sees Sydney almost immediately when they scatter on the ice for warmups, legs pumping hard to send him around the rink a few times, cool air on his face, and shouting in his ears. He got the band center ice tickets, only a few rows back, but Syd and Sky have abandoned their seats to stand at the glass and bang on it, waving, as he skates by. He waves back and then tries to focus on his normal routine: laps, stretches, drills, his good-luck handshake with Rome. There aren't many people with Hounds signs ringing the ice, considering it's the Kings' house, but Matts tosses pucks to the few kids that have them. And then he's face-to-face with Sydney again. She's got both hands pressed to the glass, smile wide and unobstructed by her hair which is tied up in a red bandana. The rest of her is still dressed in shades of black, but he appreciates the attempt.

Matts wonders if she'd wear a jersey if he got her one. It's a little too easy to picture Sydney wearing his name and number on her back. He has plenty of extras. He could just give her one and see.

Sydney bangs one palm on the glass, and he meets

her eyes.

"Is it only kids that get pucks?" she shouts.

He laughs but snags a loose one with the blade of his stick and tosses it over.

Sky gestures at herself with a look of outrage, and he tosses one to her too.

Sydney holds the puck against her chest with one hand, the other still spread on the glass. She curls the fingers of that hand into a fist, offering him her knuckles.

Good luck, she mouths.

He bumps the glass with his glove.

Matts is still grinning when the game starts, and he goes over the boards for the first time, his chest full of—whatever it is. He accepts a pass from Rome straight and flat and right to his tape, dekes around the defensemen like they're practice dummies, and passes the puck easily back to Rome for a one-timer. It pings off the crossbar, but it's damn close. The goalie is visibly pissed because he was nowhere near it, and they're barely two minutes into the game. As they go back over the boards, Matts already feels an elation he hasn't known in a while. He doesn't look for Syd in the stands.

His second shift, Matts pushes harder. He's a big target, but he's always been fast—faster than he should be for his size. He plays with the defensemen. Plays with the puck. He's showing off, and he knows he's showing off. But they don't touch him; they can't. The goalie blocks his first shot, but Matts snags the rebound and sends it back out to Asher, shoves his defender away, fakes him out just long enough for Asher to send the puck right back to him. Matts makes a no-look pass to Rome, but he doesn't need to look. The crack of Rome's slapshot is loud in the anticipatory silence, and by the time Matts has turned, Rome is colliding with him. They're up 1–0.

Matts keeps pushing.

With a minute left in the first, they're up 2–0 after Alex scores glove side, low. They're on the power play, and his lungs are burning, and the clock is ticking down when Kuzy manages to steal the puck just outside their own crease. Matts shouts for the pass and gets it, toe drag dekes around one defender, then the other, and — there.

Right there.

Puck. Net. Goal light.

Matts goes into a celly.

He doesn't look for Syd as his teammates pile onto him, but he does crane his neck to catch the replay on the jumbotron over Alex's head. The play looks just as pretty as it felt.

"The fuck's gotten into you?" Rome says, grinning wide and feral and complimentary as they grab water bottles and slide onto the bench to watch the last seconds tick down on the clock.

"Whatever it is, I want some," Asher pants.

You can't have her, Matts thinks.

He finally gives in and glances across the ice. Sydney is sitting on her knees in her seat, looking right at him, hands braced on the arm rests. Matts can't interpret her facial expression, not from a distance, but he's pretty sure it's positive.

"Just really want a win tonight," he says, probably several beats too late.

Rome follows his gaze.

"Fuck yeah," he says. "Let's get you one, then."

They do. Handily. Matts only nets the one goal, but he gets two assists for their four points and generally makes the Kings' defense look like children. It's pretty great. And in the locker room, Alex bestows the star-of-the-game fake plastic crown to Matts with much bowing and scraping and heckling from the rest of the guys. He wears it into the shower.

Normally, they'd go somewhere to celebrate, but

the band has a strict "no partying the night before a concert" rule. Matts has convinced the guys to have a quieter celebration at the hotel bar, something Devo has, apparently, approved as an acceptable compromise.

When they get back to the hotel lobby, Sydney is already there. She's sprawled in one of the squashy lounge chairs near the front desk, and she bounces up to stand on the seat when she sees them.

"Hark, the victors cometh," she says, not quite a shout, but loud enough, theatrical enough, to attract the attention of people nearby. "Lo, the defeaters of Kings! Weary from battle but buttressed by their conquest!"

"Okay, I love her," Jeff murmurs.

"Don't think you're the only one," Alex whispers back.

Matts ignores them. He walks straight to the chair until his shins butt against it, and her hands, outstretched for effect, fall like a natural thing to his shoulders. Sydney is taller than him like this, her chin tipped down, her eyes searching. He finds he doesn't mind looking up to meet her gaze.

"Hi," he says, smiling too wide, probably, but she's grinning right back at him, so that's okay.

"Hi," she agrees, all teeth and humidity-frizzed hair.

He hugs her. Well. He wraps his arms around her hips and picks her up, and she folds herself around his shoulders, laughing as he squeezes her.

"Holy *shit*," she says into the side of his face. "You were on fire tonight!" Her hands are still on his shoulders, and one of them fists, tapping to emphasize her excitement. "I knew you were good, but this was a whole other— You're so *fast*."

He loosens his hold on her, and she slips down until the toes of her boots are on the floor again, the whole of her body still leaned forward, plastered along his front. He only has a moment to enjoy it though.

"You made those defenders look so stupid with the—" She pushes away so she can pantomime a toe drag. "And then when you did the thing with the—" She mimes holding a stick and spins around before firing an invisible puck at the check-in desk. "It was just...*so* cool."

"Thanks," he says. "Rome and Alex scored most of the points."

Rome makes an exasperated noise behind him.

"Okay," Jeff says, clapping him on the back. "Why don't we head to the bar, and we can all grab some drinks. Is the rest of the band here?"

Right. That was the plan.

"Yeah, they're already at the bar." Sydney points, and then she turns to say something to Alex about his first point, and Matts gestures to the group of guys behind him.

When he glances back to make sure everyone is following him, he notices that Syd, still speaking lowly to Alex, isn't looking at Alex. She's—well, it looks like she's checking Matts out.

He abruptly forgets how to walk.

How does a person walk normally anyway? Are his steps too long? Too short? Matts feels like he's using his hips too much. Or is that a good thing?

"Hey, Matts," Kuzy says. "Walk funny. You pull a muscle?"

Matts sighs. He lets Kuzy throw an arm around his shoulder and recommend some Russian anti-inflammatory tea. He doesn't look at Sydney again until they're sitting at the bar. She's facilitating introductions, so he can stare at her without it being weird.

The way she taps her ringed fingers against the lip of her glass.

The way her too-big collarless Quiet Riot shirt slips down over one shoulder, exposing a swath of tanned mole-spotted skin as she leans against the bar, the subtle muscle in her lean bicep, the cut of her collarbone, glittering with a tangle of necklaces.

Her eyes are hooded when they meet his. She doesn't smile, not exactly, when she notices his attention, but her dimples get more prominent before she touches her tongue to her bottom lip and follows it with her teeth. She doesn't look away until he does.

He might be just a little bit fucked.

*

MATTS IS COMPLETELY fucked.

It's rare that he miscalculates something, but this is a whole different kind of math, and he's made a critical error.

Seeing Sydney perform live is incomparable to seeing her in a grainy YouTube video.

From the moment she stalks onto the stage, mic in hand, shouting, "How's it going Los Angeles?" to raucous applause, he's...

"Lost" isn't the right word, neither is "overwhelmed" or "confounded," but he's not sure what the right word *is*.

Matts knows the band is good. He's listened to every song they've created and every cover they've posted online. While he may be biased—he'll admit he probably is—they're opening for one of the biggest rock bands of all time. As young as they are, they've already reached syndicated radio and minor online notoriety, and a tour presence speaks to their talent.

Objectively, they're good.

Seeing them live, though, feeling the throb of Rex's bass and the wail of Sydney's guitar and the deep, shuddering beat of Sky's drums, hearing Sydney move seamlessly from soft head voice to a rich, rough, chest voice, to screaming the lyrics of a chorus while the audience shouts along with her—it's something else. She prowls around the stage like she's never been comfortable anywhere else, propping one boot on Sky's drum kit to play a riff and running back to the mic stand just in time for the last verse, tossing hair out of her face, eyes closed, then swaying forward, teeth bared around the lyrics.

And Matts is *there*. He's there, getting to experience it in real time, to exist in the same moment as her.

It's beautiful.

It's devastating.

It's—

Matts wonders if there's a word that means the opposite of catharsis. A word that means being so filled with emotion you hemorrhage with it; it consumes you.

Maybe that's what this is.

Too soon, Sydney is drinking water, voice lovely

and scratchy as she tells the audience they have one last song.

She pauses, shading her eyes against the lights, to look at one of the signs held up a few feet from the stage.

"Well, hello," she says. "Are you serious?"

Matts has to consult the big screen behind her as one of the cameramen helpfully zooms in on the audience member in question. It's a girl on the shoulders of another girl, with a sign that says, "SYDNEY, BE MY FIRST KISS?"

From the girl's reaction, it's pretty clear she's serious.

"What's your name?" Sydney asks, slinging her guitar around to her back. She crouches at the edge of the stage, elbows on bent knees.

The girl clambers off her friend's shoulders with the help of the people around them. She pushes her way forward to cling to the barricade and shouts back at Sydney.

Sydney glances up. "Her name is Ari," she tells the audience. "How old are you, Ari?"

Matts can't tell what she responds, but Sydney laughs.

"She says she's eighteen, folks. Do we believe her?"

The stadium erupts in cheers.

Matts is silent. He can hear his heartbeat uncomfortably loud in his ears. It's probably not just from the sudden comparable quiet after nearly an hour of 100-decibel sound, but he wants to pretend it is.

Security helps the girl over the barricade, and Sydney kneels at the edge of the stage, beckoning her closer. The stage is at least five feet tall, so Ari has to reach to pull herself up and close the space separating them. Sydney bows forward, one hand sliding around the girl's jaw, steadying her.

"You sure about this?" Sydney says into the microphone between their mouths.

"No doubt," Ari says.

Sydney moves the mic.

It's brief.

Maybe.

But for a moment, they look like a living painting. Ari's neck is extended, arms straining to pull herself closer. Sydney's rings catch and throw light where her hand rests on Ari's exposed neck, where her thumb and forefinger hold the girl's chin in place. The stage behind them is a canvas of reds.

The audience roars.

Chapter Eight

THERE'S A CERTAIN kind of high following a performance that Sydney has never been able to replicate elsewhere.

Not that she's tried to use more conventional methods, but there is nothing like the ecstatic buoyancy that comes from leaving the stage to thunderous applause, heart in her ears and sweat running down her back, throat sore and chest full, knowing she did her best, and it was enough. She was enough.

Coming off stage after a solid show makes Sydney feel as if she could do anything. Be anything. Like maybe she could live out the bravery in her lyrics.

Rex scoops her up in a spinning hug as they crash into their dressing room backstage, and then Sky jumps onto Rex's back, and they all three end up in a pile on the nearest couch, yelling incoherently at one another. Devo, following them from the wings, rolls his eyes but smiles as they press obnoxious kisses to one another's faces and muss sweaty hair and recount the best parts of the show.

"Jesus," Rex says, smooshing Syd's cheeks together. "The bridge for 'Sins of Our Father' was the best you've ever done it. I nearly forgot to come in for the chorus; I was so distracted listening to you. It's like you're a goddamn banshee. Or a siren-banshee hybrid."

"Okay, but your vocals for 'Become the Monster'" she retorts, knocking their foreheads together. "Fucking ace. And *you*!" She rolls, taking Sky with her off the couch and onto the floor, squeezing her tight enough that she makes a wheezing noise. "Best drummer in the world! Your solo in 'Divine Rights' was just— Marry me now."

"We've talked about this," Sky says gravely. "I don't believe in the institution of marriage."

"And, also, I have first dibs if she changes her mind," Rex reminds them, chin propped on stacked hands. "Get your own prospect. "

"Mm. I suggest someone around six foot three," Sky says. "Professional athlete. Socially awkward. Weirdly into you."

"Currently walking down the hallway," Rex mutters.

Sydney and Sky both look toward the door, and yes, even upside down, Sydney can recognize the bulk of Matts's backlit frame.

"Oh," Matts says as he's directed into the room by someone with a clipboard and an earpiece. "Sorry. Should we come back later?"

A whole group of men stands behind him, all peering into the room with equal curiosity. It occurs to Sydney that Sky is straddling her in a way that could be mistaken as something other than platonic.

"No, come in," Syd says as Sky laughs into her neck, completely unhelpfully. "Come in. Sorry." She tries to shift Sky off her unsuccessfully. "Rex, a little help here?"

Rex stands, tying back his hair, then scoops Sky up and relocates them to the couch.

"They all get cuddly after a performance," Devo explains to the Hell Hounds as they make their way inside. "It's the dopamine or something."

Matts offers Sydney a hand, and she lets him pull

her up to her feet and directly into a hug.

"I'm super gross," she warns him.

"I'm a hockey player," he reminds her.

She probably lingers a little longer than she should, relishing the weight of his arms around her shoulders, the firmness of his chest against hers, and the warm smell of him that shouldn't be familiar but is.

"Hi," she says, finally putting some space between them.

"Hi," he agrees.

"And," she says, looking behind him, "it appears you've brought half the Hell Hounds roster with you. A veritable *pack* of hounds. Wait, I can do better than that." She considers for a moment. "Hark! A host of hellish hounds."

"Hallelujah," Sky shouts.

"Someone please stop them before this turns into a five-minute alliteration event," Devo says.

That's a valid concern.

Matts reintroduces everyone, even though they all met the night before. Within minutes, Sky has vacated the couch and pulled her drumsticks out of her back pocket to teach Kuzy how to spin them. Rex and Jeff have fallen into a conversation about Rex's tattoos. And Sydney is left with an attentive group of very large men.

The room suddenly feels much smaller despite its tall ceilings.

"I have to admit," Rushy says, "I was mostly here to watch Matts fanboy, but you guys are amazing. Like, I typically don't go for this kind of music—"

"He prefers banjos," Alex interrupts. "And harmonicas. Mandolin, if he's feeling risqué."

Rushy ignores him. "But your energy and the *lyrics*— Do you write your own songs?"

"I write most of them. Rex helps. He wrote one of the ones we did tonight. 'Sins of Our Father.'"

"Which one is that?"

She hums the lead-in to the chorus and quietly sings.

> *'Cause what you call love, I call indifference*
> *Just fuckin' spare me your so-called deliverance*
> *I'll spit on heaven's gate and welcome hell's fire*
> *Before I kneel to a god who'd create in me condemned desire*

"Oh, shit," Rushy says. "Yeah. Kinda want to send

that to some family members of mine."

"Rex had a stretch there, senior year of high school, where he cranked out an album's worth of songs, coming to grips with his faith and his queerness not being mutually exclusive, regardless of what certain people in his life said. That's the only song that made it into the album, but there are some other bangers for sure."

"Jesus didn't say that, bitch," Matts says.

Sydney stills. Along with pretty much everyone else present.

"What?" Alex says.

"Sorry," Matts shoves his hands in his pockets. "That's the title of one of the other songs, right? And all the verses are him arguing about things attributed to Jesus that aren't, uh, biblical. It's…both educational and hilarious. The end of every line rhymes with the word 'bitch.'"

"A lot if it is slant rhyme," Sydney says. "But, yes."

The only place that song was publicly recorded was in a video posted to her personal channel over three years ago before they had a record deal or even a decent camera. Which means Matts has been watching her channel and not watching casually but going through the archives. Sydney can't deal with that right now.

"So," she says brightly. "You guys didn't want to

stay in the audience for the main event? I saw your tickets; you have good seats."

"Oh, I think we got our money's worth," Jeff says, slapping Matts's back as he moves to join the main group. "But we wanted to say hi; we're going back to our seats in a minute."

"I'm not," Matts clarifies. "They are. If that's ok."

"We're going to be hanging out here" Syd says, "until the VIP event stuff when the Killer Sunday guys are finished with their set. Won't be very interesting."

"I'm good here," Matts says again.

"Well, all right then."

"I hate to be that person," Devo says to the Hell Hounds from where he's been lurking by the snack table. "But until they hire an actual manager, I *am* that person. Would y'all be cool with taking a picture for the band's socials?"

The assorted hockey players present apparently do not mind being used for free marketing. Sky ends up on Kuzy's shoulders, and not to be outdone, Matts then insists on putting Sydney on his shoulders. At this point, Rex loudly declares he's being left out, so Alex and Rushy help him onto Rome's shoulders. The rest gather around, and a minute later, Devo airdrops a dozen photos to everyone involved. Alex and Kuzy immediately duck their heads together to argue over who gets to post which photo.

"So…" Sydney's still on Matts's shoulders, one hand cupped under his pleasantly scratchy jaw for stability, the other holding her phone. "Do you have a PR person who's going to lose their mind if I caption this 'We got high backstage with the Hell Hounds'?"

All the hockey players turn to look at Jeff.

"Why?" he says. "Why am *I* always chosen as the default adult?" He sighs. "I think that should be fine."

Sydney posts it.

The Hounds say their goodbyes and head back to their seats, Sky and Rex return to the couch, and Sydney…is still on Matts's shoulders.

He's got his fingers curled around her ankles, and he's idly walking around, checking out the snacks and drinks and the carefully organized piles of chaos surrounding the collection of utilitarian black couches.

"You can put me down, now," she points out. "Unless you need to get an extra workout in."

Matts makes a derisive noise. "Please. You're not even my warm-up weight." But he drops into a crouch, as if that's a normal thing to do with over 100 pounds of human on his shoulders, and releases her ankles so he can offer her a steadying hand to dismount. This works right up until she catches the toe of her left boot in the stretchy fabric of his T-shirt, and then she's careening toward the floor, her phone clattering to the linoleum, her arms tucked to her chest because she'd rather get a concussion than break one of her fingers. Except she doesn't have to worry about a concussion because Matts catches her. Or he doesn't so much as catch her as fall with her, twisting to take the brunt of the impact. They end up in a reckless sprawl of limbs, both cursing.

"Shit," Syd says. "Ow. Are you okay?"

When Matts answers, she can feel his mouth against her ear, feel him groan, just a little, as he shifts underneath her to sit up. "Yeah, I'm good. Are you?"

She has no idea. All Sydney knows is that her palms are pressed to his chest, and her face is smashed into his neck, and she can't complain. It's nice real estate. She would happily live and die right here.

Matts manages to push them up into a more conventional seated position and laughs, shoving hair out of her face. "Are you sure you're all right?"

For a second, her fingers curl tighter into his shirt before she forces herself to let go.

"A-okay, right as rain," Sydney says, which is not something she has ever said in her life. "Nice save." She pats his pecs, then stops immediately. That's not the thing to do if she's trying to regain normal brain function.

Matts's hands are still in her hair. She should tell him it's a lost cause between the sweat and the humidity, but if he's touching her, she's not going to give him an excuse to stop. And the way he's grinning at her is—Sydney typically rolls her eyes when romance novels describe smiles as "devastating," but— That shit is pretty devastating.

"Friendly reminder that there are other people in the room," Devo says blandly.

Matts withdraws his hands.

Sydney considers fratricide. "Sorry." She tucks her toes to stand, and Matts follows her, collecting her abused phone on the way to his feet.

"Not broken," he says, like it's a personal triumph.

When Matts passes it back to her, Sydney's middle fingertips touch his last two knuckles, and they both pause, looking down at their hands. She's stuck, for a moment, following the natural path of his wrist with a pretty set of bracelets to the subtle map of veins that climb up his tanned forearm, to the thin, clinging T-shirt stretched around his bicep. If the shirt is meant to highlight his frankly ridiculous shoulder-to-waist ratio, it is assuredly serving its purpose.

"Hey," Matts says, releasing the phone only to reach for her face. "You've got— Can I?"

She makes a noise that is meant to be a yes, and he interprets it that way, cupping one hand behind her head to hold it steady while he uses his opposite thumb to wipe from the crest of her cheekbone up to the corner of her eye.

"The wing of your eyeliner is all smudged on this side," Matts says, ducking to bring his face closer to hers. "You've got a raccoon thing going on."

"How do you know it's called a wing?" Syd asks, which isn't scintillating dialogue, but her managing a cohesive sentence when he's bent over, face inches from hers, lip tucked between his teeth in concentration, is encouraging.

"Eli," he says as if it should be obvious, and yeah, maybe it should be.

Matts uses the edge of his thumb to wipe along her waterline, looking pleased with himself.

"There," he says quietly, "better."

He doesn't move away.

"Are you seeing this shit?" Rex mutters quietly from the couch.

"Unfortunately," Devo answers.

Sky hushes them.

It's enough to break them apart, Matts looking sheepish, Sydney hoping the low light is enough to camouflage the flush creeping up her neck.

When they join Rex and Sky on the couch, Sydney leaves a calculated amount of space between them, but Matts braces his hand on the cushion beside her, overlapping their pinkies. It's somehow even more fraught than when she was sitting in his lap.

Rex and Sky pick up right where they left off, breaking down the highs and lows of their performance, and Sydney tries to breathe normally and figure out what the hell is happening to her.

She has had actual sex before.

She has touched people *carnally*.

She should not be having an existential crisis over their pinkies touching.

She's having an existential crisis over their pinkies touching.

"That kid at the end has bragging rights for life now," Rex is saying, and Sydney forces herself to focus on the conversation. "Imagine if your first kiss was a rock star on stage at a show."

"If only," Sydney says breezily, looking at Sky.

"Watch yourself," Sky mutters.

Matts's face has gone weirdly placid, probably because he has no idea what they're talking about.

"My first kiss was Sky," Sydney explains, "when she was decidedly not a rock star."

"And Sky's first kiss was me," Rex says. "Also, pre-rock star." He leans over Sydney's lap so he can speak directly to Matts, lowering his voice as though they're sharing a secret. "We didn't have a lot of options, considering our social status at school."

"Who was *your* first kiss?" Matts asks Rex.

"No," Devo says from where he's leaning against a wall. "Subject change."

Rex makes a kissing face at him. "Darling, was it not memorable?"

Matts glances between them. "It was *Devo*?"

"Come back with a warrant," Devo says.

"Huh," Matts says, "I didn't know you were—"

"I'm not," Devo mutters, aggrieved. "Which was very much confirmed when I very *briefly* kissed Rex."

"To be fair," Rex says, "I was kind of an asshole about it."

"He was crying," Devo says.

"I was not *crying*," Rex argues. "I was sixteen and emotional and simultaneously had seasonal allergies. And I thought if I was pitiful enough, my best friend's hot older brother might kiss me. And I was right, so..."

Sydney's phone lights up on her thigh, and she frowns at the notification that Devo has airdropped her—

Another photo.

In the photo, Sydney sits in Matts's lap, knees bracketing his hips, fingers splayed, bright with rings, on his chest. One of Matts's hands is on her lower back, the other has a handful of curls that he's trying to tuck behind her ear. He's grinning at her as she looks at him with enough naked affection to have her immediately angle the phone screen away from Matts's view. If he didn't notice while it was happening, she sure as hell doesn't want him to be aware now.

Fuck.

Fuck.

She needs to get her shit together.

*

SYDNEY ISN'T PARTICULARLY proficient at getting her shit together.

She manages to be normal when talking to Matts— or as normal as she gets—for the next few weeks, through five more shows with Killer Sunday. But even if Sydney manages to sound unaffected in texts and

FaceTime calls, she is, in actuality, pretty damn affected by Justin Fucking Matthews.

A significant part of the problem is that when she tries to pull back, to keep her responses short and limit the time she'll talk to him when she's most unguarded— in those drowsy midnight post-concert come-down hours—he doesn't let her. Oh, she has no doubt that if she told him to leave her alone, he would, but she doesn't want to do that because she doesn't *want* him to leave her alone. She just wants— Sydney doesn't know what she wants. No, that's not true. She wants *him*. And perhaps an even more significant part of the problem is that she's starting to think having him is a possibility. Because she knows she's not completely unfortunate-looking. Her DMs are full of prospective suitors. And sure, most of that attention isn't really for her; it's because she's quasi-famous. But all the earnest compliments, the inside jokes, the quiet attentiveness, paired with his now-constant presence in her life, makes Sydney think Matts might be interested in something more than friendship. Maybe even something more than a one-night stand.

Either Sydney has to lean into that potential or lean away, and leaning away isn't working. Leaning in, however, is terrifying.

"So," she announces to Sky and Rex the first night they're back at the ranch for their break. "I'm considering wooing Justin Matthews. Thoughts?"

Sky, sitting at her drum kit, chokes briefly on the water she's drinking, then bends to use her shirt to clean up the mess she's made on the snare.

"I like him. I thought you were just going to be friends with him though," Rex says, picking idly at his guitar.

"That was the initial goal, yes. But that's been achieved now, and I'm considering...adjusting the plan."

"You realize romance isn't part of the standard linear progression of a friendship, right?" Rex says.

"Obviously." Sydney gestures between them. "But it's not an atypical outcome either. And I like him. A lot."

"I won't lie and say I don't think you have a chance," Rex murmurs, eyes on his hands. "But do you really want one? You've seen the shit Eli has to deal with. The hockey world isn't going to be kind to you."

"The actual world isn't kind to me," she argues.

"Fair enough."

"I think you should go for it," Sky says.

"I think I might," Sydney agrees.

Rex sighs. "At the very least, you're cranking out some killer lyrics with all the pining, right now. Do you think love or heartbreak would generate more content?"

Sky tosses Sydney the water bottle, and she catches it with one hand, the other still wrapped around the neck of her guitar.

"I don't know," she says. "I guess we'll find out."

*

SYDNEY INVITES MATTS, along with the rest of the Hell Hounds and their significant others, to the annual Warren Easter cookout. The band is back for a two-week break between their last show with Killer Sunday and their first show as the headliner for a six-city stretch. The Saturday of the Easter cookout is right in the middle of the Hounds's three-day break, and by 4:00 p.m., there are close to fifty people on the property, children included, as well as a handful of dogs. But no Matts.

Sydney keeps finding excuses to go inside so she can squint down the hall through the glass door to the front yard. She knows she's being ridiculous, but he'd said he would be there at three, and, as far as she knows, he's not the kind of person to be late.

"Probably family stuff," Eli says. "Don't start worrying until he misses dinner."

Sydney spends some time petting Hawk to console herself before Hawk is enticed away by Boogie and some sort of corgi-demon mix that belongs to their neighbor.

She's brushing dog hair off her jeans, considering sneaking inside one last time before joining the others, when a hand touches her shoulder.

"Hey, sorry I'm late."

Matts is wearing aviator sunglasses and a denim jacket over his white T-shirt and work pants. His boots are the same familiar scuffed brown ones he wore to the last cookout. His hair is—well, there's no denying it's some species in the mullet genus now. Or maybe if a mullet and a mohawk had a very confused baby. His hair is clipped shorter on the sides of his head around his ears, but it's longer, thick and wavy, down the center of his skull, with half-formed curls falling into his eyes and over the collar of his jacket.

He might be the only person in the world who can pull it off.

She might also be biased.

Sydney's trying to decide if the agony of hugging him is a good idea when he makes the decision for her.

It's possible he smells even better than he did the last time she saw him in LA.

"Well," Sydney says. "You have perfect timing." She steps back, only to grab his sleeve so she can pull him toward the group of people congregating at the back gate.

"Oh? Why?"

"You're in for a treat, Matthews. It's Power Wheels NASCAR time."

He lets her drag him down the slope of the lawn past the pool. "What's Power Wheels NASCAR?"

"You know, I bet you can figure it out from the name."

"Are there…children racing little cars?" he asks.

"Better. There are *adults* racing little cars. A glorious spectacle to behold, truly."

"Are you counting yourself in that adult category?"

"I am, smartass. You want in, or are you just watching?"

"I feel like participating might violate the part in my contract where I promise not to do activities that could potentially put my health in jeopardy."

"Excellent point. Spectating only for Lord Matthews, lest he injure his royal heinie."

"Hey. Tailbone injuries are nothing to joke about," Matts says, trying and mostly failing to smother a laugh.

"You're right," she agrees somberly. "It's just so

easy to make them…the butt of a joke."

"No."

"Yes."

Her dad has mowed a track in the front pasture and marked the turns with orange spray-painted stakes. The vehicles are collected at the starting line, which is also spray-painted orange.

"What happens if a cow is in the way?" Matts asks, eyeing the herd that has started to amble forward, curious, in the distance.

"Obstacles," she says. "Part of the fun. You want to come check out my ride? It probably won't win, but I haven't had as much time to work on it this year."

Sydney leads him to her car, a bubblegum-pink Barbie Jeep plastered in band stickers with a Bluetooth speaker zip-tied to the back roll bar.

"You do this every year?" he asks.

"This is the eighth in a row. First year, we used stock kids' cars. Second year, Devo modded his without telling anyone and cleaned house. After that, we made the rules."

"Which are?"

"Helmets for everyone on the course, no drivers under the age of fourteen, no mods that go faster than twenty miles per hour. Any make or model is allowed, provided it isn't a motorcycle or four-wheeler. And your engine or battery of choice must fit within the original blueprint of the vehicle."

Sydney pops up the plastic seat and gestures for him to inspect the interior compartment with a bow. "My liege."

Matts leans over, hands on his knees, and lets out a startled laugh. "Are those Milwaukee drill batteries?"

"Yep. Two M18 lithiums."

"What comes standard in these things?"

"Twelve volts."

"Jesus. Do you just…immediately wheely?"

"Nah, not as long as I'm leaning forward. I've added extra weight to the front too."

Matts straightens, looking at the line of little plastic cars as the racers approach their vehicles.

"Are everyone's like this?"

"More or less. Devo and Sky have DeWalt's in theirs, and my mom rigged up an old gas lawn mower engine. She fudged the rules by using a truck as her base car, but technically, the engine does fit in the back of it. She'll probably smoke us all." Sydney points to the tiny Ford Raptor a few feet away. It's decorated with flower decals. "And then we have a couple extras for people that want to join who didn't bring a car."

He runs a hand through his hair, watching as Sydney's mom pulls the cord to start the engine on the Raptor. "Is this even legal?"

"We're sure as hell not going to ask," Devo says, sliding by them to get to his green Lamborghini. Alex, Eli, and Hawk approach with him, and Alex appears similarly baffled. Eli, who attended the year before, looks delighted.

"No cops at Pride, and no cops at Power Wheels NASCAR," Eli says.

"Why?" Alex asks.

Sydney opens her visor to answer, but Matts beats her to it.

"Well NASCAR was basically born from a direct competition with police."

Sydney gestures for him to continue.

"I mean," Matts says, "NASCAR only exists because there were a whole bunch of moonshiners during prohibition who needed to outrun cops. So, they started souping up shitty old trucks that didn't look like much, but then could—"

He makes a *shoom* noise, driving his hand, palm flat, fingers pointed, toward Alex. "And because humans are incapable of doing something without making it a competition, moonshiners started having races to prove who made the best cars for outrunning cops. And then those turned into bigger and bigger events that eventually turned into NASCAR. So, it was born from country folks turning their beaters into the best possible smuggling vehicles to say 'fuck you' to the police."

"Exactly," Sydney agrees.

"Thank you, Wikipedia," Alex says.

Matts sketches out a bow that looks very similar to the one Sydney gave him a few minutes before.

"Racers, to the starting line!" Sydney's dad calls through a megaphone.

The group ambling down the hillside splits into two. Half of them converge upon the cars, the other half claim spectating positions.

"Well, Lord Matthews," Sydney says, "this is where we part."

He closes her visor for her, knocking two knuckles to the top of her helmet. "Be safe."

"Alas," she says, snapping the seat back into place so she can climb into the Jeep. "I make no such promises, for the arena is unforgiving and fraught with peril."

"Fraught with cows maybe. Wait, hold on." Matts slips off one of his bracelets—the jade one—and goes down on one knee to pull her hand off the steering wheel and slide the bracelet onto her wrist. He's gentle when he adjusts the leather closure cords.

"There," Matts says, quiet and private and too serious for the previous timbre of the conversation. "A token for my knight."

"I'm honored."

She's still caught on that "my." *My* knight. My. Possessive.

"All spectators to your seats!" Sydney's dad calls.

Matts takes a step back. Then another. "Good luck."

Sydney reaches down to wrap her fingers around the steering wheel, and the bracelet slips to settle like a too-big cuff over the tendons in the back of her hand.

She is suddenly much more invested in winning.

Sydney glances over at the line of cars to her left as her dad brings the megaphone back up to his mouth.

Devo is similarly hunched in a cannonball position. Rex, too tall to fit both legs inside the vehicle, has one knee bent over the door, toes up, heel an inch from the ground.

Her mother is looking right at Sydney with an expression that says they will be talking later.

"On your marks!" her dad says.

Sydney leans forward over the tiny windscreen.

"Get set."

She tucks her elbows between her knees and

touches her boot to the gas pedal.

"Go!"

She's first off the starting line.

Chapter Nine

MATTS DOESN'T WANT to leave. It's a strange sensation. Usually, he keeps time in his head at social events, counting down whatever feels like a polite number of hours before making his escape.

But when he's well fed and relaxed from laughter and a couple of beers, sitting on a porch with a dozen other people and their various musical instruments— guitars, harmonicas, too many tambourines, and a single, ancient fiddle—when he's surrounded by friendly bickering and shared stories and casual, gentle, touches to his shoulder or arm as people maneuver around him, he feels "home" would be too cheesy. Too presumptive.

But something close to it, maybe.

Matts has spent his life trying to make a home wherever he is. First, it was at the farm, then splitting his time between the farm and his mother's condo, then his mother's hospital and hospice rooms, then a series of dorm rooms and billet bedrooms, and now, in adulthood, a shared apartment he still hasn't gotten around to decorating. He's never spent long enough in one place for it to feel like his. But some places that have felt close to home almost immediately: the farm, when he was young enough to notice the floral curtains and sprawling sunsets but not the fissures in his parent's marriage; his second billet house, with a living room full of handmade quilts and a kitchen that always smelled like a warm oven, with crayon drawings on the refrigerator and a pond hockey rink in the backyard; and here, a hallway full of photographs and a back porch full of laughter.

When Matts does leave for the night, Sydney walks him out like she did the first time. Unlike the first time, she hugs him. And she lingers.

"We're here for two more weeks," she says into his collarbone. The implication is clear enough that even *he* catches it.

"Think you'll be up for a jam session or two?"

he asks.

"I do."

"I'll text you, then."

It would be so much easier, he thinks, if everyone just said what they were thinking. If he could ask: *Will I ruin whatever this is if I kiss you?* And she could answer. And then he would kiss her, or would know better, and he wouldn't have to spend the thirty-minute drive back to his apartment deconstructing every look, every touch that had occurred that evening.

She was still wearing his bracelet when he left. He doesn't think it was intentional; he's pretty sure she forgot she was wearing it. But Matts didn't forget. And he didn't ask for it back.

It feels like a triumph, though he can't logically explain why. It's not as if anyone will know it's his. It's not as if he's marked her in some way. But he knows. And she knows. And maybe when she's getting ready for bed and she's taking off her rings, she'll look at the bracelet and think about him, and maybe that's enough.

His phone lights up with a call as he's unlocking his apartment. "Hey, Aaron," he answers as he tosses his keys into the bowl by the door.

"Hey, Matty," Aaron says.

"Is this a good drunk or a bad drunk situation?"

Aaron exhales static. "This is a 'your dad is a piece of work' drunk situation."

"Ah." Matts is intimately familiar with those kinds of situations. "I take it the trip home wasn't as smooth as you'd hoped?"

Matts's dad has been getting his chemotherapy at the hospital there in Gunnison, but he had to go back to Denver for more scans earlier that day. Matts already talked to Aaron for nearly an hour—was late to Sydney's because of it—getting a debrief on how the appointment went while his dad and stepmother got lunch. But apparently, the nearly four-hour drive back to the farm wasn't easy.

"No," Aaron says, and the word is loaded. "So now, I'm freezing my ass off in the barn with Erno and a bottle of Jack because shouting at a man with cancer is shitty, even if he deserves it."

Erno is Matts's horse—if Matts can still claim ownership. Erno is a roan blue draft-cross gentle giant named after Ernö Rubik. Matts was there for his birth at ten years old and the first person to ever ride him at twelve. Erno is, quite possibly, the thing he misses most about the farm.

"Why are you with Erno and not your hellbeast?" Matts asks, opening the refrigerator to retrieve a sports drink. Aaron's horse Trigger is a beautiful but exhausting leopard-spotted ranger mare who has tried to take off one of Matts's fingers on more than one occasion. They put up with her attitude because she's one of the best cow horses the ranch has ever had. She cuts like a dream and has more fight than flight in her.

"I moved some of the goats in with her while we're working on the goat barn; there isn't any room for me to join that party."

Also, despite her attitude toward most humans, Trigger is weirdly obsessed yet always gentle with goats.

"Ow, fuck." The line goes crackly for a minute.

"You okay?" Matts asks.

"Your stupid horse just tried to sit on me."

"He probably just wants a cuddle." Matts breaks the seal on the bottle and drinks half of it in one go as Aaron mutters back at him about stupid horses and stupid, stubborn old men. Matts sets the bottle on his nightstand and pins the phone between his shoulder and ear so he can reach for the GAN ROBOT plugged in next to the lamp. The Rubik's Cube inside the machine is still scrambled from when Matts was using the app the prior night, and he presses the button that makes the arms release the cube. Falling back onto the bed, he considers it from various angles as Aaron tells him about the litter of puppies the neighbor had a week before and how he's been on a third date with the sophomore at Western and isn't sure if that means he needs to get her a birthday present next month or not.

Matts makes encouraging noises and starts spinning segments, the familiar shift of his fingers, the soft clicks of the internal mechanism, settling the anxiety that started building in his chest.

His father's treatment isn't something he can control.

But this—this is simple. Manageable.

Matts solves it and pops it back into the robot, then puts Aaron on speaker so he can get into the app and turn on the scrambler function.

"What about you?" Aaron says. "You ever ask out that girl you were talking about?"

Matts stills, watching the bot do its work. "No. Not yet."

"What are you waiting for?"

Matts removes the cube. He hasn't told Aaron anything about Sydney, only mentioned there was a girl. That seems wrong, now, as if he's doing Sydney a disservice. It feels like minor blasphemy to hear her described as "some girl." But Matts also has no idea how the conversation will proceed if he corrects the omission.

"She's in a band."

"Okay?"

"And they're touring until May. So, I don't want to try and start something until then."

"Oh, touring. So, like an *actual* band. Guitar player? That'd be cool for you."

"Lead singer and guitar."

"Why are you being weird? Tell me the name of the band."

"Red Right Hand."

"Shit, I've actually heard of them. Couldn't tell you the name of a song or anything, but hold on."

The sound changes, and Matts assumes he's been put on speakerphone so Aaron can google Red Right Hand. Matts retrieves the cube and starts spinning it. He knows what the first few returns of that search will be because he's made it himself.

"Oh." Aaron takes an audible swallow of his whisky. "Sydney Warren? That's her?"

"That's her." Matts solves the cube too quickly. He sets it to scramble again.

"You know she's uh—"

"Yes." Matts tries to keep his voice even. The fact

that Aaron is still using the right pronouns for Sydney is, frankly, more than he hoped for.

"Right."

Matts's palms are suddenly sweaty, cupped around his knees. He feels unprepared for whatever Aaron will say, even more so than Matts usually is in awkward social situations. How is he supposed to defend something, explain something he's only just started to understand himself?

"Well," Aaron says finally. "She's hot. I never would have guessed."

Matts reminds himself that is probably the best possible response Aaron could give, all things considered. He swallows his initial reply and chooses a gentler one.

"You should hear her sing. And play. I mean, you think *I'm* good at guitar? I went to her concert in LA, and yeah, the whole band is talented, but she's something else. A lot more than just a pretty face."

"Should have known it'd be a musician who'd finally make you want something more than a night at a time. That, or a Rubik's Cube champion."

Matts freezes, halfway through retrieving his cube from the robot again.

"Does Sydney know you're a giant nerd?" Aaron asks.

"She does," Matts says as dignified as he's able.

"Well, I hope that...works out for you, then."

"Thanks."

Matts can hear Erno blowing in the background, and Aaron responds to him quietly before returning his attention to Matts.

"I'll let you go. Thanks for letting me vent."

"Thanks for keeping me updated."

"Bye, Matty."

"Bye, Aaron."

He collapses backward and breathes at the ceiling for a minute. That went...well.

Matts rolls the cube back and forth over his sternum with a flat palm, considering. He exhales, pushing himself to his feet, and sets the cube to scramble one last time. Matts pulls off his shirt, turns on the shower, and tries to reclaim the loose-limbed happiness he found on the Warren back porch. He wonders if Sydney has gone to sleep yet. He wonders if she's noticed she's still wearing his bracelet and, if so, whether she decides to leave it on.

*

THE HOUNDS PLAY the Avalanche at home the Monday after the cookout, and Matts just barely resists offering the band tickets again. He's glad he does, though, because it's a loss, and while Sydney has to know that they don't win *every* game, Matts doesn't want her to witness them losing.

Tuesday morning, they don't have practice, so he goes to Eli and Alex's apartment for breakfast. Rome and Damien are already there, which is fine. Matts likes Rome. And Damien is nice, if intimidating. But for a while there, the summer before Rome was drafted, Matts inexplicably developed a friendship with Eli despite their history, and it was just the three of them. And Hawk. It was nice.

This is nice, too, just different.

Matts spends a good amount of time on the floor with Hawk. Before arriving, he stopped at the Three Dog Bakery to pick up some cookies for her and, as typically happened, they had a rack of toys by the register, so he ended up buying one of them too. The nearly three-foot-long, rainbow-colored snake has a squeaker in each of its half-dozen body segments, and Hawk is just as delighted about it as Matts thought she'd be. Everyone else, trying to carry on a conversation over the incessant squeaking, is less delighted. But that's their problem.

Eventually, Matts drags himself away from the

euphoric, up-side-down, snake-squeaking dog and washes up to help Eli with breakfast. Over the last year, Matts has found he enjoys cooking, provided he has clear instructions. It's like math. Except when you solve the equation, you also get to eat the answer. He also just likes using knives. There's something very pleasing about the repetitive sound, the feeling, the visual of dicing something. At this point, whenever Matts asks to assist, Eli automatically assigns him to the butcher block and starts handing him vegetables. Another nice thing about cooking with Eli is that he does the majority of the talking. Matts can lose himself in the pleasure of habitual movements and the soft drawl of Eli's storytelling about the exploits of his best friend from home, Hawk's recent vet appointment, and the figure-skating kids he's working with.

Matts thinks it would be nice to have this one day himself—a bigger kitchen than his matchbox of a place now, with enough counter space to spread out all his ingredients and only have to worry about washing things at the end. He wants the friendly hip checks and ease of working with another person who's familiar with not only the kitchen but him. He wants the lull of easy conversation interspersed with compliments on his bell pepper cutting technique. He wants gentle hands on his back and quiet encouragement—

He wants more, if he's being honest.

He wants to share his kitchen with someone who shares his life.

He wants to work elbow-to-elbow with someone he loves who loves him, and when Matts passes her to rinse the sweet potatoes in the sink, he wants to stop, to gather her curls in one damp hand and duck to kiss the back of her neck. He wants her to slap him away, laughing, or maybe turn to kiss him properly and—

It occurs to him belatedly that this fictional future person has a face.

A familiar face.

Matts forces himself back to the present. He asks about Eli's summer plans and listens to the answer while washing the potatoes without any additional daydreams.

Matts knows, his mother taught him young, that counting chickens before they're hatched will only lead to disappointment. *Hope is a dangerous thing, baby*, she murmured into his hair after a lost mite championship game he was certain they'd win. *Hope is a dangerous thing, baby*, she warned him when her favorite mare was pregnant with Erno. *You're not guaranteed happiness*, she whispered when she was first diagnosed. *It's best not to expect it and appreciate it when it comes.*

He's never been very good at that in practice though.

They're just sitting down to eat when Matts's phone rings. He only answers because it's Aaron.

"You realize it's not even noon, right?" he says in lieu of a greeting.

"Hey," Aaron answers, and Matts realizes immediately that something is wrong.

"He's going to be fine, probably," Aaron continues. "But I'm at the hospital with your dad."

Matts stands up. "What happened?"

"He fell down the stairs to the basement early this morning. Because the stubborn bastard refuses to admit that the chemo's fucked him up, so he's still trying to go about life as usual against the doctor's advice. They're pretty sure he's got a broke ankle, which is not what I fucking need right now."

"Do I—"

Aaron interrupts him before he can even get the question out. "No, you're not getting on a plane over a broke ankle. I just need to vent, and you needed to know, so."

"Hold on." Matts presses the phone to his chest. Everyone is looking at him. "Can I take Hawk for a walk?" he asks Eli, and he probably should have asked a little quieter because Hawk immediately goes to sit by her leash hanging at the door.

"Yeah," Eli says, "of course."

"Okay," Matts says a minute later as he exits the elevator, leash in hand and Hawk high-stepping with excitement beside him. "Vent away."

After fifteen minutes and a very awkward juggle-the-phone-while-picking-up-dog-poop moment, Aaron winds down with "I don't fucking know. On the one hand, he's a better father than mine ever was, and he treats my mom like the angel she is. But God, he can just be so—"

"Yeah," Matts agrees.

"Guess you'd know."

"Yeah." Matts takes an intentional breath, pausing to let Hawk sniff a suspicious stain on the sidewalk. "Do you need...help? I could hire someone to come and—"

"Imagine how that conversation would go."

Matts exhales. "I'll piss him off if I have to. I'm more worried about if you can keep doing this by yourself. Even before this, you were managing most of the ranch."

"I'm fine."

"This is the second time in three days you've called

me."

"Smartass. I'm fine *for now*. It's still winter. Things are slow. Ask me again in the spring. Or if he breaks another fucking limb."

"Okay."

Aaron's voice suddenly drops to a whisper. "They're bringing him back from X-ray. I gotta go."

Aaron hangs up before Matts can say goodbye.

Matts lets Hawk pull him forward and into movement again, still looking at the phone in his hand.

It would be easier if his father were a bad man. If he was intentionally cruel or malicious or if he'd raised Matts with neglect rather than love. But his father's not a bad man. He made sacrifices Matts didn't ask him to and enforced restrictions that chafed and had a disciplinary hand he'd learned from his own father that relied more on fear than respect.

His love hasn't always looked the way Matts wanted it to, but there was never any doubt of it.

When Matts was younger, it was easier. Because first, his father was a hero. Then, in Matts's teen years, he was a villain. Now that Matts is an adult, he knows neither is true. His father is just a man repeating history, doing the best he can with the example and expectations he was given. Just a man who's fallible and imperfect and probably terrified right now. Which is a word Matts has never associated with his father. He finds it difficult to try, to picture him immobile, to picture him weak.

Matts opens his text conversation with Sydney and then remembers she drove to Austin with the band the day before for an interview and photoshoot, and they weren't getting back until late afternoon. She's probably somewhere in the purgatory of I-35 right now. Matts swipes back to his contacts and finds Devo.

Devo answers on the second ring. "You know you've called me and not my sister, right?"

"Yeah, hi," Matts says. "I need to ride a horse. Please."

The line is silent for several seconds. "Well, I guess you'd better come over, then," Devo says.

*

WORKING WITH DEVO is a lot like working with Aaron: 95 percent silence, 5 percent sarcasm.

When Matts arrived at the ranch, head no more settled than when he called an hour before, Devo answered the door in barn clothes and said, "I hope you were serious about working for your horse lease."

It was a relief to be asked for something in return, to fall into a familiar cadence of chores that Matts has been performing for most of his life. They turn out the horses, muck all the stalls in the barn, move the chicken tractor to fresh grass, and then Matts takes one of the four-wheelers around to fill the water troughs in the front pasture while Devo deals with returning some customer calls.

Boogie follows at Devo's heels for the most part, though when they take a break for a late lunch—bologna sandwiches on white bread, homemade pickles, and creamed corn—Boogie lies at Matts's feet. Probably because he knows Matts is more of a pushover than Devo, which is true. But Matts doesn't like the texture of the outer edge of the bologna slices anyway. And it would be a waste to throw them away when Boogie is *right there*.

Matts and Devo are working on one final project when they hear a diesel engine coming down the drive. And as they're putting the new tack room door on its hinges, Ben and Wade enter the barn.

"Afternoon, boys," Ben says. "Wade just got here, and we figured we'd see if you two needed any help."

"About done, actually," Devo says around the door he's holding.

Matts sinks the middle pin into place, stands, and taps in the final top one. He sets the hammer aside so he can shake both their hands.

"Does Devo have something on you, or are you here of your own accord?" Wade asks.

"He needed some horse therapy," Devo answers for Matts. "I'm just making him work for it. We'll head for the creek trail in a minute."

Wade walks over to the ancient refrigerator by the back roll-top door and pulls out two water bottles. He proffers one first to Devo, then to Matts. They both accept.

"Family stuff?" Ben asks Matts as he breaks the seal.

"Yeah. My dad is sick. Cancer."

Both older men nod. "You two close?"

He takes a drink. "We're...complicated."

"Sounds about right," Ben says. "You want to talk about it?"

"Not really," Matts admits. Or maybe a more honest answer would be *not with you*, but he knows that's rude.

"Sydney's on her way back," Ben says, perhaps understanding the subtext of his statement nonetheless. "She's an hour out. You want some quiet, or should I send her to find you when she gets here?"

"I'd like to see her," Matts says.

"Shocker," Devo mutters quietly.

Matts doesn't think so.

"Well, you boys watch for snakes and keep an eye on the weather. Storm is supposed to roll in around dinnertime tonight."

"Yessir," they both say.

But neither Wade nor Ben appears interested in leaving them. And they're both looking at Matts. He glances at Devo, but Devo appears just as stymied.

"I heard you came to the cookout last weekend," Wade says. "I was disappointed to miss it this year."

"Yeah," Matts agrees. "It was great."

"What'd you think of Power Wheels NASCAR?"

"Sydney's a cheater," Devo says.

"Didn't ask *you*, son," Wade answers.

Matts takes another drink, stalling. He has no idea where this line of questioning is going, and he doesn't like not knowing. "More entertaining than actual NASCAR, I'd say."

"And you met the rest of the family?"

He met a couple aunts and uncles and a pair of grandparents on Ben's side, a great-aunt and a handful of second cousins on Tricia's side.

"I did," Matts agrees. "Pretty cool that nearly everybody plays instruments or sings. I've never had a big jam session like that before."

Wade nods.

"The music gene is hit or miss on my side," Ben says. "But seems everyone on Tricia's side got it. Syd and Devo's biological parents used to sing the most beautiful duets, back in the day."

"Do they ever come to the cookouts?" It only occurs to Matts after he's asked the question that it might be indelicate.

Devo ducks his head, scuffing the heel of his boot against the concrete. "Nah."

"Good riddance," Wade confirms.

"I'm assuming she told you about them?" Ben asks. "Why she left?"

"She did."

They all stand in silence for a minute, arms crossed, not quite meeting anyone else's eyes.

"I never could understand," Ben says finally. "When they were pregnant, everyone asked if they was hoping for a boy or a girl, and they said the same thing, every time. 'We don't care, long as the baby is healthy.' For some reason, that changed for them after the fact."

Ben shakes his head. "Don't make much sense. That you'd want a dead son over a living daughter. But that's the choice they made. They haven't seen Sydney since Wade brought her here."

"And I stopped seeing them as soon as I turned eighteen, and they couldn't use the legal fact of them still being my parents on paper as coercion," Devo says. "They refused to come here, but they'd make me visit them a couple times a year before that."

Matts is extremely out of his depth. "Good riddance?" he repeats.

Devo laughs softly. "Yeah, good riddance." The timer on his phone goes off, and he throws a thumb toward the front of the barn. "I've gotta go turn off the sprinkler. We can head out after."

Matts waits until he's out of earshot, then turns to Ben. "Does it bother you that you're not biologically related to them?" It's probably a rude question, but he's curious.

Ben exhales, hands on his hips. "It does. Not in the way you might expect. I couldn't love them more if they was my own flesh and blood. I just wish I could say I was partially responsible for making them. I wish I could take credit for some little portion of what they are. What they'll be."

Matts has no response for that, but it makes his chest feel tight. He doesn't think he ever wants kids, but he hopes he could love them like that if he did. Kids deserve to be loved like that. And he knows a lot of them aren't.

"I think you can take some credit," he says finally. "There's a reason for the nature versus nurture debate, right? And you— I think it's clear you've done a good job on the nurture front."

Ben whistles for Boogie. "Well. That's nice of you to say. Anyhow. I'll send Syd out after you whenever she gets here."

When Devo returns, wiping wet palms on his jeans, they walk down to the pasture. They collect and tack the horses in silence, and then Matts is swaying in a creaking saddle with cloud-diluted sun on his face and age-soft leather reins in his hands. He feels like he can properly breathe for the first time in weeks.

"We'll follow the fence to the back pasture," Devo says, pointing. "There's a gate there and a trail that follows the creek for several miles. It crosses a couple folks' properties, but everyone's neighborly about using it, provided you don't leave any trash behind. Sound good?"

That sounds good. Very good.

"Is there space on the trail for a gallop once we get them warmed up?"

Devo grins over his shoulder. "There is."

*

THEY'VE HIT THE end of the trail and turned around when the sky starts to get dark. A bank of cumulonimbus clouds masks the beginnings of sunset, casting long, reaching shadows over the open trail in front of them.

Ten minutes later, they hear the first roll of thunder.

"We might want to pick up the pace," Devo suggests.

Matts finds that wise.

They leave the trail to take a shortcut through one of the neighbors' unfenced fields, and it's then that Matts recognizes a figure approaching them on a horse, bareback, at a lope.

"Is that—"

"Yep," Devo says. "Show off."

Sydney pulls her horse to a walk once she's a few feet away, one hand on her reins and the other holding her hat to her head. "Y'all somehow miss these fuckoff huge storm clouds?"

Her cut-off shorts trail white frayed edges down her tanned thighs. Her knees are scarred, her calves mud-smeared, and her bare feet press, easy and familiar, to the heaving belly of her horse. She's still wearing his bracelet, too big and halfway down the forearm of the hand holding her hat against the wind.

The thunderhead roils behind her, dark and foreboding in an otherwise pink and orange sky. A sea of grass pitches like waves in the wind in the middle ground between them.

Sydney looks like the main character in a movie clip. Or maybe one of those giant southwest aesthetic oil paintings so many wealthy Texans seem to have on their entryway walls.

She is so, so beautiful.

"And that's my cue to leave," Devo says. "Thanks for your help today, Matts."

"Yeah," Matts says. "Any time." He means it. "Thanks for this."

Devo kicks his horse into a gallop, leaving them behind in a scatter of dirt clods.

"Hi," Sydney says, reining her horse so they're side by side. "My dad says you're having an existential crisis."

"Little bit," he admits.

She glances heavenward. "Will it keep until we have a roof over our heads, or do we need to hash it out now?"

Matts likes the implicit assumption in that statement. That his existential crisis is theirs to work out.

"I suspect it will be ongoing," he says.

"Well, in that case, we can start working on it after dinner, okay?"

"Okay."

Their horses both pin their ears, and they look north, where the clouds are gathered, watching as purple lightning spider-webs down to make landfall in the distance. The thunder follows, low and rolling, several seconds later.

The air feels damp and full of static.

"I'll race you back to the barn," she says.

*

THEY GET BACK shortly after Devo. Wade comes down to help them get the horses all buttoned up and away, but the drizzle has turned into a proper downpour by the time they're finished and running back to the house. They take turns showering and changing into dry clothes; Matts ends up wearing one of Sydney's oversized Judas Priest shirts that fits him rather well and a pair of Ben's shorts that do not.

They eat their dinner on the porch—leftover lasagna and vegetables warmed in the microwave with sweet tea in mason jars. It reminds him of being a kid, a warm plate in his lap and a quilt around his shoulders that smells like sun, likely dried on the clothesline in the distance. The rain on the metal roof and the wind chimes hung in the eaves are a familiar kind of music. And there's Sydney, bedraggled and grinning at him between bites as she checks the weather forecast on her phone.

"Yeesh," she says, tipping the phone screen so he can see the swath of yellow and red moving across the radar. "Probably isn't safe to drive in this."

Matts takes the phone from her. "Looks like there'll be a break in thirty minutes."

"Or," she presses, "to be safe, you could just stay."

"Stay," he repeats, glancing up.

"The night, I mean. You said you're contractually obligated to not do things that would potentially put your health in jeopardy."

"True." He draws the word out, then looks first at her left eye, then her right, as if one of them has some additional context he's missing. "But I wouldn't want to be an imposition."

Sydney rolls her bottom lip between her teeth. "Matts," she says, holding his gaze.

"Sydney," Matts says.

"I'm trying to engineer an excuse for you to stay."

"Oh." The tension in his shoulders evaporates. He

wants to ask at least a dozen follow-up questions, but he resists. "Then I could stay because we both want me to stay?"

"That works too," she agrees.

He considers pointing out that there are four bedrooms in the house, and with Wade visiting, they're all taken. But Matts doesn't know how to do that gracefully or how to ask without making it sound as if he's angling to share her bed, even if that would be his preference.

"You know," Sydney says. "We got some strawberries from one of the neighbors on Friday. I was thinking I'd make a cobbler for dessert. You want to help me?"

He glances toward the kitchen and thinks about his daydream earlier. He can't have all of it—can't kiss her yet. Not now. Maybe not ever. But something is better than nothing. Something might even feel like everything.

"Yes," he says. "Please."

Chapter Ten

JUSTIN MATTHEWS IS in her bed, and despite being the one who invited him there, Sydney Warren has no idea what to do about it.

She was hoping for a yes and ready for a no when she asked him to stay. But she hasn't fully thought out what would happen if he *did* say yes.

Sydney has never slept next to anyone other than Devo before.

She knows people do it all the time, but she doesn't understand how they can act as though it doesn't mean anything to share a bed at night with strangers they've only just met at a bar or a club, as if it's anything other than a huge, terrifying show of trust.

Sydney never had sleepovers as a kid, not for lack of wanting but because it was too much of a risk. A risk she already understood too well at twelve years old when she made no complaints about her mom picking her up early from the few slumber parties she was invited to. Even staying in the same hotel room as Sky and Rex the first time the band went on tour, Sydney struggled to sleep on the rollaway bed. And the few times she's hooked up with someone, they never got anywhere near sleep.

This is something more than unfamiliar territory.

Her phone has already lit up with messages from every other person in the house, ranging from cautious concern—her mother—to *What the fuck are you doing?*—Devo.

But Sydney wanted Matts to stay. She wanted him in her bed. And she's allowed to want things.

But he's here now, wearing her shirt and her headphones and smiling softly at her as she frantically tries to tidy the organized chaos that is her room.

"You don't have to clean up for me," he says.

"On the contrary. I refuse to be responsible for benching the Hell Hound's star player because he tripped in the night while trying to get to the bathroom, and broke…I don't know…one of the important hockey-playing bones."

"All of my bones are important for hockey playing. Also, Alex is the star player. Rome is a close second now. I'm third, and only if we're not counting goalies. And we should. In which case, I'm fourth. I don't even make the podium."

"Oh, go away. Neither Rome nor Rushy were selected for the Olympic team. You're on the podium."

Matts slides the headphones off his ears, sitting up. "How did you know I was selected for the Olympic team?"

She pauses, a pile of laundry in her arms. Shit. "You follow my tag," she says, aiming for cavalier and probably missing by a mile. "I follow yours."

"People don't always say nice stuff about me." Matts has the audacity to look concerned about it.

Sydney shoves the clothes into the hamper and looks at him for a minute, hands on her hips. "You see all the shit people say about *me*, and you're concerned I'm going to…what, judge you? Based on the opinions of internet idiots? I understand better than most that social media commentary is a never-ending case study in the Dunning–Kruger effect."

"But the stuff about you isn't true. I *am* shit at

interviews, and I *do* play too aggressively, and my hair *does* look dumb, and—"

"Stop talking."

Matts stops talking.

Sydney abandons her cleaning vendetta and knee-walks across the bed until she can get in his face to ensure he's listening. "You're endearing as hell in your interviews because you're not a robot regurgitating the same five PR-approved statements everyone else does. And yeah, you're too aggressive, but it's because you're stupidly loyal, and other players have realized targeting Alex or Jeff is an easy way to get you into the penalty box. And your hair is *not* dumb; it's charming. And if you like it, which I'm assuming you do, fuck what anyone else thinks."

"Oh," he says. "You think my hair is charming?"

All of him is charming. It's terrible.

"I do, but that is literally the opposite of the point."

Matts sets the headphones on her nightstand and then carefully nudges her with his elbow. "The path to the bathroom looks pretty clear to me."

She must admit it does. "Right. I'm going to brush my teeth; you want to join me?"

A few minutes later, Sydney discovers there's something shockingly domestic about brushing your teeth with someone. Matts stands next to her at the sink, hair mussed from the headphones, taking twice as long as he should because he keeps stopping to gesture with the spare toothbrush she gave him—a free pink plastic thing from her dentist. Sydney asked him his thoughts on the songs she assigned him that week as she handed over the toothbrush. Now, he's talking about "Call Me Little Sunshine" and Ghost's general lyrical prowess, with toothpaste foam in the corners of his mouth and adoration in his voice, and it's almost unbearable.

In the mirror, their size difference is apparent, something Sydney typically forgets. She's used to feeling too tall and gawky compared to other girls. She has a couple inches on MJ and Sky and is nearly as tall as Devo and Rex. But next to Matts, Sydney feels small. Delicate.

She slides off her rings and deposits them one at a time in the old paisley teacup she keeps for ring-holding purposes as Matts bends at the waist to spit and rinse his mouth. He goes quiet for a minute, sink running, watching her.

She takes the bracelet—his bracelet—off last and proffers it to him.

"My liege," she says.

He turns off the faucet. "I think you should keep it."

"Matts."

"It's good luck. It helped you win the race."

"I won because I cheated. And don't you need luck more than me right now? Playoffs are about to start."

"I can make my own luck."

He rubs the back of his wrist over his mouth and then crosses his arms to drive home the point that he has no intention of taking it from her.

On impulse, Sydney reaches for the teacup and dumps the contents back into her palm to find the least ostentatious ring she owns: a flat silver band with a small, raised heart as its only ornamentation.

When she holds it out to him, for once, she's at a loss for words. So, she doesn't say anything at all.

Matts uncrosses his arms, considering. "Luck exchange?" he asks quietly.

"Luck exchange," she agrees.

As he takes the ring, it occurs to her it probably won't even fit his smallest finger. He must have the same thought because he tries it on his pinky first. It takes a little wiggling to get it over his knuckle, but then it slides just fine. Matts holds his hand out, studying it, using his thumb to spin the band so the heart is centered.

A ring has different connotations than a bracelet.

And it feels belatedly obvious, looking at his otherwise naked hands, that her offering him one of her rings means something.

His mouth is tucked into a pleased, crooked smile, though, as he studies his pinky. And when Matts finally stops looking at it, he directs his attention to her wrist, raising his eyebrows pointedly.

Sydney sets the cup and its remaining rings back on the counter. She slides the bracelet on and uses her teeth to tighten the cord. She doesn't look away from him while she does it.

Matts nods approvingly. "Bed?" he says, flipping off the lights.

Bed.

Right.

She might not survive this.

Lit only by LED lights strung up behind her bed, Sydney watches as he pulls back the comforter and makes himself comfortable on the left-hand side, closest to the door.

Matts pauses halfway to depositing his phone on the nightstand, then swipes in to type a response to someone.

"Everything okay?"

"Yeah. Well. No. My dad broke his ankle this

morning. Chemo's made him pretty weak, and he fell down the stairs to the basement. He'll be fine. Probably. But he's…"

She pulls back the covers on the right side. "Not a good patient, I take it?"

"No." Matts sets the phone aside. "My stepbrother is doing the best he can, but their dynamic is already awkward. And he's basically running the ranch now on top of dealing with my dad's health stuff."

Sydney stacks two pillows so she can sit against the headboard and face him. "Tell me about the ranch?"

He has no difficulty fulfilling that request.

Matts tells her about his horse, the house, and the land and its history; crop rotations and boundary disputes; a tree that got struck by lightning; the reportedly haunted outhouse; and about growing up in the shadow of mountains and beneath sunsets like forest fires.

"You said you do an actual cattle drive twice a year?" she asks.

"Yeah, in the spring, we take them up to higher elevation land and then bring them back home again before winter sets in."

Sydney glances at the spot on the wall behind Matts's head that is currently empty but displayed a bookfair horse poster for an embarrassing number of years. "You know, I used to dream about going on a cattle drive. I was a weird music freak as a kid, but I was also a certified horse girl. I would have killed a man to go on a cattle drive." She attempts to untangle two curls in her peripheral vision, considering. "Still might. Depending on the man."

"You should come."

She pauses, her fingers now also part of the tangle. "What?"

"If you're not doing shows then, you could come with me. Just for a couple days. We'd appreciate the help."

"Are you serious?"

"Why wouldn't I be serious?" Matts beckons her forward and ducks down, squinting, to sort out the knot. "It's typically two full days of riding. Half the herd one day, the other half the next. You don't get much sleep the night between, but at least you're in a bed. No camping required. And the route itself is easy. One river crossing, and from about mile marker eighteen to twenty-three, we're on the road. Lots of folks driving up to Crested Butte stop and take pictures. It's slow but nothing treacherous."

"You gotta stop talking about this, or you're going to get me all riled up, and I won't sleep."

He laughs softly, tucking her now-untangled hair behind her ear. He leans back against the headboard, arms crossed. "Well, just think about it."

As if she'll be doing anything else.

"So—" Sydney tries desperately to find a topic of conversation that doesn't encourage her to revisit every romanticized teenage fantasy she had about falling in love with a cute cowhand on the open range. "How did you get into cooking? I felt like I was deadweight in the cobbler-making process earlier."

He shrugs. "As a kid, I liked helping my mom in the kitchen whenever I was allowed. And now, I like helping Eli. It's kinda like…the recipe is an equation. As long as you solve it correctly, you can't go wrong."

"Makes sense. Water plus flour equals bread."

"You need a little more than that for bread."

"Tell that to medieval peasants."

"I know you're trying to be witty, but you don't want to go down this path with me," he says seriously. "When Eli taught me to make bread last year, I spent a month researching bread-making techniques around the world, historical and present-day. So, if you want to talk about medieval breadmaking techniques with, you know, at minimum, salt and a variety of different rising agent methods in addition to flour and water, we can do that. But if not, you should probably take the L on this one."

She doubles over laughing. "You're good at trivia, huh?"

"I am."

"Well, then" —Sydney scootches down into a more typical sleeping position, unstacking her pillows so she can hug one—"lay some cursed knowledge on me. As a bedtime treat."

"Cursed knowledge?"

"You know. Something weird. Unsettling."

Matts's expression is hard to read in the dark, but she thinks it's probably fond.

"One of the few natural predators of the moose is the orca whale," he says finally.

"I...uh. Huh. Okay. How are whales eating moose? Do moose swim?"

"Pretty regularly, yeah. They can dive twenty feet and hold their breath for over a minute. And they swim between islands off the coast of Canada and Alaska, looking for food."

"Except they *become* food. Because whales."

"Yeah."

"A-plus cursed knowledge, thank you."

"You're welcome."

Matts yawns and then mimics her position, curled toward her like an oversized parenthetical. His arms are tucked to his chest, and Sydney's attention catches on his right pinky finger, her ring glinting in the scant light.

The rain on the metal roof is a soft susurrus of background noise, the rolling thunder far enough away to be ambient and not frightening.

Matts is a study in contrasts, painted in sepia light. His eyes are dark, and his jaw is sharp, and she knows she either needs to stop looking or do something about the want in her chest that's slowly threatening to choke her. Sydney wants to touch him. She wants to kiss him. But even more than that, she wants him to *want* her to touch him and to kiss him, and she's not sure if he does. More than anything, she wants to be certain.

"Goodnight," she says and searches for disappointment but doesn't see any in his face.

"Goodnight," he agrees and closes his eyes, just like that.

Sydney closes hers, too, knowing it won't make much difference.

An hour later, well after Matts's breathing has evened out, she eases back the duvet and slides as quietly as possible out of bed and into the hallway.

The under-counter lighting is on in the kitchen, and

Devo sits at the breakfast bar with a beer and the cobbler tin in front of him. He's eating directly out of the tin with a fork.

"Can't sleep?" he asks.

"Nope." She moves to sit beside him.

"Maybe it's the professional hockey player in your bed."

"Maybe you should mind your own business."

Devo rolls his eyes but deposits his fork in the tin and shoves it toward her.

Sydney accepts the unspoken peace offering and takes a bite.

"So," he says as if he'd rather be saying anything else. "Are you two…"

"No."

"You planning to actually make a move at some point, or just keep doing less and less platonic shit until one of you caves and admits your feelings?"

She ignores him. "Matts invited me to his family's spring cattle drive. I think I want to go."

"Spring cattle drive," Devo repeats, his tone suddenly flat.

"Yeah. His family has a ranch in Colorado. They move their herd up to better grazing land in the mountains every spring and back down in the fall. Two days of movement but no camping. Sounds amazing."

"You sure that's a good idea?" Devo is looking at his hands, picking at one of his nails.

Sydney pushes the dish back to him. "It'd probably be between the spring and summer tours, and I'd only need a week off, tops, with travel. It shouldn't impact practice much."

"But do you know anything about his family or this ranch?" Devo's playing with the fork now, still not meeting her eyes.

"Why? What do you mean?"

"I'm just saying."

"*What* are you just saying? Jesus, Devo, this is only a childhood dream come true for me. Why are you being so fucking weird about it?"

"Because I can't *protect* you there," he says, and it's a shock, the sudden, urgent volume, cutting through the soft blur of rain and thunder outside; the refrigerator humming in the corner.

"What?" she says.

"I can't—" He presses his palms to the edge of the table, glancing at their parents' closed bedroom door. He sucks in a breath, lowering his voice. "The bullies at school and the internet creeps and the weirdos at concerts I can handle for you, but this... I won't be there.

And even if I could be there, you'll be surrounded by men we don't know in a rural part of the country that isn't known for being progressive. And maybe that's a shitty assumption to make, but I'll make it if it means keeping you safe."

"Matts wouldn't let anyone hurt me," she says blankly.

"Matts might not have even considered it could be dangerous, Syd. He hasn't spent his life watching the world do its level best to shit on you at every possible opportunity. He doesn't understand. And even if he did, he's only one person. It might not be in his power to promise you safety."

Devo is right. She hates that he's right, but... He's right.

"I'll talk to him."

"I'm sorry."

"No, you're right. You guys let me forget, sometimes. That I have to be cautious."

"I'm still sorry."

She's close to tears, and he can probably tell, which is why he stands and pulls her into a tight hug, one arm looped around her shoulders, the other hand cupped to the back of her head.

"You want me to talk to him about it?" he asks.

"No." She cinches her arms around his waist so she can squeeze him back. "I'll do it."

They stand there for a while, through several rolling rounds of thunder, before Devo clears his throat. "You've still got his bracelet on. You planning to give it back at some point?"

"I tried. He didn't want it back."

"Shocking."

She should stop there, but she doesn't. "I gave him my heart ring in exchange."

"You think maybe you should just kiss him at this point?"

She exhales into his chest. "Not sure I'm ready for what would happen after," she admits. "Either way."

"Fair enough."

He rocks them back and forth.

She wonders if they're both thinking about the same thing—about the summer between her sophomore and junior year of high school. About Bryce Shaw. Neither of them says his name.

"He seems decent," Devo says finally. "He'd probably give you time to figure things out if you asked for it. And if he *didn't*—"

"Matts could kill you with very little effort, don't even."

"Yeah, that's true."

She pushes at him, and he pushes back as if it hadn't been his idea to initiate the contact. After the ensuing slap fight knocks the fork leaning out of the tin onto the floor in a loud clatter of metal on tile, they both freeze, waiting to see if their parents' bedroom door will open.

After several beats of silence, Devo retrieves the fork and retreats to his seat. They shove the pie plate back and forth until the cobbler is all gone, and Sydney is warm and tired and full and maybe, possibly, feels like she could sleep.

The rain has slackened, and the thunder has all but died off by the time she finishes brushing her teeth for a second time and tiptoes back to the bed.

"Syd?" Matts asks blearily as she pulls the comforter up.

"Hey," she whispers. "Sorry. Go back to sleep."

"You okay?"

"Yeah. I'm good."

But he's rolling to face her, to reach for her. His hand lands on her shoulder and slides down to encircle her bicep.

"What's wrong?"

She breathes. "I want to go. With you. On the drive."

"Yeah?" His thumb moves in a lopsided circle on her skin. "Cool."

"But will I be safe? If someone recognizes me. If your family or the people who work for them found out about me, I mean. Will I be safe?"

His thumb stops moving. "Of course."

"Are you sure? Because I need you to be sure."

A heavy silence stretches between them and settles in the space between their mouths, where they're breathing each other's secondhand air. His eyes are dark and liquid and serious when they meet hers.

"I can make sure," he says. "I'll talk to Aaron and see if we need to worry about any of the part-time guys. And Aaron or I, or both of us, will be with you at all times. I can make sure you're safe. I promise."

"Okay," she says. "I trust you."

And she does, she realizes. Wholly and without reservation. It is an uncomfortable thing to acknowledge.

"Okay," he agrees.

His hand slips down to her elbow, her forearm, her wrist. He tucks two fingers between the bracelet and the meat of her palm, thumb against her wristbone. And then he leaves his hand there, not quite holding hers, but pretty damn close.

"Night," he murmurs. And to all appearances, he

goes back to sleep.

Unbelievable.

She does not sleep. She lies there with her hand under his hand, watching him breathe, and writing lyrics in her head that she commits to memory rather than dislodging him to reach for the journal on her nightstand. Lyrics about hands and fingers and full bottom lips. Lyrics about longing and hope and want tempered by fear.

If she isn't a little in love with him already, she's getting there.

*

SYDNEY MUST FALL asleep at some point because sleeping is the predecessor to waking up, which she does with a lurch to the sound of Rex's motorcycle pulling into the yard.

She shoves her face into her pillow with a groan before remembering—

Matts.

Who is similarly trying to block out the noise by pulling the duvet over his head.

The engine cuts, and they can hear Sky and Rex talking indistinctly as they approach the front door.

Matts sighs, sitting up.

He has a glorious case of bed head and a sheet

imprint on his cheek; his eyelids are puffy, and his lips are chapped, and he is still the most beautiful person she has ever seen.

"Morning, Goldilocks," she says.

"What?"

"You're sleeping in my bed. Seemed apropos."

"If either of us is a bear, it's me." He blinks, then digs his knuckles, a little more vigorously than she would prefer, into his eye socket. "What time is it?"

"Almost eight-thirty."

"Why are they here so early?"

"Practice. We're supposed to start at nine, and they always come early to steal food."

Matts exhales, long and slow and intentional. "Well, shit. I've got practice, too, so I should probably go anyway."

"You have time for breakfast?"

He blinks a few more times, and she tries not to get a thrill from seeing him like this—rumpled and un-guarded and striped with pale morning light coming in the blinds. His eyes look gold where the sun hits them.

"Yeah," he says, "okay."

He's still wearing her shirt when they emerge from the bedroom a few minutes later, the worn fabric stretched thin and tight over his chest and around his arms.

He has nice shoulder blades, Sydney thinks absently as she follows him into the kitchen.

Her parents and Sky are at the dining table. Rex is in front of the open refrigerator. Devo is scrambling eggs and looking hungover about it.

"Good morning, family," Sydney says. She nods formally to Sky and Rex. "Business associates."

"Esteemed leader," Sky responds, equally formal, with a bow.

"Commodore," Rex salutes.

"Weirdo," Devo says.

"Not your best," Sydney murmurs to him, sotto voce, as she pulls her own pan out of the cabinet. "You wanna try again?"

"Oh, hey, Matts," Devo says loudly. "I didn't know you stayed last night. You sleep well?"

Matts, standing awkwardly in the doorway, somehow manages to look even more awkward without actually moving.

"Yes?" He sounds unsure.

"Ignore him," Sydney advises. "You want some eggs? I'm sunny-side-upping mine."

"Please." Matts still looks like a deer in headlights.

"Sausage is on the counter and oatmeal is on the

stove," her mom adds.

"Toast?" Sydney asks, and then, before Matts can respond, "Wait, how do you eat your toast? Eli said it was a war crime."

"With salt and pepper and hot sauce."

"Hot sauce."

"I like spice; it makes textures easier to deal with."

"Yes!" Sky says. "Because if your mouth is numb, your tongue can't have opinions about the way things feel. I keep *telling* people this."

"Yeah, that's it exactly."

"I think we just became best friends," Sky says. "Adjust your internal hierarchy accordingly."

"My…internal friend hierarchy?"

"Obviously."

"Ignore her too," Sydney further advises.

"Pass on the toast," Matts says. "But I can cut up some peppers to eat with the eggs?"

Sydney nods to the pile of cutting boards, and Matts looks pleased as he selects one and starts chopping, pausing occasionally to flip his knife and scrape the board over her frying pan. He keeps the peppers in a tidy pile away from the cooking eggs.

Conversation resumes, and Sydney basks in the domesticity of it all: the smell of breakfast and coffee, the soft murmur of her parents' voices, Sky's sarcasm, and Rex's laughter. Matts gently hip-checks her as she pokes the half-cooked eggs with a flat-edged wooden spoon, the egg whites' edges bubbled and popping in a thick puddle of olive oil.

"Breaking news," Rex says, reading from his phone. "Red Right Hand is emblematic of the downfall of traditional values in America."

"Are we really?"

"Gunna put that on my resume," Sky murmurs, head lolled against the high back of her chair.

"Good parents," Rex continues, using a broadcaster voice, "will keep their teens away from such pagan music lest it confuse their minds and lead them down a road of *depravity*."

"What does that make us?" Tricia murmurs rhetorically to Ben.

Rex tosses his phone to Sydney, and she puts the wooden spoon in her mouth so she can use both hands to scroll through the article. "Sho 'nuff," she drawls around it, "lookit us, corrupting the youth."

Matts takes the spoon from between her teeth.

She keeps reading, making progressively more unattractive noises the further she gets into it. "Wow. Just going for the full discrimination bingo card, here, huh.

Who writes this stuff?"

"What?" Matts says.

"They're talking shit about Rex."

"Mm," Rex agrees. "Insulting the Asian man by calling him effeminate. Groundbreaking."

"O God, that I were a man!" Sydney quotes, tossing the phone back. "I would eat his heart in the market-place."

"Pretty sure a woman wrote that article," Rex says. "But I agree with the sentiment."

"Well, in that case, muskets at dawn or whatever."

"She gets more intelligible the more time you spend with her," Devo says to Matts, "unfortunately."

Sydney kicks the back of Devo's knee gently but with enough surprise force to cause a brief collapse. He catches himself on the countertop and throws a dish towel at her.

"I understood the muskets at dawn part," Matts says, stepping between them, ostensibly to hand back her spoon, but more probably so he can prevent Sydney from retaliating.

"First bit was from *Much Ado About Nothing*," Rex says. "Shakespeare. This lady is saying she'd fight a guy who slandered her friend if she was able. I remember that one because of all the sexual innuendo."

Matts turns to face Rex. "Shakespeare has sexual innuendo in it?"

"The US education system is in shambles," Sydney says with a sigh.

Matts looks between them, arms crossed. "I thought Shakespeare was highbrow. Fancy."

"Not even a little." Sydney nudges him out of the way so she can transfer the eggs to two plates. "His work is full of dirty jokes; they're just not as obvious to us now because language has changed."

"Dirty jokes like what?"

Tricia sighs loudly.

"Like even the title of *Much Ado*," Sydney says. "Sure, it can mean 'people freaking out about nothing,' but 'nothing' was also Elizabethan slang for 'vagina.' So it's possible he meant it to be interpreted as, 'a whole lot of fuss about vagina.'"

"Can we please not say the word 'vagina' at the breakfast table?" Tricia asks.

"I'm not at the breakfast table," Sydney says.

"Aw, but we're talking about *literature*," Sky adds.

"And you've always said it's important to use correct anatomical language," Devo points out.

"Fine," Tricia says. "Just don't start on that *Twelfth Night* shit."

"What's in *Twelfth Night*?" Matts asks quietly, one hand on Sydney's lower back as he maneuvers around her.

It takes her a moment to respond because of that hand.

"Probably the dirtiest joke in any of Shakespeare's plays," she murmurs back. He ducks closer to hear her, and she does not get a thrill from it. Much. "I quoted the joke in a paper my junior year, and my English teacher took exception to the inclusion, even though I was quoting from the source text she'd given us."

"That's not fair."

"Which is exactly what the administration decided when my parents objected to my failing grade. But I think my mom has *Twelfth Night*–related trauma now, considering she had to take part in a very serious meeting with school officials in which she defended her daughter's right to use the word 'cunt' in a paper."

Matts coughs on a laugh. "I'm going to need additional context for that at some point."

"Later," Sydney whispers, "or my mom will break out in hives."

Matts finishes sliding past her, removes his hand, and tips the peppers onto their plates. She tries not to think about the warmth of his palm and the fan of his fingers, how his hand had spanned most of her lower back. That he'd absently pinched the fabric of her shirt between thumb and forefinger as though he'd wanted to linger before letting go.

"Anyway," Rex says, moving into the kitchen to get a bowl. "No need for dramatics, Syd. We agreed to ignore the haters, right?"

"I guess. My musket needs cleaning anyway. Also, I'm not *that* dramatic."

Devo pretends to choke on a sip of milk.

"I think we can all agree," Sky says, "that of the life-forms present on this property, you are the most dramatic."

"Aside from the horses, on occasion," Tricia says.

"Aside from the horses, on occasion," Sky allows.

"Et tu, Brute?" Sydney mutters.

"Oh," Matts says. "I know that one."

Chapter Eleven

MATTS HAS A reputation for being violent.

He's not a goon; he's not an enforcer. But he's made toeing the line between legal and illegal hits something of an art form, and while he doesn't start many fights, he certainly welcomes them. He's not *violent*, though, or at least, he's never considered himself violent before. Until he opens his door to Sydney with blood on her face. Then, he thinks maybe he is a violent person after all.

He was practicing guitar before going to bed, trying to get the solo from "Master of Puppets" down, when his phone lit up with a text from Sydney.

can I come over

No punctuation. No context.

Red Right Hand had a concert at House of Blues that night. It was the first real venue that ever booked them, nearly three years prior, and they wanted to play there again before kicking off their first ever headlining stadium tour. For nostalgia, Sydney said. For excellent drinks, Rex said. For hot bartenders, Sky said.

House of Blues isn't far from Matts's apartment. He would have gone if tickets weren't sold out by the time he talked himself into looking for them. So, he knew something was wrong when he got the text from Sydney a little past 11:00 p.m.

Do you need me to come get you?

give me your address

Matts sent his address.

And now, he opens his door to Sydney, standing on the mat with half-dried blood running from her nose to her chin, cracked and starting to flake over the bow of her swollen lip. His heart feels too big for his chest. Matts wants to hit something. Someone.

"Who did this to you?" he asks, pulling her inside.

She laughs, a raw, hysterical edge to it.

"Who did this to you?" she mimics, low and mocking.

His fingers are on her face. He's not sure how they got there. "Is that supposed to be my voice?"

"Stop," she mutters roughly, pushing at his hands. Blood smears on his thumb. "You're like a romance novel cliché right now."

"Sydney," Matts says and doesn't recognize his own voice.

She stops.

She swallows.

"It doesn't matter. I'm fine. Security took care of it. I need—" Sydney sets her motorcycle helmet on the entryway table and hugs herself, hands wrapped around her biceps. Her hair is a frizzy mess, her eyeliner is smeared halfway down her cheeks, and her tongue keeps probing at her swollen lip. "I don't know. I don't know what I need. I—can you—"

Matts is intimately familiar with wanting something and not knowing how to ask for it. He hopes he's right when he assumes. "Yeah. Yeah, come here."

She folds into him as if all she needed was an invitation, as if she didn't know she already had one. He should probably ask for permission before manhandling her. But he doesn't have the words; he needs her closer, needs tangible proof that she's okay, that there aren't other injuries hidden under her clothes. Sydney doesn't flinch away from his searching hands. She doesn't protest when he lifts her off the floor entirely. She clings, wraps her legs around his waist, hooks the toes of her boots together behind him, and pushes her bloody mouth against his neck with something close to a sob.

"I'm sorry," she says, smearing the exhalation damp and miserable into his skin. "I'm sorry, I don't—"

"No, hey. You're fine. Don't apologize. You're fine. You're *perfect*."

She shakes, and the world shakes with her.

Matts walks to the kitchen and sets her on the island, putting enough space between them so he can get a better look at her. He doesn't like what he sees. Her shoulders are a sharp curve of defeat, her jaw is clenched like she's trying not to cry, and her fingers are knitted together like she's uncertain if she's allowed to touch him.

He didn't think it was possible for Sydney to look so meek. It's terrible. It doesn't suit her at all.

"Just your face?" Matts asks.

"Yeah," she says roughly, her eyes wet. "Two

punches. Nose and mouth."

Sydney holds up her right hand, and the sight of her swollen knuckles, the rust-brown patina on her silver dragon ring, gives him a sick satisfaction. "I got one in between though. I think I took some skin off."

"Good," he says fiercely.

Matts lets his hand around her neck slide down her arm, forces himself to let go of her hip so he can use both hands to gently—so fucking gently—remove her rings. He leaves the bracelet on. "Tell me if this hurts."

He tests each of her joints, bending and unbending each finger, pad to palm, using his thumb to press each curled finger flat again. Sydney watches without fighting him.

"Hurt?" he asks.

"Only a little."

"Okay. That's good. And nowhere else?" He has to ask again just to be sure.

"Nowhere else."

"Let's get you cleaned up, then."

Matts digs the first aid kit out of the hall closet, washes his hands, and lays out a handful of alcohol wipes.

"Sorry," he says, ripping open the first one. "This'll sting. And stink."

But she stays motionless on the counter as he cleans up her lip, wipes the blood off her chin, the smeared kohl from around her eyes, and presses his thumbs to either side of her nose.

"It doesn't feel broken," he murmurs, more to himself than her. "Noses just bleed a lot."

"You'd know," Sydney says.

He thinks it's supposed to come out joking, judgmental, but she mostly just sounds exhausted.

"I would," he agrees, holding up a penlight. "Let me check you for a concussion, and then we'll be done."

Her pupils are normal. She follows his finger. She doesn't have a headache.

Matts feels like he can breathe again.

"You wanna tell me what happened?" He's still standing between her splayed legs, still touching her, palms cupped around her elbows, thumbs against the soft skin in the crease of her arms. He doesn't need to be this close anymore, but he can't seem to stop.

Sydney kicks the heels of her boots against the cabinet. "No."

Matts doesn't get a chance to press because his phone, sitting on the counter next to Sydney's thigh, lights up with a call.

"It's Devo," he says. "Does he know you're here?"

"No. I gave the police my statement, and then I…" Sydney falls into him, forehead knocking against his sternum. "…left."

So, Devo is probably panicking.

Matts answers the phone. "She's here."

Devo exhales rough static in his ear. "Is she okay?"

"Yeah. We just finished cleaning her up. No concussion or broken bones."

"Good. Tell her I'm going to fucking kill her."

Matts laughs. "Is everyone else okay?"

"Yeah. We split up after the set because she took her bike, and we were supposed to meet at Dirt, but when we got there the cops said—" He cuts himself off. "Sorry. No. Everyone is good. Are you sure she's okay?"

Sydney takes the phone. "I'm fine. I'm sorry I freaked you out; I wasn't thinking when I left. I just needed to get out of there." She clears her throat, summons a smile, and gains back something of her standard lilt. "I figured I should get myself checked out by an expert brawler, so."

"Right," Devo says, his voice muffled, but Matts can still hear him. "I'm sure medical advice is the only reason you went to Matts's place—"

"Oh, no," Sydney interrupts, with zero inflection in her voice. "I'm going through a tunnel. I might lose you."

"Oh, fuck you," Devo sighs. "Give Matts his phone back."

She hands it over willingly.

"Hey, Matts?"

"Yeah."

"Don't let her back on that motorcycle tonight. If she doesn't want to stay, I'll come get her."

"I want to stay," she says into Matts's chest. "If that's okay."

What a joke. He'd keep her here forever if that was an option. He knows better than to say it though.

Instead, he says to Sydney, "Yeah, of course," and then to Devo, "She'll stay."

"Okay. Take care of her, please. I know she can take care of herself, but—"

"She shouldn't have to. Not all the time."

Devo is silent for several seconds. "Yeah. That. Thanks."

He hangs up.

"Well," Sydney mutters. "That wasn't mortifying or anything."

Matts scoops her off the counter before she can say anything else because he knows it will make her laugh. She protests as he carries her through his bedroom and into the attached bath.

He shows her how the shower works and leaves her with a shirt and a pair of boxers. When she emerges a few minutes later, swallowed in his clothes, hair wet, face flushed with warmth, he briefly considers kissing her. Because how could he not? How could he look at her like this and not want to—

But her lip is split, and her eyes are rimmed in red, and he's not going to let selfishness make a long day any longer for her. Even if she *wants* him to kiss her, tonight is not the night to try to start something.

Instead, Matts shows her the GAN ROBOT and lets her play with the shuffle function on the app while he takes his own shower.

When he comes out again, turning off the lights behind him, his electric guitar is no longer on its stand on the floor of his closet. It's in her hands.

He freezes.

"How long have you had this?" Sydney asks, absently plucking at the strings.

"A couple months."

"Will you play something for me?"

He wants to. Desperately. Matts wants to show her everything he's learned, wants to see her face when he plays the songs they've been deconstructing each week. He wants to play one of *her* songs—to impress her, to show her exactly how much he fucking cares.

But tonight is not the night.

"It's late." He moves to pull back the duvet on the bed. "We should go to sleep. But I do want to. Next time?"

She watches him for a moment, head tipped, with wet hair and heat-pink cheeks, before she returns the guitar to its stand. "Next time."

Sydney climbs into the bed next to him like it's normal, as if she tucks herself into his space every night, head on his shoulder, knees butting into his stomach, fingers curled like an anchor in the fabric of his shirt.

"Did you get it just so you could play with me?" she asks quietly.

"I did." It's damning, but it's true.

"And you've been practicing?"

"I have."

She doesn't say anything for several seconds, and then, "You don't do anything by halves, do you?"

"No." Matts slides his hand, more possessive than it should be, around her shoulder and down to the curve of her flank. He presses his fingers to the divots between her ribs.

"No," he says again. "I do not."

*

MATTS HAS A very particular way he tapes his stick.

Not a euphemism.

When the PR intern stops him after practice the next morning to shove a couple rolls of tape at him, it takes him a minute to understand what he's looking at.

And then the intern tosses a few rolls to Rushy in a different color scheme, and Matts recognizes the pink-white-blue pattern in his hands. It's the trans flag tape he requested because the Pride game is that night.

And he'd completely forgotten.

> He texts Syd: *If you're not tired of me yet, come to the game tonight?*

> She answers almost immediately: *As if I'd miss Pride night? It's a shame I don't have a jersey to wear though.*

Matts once again finds himself standing, half-dressed in the locker room, staring at his phone, uncertain how to respond to a text from Sydney.

He reaches up to tug on his necklace, the tiny ring now hung there beside his customary St. Jude pendant.

Rome and Alex, in their stalls on either side of him,

are looking at each other in a way that is probably significant but Matts has no hope of discerning.

"Matts," Rome says.

"Rome," Matts says.

"What's the face for?"

Matts doesn't ask what his face is doing. He tosses the tape and his phone into the top of his unzipped bag without responding. He thinks about the way Sydney clung to him last night. About the way she said goodbye to him that morning after making breakfast together in his kitchen. The way she breathed him in like it meant something.

"How do you know if a hug is platonic or romantic?" he asks.

"Uh," Alex says.

Rome ducks into his hoodie, scrubs a hand over his buzzed hair, and then holds out his arms. "Reenact it with me."

"What? No."

"Why not?"

That's a good question. "It'd be weird with you."

"Why? Because you don't want to make sweet, sweet love to me?"

"No, because I already know that I want to— No. The question is if *she's* interested in *me*."

"Okay," Rome says. "So, pretend you're Sydney, and I'm you. And hug me the way she hugged you."

"That won't work. I'm taller than you."

"Hi," Kuzy says, sidling up to him. "I'm Matts. Very good looks. Very good hockey. Very bad talk to women."

Kuzy, admittedly the tallest person on the team, has a couple inches on Matts. It's not quite the difference between him and Sydney, but it's the closest they'll get.

Matts steps into Kuzy, slides his arms around his waist, and wraps a hand around his own wrist so he can squeeze tighter, so he can rest his left ear on Kuzy's collarbone and turn his face into Kuzy's neck and —

"Nope," Matts says, stepping back. "No. Absolutely not."

"Okay," Alex says while Rome and Kuzy laugh at him. "I think you have your answer then."

Matts thinks he might.

On his way out of the igloo, he stops at the front office. More specifically, he stops at the cubicle where he knows the social media interns lurk.

"Would it be completely inappropriate if I asked one of you to run an errand for me?" Matts asks. "It'll take around an hour and a half. I'll pay you, and I'll let you do one of your tiny microphone interviews with me tomorrow."

One of the interns, mid-spin on a rolly office chair, stands up so quickly she falls over into the wall. "I volunteer as tribute!" she says.

Matts reaches past her to grab a sticky note and pen from the desk and writes down Sydney's address. "Can you get one of my jerseys in a size small and take it to this address?" He fishes out a couple hundred-dollar bills from his wallet and hands them over.

"This is way too much," she says, looking suspiciously at the cash in her hand as if it might suddenly gain sentience.

"I'll take it if you don't want to," the other intern says.

She shoves the bills in her pocket. "Any message you want me to deliver with it?"

"Oh." Matts is stymied. "No? Only that it's for Sydney." Whoever answers the door at the house will know, but he figures it's good to clarify.

The intern salutes.

Matts goes home.

He sets the trans flag tape on the island and gets a couple of his sticks out of the closet. Matts spends the half hour before his nap practicing, getting used to the color, the slightly different heft and texture of the tape as he goes through the habitual motions: the turn of the tape roll on his pointer finger, the pull from his wrist, the press of his thumb. Usually, Matts doesn't use much tape, just enough on the toe of the blade for catch and spin and plenty of slick space behind to feed the puck. But he figures, in this case, the visuals are more important than utility, and it'll only be for warmups anyway.

So, he uses twice the amount of tape he usually would and gets a little overly critical about the spacing, trying to line the colors up. Finally, Matts decides he's happy with his approach a few minutes before the nap alarm goes off. He's probably spent too much time worrying about it, but that's fine. No one needs to know.

Matts doesn't hear from Sydney again until he's in the locker room before the game, headphones and hype playlist on, taping his stick with the colors all lined up, just like he practiced.

His phone pings.

The alert is from Eli, and there's no text—just a picture. It's a slightly blurry candid of Sydney, walking up the strip in front of the stadium. Her back is to the photographer, and she's looking over her shoulder, curls swinging to one side, clearly midconversation.

The jersey fits her like a dress, with only the telltale

sign of ripped black shorts where the hem hits her thighs. His name is right there in the center: a bright white *Matthews* stretched from shoulder to shoulder with a background of Hell Hounds black and red.

Matthews.

72.

On Sydney's back.

His stick is perfect, but Matts retapes it again just to have something to do with his hands while he processes that.

He never really got it before, when the other guys talked about seeing their partners in their gear—why Alex's phone background is Eli in Alex's jersey and Jeff can't seem to keep his hands off his wife when she's wearing his hoodies. Objectively, Matts understood there was some sort of possessive thrill they got out of it, sure, but he didn't *get* it.

He gets it now.

When they skate out for warmups, it takes a while for him to find Sydney in the riot of signs and flags. The stadium is packed, and a larger-than-usual crowd presses forward for pictures and pucks.

When he finds her, she's grinning widely, fisted hands on the glass. For a second, they just stand there, smiling stupidly at each other while the world spins on around them.

Until Sydney notices his stick.

And then her fingers uncurl, slack with surprise, palms smearing on the glass, smile fading into…something else. It's not a *bad* expression, but he has no idea what it means.

Matts flips his stick to allow her a better look at the blade. He wiggles it a little. He gives her a thumbs-up. But Sydney's not looking at him anymore; her eyes slide from player to player on the ice like she's searching for something, and he lets his attention be similarly pulled away by a group of kids with a sign beside her. He tosses them some pucks and skates in close to take a selfie with someone, then tosses a few more pucks farther down the glass. And then Rome skates over to complete their pregame handshake. He's lost sight of Sydney by then and doesn't have time to find her again because he does actually need to warm up and do his job.

At the end of warmups, before he leaves the ice, Matts finds her again up against the glass with flat palms, dark eyes, and a flush riding high on her cheekbones. He taps his gloved knuckles at her.

"Catch," he says.

"What?" she yells back.

He balances the butt of his stick in his palm and

mimes throwing it.

Her hands go up immediately, the too-big sleeves of her jersey sliding down her forearms, and something catches his attention. His bracelet, also too big, slips down her forearm before it's out of sight again in the pooled fabric bunched at her elbows.

He hefts his stick up and over the glass.

The guy standing next to her, taller and with a longer reach, snags the blade before Sydney can. Matts bangs both hands to the glass, probably harder than is necessary, pointing at Syd.

"Hey! No," he shouts. "Let go. It's for her."

The guy lets go.

Matts meets her eyes again as he skates backward toward the tunnel. She's holding the stick with both hands against her chest, her bottom lip tucked between her teeth, dimples showing as she watches him. He waits until the last possible minute to turn around.

"Giving a girl your stick is definitely not platonic," Rome says, shoving Matts's shoulder as they leave the ice. "If you were still wondering about platonic versus romantic behavior, I mean."

"I was not," Matts says.

*

MATTS LIKES PREDICTABILITY. Numbers, equations, Rubik's Cubes—he likes the knowledge that some things are structured and immutable. Axioms may change, but math does not. There's comfort in that.

In many ways, hockey is predictable, like plane geometry. The neutral zone is both a quadrilateral and a parallelogram. The angle between the blade and the shaft of his stick is 135 degrees. Better edge control depends on the angle of his ankles, better ice coverage depends on the angle of his knees, and better speed depends on the angle of his hips. Crossunders are more effective because he can skate faster if he uses his interior skate less than his exterior skate, if he only takes full strides with alternating outside skates. And passing, shooting—well, that's all angles too—angles of incidence and angles of reflection: knowing how to bank a shot off the boards to sit on a teammates' tape, to ricochet off the pipe and into the acute space between the goalie's pad and the net. It's all numbers. Angles and lines, circles and triangles.

When the puck drops in a face-off, there's a circle at the center: an equal probability each player on its radius will get the puck. But geometry can't account for the human component of hockey: the player in the face-off with split-second faster reflexes; the player with the longer reach; or the player who doesn't play the angle game at all.

In many ways, hockey is predictable. But in many ways, it's not.

Like when an opposing defenseman targets Alex from the moment he steps on the ice in the first. Petty shit that escalates. Like when he checks Alex from behind two minutes into the second. Like when Alex goes down and doesn't get back up.

Matts isn't on the ice when it happens, but his line change is coming up, and he's got one leg over the boards, tapping his heel, ready.

And then Alex is down, and Kuzy is trying to kill the player who hit him, and Matts is throwing himself onto the ice with the rest of the emptying bench to pair up and swing.

Alex limps down the tunnel with an arm over the trainer's shoulders, and both penalty boxes end up crammed with players. Their lines are totally fucked when Matts skates out to take the next puck drop, but despite the chaos, a fight also has a way of changing the way the air feels. It reminds him that hockey is more than just a game of angles and shapes. It reminds him that, for hundreds of years, humans have thrown their bodies into competitions for the sake of the unpredictable nature of sport. Rome says fights "summon up the blood," which Matts is pretty sure he stole from Damien, which means it's probably Milton or Shakespeare or something. Syd would know. He should ask her.

The point is that Matts isn't thinking about geometry when he takes the next puck drop. He's not thinking about the law of cosines. In that moment, he doesn't want predictability or comfort. And maybe it's a residual effect from the night before. Maybe he's projecting. But he wants anger and violence and the thrill of uncertainty. He wants someone to try to hit him the way they hit Alex. He wants someone to *test* him.

Matts wins the face-off and sprints, manages a fucking beauty of a spin-o-rama to split the defense, and then he's on the breakaway. The goalie is good, Matts will give him that. He manages to get his stick down just in time to block the shot, but Jeff battles for the rebound, wins it, and they reset. Again, down the center line, a toe drag fake out, a give and go.

There's nothing calculated about the shot Matts takes; it's just anger and muscle memory, and that's all he needs. He doesn't even feel like celebrating when the goal horn goes off.

He just wants to do it again.

So, he does.

*

DESPITE THEIR WIN, the locker room is subdued after the game.

Alex has a concussion and will be out for the rest of the regular season. No one has brought up playoffs, but they're all thinking it.

Matts follows Eli and Alex home after the game.

He says it's so he can help Eli keep an eye on Alex, and it is. But Asher has started spending more and more nights at his girlfriend's house, and Sydney had to go home right after the game to sleep since the band has an early morning departure the next day, and he just... doesn't want to be alone.

Matts helps get Alex settled on the couch with ice, Gatorade, and meds. He then retreats to the guest room so Eli can curl up under Alex's arm to distract him, and so Alex can be vulnerable in a way only possible when you're alone with someone you trust. Someone you love.

Matts likes listening to them through the cracked guest room door, the soft murmur of Eli's muffled voice as he recounts some story from his childhood involving goats and the quiet appreciation of Alex's laughter.

Eventually, Matts calls Aaron, stretched out on the guest bed with Hawk mostly on top of him.

"Hey, Matty," Aaron says after the third ring. "Are you petting a dog in some back room at a party again?"

Matts sighs into the phone. "No. Well." He looks at Hawk. "I am petting a dog, but it's not at a party. And I'm not drunk. I need to talk to you about something."

"Okay," Aaron says, immediately guarded. "What's up?"

"I want to bring Sydney with me to the spring drive."

"Oh."

Matts waits.

"Are you two together now?"

"No."

"Matty."

"I think there's a chance though. I mean, I think she might— She's always wanted to go on a cattle drive, and we could use the help."

"You can't use a drive to *romance* someone."

"I think there's more than one western movie that would disagree with you."

"Look, I know you said she's familiar with horses and cattle, but if you bring her here, all folks will see is some city girl you're trying to impress, which will cause plenty of problems even if no one knows she's...you know."

"Transgender," Matts says for him. "It's not a bad word."

"I'm just saying."

"I live in a high-rise and get my groceries delivered," Matts says. "When she's not on tour, Sydney lives with her folks and pulls her weight. She does more barn chores annually than I do. So, at this point, I'd say she's more suited to a drive than I am."

Aaron makes a noise somewhere between a groan and a whine, and Matts can practically see him pacing, digging the heel of his free hand into one of his eyes.

"Can you imagine," Aaron says finally, "how your dad would react if he found out about her? You realize that would be a shit show, right?"

"I need you to understand that I do not fucking care about my dad's opinion of Sydney." Matts is a little bit shocked to find that the statement isn't all bravado. Does he want his father to like Sydney? Yes. Does he *need* him to like Sydney? No.

Aaron is silent. He lets out a low whistle. "Man, who *is* this girl?"

"She's important, okay? And I'm bringing her; I've decided. And I need to keep her safe while she's there.

Will you help me with that or not?"

"Obviously."

"You think any of the guys will be a problem?"

Aaron makes an ambivalent noise. "If they are, we can take them."

That's probably accurate. Aaron is nearly as tall as Matts and easily outweighs him in the offseason, much less when Matts is playoff lean.

"Okay," Matts says, "but should I be expecting trouble?"

"Nah. Don't think anyone here will have heard of her, and even if they've heard of the band, they wouldn't know her face. Except for maybe Ellie. She'd want Sydney's autograph before wanting to take a swing at her though."

"Ellie?" Matts doesn't know an Ellie.

"Eloise. New part-timer. Girl who lives down the road. She's into that punk music shit."

"Red Right Hand isn't punk," Matts says absently, and then, "My dad hired a girl?"

"*I* hired a girl."

Huh. "Good for you."

"Isn't like I'm trying to be progressive or anything," Aaron mutters. "She's a good fit for the job. Local. Strong. Hard worker. Doesn't take any shit. And Trigger likes her."

If anything is a ringing endorsement, it's the latter.

"Still. That's cool," Matts says.

"It's whatever. Listen. Speaking of the drive. The weather has been warming up earlier than expected. We're probably going to need to move the herd sooner rather than later."

"Like, before playoffs?"

"You've got a week between the regular season and the beginning of playoffs, right? Could you come then for a few days?"

"Yeah, that could work. You know my game schedule?"

"You're an idiot. Also, you need to stop punching people. You're not an enforcer."

"You were watching the game tonight?"

"I'm hanging up now," Aaron says.

Chapter Twelve

SYDNEY SPENDS THE first week of the headlining tour writing some of the best lyrics of her life and having a small crisis. She keeps replaying in her head the last few times she saw Matts. The way he looked at her. The way he touched her.

She calls Eli from her bunk in the tour bus one night.

"Is there a straight version of gay chicken?" Sydney asks in lieu of saying something normal like "hello."

"I think that's just called denial," Eli says.

Sydney makes a distressed noise.

"Might you be having feelings?" Eli suggests. "Perchance giving a fuck?"

"Perchance," she admits.

"How embarrassing."

"Tell me about it."

"Does it make things better or worse if I tell you Matts has been moping ever since you left?"

"Better. Does that make me a bad person?"

"Nah. Are you admitting you want to kiss him now?"

"I want to do considerably more than that," Sydney says, shoving her free palm into one eye.

"I'm not seeing the problem."

"You mean besides the fact that I have minimal sexual experience, *no* dating experience, and he's a *professional hockey player*? Normal people have awkward teenage fumblings and even more awkward college hookups by the time they're my age. I have a half-dozen kisses and two sort-of hookups. And when Matts and I first met, I may have implied that I was a much more sexual being than I am. He thinks I have experiences, Eli. *I do not have experiences.*"

"You realize who you're talking to, right? Alex was nearly all of my firsts. Also, from what Alex has told me, Matts doesn't have any dating experience either. Just hookups."

Sydney exhales, eyes closed, gently thumping her fist against her forehead. "That's not a consolation."

"Syd."

"I don't think I'd survive something casual with him."

"So don't do something casual with him."

"Our very first conversation included Matts telling me he wasn't interested in anything other than one-night stands."

"Your very first conversation included you telling Matts you weren't interested in *him*. Clearly things change."

"Eli."

"*Sydney*."

"Fine," Sydney says. "The next time I see him in person, I'll…do something."

"Something romantic?"

"Something embarrassing, probably, but it'll get the point across."

She exhales, swallowing around the scratch in her throat that says she needs to be more careful with her voice. "Tell me about your kids, please?"

"Ah," Eli says knowingly. "One of those nights?"

"Yeah. You mind?"

"Obviously not. I am happy to charm you with tales of my tiny humans until the melodious sound of my voice puts you to sleep. Who do you want to hear about? The gremlins or the angels?"

"Diversity is the spice of life. But first, I want an update on the kid who thinks he can throw any trick he sees on TV. What's his name—Julius?"

"Julian, oh my God. Natural selection should have taken that child out years ago." The overwhelming fondness in Eli's voice softens the words. "If he survives to adulthood, he will do great things. Okay, so last week he comes in for his lesson wearing a Spider-Man costume, mask included, which should have clued me in we were going to have an *extra* special day, and before we've even finished warmups—"

Sydney closes her eyes and imagines she's lying on a beach at the waterline with sand and sky and the hush of twilight. She lets Eli's voice wash over her, the ebb and flow of his inflection like waves.

He's a good storyteller, and his job as a children's ice-skating instructor provides plenty of content. Half an hour later, when Sydney hangs up, she's feeling a little more settled but almost too tired to sleep.

Being on tour is exhausting in itself, but being on tour also means more press, particularly now that they have *two* songs playing regularly on Top 40 stations. More media attention has come with its own challenges. Sydney's turned off comments on her personal Instagram posts, and the band's socials are getting more death threats than usual. They don't go out to bars or clubs after concerts anymore unless they have security. They're quickly becoming recognizable, not just by niche underground kids and the sort of people who frequent rock venues, but by people on sidewalks and in grocery stores. When the band is together, they're most noteworthy. When they're apart, Sky and Rex can fly under the radar as long as Rex has his tattoos covered. But Sydney—Sydney has been putting her face on the internet for close to a decade, and between her hair and her jaw and the sharp cut of her cheekbones, she has a memorable face. Not to mention her aesthetic choices.

She knows she stands out.

Initially, when she was twelve and terrified, it was by design. She's never been good at being subtle. She's always been loud and opinionated and too full of movement to contain. When Sydney went shopping for new clothes, preparing for her first year as a girl—a *girl*—at public school, she figured people would stare anyway. So, she decided she'd give them something to look at.

It was a little like designing a character, except the

character was herself. She picked out thick-soled lace-up boots, ripped jeans, and black band shirts; she thought it would be easier to BS her way through acting brave if she looked the part, and it worked.

Maybe a little too well.

Because now she's not entirely sure she wants to be that character anymore. Not all the time, anyway. The character she created is brash and cool and sexy and isn't afraid of anything. She prowls across the stage and kisses fans and answers interview questions with wit and sarcasm and aplomb; she responds to criticism and cruelty with unflappable, dismissive confidence.

The problem is that the persona Sydney built for herself leaves no room for public vulnerability. And as her life becomes more and more public, it's becoming harder and harder to find spaces where she's allowed to be soft and scared and capable of being wounded.

She knows it's a good problem to have and one not to complain about. Oh, poor thing. So famous from her songs and her sold-out concert tour that she has to deal with the inevitable negative attention that goes hand in hand with visibility. So sad. So hard. Poor little rock star.

But maybe worse than the negative attention are the people lauding her as a queer martyr, paving the way for future generations or what the hell ever.

You're so strong. They say.

You're so brave. They say.

Some days, Sydney is so tired of being brave.

She wants to just be. Without witnesses or expectations or the burden of representing an entire fucking group of people in the public eye.

She wants to write her songs and play her music, and when someone comments that her parents should have killed her, that she should do the job herself, she wants to rage back at them, to destroy something, to cry.

Sydney remembers two years before, watching Alex's press conference shortly after he came out. He said, over and over again, with a painful husk to his voice, that he just wanted to focus on hockey. He didn't want to be some public queer figure. He *just wanted to play hockey.* Except the press won't let him forget what he is and who they've built him to be. If he wants hockey, he must put up with the rest. He's handled it well, or at least, he seems to. And at least now, there are other out players. Now, Alex is one of a small subset, some with behavior far more tabloid-worthy than his.

But Sydney doesn't have that luxury.

There aren't many queer rock bands fronted by trans women with songs on syndicated radio. Certainly, none whose trans frontwoman has a decade of YouTube videos chronicling their transition available for easy public access. Often for easy public ridicule.

Sometimes, Sydney wonders what it would be like if she never posted that first video. If they formed the band and played behind closed doors for a few years as she transitioned or took a more traditional path toward finding venues and securing a record deal. Something that didn't depend on her forfeiting the right to ever be stealth.

She could just...be a girl in a band.

Wouldn't that be something?

Sydney tries not to think about it too often, mostly because she doesn't know if she'd do it again if she had the choice to go back and never post a single video but still achieve the success they have today.

She's a little ashamed to say she probably wouldn't because it'd be so much easier if she wasn't out. And that recognition comes with its own guilt. It feels like a betrayal to her community and to herself.

She's just so *tired*.

Her phone lights up, illuminating the ceiling in her bunk. She's stuck a couple glow-in-the-dark stars up there, but they never get enough light during the day to glow for more than a few minutes.

Sydney rolls to her side and squints at the screen.

It's Matts.

They've gotten into the habit, most nights, of talking on the phone before going to sleep or texting if Sydney's voice needs a rest.

But with the time difference, with her on the East Coast and him at an away game in Seattle, she assumed he wouldn't want to talk tonight.

Apparently, she was wrong.

Syd calls him instead of responding to the text message.

"Hey." Matts sounds just as exhausted as she feels.

"Rough game," she says.

She's been keeping track on the NHL app. It's on the home screen of her phone now, the Hell Hounds logo black and red and damning.

"Not the best, no," he agrees. "Hopefully, your night was better?"

"Mm…" She tries for levity. "Just another day in paradise."

"You sound tired."

"I am."

"You up for questions, or no?"

They've started doing this thing where they take turns asking each other questions until one or both are too tired to continue.

Most of Sydney's questions are like: "If a vampire was a detective and she had a warrant to search someone's house, would she still need to be invited in?" or "Do you think pop tarts technically qualify as ravioli?"

Most of Matts's questions are harder. Like: "If you had the ability to know the exact date of your death, would you want to know?" and "If you could spend ten minutes with your ten-year-old self, what would you say to her?"

"Jesus," she said one night after he laid *How could your parents have loved you better?* on her. "Where are you getting these from? A therapist?"

He muttered something incomprehensible.

"Come again?"

"I got a deck of cards."

"Okay."

"They have questions on them."

"Questions."

"I want to know things about you," he said with the honest vulnerability she adores. "I just don't know what to ask. The cards help."

So, Sydney has started keeping a list of questions in her notes app, collected from the band and their bus driver and the techs at their venues. She answers the questions he asks her from his deck of cards in the dark, warm, quiet of her bunk where she can speak softly into the still pocket of space that feels safe.

Sydney doesn't know if she can handle much of that now though.

"Maybe one or two," she says. "And then you could give me some cursed knowledge?"

"It would be my pleasure," Matts says seriously. "What's something mundane that makes you happy?"

She doesn't even have to think about that one. "Oh, easy. The lighting aisle at hardware stores."

"What?"

"Yeah, like…when you go to Home Depot or wherever. There's always a section that's all lamps and chandeliers and string lights. And when you walk down the aisle it's like stepping into a different world. All bright and magic and—" She cuts herself off with a yawn. "—happy."

"Huh. Fair enough."

"What's yours?"

"Uh. Hm." Matts considers for several comfortable seconds of silence. "You know how some things have those looped silk or satin care instruction tags?"

"Like blankets and pajamas?"

"Yeah, exactly. I love those stupid things. My pillowcase has one, and I'll drag it between my fingers over and over again. It's nice. Calming."

"Are you doing it now?"

"Maybe."

"All right, keep your secrets." Sydney finds the tag on her own pillowcase. She runs it through her fingers. He's right; it is nice.

"Okay, flip side of that," she says. "What's something mundane that makes you angry?"

"Referees."

"Maybe think of a more...universally relatable experience."

"Touching wet food."

"I'm going to need more than that."

"You know. Like when you're washing dishes and you accidentally touch some wet food in the bottom of the sink. It's a texture thing."

"You realize that every piece of food you eat is wet by the time you swallow it. So your tongue touches wet food all the time."

There is a brief, horrified silence.

"Why would you say that to me? That was unnecessary."

Sydney laughs softly. "Sorry."

"Are you okay?" Matts asks. "You sound off. Did something else happen?"

"No, I'm fine. Just tired."

"Maybe instead of cursed knowledge, I could play for you until you fall asleep? I don't have a roommate this trip, so we won't disturb anyone."

"Please," she says.

After a minute of muffled fumbling, Matts plays a quick scale, and Sydney can almost see him propped in bed, phone on the nightstand, lamp casting long shadows. She knows what he looks like in bed now. Knows what he looks like rumpled and bleary and soft. The visual makes something in her chest go tight.

"Anyway," Matts says, "here's 'Wonderwall.'"

It surprises a laugh out of her. "Don't start that shit again."

He doesn't play "Wonderwall."

He plays "The Sea" by Haeven. He sings along, soft and slow and aching.

And despite having no resolution to all of the everything that prevented her from falling asleep previously, this time, when Sydney closes her eyes, she sleeps.

*

THEY'D WORKED WITH a choreographer before they left for the tour—well, not a choreographer exactly.

A…performance coach? Sydney can't remember what the man's official title was, but the point is that there was a routine they had to follow. They didn't have *dance* routines or anything. But there was a basic script, certain beats, movements, and marks they were supposed to hit during each song as they worked their way through the set list.

Sydney can't decide if she misses the freedom of being an unknown band on a tiny stage at the back of a bar. When she could do whatever the hell she wanted, depending on the music or the night or the well of energy under her skin demanding an escape. Probably not, since it means she gets this in exchange: thousands of fans and venue-shaking sound systems and lighting techs who paint an ever-shifting fantasy world of color across the stage and the audience and Sydney's skin.

So, she hits her marks and accepts that they've reached an echelon where the music is only part of the performance and pageantry is the other. It's not a trial. Sydney gets to throw herself around the stage, prance, pose, and let straining hands touch the blocky platform heels of her boots as she stands at the edge of the stage and opens her chest and gives all of herself for as long as they'll take her.

She'd like to do more—climb light scaffolding and

show off the backflip she spent a month perfecting the year before. But playing guitar in addition to singing limits her, which is part of the reason they've started actively looking for another guitarist.

It'd also be nice to get the occasional break, which is why they've been pulling a fan onto the stage to play "Victor's Loss" each night.

It's not their best song, by any means. Mostly because Sydney wrote it when she was sixteen, and it's just as dramatic and overwrought as a song written by a sixteen-year-old should be; it only barely made it onto their album. But she's still proud of the play on words in the title. Sydney wrote "Victor's Loss" after reading *Frankenstein* for school when she was full of outrage on behalf of a creature created without consent, cast as a monster, and given no opportunity to escape the inevitability of fulfilling the role. She got detention when she tried to argue with her teacher about how unfair the ending was—that the other students thought the creature's plans for suicide were earned and somehow commendable. Sydney probably empathized more with the creature than anyone else in the room, considering she regularly attended detention for retaliation against the bullies who found her mere existence a problem.

It's funny, she thinks, to play the song now,

grinning on a stage under bright lights, surrounded by thrumming speakers and bolstered by the fervor of a screaming audience when she tearfully wrote it alone on the floor of her bedroom, back against the closet door, guitar tucked between chest and skinned knees. Sydney survived high school though. *She* lived. And she didn't let them turn her into the monster they wanted her to be. So now, she sings the lyrics composed between breathless, angry sobs to shouted accompaniment by adoring masses. It feels like restitution, maybe.

Besides having a special place in her squishy emotional parts, "Victor's Loss" is also the easiest song on their album to play on guitar. They've advertised it all over their social media, and at every venue, hopeful attendees hold dozens of signs telling the band to pick them.

The song is halfway through their set. Provided the person they pull knows how to play it, which they more or less have so far, it gives Sydney's fingers a break. And the audience eats that shit up.

When they take the stage in Denver, she looks longingly at the scaffolding and gives it a brief salute. One day.

The energy in the stadium is perfect from the moment Sky counts them in for the first song. They start with a bang, the first three songs in the set winding up to the frantic crescendo of "A Prayer for Arson" before segueing into the slower "Godless Martyr" and even slower "Black Star Night." She gets to sink to the stage and play on her knees, head bowed, guitar plaintive and wailing.

And then it's time for "Victor's Loss."

When the lights turn to illuminate the crowd, Sydney and Rex move to the front, searching for volunteers.

She spots a kid—man?—almost immediately, right in the center. He's on his buddy's shoulders and holding a sign with an artistically rendered guitar pick and the words *"PICK" ME FOR VICTOR'S LOSS* underneath it in all caps. In smaller words, it says: *I promise I don't suck.*

She does love a good pun.

Sydney points him out to Rex, who gives her a thumbs-up. Security helps the guy get to the front of the crowd while the lights pan back to them, hot and blinding.

They sling their guitars to their backs; each takes one of his hands and pulls him onto the stage.

"Hey, man," Sydney says. "What's your name?" She extends the microphone to him.

"Paul," he says, blinking. She gives him a minute to orient himself.

"Okay, Paul. You know 'Victor's Loss'?"

He grins, looking more confident. "Sure do."

"You ever played it for this many people before?"

He shades his eyes with one hand and pretends to count with the other for a moment to rolling laughter from the audience.

"Hard to say," he responds, leaning back into the microphone, "but probably not."

Sydney walks him back a few paces to collect the second guitar from its stand and proffers it to him. "Will this do?"

He accepts it, adjusts the strap, and fishes a pick out of his pocket to play a quick complicated riff from the song they just finished.

"All right, all right, show off," Sydney says as the cheers build.

She ducks to leave her own guitar on its stand, taking a moment to pull her sweaty hair off her neck. She snags her water bottle and takes several long pulls from it as Rex starts the bassline. Sydney licks her lips, maybe a little more dramatic than is actually necessary, as she sashays back to her spot on the stage, foregoing the mic stand that usually tethers her in place.

"Are we ready, kids?" she asks. The cheers becoming deafening. Sydney shoves hair out of her face and checks in with Rex and Paul. Yeah, they're good.

"Sky," she says, glancing over her shoulder, "if you would?"

Sky counts them in, and they're off.

It's clear by the end of the first verse that Paul is talented. He moves seamlessly between them, making eye contact with Rex as he fits the notes he's playing, a higher mimic to Rex's deeper chords, between the bassline and Sydney's voice. He headbangs along to Sky's little drum solo just after the first verse, and by the chorus, Sydney's eyeing the scaffolding to her left with actual consideration.

For once, she's not worried that she'll need to grab her guitar and assist.

Paul clearly has it covered.

As Sydney finishes the second verse, knowing she has about fifteen seconds worth of drum solo before she has to sing again, she moves.

She *climbs*.

The third verse isn't her best vocal performance because she's out of breath by the time she gets to the cross bar and can hook her knee into the truss ladder, anchoring herself into place. But judging by the tumult of riotous energy from the audience, they don't care that much.

She gets her wind back for the final chorus and pushes it hard, probably harder than she should considering they've still got five songs to go in the set. But there's something about being able to look down on the stage—at Sky, half standing over her drum kit, her corded arms slick with sweat, teeth bared and white under the red lights, hair a mess of tangled blue; at Rex and Paul, standing hip to hip, legs braced, forearms, heads, and mouths moving in sync as they lean forward to share Rex's mic. There's something about looking out at the arena spread before her, at the sea of moving bodies and lit-up phones, at the mass of fans shouting her lyrics back at her.

It feels like maybe, somehow, the people the lyrics were meant for might hear the words if she sings them loud enough now. So, she does.

> *Because, see, I've got in me*
> *love unimaginable, rage unbelievable*
> *And if I can't have one, I will indulge the*
> *other*
> *It's your choice, villain or lover*
> *But when I become the monster*
> *Don't forget who made me*
> *Don't forget you made me.*

Sydney pulls out one of her ear pieces before the final lines repeat again, points to the audience around her mic, and they shout like a wall back to her:

Don't forget who made me

Paul plays his riff with perfect timing, and she points out again to the sea of moving, jumping people, their phones and voices raised.

Don't forget you made me
Don't forget you made me.
Don't forget you made me.

And Sydney can hear it. Every word. Clear as a fucking bell.

She feels dizzy with it. It's amazing. It's exhilarating. It's—time for a guitar solo.

The solo isn't particularly complicated, or at least, it's not supposed to be, except Paul changes it.

Not a lot. Not so it's unrecognizable. But it's a hell of a lot more intricate than the original. And Sydney has to admit, it's better. The way he pauses just when the bassline hits, goes thin and high and whiny at the clash of Sky's cymbals. It's good. *He's* good.

Sydney finishes out the rest of the song with a birds-eye view of the stage, the fans, the expanse of it all stretched out before her like something out of a dream.

And then she climbs down.

"Holy shit, you guys," Sydney shouts once her boots are back on the stage. "Paul can shred! Give it up for Paul!"

He meets her halfway, grinning with euphoria that only comes from moments like this, a musical battle won and a clamoring mass of fans who bore witness to it. Who *participated* in it.

Paul leans into her. "I took a little creative license there," he says as if they wouldn't have noticed. "Hope that was okay."

"More than."

Sydney slings an arm around his shoulders so they can share the mic more easily. "Paulie, my man, what do you do for work?"

"I'm about to graduate college, and I currently have no prospects."

"Are you a burden to your parents? Are you frightened?"

"Alas, I am."

"How would you feel about auditioning for a more permanent position?" Rex asks, which is exactly what

Sydney was thinking.

"I mean, I'd feel pretty okay about that, yeah." Paul pauses, looking between the two of them. "Hold on, are you serious?"

"We'd probably need to do a background check," Sky says.

"And there are some important office culture questions we'd need you to answer," Sydney adds.

"Like are you gay?" Sky asks. "Because being queer isn't an *official* prerequisite, but—"

"Oh my God, Sky," Sydney interrupts. "You can't just ask people if they're gay."

Paul leans into the mic as the audience laughs. "Unfortunately, I'm straight. However—"

He reaches for the hem of his shirt, and at first, Sydney doesn't understand what he's doing. Does he think having nice abs is somehow a substitution for queerness? They're nice, but not *that* nice. Until she realizes—surgical scars are tucked in the bottom curve of his pecs.

Top surgery scars.

It takes a minute for the camera feeding the massive screen behind them to zoom in enough that the audience understands what's happening, but when they do, they lose their goddamn minds.

Which is fair because Sydney is losing her mind a

little bit too. What are the chances?

"Well shit, dude," Sky says. "Now we practically have to keep you."

"Gender-affirming chest bump on three?" Sydney asks.

"Oh, definitely," Paul agrees.

They miss the first time because he has significantly more ups than she does, but he moderates his enthusiasm, and they get it the second try.

"Okay, okay, wait," Sydney says. "Dude. I don't want to make assumptions here, but you picked your name, yeah?"

"Yeah."

"And you picked *Paul*?"

"Middle name Atreides."

"Acceptable."

"I appreciate your approval."

She bows accommodatingly. "All right, we should probably go ahead and, like, finish the show. We'll let you go back now, but we'll talk later. Everyone, give it up for Paul again!"

They do.

*

SYDNEY IS STILL buzzing with energy in her bunk when Matts calls her that night. She talks for probably ten minutes straight about how they may have found a second guitarist, and he was originally trained in traditional flamenco guitar-playing as well as piano and is super fucking talented, and he's trans, and also, did she mention she got to climb the scaffolding?

He listens with encouraging noises and leading questions. When she finally starts to run out of words, throat raw and chest full of warmth, Sydney remembers he had a game that day. For once, she hasn't had a chance to check the highlights.

"So anyway," she says. "I'm killing it. Band is killing it. Tour is fab. How was your night?"

Matts clears his throat. "Fine."

She squints at the ceiling. "Matts."

"Tensions are always high at this point in the season." He sounds like a press conference.

"Oh my God. *Another* fight?"

"No. I mean, yes, but listen. They targeted Kuzy. I couldn't just let that go."

"How is he?"

"He'll be okay. He'll probably be out for the start of the playoffs though."

"Hold on, I'm finding a video." Sydney puts Matts

on speaker and thumbs to the browser.

"You don't need to do that," he says.

Oh, but she does.

The first video she clicks on is a post-game locker room interview with Matts in his customary black Hell Hounds–branded T-shirt and stupid short shorts that show off way too much of his stupid hairy thighs.

She'll come back to that one later.

The second video is the play. The hit. The fight. Kuzy very distinctly yelling, "Revenge me!" as he's carted off down the tunnel. And Matts...following his instructions moments later. Sydney tries not to enjoy watching the fight, she really does. Because fighting is dangerous, and she knows from Eli that concussions are no joke. But there's a part of her, watching him pick up another man by the front of his jersey, that's thinking, *He could probably hold me against a wall for a while with very little effort.* But she's not going to dwell on that right now. That's also maybe something to consider later.

"I won," Matts says hopefully.

"And you're okay?"

"Completely."

"Well, nice job, I guess. But you should be more careful."

"I wasn't the one climbing scaffolding tonight."

"Okay, no, that's not even—"

They devolve into a companionable argument backgrounded by the occasional now-familiar whir of the GAN ROBOT shuffling Matts's Rubik's Cube. Only a few minutes later, the exhaustion from the day starts to hit her though.

"I need to tap out in a minute," Sydney says around a yawn. "You got any good cursed knowledge for me tonight?"

As usual, Matts doesn't need time to think. "The, uh, the breakup of Yugoslavia could possibly have been delayed if a guy had a dildo."

"Holy shit. Please explain."

"So, obviously tensions were already high between the Serbian and Albanian populations of Yugoslavia in the early '80s—"

"Oh, yeah, obviously."

Matts sighs at her. "But in 1985, there was this Serbian guy who ended up at the hospital with injuries."

"Butt injuries?"

Matts sighs louder at her. "Yes. Due to a broken bottle. And at first, he said Albanian men attacked him who, you know, inserted the bottle and gave him the injuries."

"Oh, damn."

"It turned into a whole thing, especially once the Serbian media outlets got a hold of the story, and the supposed attack became this driving force for worsening tensions between Serbs and Albanians. The guy did admit afterward that he was just masturbating and slipped and broke the bottle himself and was too embarrassed to say so when he went to the hospital. But by then, there was this whole inquiry happening, and some people, like politicians, were claiming the attack did happen, but the guy was scared and covering for the attackers. Things snowballed from there. It's called the Martinović affair if you want to read up on it."

"Wow. Excellent cursed knowledge, thank you."

"I live to serve. Hey, so… You've got a ten-day break coming up the week after next, right?"

"We do."

There's a funny little hitch in his voice. "I know it's sooner than expected, but do you want to spend four of those days in Gunnison for a cattle drive?"

She pauses. Rex is planning to spend a week of their break with his family in Austin before the band leaves for the West Coast portion of the tour, and Sky is going with him. Sydney was planning to spend the time sleeping and helping at the farm with Devo, but they don't *need* her.

And it would be a little magical getting to fulfill a childhood dream.

But she'd also be in constant contact with Matts for the duration of the trip and probably sharing a room, if not a bed, with him. And yes, Sydney told Eli she would make a move at the next opportunity, but doing so during a trip like this feels dangerous. Not because Sydney's afraid of Matts, but because she learned early and well to temper hope with caution and always have an escape route. Sydney thought she'd have the opportunity to tell Matts how she feels on her own turf, with a plan for all potential reactions, not when sharing a room with him a thousand miles from home. But Sydney also doesn't think she can share a bed with him again *without* kissing him.

So. Going with Matts is probably a terrible idea.

"Yeah," she says. "Absolutely. Just text me the details, and I'll be there."

Chapter Thirteen

MATTS IS NOT a jealous person.

He grew up good at hockey and bad at girls. He didn't have much competition in the former arena and was used to coming dead last in the latter. Matts was always picked first for sports teams and never had a date to dances, and he was okay with that dichotomy up until his physical prowess overshadowed the social weaknesses. He may have looked at other guys who flirted easily without second-guessing every other word and felt envious sometimes. But Matts has never been *jealous*, or at least, he's never considered himself jealous before. Until he answers his phone one night to Sydney raving about some guy named Paul who's *such* a good guitar player and *so* sweet and totally *gets* her, and maybe, he thinks, he is a jealous person after all.

Matts feels like a dick about it. Sydney is happy, and he should be happy that she's happy, even if it's some asshole named Paul who's making her happy and not him. She's been...not sad. Not exactly. The videos from her concerts and interactions with fans are still just as wild and colorful as ever. But ever since the fight after the House of Blues concert, when she's texting him or talking to him on the phone, she's been muted in a way that makes something in his chest feel tight. Sydney isn't built to be quiet or subdued. She's a feral creature not meant for restraints. And this Paul guy, as much as Matts is loath to admit it, has broken her out of whatever funk she's been in.

Paul isn't officially signing on with the band yet, not until he graduates and can join them on the summer tour, but they've been talking on the phone and making plans and —

Matts is jealous.

Which is why, in addition to getting Sydney a first-class ticket to Gunnison for the drive, he also buys her a gift.

Matts runs the idea past Devo first, and with his

blessing, Matts commissions her a custom drive hat out of Australian wool with a stiff brim, a copper-leather band, and a small clutch of red pheasant feathers laid along the right side. The custom bit is the dark brown burn work around the brim. Blooming roses surround a rattlesnake, curled tip to tail around the crown. Matts sends the hatmaker a picture of the rattlesnake tattoo on Syd's arm and asks her to match it.

He pays double for a rush order and then tips the lady extra when it arrives two days before he leaves. It's the most metal western hat he's ever seen. Matts may not be good at people, but he's starting to be good at Sydney, and he's almost certain she's going to love it.

He texts a picture to Devo, though, to make sure.

Just kiss her already, he answers.

Matts is planning to. Eventually.

When Matts doesn't respond, Devo texts him again a few minutes later: *It's fucking gorgeous. My birthday is February 8th if you were wondering.*

Noted, Matts answers. *Thanks.*

The following day is the last game of the regular season, and it's just as brutal as Matts anticipated, seeing as Kuzy, Rushy, and Alex are all out with injuries. The less said about it, the better, which is what he tells Sydney when she gently asks how he's doing that night.

She doesn't push, which Matts appreciates.

"Well, I haven't the time for queries tonight," Sydney says, with what is probably supposed to be an English accent. "But please, sir, may I have some cursed knowledge?"

Of course she can. She can have anything she wants.

*

AARON PICKS MATTS up from the Gunnison airport in Matts's dad's truck, a 1960 white Chevy that's more rust than paint. The Mexican blanket on the bench seat is new and covers what's left of the original fabric. The rest is the same: the rosary hanging from the rearview mirror, the can of Skoal on the dash, the peeling seal around the back window. It smells like decades of cigarettes and the air freshener his stepmother uses to try to cover up the smell.

When Matts pulls himself into the passenger seat, he remembers similar movements as a kid when his feet couldn't touch the floorboards, and he'd slide across the bench to sit against his dad's side. He'd watch his dad's hands on the wide steering wheel and the small radio knobs. At ten years old, Matts lived for the three-minute span of time it took to get from the mailbox to the house, when he'd jump out of the passenger seat to open the gate, then scramble back inside after closing it, and ask if he could drive the rest of the way. His dad would hem and haw about it, like it was such an imposition. But he'd nearly always slide along the cracked leather and let Matts clamber over him to perch, half standing, with his butt barely on the edge of the seat so he could reach the pedals and see over the wheel at the same time. Matts would cautiously, earnestly drive them up the pitted dirt road. He'd grin at his father's approving nod after he put the truck in park beneath the oak tree in the yard, then run up the front steps to tell his mom.

Now, Matts sits on the passenger side, his feet touch the floorboard, and the radio is silent.

"I feel like I should warn you," Aaron says as they bounce down the muddy driveway, rosary swinging from the rearview mirror. "He doesn't look the same."

"What, he's lost his hair? I figured."

"No. I mean, yeah, he's lost some of it, refuses to shave the rest. But he's also smaller. Lost weight, but…I don't know how to describe it. It's like he takes up less space now. You should just prepare yourself. I've seen it happen slowly, you know? I'm used to the way he looks. But it'll probably be a shock for you."

Matts isn't sure what to do with that information. But he doesn't have a chance to ask for further clarification because they've arrived; Aaron's mom—his stepmom—is on the porch, pushing the screen door open, waving.

Matts pulls his bag out of the truck bed and goes to give her an awkward hug. He steps into the kitchen that used to be synonymous with his mother and now is just…a kitchen. Red curtains instead of yellow. An empty wall where the china cabinet used to stand.

His father, shuffling slowly into the kitchen from the living room, cursing quietly about the boot they've got him in, pulls Matts's attention away from the pictures on the refrigerator.

The sight of his father *is* a shock.

Aaron is right. He's smaller. Thinner. But "thinner" doesn't encapsulate the jarring transformation he's undergone since Matts saw him last.

His father has always been a big man—not just in height but in the way he demanded people's attention and respect. He had a confidence, both intimidating and reassuring. When Matts was a kid, he thought there was nothing his father couldn't do. And even after Matts surpassed him in height, somewhere around sixteen years of age, Matts constantly forgot that he was technically the taller of them. His father was a presence.

That presence is now diminished in a way that makes Matts feel unmoored.

For the first time in his life, Matts has to be careful when he hugs his father.

When he does, the smell of him is a second, though lesser, shock. Matts has always associated the scent of tobacco with his father, something he never thought about until now that it's missing. Now, his father smells of aftershave and warm flannel and something vaguely chemical Matts can't pinpoint.

"Hey, Dad," he says, stepping back, uncertain what else to say.

"Boy," his dad says, "*what* are you doing with your hair?"

Matts reaches up to touch the curls that now spill just over his collar. "It's good luck," he argues faintly, still trying to adjust. "My scoring percentage is higher when I keep it like this."

"You look like a damn fool." His dad's face is different, sunken, his beard patchy and nearly gone.

"Well." Matts tries to rally, tries not to look like he's staring. "Sydney likes it."

"The girl who's coming tomorrow?"

"Yeah, that's her."

"Doesn't speak much to her taste, then," his dad mutters, easing himself into one of the chairs at the kitchen table. His stepmom puts a cup of tea in front of his father with a gentle touch to his shoulder before re-treating to the sink—giving them space, maybe.

"Dad." Matts's voice, embarrassingly, cracks.

His dad sighs. "I'm assuming someone's told you already."

Matts carefully doesn't look at Aaron. "About?"

"The cancer."

"I heard, yeah." And then, because he's up for pushing his luck today: "I'd like to know why I didn't hear it from you."

"Didn't want you to worry."

"Dad."

"It's hardly a thing. Treatment will be over and done within another month, and I'll be just fine. Back to normal."

Matts looks to Aaron for confirmation because that isn't the timeline they last discussed. Aaron shakes his head minutely, and Matts resigns himself to a conversa-tion he'd rather not have at some point during his trip.

"Listen," he starts, "I know—"

The front door opens, interrupting him.

"Hey, dipshit," a female voice yells over the slamming screen door. "Your hellbeast is taken care of, and I made the new feed order." There's the distinct sound of boots being dropped on the floor by the door. "Charlie tried to hike the prices on me like I didn't know full well what you typically pay, but I got it sorted. Are you ready for—oh. Uh. Hi."

The girl entering the kitchen has to be six feet tall, and the thick blonde hair in a messy knot on the top of her head makes her look taller. She's wearing a hoodie over well-worn jeans and mismatched wool socks with a backpack hooked over one shoulder. She's not pretty exactly, but she's certainly interesting to look at with her high cheekbones, sharp jaw, and shoulders that are probably nearly as broad as Matts's.

More importantly, Aaron is looking at her with a soft expression that Matts has never seen on his step-brother's face before.

"Matty," Aaron says, "Ellie. Ellie, Matty."

He shakes her hand and tries not to overthink it. "I thought you were a high school student."

"Oh, I am," Ellie says brightly. "A senior. I was held back twice on account of being dumb as a rock. If my mom wouldn't cry about it, I would have dropped out by now."

"You're not dumb," Aaron argues.

She rolls her eyes. "Anyway, it's nice to meet you, Matty." She glances between them. "Y'all have plans tonight?"

"No," Aaron says. "Matty is going to dump his stuff and then head back out again to pick up his girlfriend. 'Cause God forbid we wait at the airport for an hour and save twenty dollars on gas."

"Not my girlfriend," Matts corrects. "And I'll pay you back for the gas."

Aaron ignores him. "I'm still free," he tells Ellie. "If you want to go get set up."

Ellie salutes and moves through the kitchen toward the sewing room with a friendly hello to Matts's dad at the table and his stepmom, elbow deep in dishwater.

"What are you working on with her?" Matts asks.

Aaron looks shifty. "Nothing."

"Math," his dad says.

"Just a little calculus. She's got a test next week."

"Since when do you know calculus?" Matts asks.

"Well, I passed the same godforsaken curriculum three years back."

"Barely, if I remember."

"And I've watched a couple YouTube videos," Aaron mutters.

"Oh, have you? Also, you let her call you 'dipshit'?"

"Nobody *lets* Ellie do much of anything," his dad says. Bizarrely, it sounds approving.

"She only calls me that when the others aren't around," Aaron says. "She does have some concept of professionalism."

"They were in 4-H together in high school," his dad adds. "She started hanging around more last year, and Aaron hired her a few months back. She's a hard worker." Which is just about the highest praise that will come out of his mouth. "Healthy girl too. Strong. Got good childbearing hips."

The last bit is pointed.

"Honey," his stepmom chides.

"All right, that's enough," Aaron says. "She's an employee, not a broodmare."

Aaron hands Matts his keys. "You're picking up Sydney at six, right?"

"Yeah, I'll"—Matts points toward the stairs—"put my stuff up and head back out." He raises an eyebrow, jerking his chin toward the sewing room. "Let me know if you two need any help."

"Yeah, yeah. Thanks, boy genius."

*

IT'S CLEAR NO one at the Gunnison airport has the slightest clue who Sydney is. Her aviators are pushed up into her wild hair, and she's dressed in her typical uniform: black jeans, boots, mutilated Slipknot shirt. The sides of the shirt are cut so deep Matts can see the black lace bra she's wearing and the tattoos on her ribs. She does this cute little hop when she sees him, then breaks into a run, dragging her suitcase awkwardly behind her, wincing when it hits her heels until she abandons it entirely to hug him.

Matts might pick her up and swing her around a little. Just a little. The guitar case on her back gets in the way, but he doesn't even care because she's here and she's real and she smells fucking amazing, and she's still wearing his bracelet.

"God, it's good to see you," Matts says when he puts her back down again.

"Yeah?" Her palms are on his chest, slid down from his shoulders, elbows trapped between their bodies. Sydney looks at him searchingly, as if she's trying to decipher what the words mean. He thinks they're pretty clear.

"Yeah. You ready?" Matts asks, and she takes a step back, collects her bag. She pulls it with her left hand, her right arm nudging against his as they walk to the parking lot. Matts considers reaching for her hand. It's right there, and he's reasonably sure she wants him to take it.

But now is not the time, not when, if he's read this all wrong and she's not actually interested, it would mean three days of awkward interactions. Or worse, three days of Sydney, uncomfortable, wishing she never came.

"So," she says once they're in the truck and back on the main road. "How much do I need to tone things down while I'm here?"

"Tone things down," he repeats.

She recognizes it's a question. "Tone *me* down. I know I'm not everyone's cup of tea, and I don't want to cause any problems for you. I'm assuming I should put on a jacket and shouldn't mention any recent protests I've attended? Or my political affiliation?"

"Do whatever you want; I know how to fight."

"Matts."

"I'm serious," he says, and maybe it comes out too hard, too aggressive, but he wants to make sure she understands. "I don't want you to be anything but yourself."

"Well, all right, then." Sydney's looking at him again as though he's speaking a language she's only just started learning.

She hooks her thumb toward the guitar case in the truck bed. "I've been practicing some country songs to charm your family. Brought my acoustic."

"It'll get used every night if you're willing."

"I am. Should probably give me a list of approved songs though. Don't want to insult anyone's delicate sensibilities."

"I don't think you're hearing me," Matts says. "Wear and say and sing whatever you want."

"So if I wanted to play the Kasey Musgraves song, 'Follow Your Arrow,' you'd be okay with that?"

"I'll sing it with you," he says.

She smiles.

*

THEY DO PLAY the Kasey Musgraves song.

Dinner is a small casual affair, nothing like it will be the following night when all the folks helping with the drive are there. Tonight, it's just them—Dad, Aaron's mom, Aaron, Ellie, Sydney, and Matts.

His dad tells him to play them something after dinner, which is typical, and Aaron notes Sydney brought her guitar. Five minutes later, they're in the living room, playing "Folsom Prison Blues" and then "Jolene."

Matts lets Sydney decide what they'll play and does his best to keep up. It's only after she's lulled them into a false sense of security with a few classics that she meets Matts's eyes, one brow raised like a challenge, and starts "Follow Your Arrow."

Ellie, who's been singing along with them, knows all the words, her voice soft and lilting and completely at odds with the rest of her in a way that Matts finds charming. Aaron clearly does too. He sits in his chair with a beer and watches Ellie sing, looking hungry even though dinner's over. Matts wonders if he looks at Sydney the same way. He thinks he probably does.

Nobody says anything about the lyrics, though his dad's eyes do get a little narrow at times. But Sydney segues them directly into "Mammas, Don't Let Your Babies Grow Up to Be Cowboys," which actually gets a laugh out of his dad.

Too soon, she's leaning into Matts, saying she's beat and needs to get ready for bed. Matts is helpless to look away.

A trio of beauty marks hug the curve of her jaw on the right side. A scar pales a section of her left eyebrow.

When she smiles up at him, it's—

Simple. Perfect. Life ruining.

If Sydney doesn't want him, he's not sure what he'll

do with himself. Leave her alone, obviously, but then what's he supposed to do? He doesn't think Sydney is someone you can ever recover from.

She goes up the stairs to take a shower; Matts watches her leave, not even trying to hide it. Ellie is next to slap her thighs and say goodbye, and his stepmom goes to take her own shower at Aaron's insistence that he'll take care of cleanup.

Matts helps Aaron in the kitchen, rinsing the dishes he's washing, trying to fight the wall of fatigue that's suddenly hit him.

"Okay," Aaron says after several minutes of working in silence. "I get it. Why you like her so much. She's really something."

"She sure is," Matts agrees. "Ellie also seems—"

"Nope," Aaron says.

"You're learning calculus for her. You didn't even learn calculus for *you*."

"No. Stop talking. She's a *high school student*."

"She's twenty. And she'll graduate in a month. And I've heard Trigger likes her."

Aaron throws the dish towel at his face. "Goodnight," he says and heads for the hallway.

Matts grins as he finishes the last bowl. He pulls the plug in the sink, grimacing because, yes, there's some wet food collected around the drain.

He wipes down the counters, turns out the lights, and then stands at the periphery of the living room, watching for a moment as his dad talks back to the TV playing the end of some baseball game.

"Goodnight," Matts offers, hand on the stair railing.

His dad leans to the side, squinting at him, and says, with his usual level of tact, "You fucking her?"

Matts rubs the heel of his palm against his forehead. "Jesus, Dad."

"Are you?"

"No."

"See," his dad says, more to himself than Matts, "I figured we didn't have anything to worry about."

Matts stills. "Why's that?"

His dad laughs.

Matts doesn't.

"I'll allow she's pretty enough, and she sure as hell can sing, but she's not really our type, huh?"

Matts does laugh then, a humorless bark of a thing. "Our type," he repeats.

His dad waves a dismissive hand. "You know what I mean."

"I don't. Because she is beautiful, and capable, and kind. She is the *definition* of my type. My type currently has one entry, and it's her. But she's also incredibly out of my league. So, no, Dad, I'm not *fucking* her, but if she so much as showed a hint of interest, I'd get on my knees for her."

"Enough." His father's voice is dangerous.

But he's right. It is enough. Matts does something he's never even considered before in the kindling stages of an argument with his father. He walks away. It's not an argument worth having with him.

He starts up the stairs but pauses at the landing, trying to convince his heart to chill the hell out. Years of arguments have created a Pavlovian response to his father's raised voice, and it takes a few steadying breaths to convince his body that he doesn't need to gear up for an hour-long shouting match.

Matts tries to look casual when he slips in the guest bedroom door a minute later. "Hey," he says.

Sydney sits on the bed, legs pulled to her chest, one elbow slung around her knees, hand curled around the opposite bicep. Her hair is a riot.

Not his type. That would make things a lot fucking easier, wouldn't it?

"Hey." She chews on her bottom lip for a second. "I feel like you should know that I chose a very inopportune time to go get a drink of water a second ago."

He shuts the door and leans back against it. "Shit. Okay. How much did you hear?"

Her gaze is steady. "I heard you say you'd get on your knees for me if I showed so much as a hint of interest."

He closes his eyes. "I did."

"Did you mean it?"

He opens them. "I did."

Sydney stands, long legs bare under the hem of a hoodie she's stolen from his bag. The shoulder seams hit her mid bicep. Her fingertips barely peek out of the sleeves. He never wants that hoodie back.

She paces to the window and then abruptly changes course to stalk back over to him. She knots her fingers in her hair and then just *looks* at him. He has no idea what the look means.

"What?"

"Fuck," she mutters, pulling harder at her hair. "This is a terrible idea."

"*What?*"

Her arms fall to her sides with her next inhale, palms open, fingers spread, sleeves falling down over her hands. "This," she says, "is me showing interest."

It takes him a second. But only a second.

He gets on his knees.

It's not slow or seductive. It can't be interpreted as anything other than desperation. He's not ashamed. Matts catches the back of her thigh with one hand when she startles and tries to step back, then steadies her with his other hand around her opposite hip. He presses his thumb to the sharp jut of her hip bone and tries not to look too pathetic when he meets her eyes.

"Holy shit," she says, more an exhalation than words. "And you say I'm dramatic."

"That doesn't preclude me from being dramatic too," he points out.

"Preclude. Good word."

"Thanks."

Her hands alight gently, uncertain, on his upturned face, palms to his jaw and fingertips to his temples. Her rings are cool points of contact against his flushed skin, and when he doesn't move, she taps one thumb to his bottom lip and drags it from one side to the other.

"You don't even know what's in my pants," she says quietly.

"I couldn't care less at this point." It comes out more breathless than he would have preferred. "Unless you've got, like, a carnivorous plant down here. No, I'd still be willing to work with that. I like plants. And the carnivorous ones are evolutionary marvels. I've got some cursed knowledge I can share about giant montane pitcher plants if you'd like."

"Matts."

"Right. Sorry."

"I'm serious."

"Do I *not* look serious to you?"

She looks at him. Looks at him again in a way that makes him feel somehow more than naked despite being fully clothed. He thinks about refinishing old furniture, stripping away decades of seal layered on paint layered on stain. That's how he feels—like freshly sanded raw oak, breathing for the first time in years, no varnish, entirely vulnerable, but also entirely himself.

"Terrible idea," she repeats, a whisper this time. But then she's kneeling with him, first one folded leg, then the other, knees tucked between his in a far more elegant descent.

Sydney braces her hands on his thighs. Digs in her fingers like she means it.

And then she leans up to kiss him.

Chapter Fourteen

SHE DOESN'T KNOW how to do this.

Kissing, sure. She's kissed people.

Curiosity and lust and even boredom are simple, familiar motivations, but *this* is something else. It's not love, or at least Sydney's pretty sure it isn't love, not yet. But saying she *likes* Matts seems trite and laughable.

Like doesn't even begin to cover all of the everything she feels when finally, *finally*, she's allowed to slide her fingers into his ridiculous hair and know how it feels to catch his full bottom lip between her teeth.

He makes an aborted noise, soft and a little desperate in the back of his throat and pulls her closer, elbow hooked around her lower back, palm splayed on her ribs.

Upon further reflection, Sydney thinks that whatever is sitting like a roaring thing in her chest, bright and hot under his hand, may be uncomfortably close to love after all.

She doesn't know what to do about it. Sydney doesn't know how to kiss someone when it means something for her, and she needs it to mean something for them too. She doesn't know how to touch him when it feels like every moment since the day they met has been leading up to this chance for something more, and now that they're here, she can't fuck it up.

Sydney's never been almost in love before. She hasn't let herself. Or maybe no one seemed worth the risk until Matts. Crushes are all fine and good, but *love* is dangerous. Love is giving someone, every day, an invitation to hurt you and hoping they don't.

But she doesn't think she can stop herself. Not when it's right in front of her. Not when *he's* right in front of her, and he's holding her like he's feeling the same mixture of fear and elation.

She might be projecting. She hopes she isn't.

He kisses the side of her mouth, her cheek, her temple, her forehead.

He slides his hand up to cup the back of her skull and exhales, mostly in her hair.

"I have wanted to do that," he says, "for so long."

"Yeah? What took you so long?"

"Waiting for tenure."

It takes Sydney a minute to understand the callback. To remember their first conversation when she'd been trying so hard to be flippant and probably succeeded too well. She'd joked that she fucked her friends, but only when they had tenure. She manages a shaky laugh, trying not to let him see what the implication does to her.

"Congratulations, Dr. Matthews," she manages.

Sydney knew going into this that he wasn't looking for a serious relationship, and he's clearly still under the assumption that she isn't either. That's fine. That's whatever. She can deal with that. Having any of him is more than she could have hoped for; she's not going to get greedy before they've even started.

Matts seems to notice she's gone maudlin.

He rubs his thumb against the hinge of her jaw. "I'm sorry about my dad."

Not the reason, but sweet nonetheless.

"About what I expected."

"I'm still sorry."

She exhales. "I could have worn a shirt that didn't show off so many tattoos."

"I like that shirt."

"You also like my tattoos."

"I do. I'd like to see all of them," he says carefully. "If that's allowed now."

"It is. But I need to not be in your father's house the first time I get naked with you, and we'll need to talk about some things. Even if that's not particularly sexy. Sorry."

"No. I want to make sure anything we do is good for you, and I—" He's not one to flush, she's noticed, but his cheeks are a pinker than normal. "I like direction."

"*Do* you?"

He grins. "I've been told I'm very coachable."

"An admirable quality in both a professional athlete and in a paramour."

"Paramour. I like that. Why did you say this was a terrible idea?"

"You mean besides that you're a professional athlete, and I'm a professional musician, and our schedules alone are going to be hell to contend with. But also, if people find out you're sleeping with a trans woman, they're going to have shit to say about it. Experience tells me a lot of it won't be kind. Oh, and we could ruin our friendship if this goes badly, and you're one of my best friends, currently, so that would suck?"

"Yes," he agrees, "besides all that."

She sighs at him.

He sighs back louder.

"Too late, now, I guess," Sydney says.

Matts looks pleased. "Kiss me again?" He asks it cautiously as if there's the possibility she might say no.

She kisses him.

Eventually, they get in the bed because the wood floor is hard under their knees and the room is cold, and they have to wake up at the crack of dawn to move several hundred head of cattle multiple miles the following day.

Sydney ends up sprawled mostly on top of him, face tucked in his neck, and she takes a long, slow inhale to commit him to memory.

After her second deep breath, Matts wiggles a little underneath her.

"What are you doing?" he asks.

"Basking. Don't interrupt."

"Okay." He sneaks a hand up her shirt. His palm is wide and warm and spans a good portion of her back. She knows it's cliché as hell, but she loves how small he makes her feel.

"Do you want some cursed knowledge while you bask?" he asks.

"Always," she murmurs.

"Okay, so giant pitcher plants," Matts begins, then makes an offended noise when she laughs. "They're technically called 'Nepenthes attenboroughii' or 'Attenborough's pitcher plant.'"

"After David Attenborough?"

"*Sir* David Attenborough," he corrects.

"Oh, excuse me, of course."

Sydney grins into his neck as he tells her about the genus of carnivorous plants to which they belong and how Nepenthes attenboroughii have been known to eat small mammals. As he describes the horrors of the digestive process, Matts drags his fingers in soft, barely-there patterns up and down her back, pausing occasionally to tuck his thumb into the shallow spaces between her ribs, then follow it down her flank before starting over again.

They fit together like a habit.

Like an inevitability.

Like a gift.

Like a death sentence.

Sydney traces lyrics on his bicep and reminds herself not to get greedy. She'll take what she's given until it's no longer offered, and she'll be grateful for it. And she'll write some kickass songs when it's over. Sydney tries to convince herself that she's looking forward to the devastation. For creative reasons.

She doesn't quite manage it.

*

THEY WAKE UP early, just as the sunrise casts the room in muted blue. Matts sits up, rumpled and bleary, and throws an arm over Sydney so he can give her an off-center kiss before rolling out of bed.

She allows herself ten seconds to grin into her pillow before following him.

Sydney's used to early mornings and manages to get dressed and ready in less than five minutes. She's in the bathroom, French braiding her hair and frowning at her reflection—her skin is already looking dry in the high altitude—when Matts knocks on the door.

"Hey, Syd," he calls. "I'm leaving something for you on the bed. You don't have to wear it if you don't want to. But if you do want to, it's…on the bed. Which I already said. I'm going downstairs now."

That's certainly incentive to finish quickly.

When she exits, it's to find a round box waiting for her. Sydney can guess what's inside; a hat box typically contains a pretty singular item. But when she removes the lid, her breath catches.

It's the most beautiful hat she's ever seen.

The felted rim is thick and smooth between her fingers, and the intricacy of the burn work is exquisite, almost a mirror image to her tattoo. The feathers change color in the sunlight. Sydney takes the hat back to the bathroom and settles it on her head.

She looks good. Better than good. She looks fucking badass.

It almost seems a shame to wear it on the drive under the sun and in the dust. It's more suited to wearing on stage. Sydney pictures it—thinks about pairing the hat with a pair of black crocodile boots she has. She just might. Maybe when they play Nashville.

"Syd?" Matts calls from downstairs.

"Coming!" she yells back.

Obviously, she'll wear it today, if only to let Matts know she likes it. Loves it.

Sydney tips the brim a little lower over her eyes and lets the confidence of a last lingering look in the mirror carry her downstairs and straight into Matts's space.

She goes up on her tiptoes to grab his face and press a—probably too aggressive if she's being honest—kiss to his mouth.

He looks delighted.

Aaron, an energy drink in hand, raises his eyebrows at them.

"I guess that means you like it?" Matts says.

"I love it so much I want to eat it."

"Don't do that," he advises.

Sydney tucks one of the ends of the stampede string in her mouth and pretends to gnaw on it. "No promises."

Matts rolls his eyes, but he watches her with undeniable fondness as she shifts past him to open the refrigerator.

"Can I steal some baby carrots?"

"Why? I mean, yes, but why?"

She dumps a few out of the bag and into her hand, then tucks them into her jeans pockets.

"If we're leaving in less than an hour, I'll need to speedrun making friends with whoever I'm going to ride today."

Aaron says something under his breath that Sydney doesn't catch, but from Matts's immediate response—punching Aaron hard enough in the solar plexus that he falls back against the counter, laughing—Sydney assumes it was sexual.

She did set herself up for that.

"Sorry about him," Matts says solemnly, offering her a protein bar.

"You might recall that I also have a brother whose primary purpose is vexation." Sydney takes the protein bar and shoves it into her coat pocket as she makes her way outside.

Matts's father is sitting on the porch, his booted broken ankle elevated on the ottoman beside his chair. His eyes track her as she steps out the screen door, squinting against the early-morning sunlight, buttoning the pearl snaps on her outer flannel shirt against the chill.

"That's a fine hat," he says.

"Your son has good taste," she says evenly.

Matts coughs abruptly in the kitchen behind her. Like maybe he's choking. Or trying to cover a laugh.

Aaron doesn't try to cover *his* laugh.

"He does," Matts's father says finally, rubbing the heels of his hands on his thighs. "Occasionally. Y'all be safe."

"That's the plan," she agrees.

And then Matts is behind her, one hand possessive on her lower back, urging her forward down the steps and toward the horse barn.

Sydney doesn't look over her shoulder at Matts's father. Mostly because she doesn't think she can without smirking.

Matts's hand lingers.

*

MOVING CATTLE IN Colorado is mostly like moving cattle in Texas. The air is cooler, but the sun burns faster. The grit of dirt in her teeth is the same. In Texas, nearly everywhere is flat. In Colorado, the land pitches and rolls from grassy plains to jagged, rocky peaks. Shallow creek beds cut through the terrain like bright, blinding wounds with raw red dirt edges. Sydney's used to feeling small in Texas terrain, but it's in a distinctly different way here. In Texas, the sky overwhelms; in Colorado, the land makes her consider religion.

The cattle, the horses, the easy comradery—that's all the same.

Around a dozen people help to move the herd: Matts, Aaron, Sydney, Ellie, three hired hands, and a collection of neighbors.

Everyone's the same brand of laid-back country friendly Sydney is used to. Aaron claims the point man position from the onset, which causes some raised eyebrows. The assembled people seem to be waiting for something, eyes moving between Aaron and Matts. But Matts doesn't say anything aside from "I'll take flank with Sydney." And that's that.

They've got her on a big, friendly gelding named Reacher, who's clearly old hat at moving cattle. She and Reacher settle into their place with an ease that seems to have very little to do with her horsemanship abilities and everything to do with her mount's confidence. They quickly move out of hearing distance of everyone other than Ellie, who is relegated to the back as the drag rider since, other than Sydney, she's the greenest rider. Sydney wonders if that was part of the odd little power play that just happened. Did Matts give up his usual position as point man so Sydney didn't have to ride drag?

Regardless, she endeavors to be as useful as possible, pushing in when the cows try to start fanning out, pulling back to help Ellie encourage a few reluctant stragglers forward. At first, Sydney hears bits and pieces of someone singing up ahead, his voice practiced and well-pitched. But by the time they hit the road, the herd has gone long and narrow to move up the pass. The wind has changed, and it's quiet again except for the noise of hooves on pavement and the breathing of the animals around them.

Sydney's dad swears that singing keeps cattle calm, and she figures if they're singing up ahead it's not like she's purposefully showing off if she does too.

She takes in the expanse of it—cattle and cowboys and a two-lane road bookended by wild-flower valleys, backgrounded by snow-capped mountains. She settles back in her saddle letting her spine go loose. And she sings.

At first, it's country music because it seems fitting, and she knows Matts will like it if he's in hearing range.

Then, it's fragments of a song she's been working on, something about love and uncertainty. Something about pain. She switches to blues for a bit as they move off the road and into the higher elevation foothills. By the time they hit the river, her voice is warm and her hands are cold. The clouds that were previously banked far in the distance have spilled over the mountains and into the cup of the valley, blocking the sun and casting long-fingered shadows over the slow-moving water and slower-moving cattle.

The herd treks forward without complaint, a dark arrow through darker water beneath the cloud-strangled sky. The water is shallow—she probably won't even get her boots wet, tall as her horse is, but Sydney hangs back to help Ellie while Matts pushes forward. She waits on the embankment, chooses one of her own songs, but sings it in a way befitting the world before her, a landscape cast in watercolor shades of gray, barely bleeding blues, and greens and browns.

Steam rises off the river from the heat of the cattle moving through it. Over the susurrus of lowing and men calling to one another, it feels fitting to slow the cadence, soften the vowels, and push her voice higher, whimsical and maybe a little haunting as she watches the animals and valiant rays of sunlight knifing their way through shadows to paint the muddy water gold and copper.

It isn't beautiful, exactly. But it sure is something.

"I think I know that song," Ellie calls as she approaches with the last of the cattle. "It's uh—" She hums under her breath to the chorus. "—'Godless Martyr' by Red Right Hand, right?"

Sydney doesn't think she visibly reacts, but her horse's stride falters, and his ears go back, so she imagines she's tightened her legs.

"Yeah," she says finally.

"I like your version better," Ellie says, blissfully unaware.

"Thanks," Sydney manages.

She takes advantage of two calves attempting to escape to leave the conversation.

However, twenty minutes later, when someone has

called a halt up ahead, Ellie circles back to find her again about the same time Matts does.

"Have you ever thought about doing an American Idol audition or something?" Ellie asks. "Because you're crazy good. Like, you could sing professionally."

Matts, Sydney has learned, has a very poor poker face. Which Ellie notices before he can make a quick one-eighty away from them.

"What?" Ellie says, glancing between them.

"Nothing," Sydney says.

"Why is Matts being weird? Do you sing professionally?"

Sydney sighs. "How much do you know about Red Right Hand?"

Matts pulls his now-thoroughly-annoyed horse around again.

Ellie looks stymied. "They've got a couple songs on the radio right now. And I think all the band members are queer. And the lead singer is—"

Ah. Sydney thinks. *There we go.*

"Oh my God," Ellie hisses. She pulls one glove off with her teeth and stands a bit in the stirrups so she can fish her phone out of her pocket. After a moment of thumbing at the screen, in which Matts sidles closer and closer to them, she looks up at Sydney, pointing.

"You're her! I mean, you— You're—" Ellie holds up her phone. "Sydney Warren."

"I am, yeah."

"Holy shit!"

"We're trying not to advertise it," Matts says pointedly. "Since we don't know how some folks here would react to, uh—"

"Oh, right." Ellie glances back at her phone. "The trans thing?"

"The trans thing," Sydney confirms.

"Aaron would probably be cool about it," Ellie muses. "I mean, he'd probably be awkward as hell, but he won't be a dick intentionally. He's been cool about me."

"You," Sydney repeats.

"I'm bi. Or pan. Or whatever. I like people. And I know that's not the same, but Aaron was chill about that, so..."

"How did he find out?" Matts asks.

"Couple months back, I went on an absolute disaster of a first date with one of the few other queer women in town, and I frantically texted him from the bathroom that I needed him to call me with a fake emergency so I could escape."

"Did he?" Matts asks.

"Oh yeah. Nice and loud so she could hear too. Cow with a prolapse, blood everywhere, need help right now while waiting for the vet, et cetera."

"That'll do it," Sydney says.

"What did he say about the...bi thing," Matts asks.

He's only wearing one glove on his reining hand. His other hand, cupped easy and habitual around his saddle horn, is bare. On the pinky of that hand, he still wears her heart ring, bright and too small and jarringly obvious, which makes her chest warm despite the chill in the air.

"Nothing, really." Ellie pushes back at a cow trying to wander. "He asked if I like girls, and I said 'no better'n boys,' and he just nodded, and that was that. You know how he is."

"Hm," Matts says. "Well, he already knows about Sydney. And you're right. He was awkward but cool."

"Good." Ellie tucks her phone back in her pocket and slowly pulls on her glove as she studies them. "No offense, but what are you doing here? Shouldn't you be on tour or something?"

"We've got a two-week break. And Matts invited me. I've always wanted to go on a cattle drive, and he knows that."

"Well"—Ellie gives their surroundings a slow

pass—"you won't find a prettier place for a drive. Even if it's a little cloudy. Thoughts so far?"

"Definitely living up to my expectations," Sydney agrees.

"So, are you two together or—"

"Uh—" Sydney starts, at the same time that Matts says, "Oh, we're just—"

Someone whistles, shrill and cutting up ahead; the animals start moving again, and a little pack of six cows, which had been drifting as they spoke, make a break for it. Matts goes after the runaways, Ellie drops back to drag, and Sydney does not groan. She also does not spend the next half hour replaying the conversation with her own preferred ending: Matts saying "Yes, of course," or something, *anything*, more substantive than a phrase that starts with "Oh, we're just."

Sydney tries to rework it and formulate a response that's positive, such as, "Oh, we're just starting to date," or "Oh, we're just beginning to fall in love," or "Oh, we're just about to embark on a committed partnership if Sydney will have me." None of those seem likely. What does seem likely is: "Oh, we're just friends" or "just hanging out" or some other *just* that will eventually break her heart. God, she hates words sometimes. Today, she hates the word "just." Then again, it could have been worse. He could have said, "Oh, *no*, we're just—" But he didn't. There was no explicit disagreement, but then again—

By the time they get to Gothic, Sydney's replayed the cadence, the tone of those three words so many times they've lost all meaning.

External to the small crisis she's given herself, the gathering storm has finally reached something of a breaking point. The clouds have won their mutiny against the last, dying vestiges of blue and settled low over them in an oppressive, static blanket. She can taste the electricity in the air like an itch on her tongue.

From up one side of the pass, Sydney watches the men disperse their positions, and the cattle spread through the valley like they know they've reached their destination. The impending storm doesn't appear to concern them as they duck their heads to graze, rub against trees, or for the young ones to kick and run.

"We're probably going to get rained on," Matts says, jogging his horse up to join her. His non-reining hand is lax on his thigh. The ring on his pinky finger quiets some of the anxiety still milling around in the back of her head.

"Good thing I've got a solid hat, then," Sydney answers, touching two fingers to it.

His bracelet slides softly from her wrist to catch on the cuff of her jacket. She watches his eyes follow it.

The way he looks at her doesn't feel friendly. It feels possessive. It gives her a terrible amount of hope.

"You like it?" Matts asks, several beats too late, his attention flicking back up to the hat.

"I do. I think I'll wear it on stage."

"You should. It looks good. You look good."

And then they sit there, swaying with the minute shifts of their mounts, staring at each other. Sydney thinks her horse is probably judging her.

"What's that?" She nods toward what appears to be a small town in the distance. It doesn't seem likely, considering the remoteness of the valley they're in, the elevation they have to be at. But the buildings look well-kept.

He follows her gaze. "Rocky Mountain Biological Laboratory. It's one of the highest-altitude biological field stations in the US, I think. It used to be an old mining town, but now they've got dorms, laboratories, science-y stuff. There's a bunch of protected research sites all over. We passed some on the way up—all those little fenced off areas?"

She does recall this.

One of the guys whistles again, and Matts nods toward the pass. "After you."

She nudges her horse into a trot and glances at the sky again.

They're definitely going to get rained on.

*

BY THE TIME they get back to the ranch, the rain has slackened to a heavy, frigid mist, and Sydney can't feel her fingers. She's fumbling so badly Matts has to help her untack her horse. Embarrassed enough by the betrayal of her Texas blood in front of Matts, she's grateful everyone else has already started the trek to the house. Having more people witness her inability to operate a buckle in only moderately cold weather is not on her to-do list.

However, the delay at the barn means that by the time they get to the house, all the showers are taken.

Matts ushers her upstairs with a stack of towels from the laundry room and then helps her strip out of clinging flannel and sopping jeans. It might be romantic if not for her chattering teeth, and there's absolutely nothing sexy about the sports bra and compression shorts she's wearing.

"Shit, I didn't think it was possible for someone's

lips to actually turn blue," Matts says, wrapping one of the towels around her and chaffing his hands up and down her arms. "It's not even freezing out."

"I have poor circulation," Sydney mutters.

"I can see that. Are you going to be okay? Do I need to go kick someone out of a shower so you can heat up?"

"My hero. But no. I'll be good." The shiver that wracks her body as she says it undermines her credibility a bit.

Matts frowns at her. "Here, hold on."

He strips out of his own clothes, down to very clingy boxers that she would like to revisit at some point when she isn't impersonating a Victorian waif likely to expire from a slight chill.

Matts gives himself a cursory once-over with the second towel and then scoops her, bridal-style, into his arms. He sits them on the bed, tucking her close to his chest, curling himself around her like a very large, very muscular space heater. Cupped in the pocket of warmth between his lap and his shoulders, Sydney immediately feels warmer. And she feels warmer still when he tugs the towel she's wrapped in closer around her throat, using the side of his hand to rub away a line of water left by her hair on her cheek.

"Better?" he asks.

"Better," she agrees faintly.

He kisses her, and she forgets she's cold.

Matts's hand is hot on her face, and his mouth is warm and persuasive. He touches her like she's always wanted to be touched—like she means something, like he's desperate for her but restraining himself because she's worth being careful.

Sydney likes how her name tastes when passed from his mouth to hers, how it sounds breathy and reverent as he exhales it against her lips.

She likes the way he looks at her between kisses, eyes dark and searching, and maybe a little violent, the way he reaches for her with a tempered aggression that makes her want to push him to see what he'd be like if he stopped controlling himself.

"Hey, shower's ready if you—ohhhkay then. Maybe shut the door if you're going to—"

"Oh my God, Aaron. Fuck off," Matts says.

Sydney laughs into his throat while Aaron protests and Matts argues back, and then Aaron's mom is yelling upstairs that dinner is almost ready.

"You should shower," Matts says into her hair. He makes no move to let her go.

"I should," she agrees, kissing his throat.

"I'm eating your steak if you're not down in time," Aaron says.

*

DINNER IS A lively affair, composed of not only Matts's family but also the folks who had helped with the drive. Three or four separate conversations occur at all times and occasionally come together for a minute or two before diverging again. Sitting between Matts and Ellie, Sydney is content to eat and listen.

"If it shifts, it drifts," Aaron is arguing, mouth full.

"Except it didn't drift; it turned over," Matts says.

"Wait," Ellie interrupts, "you turned over a *tractor*?"

"I was sixteen," Aaron mutters.

"How am I just now hearing about this?"

"Because Dad about killed him," Matts says. "It took eight guys and two trucks to get it upright again, and he's been trying to erase the moment from living memory ever since."

"Thanks for your help with that goal," Aaron mumbles.

From the other end of the table, an older guy—Sydney thinks his name is Karl—responds to something Matts's dad said. "Still better than when the Western kids had traffic blocked on Main Street for half an hour with their rainbow shit."

Matts's dad makes a commiserating noise.

"They try to tell us they're born gay and then want us to throw them a parade about something they supposedly can't control. Make up your mind, right?"

Suddenly, Sydney is no longer paying attention to the ongoing tractor conversation.

Neither is Matts because he raises his voice to say, "I think it's a little different, considering it's only recently that they can be open about who they love without fearing for their safety. I'd probably want to celebrate that with a parade, too, if it were me."

His dad's mouth purses, forehead wrinkling, but Karl just rolls his eyes, gesturing with the roll in his hand.

"I'm not being homophobic or anything," he says. "I just don't want it shoved down my throat is all."

Sydney restrains herself from making a dick joke. As much as Matts has encouraged her to be herself, that would probably be a step too far.

"Huh," Matts says, clearly feigning confusion. "I guess I figured you'd be more supportive."

The clink of silverware goes quiet. The other conversations halt.

Karl appears stymied. "Why'd you figure that?"

"Well, the Christmas card you and Annie sent—" He points toward the kitchen with his fork. "—had the gay cardinals on it."

Sydney has no idea where this is going, but she can't wait to find out.

Judging by Ellie's facial expression, Sydney isn't the only one.

"What?" Karl says.

"The— Here, hold on."

Matts stands, taking his time as he ambles into the kitchen to pull something off the refrigerator. He returns with a Christmas card showing a snowy forest scene and two bright red birds cuddled on a tree limb together in the foreground.

"This," Matts says.

"What about it?" Karl answers.

"Well"—Matts points to the birds—"the bird couple on the front. I mean, I'm assuming they're a couple what with the framing and the context and such. But they're both red."

"So?" A vein in Karl's forehead slowly becomes more visible.

"So, boy cardinals are red. Girl cardinals are brown. That's two boys all cuddled up together." Matts taps the card for emphasis. "Gay cardinals."

Sydney doesn't know what her face is doing, but it's probably no less subtle than Ellie's.

"And that makes sense," Matts continues, "because birds are, as a class, one of the animals with the highest percentages of homosexuality. I'm not sure what the estimated rate for cardinals is, but I think black swans are the highest in the US at a little over 25 percent, and I know mallard ducks aren't that far behind them. Though *outside* the US, there are higher percentages. Like, there's a species of cotinga in Eastern Colombia that's 40-something percent."

"No kidding," Ellie says. "What about penguins? I saw a story on the news the other day about gay penguins at the Denver Zoo. The keepers gave the couple a chick that was abandoned, and they were raising it together. It was cute as hell."

"I think they're also around 25 percent," Matts says. "Maybe a little less."

"Neat."

Matts's dad clears his throat. The table goes quiet.

"Annie picked the cards," Karl says eventually. "And since when did you become a champion for the gays? Didn't think Texas was much for that."

"Well—" Matts sets the card aside so he can cut

back into his steak. "My captain is gay. And one of my linemates is bi. So's my goalie. And my— I have other friends now who are bi and trans and stuff. I went to Houston's Pride parade last year with some of them. It was fun. And it was important to them."

"Well, *I* appreciated the parade here," Ellie says, "seeing as I wouldn't turn down a date with a lady, provided we get on all right. Not that there are many takers around here, so mostly, I stick with the boys, you know? But still. Nice to see I'm not alone. Even if the parade held up traffic a little." She addresses the latter part to Karl who appears to be shocked into silence.

Sydney thinks Ellie would have no issues pulling women in Houston, but she doesn't say it out loud because she's within kicking distance of Aaron.

Matts's dad looks as similarly stricken as Karl.

"You know about this?" he mutters quietly to Aaron.

"Didn't think it mattered much," Aaron says back, but he looks pretty damn uncomfortable saying it.

Sydney notices that despite her calm demeanor, Ellie's fingers are clenched tight around her knees.

As she's watching, though, Aaron slides one of his hands over to encircle Ellie's wrist, squeezing. Ellie glances at him with a small, private smile. She turns her hand palm-up so they can lace their fingers together.

"Well," Matts's stepmom says. "More potatoes, anyone?"

Chapter Fifteen

MATTS TAKES SYDNEY to the airport.

It's an early morning flight after a late night follow-ing a second full day in a saddle. She's sore and sleepy and pliant in a way that makes him feel fiercely, almost embarrassingly, protective as he practically carries her to the truck. He tucks her against his side on the bench seat and coaxes the heater to life before pressing a kiss to her head where it's leaned against his shoulder.

They don't talk on the drive, and the radio has been silent for years, which means tires on pavement and wind and the rattle of the dash are the only soundtrack to their journey. Sydney wears his hoodie again; the sage-green makes her olive skin look gold in the sunrise light slanting in the front window. It paints copper highlights in her dark curls and accents the cut of her jaw and the slope of her nose.

She is so, so lovely.

And she's his. Maybe. At least a little. At least for now. His to kiss and to touch and to please, as best he's able. The responsibility might overwhelm him.

When they get to the airport, Matts pulls her bag and her guitar case out of the back and then just stands there, wrapped around her, holding her as long as she'll permit it.

"You think they'd let you carry me onto the plane?" she asks blearily. "If we ask nicely?"

"Probably not."

"Ugh. Why did I stay up so late last night?"

He'd tried to coax her to bed multiple times, but there had been a full-on concert happening in the living room—guitars, harmonicas... Ellie even brought her ukulele. Sydney was in her element. And then, even when they went upstairs, she was so wired she stayed up long after Matts fell asleep. He's not entirely certain she slept at all.

"Oh, no," he says. "Are you reaping the 'cussions' of your actions?"

"Alas," she says, "the 'conses' are 'quencing.'"

"You're adorable."

"I'm not," she mutters adorably into his chest. "I'm a sexy, stoic enigma."

"That too," he agrees.

He wants to gather her up and put her back in the truck. To head for the mountains through Crested Butte to Emerald Lake. To sit by the water in the truck bed with a blanket and the blue sky and to have her all to himself. Just for a day. Just for a while. Before he has to share her again.

Matts wants to see all her tattoos. All of her scars. All of her. To lay Sydney down in the sun and map all the things that make her body hers. He wants her to teach him the way she likes to be touched and then do it better than anyone else ever has.

He wants to say: *I think I'd love you, if you'd let me. Please let me.* But people aren't supposed to say things like that, especially not so soon, so he doesn't. Instead, Matts says, "I'll see you in a month."

And she kisses him.

And she leaves.

And he watches her go with an ache in his throat that feels like an omen.

*

IN THE FOLLOWING weeks, it's both surprising and not surprising how little things change.

They still text. They still talk on the phone nearly every night. Matts is on his second box of question cards and has started keeping a spreadsheet of cursed knowledge to share with her. Sydney sends him pictures of the band backstage and on their tour bus and watching his games. Sometimes, she wears his hoodie. Sometimes, he can see the stick he gave her wrapped in trans Pride tape in the background, mounted on the wall above her bunk in the bus. Always, she wears his bracelet.

It doesn't seem right that everything is so similar to how it was before because he feels like something has shifted. Some kind of tectonic event has destabilized the foundation of his existence in the process. Except he's still meal-prepping and working out and lacing his skates exactly as before.

Part of the problem is that no one knows. He hasn't told anyone. He wants to tell Eli and Alex, but if Eli hasn't come to Matts about it, then *Sydney* hasn't told Eli. Maybe Sydney wants to keep this—them—private. Which is understandable, but Matts wants to tell his closest friends that he's kissed possibly the most important person in his life. He should have asked Sydney what she wanted. What they were. But he didn't, and now he's not sure how. Matts doesn't want to scare her away by asking too much, by *being* too much. It wouldn't be the first time he ruined something with a shameful level of enthusiasm.

There are some small changes, though, that he notes as a consolation: the warmth in her voice at night; how her implicit teasing has become undeniably, explicitly flirtatious; the way she says his name as if it means something; and how she pauses at the end of their conversations when they say goodbye, as though she'd like to say something more.

God, he misses her. Misses her like—he doesn't even know. Matts has nothing to compare it to. And it doesn't make sense because he's never really had her. Maybe that's part of the problem. Matts feels like he's in his own special brand of purgatory, counting down the days until he gets to see Sydney again in person, and they can progress whatever this is to a place where he can name it.

When he pulls into the garage at Alex and Eli's place the night before their first game in the second playoff series, Matts is listening to the final song of the most recent playlist Sydney has sent him. He's still trying to formulate his thoughts about it when he gets upstairs. Neither Alex nor Eli are home, so Matts lets himself in with his key—he's been practically living with them since Asher officially moved in with his girlfriend—and twenty minutes later, he's typing up his thoughts when Eli gets home.

Matts helps him dump the bags he's carrying onto the island, crouches to unvest Hawk and kiss her, and then stands to hug Eli.

"Hey," Matts says. "How's your head?"

"That's a pretty personal question."

It takes him a minute. "Oh, gross." He steps back. "I meant because you had a doctor's appointment today."

"General consensus is that my brain is still fucked but not as badly as before," Eli says brightly.

"Good?"

"Eh." Eli starts emptying the cold bag onto the counter. "The more pressing concern is why our refrigerator still refuses to work properly." He opens the door to the appliance in question, flipping it off with his other hand before reaching for the items on the counter. "They shouldn't be allowed to market this thing as 'smart.' The technician came out three times in the last month, and the doors still aren't closing right. And the touch screen won't let us control the temperature, which, naturally, is the only way *to* control the temperature."

The front door opens with Alex's entrance. He kicks off his shoes, sheds his jacket, and greets Hawk on his way to wrap both arms around Eli's neck from behind and smash a kiss against the side of his face.

"Hi," he says, draped over Eli's back. "What'd I miss?"

"Not much. I just got home. I was telling Matts I can't wait to buy our own place and fill it with the stupidest appliances on the market. No touch screens, no Bluetooth connectivity. I want the himbos of the appliance world. Big. Stupid. Pretty. Easy to maintain. Indestructible."

"And you shall have all the himbo appliances your heart desires." Alex presses another gentler kiss to Eli's neck and then releases him to help put away groceries.

"How long have you been here, Matts?"

Matts doesn't have a chance to answer because Alex leans around the island to look at the laptop Matts left open.

"What is this?" Alex asks.

Matts freezes as if he's been caught doing something inappropriate and not as if he's updating a spreadsheet in one tab while writing what is quickly becoming a multi-paragraph song analysis in the other.

He has no idea how to explain this.

Eli joins Alex to squint at his screen. "Is this a Sydney thing?"

Or maybe it is that easy.

"Yeah."

"She's having you write essays?" Eli raises an eyebrow. "About music?"

"No, but she gives me a list of songs every week to listen to, and then we discuss them. I just wanted to get my thoughts organized before we talk next."

Eli smiles at him softly. "You've assigned *yourself* essays."

"Yes…"

"That's adorable." Alex gestures between Matts and the laptop. "Are you planning to actually do anything there, or—?"

"Yeah," Matts says. "When she's back next month before they start the second leg of their tour."

Eli moves back to the island. "And your plan is…"

"Tell her how I feel."

"Which is?"

"Too much, probably." Matts exhales when they both just look at him. "If I'm not in love with her already, I'm probably close."

"I knew it," Alex says. "Kuzy owes me twenty dollars."

"What?"

"I bet him you'd admit you were in love with her by the end of playoffs. He didn't think you'd get there until after the summer."

"I haven't even slept with her," Matts says faintly. That would be a compelling argument, maybe, if they were talking about anyone but Sydney. But they are talking about Sydney.

"I mean, do you think the sex would be bad?" Alex asks.

Matts swallows. He's thought about that quite a lot, actually. The answer is definitive. "No."

Alex shrugs at him, moving to help Eli unload groceries into the pantry.

"If it helps," Eli says, "I'm pretty sure Syd is in the same place, feelings-wise."

It does, a little.

"Enough about love," Alex says. "Did you watch the tape coach sent yet?"

Matts exhales in relief and pulls up the video file on his laptop, then slides it over so Alex can take the stool next to him.

He can talk about hockey.

Hockey, at least, is easy.

*

HOCKEY IS HARD.

Matts loves hockey. He does. It's been a constant in his life for so long that he can't imagine a day-to-day existence without the accompanying soundtrack of blades on ice or the echo of pucks ricocheting off boards. But hockey is a constant in the same way that family is a constant. Sometimes, even when he loves it, he hates it. Sometimes, Matts feels like it takes up so much of him that it doesn't leave space for anything else. Sometimes, he wonders what he'd have become without hockey. If his mom hadn't signed him up on a whim at nine years old. If he hadn't scored six goals his first game and immediately been moved to a team of kids two years older than him.

Because hockey itself is easy. Scoring those six goals that first game was simple. The defense wasn't defending, the goalie was mostly trying to stay upright on his skates, and the offense was laughably easy to intercept. Later, even on the older team, he was one of the larger players. He was fast; his balance was good; his hand-eye coordination was better. So, the hockey was easy. What was hard was the people, the other boys who envied him, his own teammates who tripped him when the coaches' backs were turned, who called him a freak and a show-off and didn't invite him to birthday parties even when everyone else on the team received an invitation. The parents in the stands were worse, adults screaming at their kids to target him, not to let him score on them again, screaming at *him* that he shouldn't be there at all.

And then there were the coaches, who weren't bad, exactly, but they quickly had expectations. Other kids could have bad days. Matts couldn't. He carried the team, and he wasn't allowed to set them down. If he did, the coaches let him know what a disappointment he was. And if he tried to talk back, to point out that he wasn't the only one who had missed a pass or shot too wide or *needed a fucking break*, they said the same thing in different voices and different phrasing, but always the same thing: We expect more of you.

When Matts was sixteen, the equipment manager at his boarding school found him alone in the locker room one night, fighting tears after a game they'd won—*won*, but he was still too much for the parents in the stands and not enough for the coaches. And the equipment manager sat down and patted Matts's back and said,

"Skill comes with its own punishments. But just re-member that you're only feeling this way, you're only being treated this way, because you're the best one out there. And one day, you'll get to a level where you won't be. You'll find your peers, and you'll share the burden. And things will be easier. I promise. You just need to hang in there until you reach that level. Until you find your people. Okay, kid?"

Matts clung to that promise until he was drafted. And then he went to the first Hell Hounds training camp and reveled in being one of the better players on the ice, but he wasn't *the* best.

The equipment manager was right. Matts found his people.

Alex was an undisputed prodigy. Kuzy was a force of nature. Jeff was the fastest skater he ever saw. Rushy had his own goalie magic. Then, Rome joined the Hounds and further emphasized that Matts was part of a *team*.

Except now, he's feeling the burden of expectation again.

Coach told him, flatly, of the expectation.

Because Alex and Kuzy and Rushy are all out with injuries. The coaches have split him and Rome between the first and second lines, and there are green callups on the third and fourth lines. No one is comfortable; everyone is desperate. They won the cup two years before, and they made it to the final round of playoffs last year. The Hounds is the team with the most out queer players in the league. They're the team with the most attention. There are *expectations*.

Which makes the *A* on his chest feel weighty and terrible as Matts sits on the bench and chews on his jersey and watches the time on the clock tick down while the score stays the same:

Two-zero, Stars.

It's the second game in the second series, and they're already down one.

Five minutes left, and he's pretty sure they're about to be down a second.

Matts touches gloved fingers to his chest, absently feeling for the bump of Sydney's ring on the necklace beneath his jersey. He hopes she isn't watching.

He pushes himself forward, throws a leg over the boards in anticipation of his shift, and then throws himself over.

He does his best.

Coach pulls their goalie at four minutes, and with Rome on the ice with him again, Matts is able to push through the exhaustion.

Rome intercepts the puck with a truly stunning reach that overbalances him, but he manages to send the puck right to Matts's tape as he dives.

Matts doesn't try anything fancy. He's too tired for that. But he manages to split the defense with a quick fake out.

His first slapshot is blocked, but Matts gets the rebound and sends it back to Rome.

Rome's shot is blocked, too, and Matts ends up chasing the puck in a dangerous grapple with one of the Stars defensemen that takes them behind the goal and against the boards. Matts manages to tap it between his skates, twist with the man pinned behind him, and then pushes himself forward, lungs somehow cold and burning at the same time.

He wraps his stick around the goal at the same time that the defender crashes into him.

Matts doesn't see the puck go in because he's face down on the ice.

But he hears the goal horn.

They don't celebrate. First, because his brain feels like it's been rattled around his head, and his usual celly involves one-footed balance, which he isn't certain he can achieve at the moment. Second, because one goal isn't enough.

It's 2–1, and they have two minutes left to tie.

He meets Rome's eyes as Rome moves to take the next face-off.

Matts recognizes the grim desperation there.

They nod to each other, breathing heavily.

They'll do their best.

Except their best isn't good enough.

The Stars score an empty-netter forty seconds later.

The game ends 3–1.

The locker room is heavy with the quiet of disappointment.

No one talks on the bus.

An hour later, as they're checking into their hotel, his phone rings.

"Hey," Sydney says.

Matts makes a noise that might be a greeting.

"You tried so fucking hard," Sydney says. "So please tell me you're proud of the game you played and not beating yourself up about the loss."

"Don't wanna lie to you," he mutters, accepting his room card from the lady at the desk.

Sydney sighs at him.

Matts shifts his guitar case onto his back as he waits for the elevator and for Sydney to continue. He's too tired to put in his usual conversational effort.

"Are you still planning to go to the Drag Bingo thing tonight?" she asks.

Matts exhales. He was. There's a charity thing in Dallas—The Resource Center—that puts on a Drag Bingo night every month. Eli convinced several of the players to go with him that month because their game was early. And it'd be good PR since marketing was leaning into their whole accidental Gay Team branding and *it's for charity; come on, guys.*

"I don't know," Matts says. "Don't feel like going out. What are you doing?"

"We're watching some pretentious BBC thing on TV. We have to leave for the venue in ten minutes though," Devo says.

"Oh," Matts says. "Hi, Devo."

"You're on speakerphone," Sydney says belatedly. "Sorry."

"BBC thing?" Matts asks.

"Recording from Donmar's. The Scottish Play." She says it with an English accent.

"The Scottish Play," Matts repeats. "What's that?"

"'Macbeth,'" Devo says. "Shakespeare."

"Why not just say Macbeth?"

"I cannot," Sydney says solemnly.

"You can, you dramatic ninny," Devo mutters.

"We're not in a theater."

"What the hell are you talking about?" Matts says.

Devo sighs. "There's this superstition that you can't say 'Macbeth' in a theater, or terrible things will happen. But, again, we're not in a theater. We're in a tour bus."

"All the world's a stage," Sydney says.

Matts smiles as Devo makes vexed noises, and then he's pretty sure they devolve into a pillow fight. He reaches around to unhook his necklace, to slide the ring off the chain and put it back on his little finger.

"Okay, but you should go," Sydney says a moment later, sounding breathless. "Because A, it will maybe get you out of your post-loss funk, and B, I would love to go, but I'm in Kansas being a rock star. So I need to attend vicariously."

"Okay," Matts says, refastening the chain.

"Yeah? You'll go?"

I would do literally anything you ask me to, he doesn't say.

"Yeah, I'll go," he does say.

"Take pictures," she instructs. "And if you're up for it, call me after the show tonight?"

"Okay," he says. "And yes, please. Just text me when you're done."

*

THEY GET TO the club hosting bingo five minutes before the event is supposed to start.

"Holy shit," Rushy says as they join the line to collect their tickets. "How did I not know about this place?"

Matts doesn't think he's just talking about the club. Rather, the whole street it's located on is like some sort of…queer oasis. All the shops, restaurants, apartments, and bars are decked out in rainbows. Matts has never seen so many people of the same gender—or, in some cases, completely unidentifiable gender—in one place.

"The gayborhood is a beautiful place," Eli says. "It's probably good I didn't discover it until after I was in a committed relationship."

"I can pretend to pick you up at the bar later," Alex suggests. "And you can be as slutty as you want."

"Oh, *sir*." Eli bats his eyes. "You're too kind."

Matts shows his ID and ticket to the bouncer and then enters to buy an overpriced blotter. Up the stairs and past the stage, he follows Eli, who several people recognize and stop for hugs. Matts finds his seat at a table near the back, organizes his bingo cards, tests the lip balm that came in the little gift bag, and tries not to stare at…any of the people around him.

Apparently, they have a theme each month, and this one is disco-related, judging by the crowd's attire. There is a lot of spandex and sequins and neon and skin.

He feels extremely out of place.

Rushy and Eli appear at ease, but Rome looks just as uncomfortable as Matts feels.

"Have you ever been to something like this before?" Matts asks.

"No," Rome mutters. "Damien said it would be good for me."

"And we're not going to say 'bingo,'" a woman—is she a woman?—on the stage is saying. "We're going to say…"

"GAYBINGO," everyone in the crowd shouts back.

Matts glances back at Rome, but Rome is staring at the stage like he's not really seeing it.

"Make sure you don't use your phone while they're calling numbers," Eli murmurs to them. "They'll stick you in the little jail on the stage until someone pays to bail you out. It's one of the ways they raise money."

Matts tuck his phone securely in his back pocket. "What are they called?" He tries to keep his voice as low as possible.

"Who?"

"The…people all dressed up. With the microphones."

"The drag queens?"

"Are they women or men?"

"Oh. If you mean pronoun-wise, most queens like to use she-her when they're in drag."

The woman on the stage calls the first number.

They're three numbers in, and Matts is just starting to settle into the familiar pattern of blotting a bingo card. He grew up in a small town where there wasn't much to do on the weekends, and his mom loved bingo. Matts suspects this won't be like bingo in Gunnison though.

The queen pulling numbers calls out, "O-69."

Matts jumps when a good portion of the audience, including Eli and Rushy shout back, "OOOOooooh sixty-nine!"

It sounds…distinctly sexual.

Matts glances at Rome, who looks just as baffled.

"Oh dear," the queen in the crowd says, picking on one of the guys near the stage. "Judging by that lackluster performance, he's never had an *O* from sixty-nine, poor darling."

The guy sputters while his tablemates laugh.

The queen on the stage shouts, "I-16."

"…going on seventeen," the crowd sings.

Matts marks his card but looks up again, trying to figure out if he's missing prompts or something.

"B— Oh no, it's our least favorite number," the woman on stage says.

"Forty-five," the audience shouts back.

"Is there some kind of manual that you're supposed to read before coming to this?" Matts whispers to Eli.

"They're pretty typical calls and responses," Eli murmurs back. "You get used to them. I should take you to *Rocky Horror* sometime."

They both look at their cards to check for G-32.

"The movie? What do you mean 'take me'?"

"There are a bunch of theaters that run it during Halloween every year. People dress up and do callbacks. It's a whole thing."

"I went last year," Rome says on Eli's other side. "At Alamo in Katy. It's fun. Though some of the costumes are a little—" He pauses as they call O-61, and Matts realizes he's now one square away from a bingo.

"Not that I was complaining," Rome continues. "Damien went dressed as Rocky. Literally, gold shorts and nothing else. Though he ended up wearing my hoodie most of the night because it was fucking cold."

They pause again to mark G-43 and watch as someone who's been caught on their phone is hefted up to the stage while the people below chant, "Lock him up."

Matts is so preoccupied watching the guy laughingly protest as he sits in the little pretend jail that he nearly misses B-11.

And that's—

"Bingo!" he says, raising his blotter. "I mean, uh, *gaybingo*!"

One of the queens with a mic who had been doing some crowd work a few feet away, collecting bail money for the phone user, sashays over to him.

She says, "Let's see it, darling."

He hands over his card and tries not to be overwhelmed by the amount of perfume she's wearing. Or the amount of cleavage she's showing. It's shockingly realistic.

"All right, big boy, stand up and let us have a look at you."

Eli laughs unrepentantly beside him as Matts awkwardly stands, making sure to avoid accidentally stepping on Hawk.

"Honey, I could climb you like a tree," the queen says with a whistle. "How tall are you?"

"Six three. Six eight in skates," he answers automatically.

"An athlete!" she carols. "You know, around here,

we typically give our height in heels. But quick, some-one who knows sports—what's the Dallas hockey team called?"

"Stars!" multiple people supply.

"Are you one of our Stars, baby?"

"Uh, no. I play for the Houston Hell Hounds. We're…the Stars' biggest rival."

"The gay team!" someone shouts. Several others cheer.

"Ohhh, an *enemy*," she says, facing the front of the room. "And we've let the sly fox infiltrate our den."

"He can infiltrate my den anytime," someone close to the stage yells.

"Down, boy," she chastises, then returns her atten-tion to Matts. "Completely unrelated. Are you a single gay or a taken gay? I may not know hockey, but I know the captain of the Hell Hounds is married to that cutie chef with the dog."

Eli makes a strangled noise next to him.

"Oh, I'm not one of the gay ones," Matts says. "That's Alex. And Rome and Rushy? But only Alex is gay; Rome and Rushy are bi. So if you mean gay as a term including everyone within the, uh, spectrum of— It's a spectrum, right?"

"Oh, I could eat you for breakfast," the queen says.

"Please do not," he says. "But anyway, they're all taken. Sorry."

"What's your name, sweetheart?"

"Justin Matthews?" He says it like he isn't sure.

"Justin Matthews." She wiggles his card in the air. "You *do* have a gaybingo, and you *may* go collect your prize. Now, off with you. I believe I've just spotted Elijah Rodriguez, and is that Hawk? Oh, my word, I will not pet her. I know I can't, but the temptation is *strong*."

Matts makes his way to the table off to the side, where she points. He hands over his card to a girl with immaculate pink and purple eyeshadow. Her dress has so many rainbow sequins that he feels briefly off balance as if trapped in one of those rainbow kaleidoscope toys he used to play with at his grandmother's house when he was a kid. She's like a living disco ball.

Matts says this out loud, and she laughs while handing over his prize money.

"Don't spend it all in one place," she jokes.

"I was planning to just donate it back to one of the people walking around with the money tins."

"Well, in that case, by all means, spend it in one place."

Matts does end up tucking all the money, a few twenties at a time, into the various collection tins by the time the night is over. No one else in their group gets a bingo, but Eli, Alex, and Rushy clearly have an excellent time regardless.

Rome is quiet for the majority of the evening, laughing occasionally at the queens' antics and cursing colorfully when he's close to a bingo two different times but someone else wins first.

When the event is over, Alex and Eli stay at the club to dance, while Rushy heads to a nearby bar to meet up with one of the Stars players he's friendly with.

"Split an Uber to the hotel?" Matts asks Rome.

"I think I might walk around for a while, actually." Rome's looking at a teenage couple passing by holding hands. The taller girl is being pulled along behind the smaller one, laughingly protesting something. Rome's facial expression is difficult to read, but it almost looks like he's in pain.

"You want company?" Matts asks.

Rome's eyebrows go up. "I wouldn't turn it down. But I figure this isn't your scene."

He isn't wrong.

But Matts knows Rome's body. He knows how it's supposed to move. And Matts doesn't like the strange, tense way Rome has been holding himself for most of the evening.

"Let's go," he says.

Sydney's concert won't be over for another hour anyway.

They make their way past the shops and bars and apartments, maneuvering around the club-goers. When the crowds thin and the air quiets—no longer full of music bleeding from open doors—they turn back. After two circuits, Rome exhales in a way that might be a laugh. Matts doesn't like that either.

"We can call an Uber now," Rome says.

"Or we could make one more round," Matts suggests. He's out of his depth here.

Rome studies him, hands in his pockets, eyes pale and bright, reflecting the neon of club sign lights. He bites his bottom lip, and his teeth are a jarring contrast against his dark-freckled skin. "I appreciate the show of solidarity, man, but I don't think it'll make a difference."

"Make a difference with what?"

Rome looks away. He rubs one palm over the crown of his buzzed head as he shakes it. "I have no idea how to even begin explaining that to you."

"Because I'm not...gay?"

"No. Yes. I don't know. It's just—" His hand comes off his head to gesture, to encompass the everything of the rainbow-lit street. "Half of me feels like I've finally found a place where I can take a full breath, and the other half feels… I don't know. Even more out of place than I usually do."

Matts doesn't follow.

"I wasn't closeted," Rome says. "As a kid. Not exactly. I just didn't date anyone. Boys or girls. I wasn't tortured or depressed; I never had a crisis or anything. I liked who I liked, and I ignored all of it because I had hockey. And I was so focused on hockey the rest of it didn't matter until—"

"Damien," they say together.

"I'm not like Alex," Rome says. "I didn't suffer because of what I am. But I'm not like Eli or Damien either. I didn't fight for acceptance. I wasn't brave. I didn't have any of the—"

Rome exhales hard, lacing his fingers together at the back of his neck as he looks up at the sky. "I feel like either pain or triumph or some combination of both is the foundation of being queer. I'm— I probably have nothing in common with the people here. I can't imagine we share many of the same experiences."

Matts thinks about his conversation with Sydney the week before when he told her he was going with Eli to the fundraiser.

Oh, I'm jealous, she'd murmured. *The Gayborhood in*

Dallas is one of the few places in Texas I feel completely safe. I cannot describe the relief I felt walking down Cedar Springs for the first time. It was like dropping something heavy I didn't even realize I'd been carrying.

"Do you feel safe here?" Matts asks.

Rome rocks his head to one side and squints at Matts. "Yeah?"

"Like, safer than you would walking downtown or something?"

"Sure," Rome says. It sounds like a question.

"I'm not good with body language. But you walk differently when you hold hands with Damien in public. And you look around like you're expecting a fight."

"I mean, 95 percent of the time, people don't give a shit. But that 5 percent makes you overthink things the rest of the time."

"So, you wouldn't overthink things if Damien was here now. You wouldn't look over your shoulder before you kissed him?"

"No," Rome says slowly. "I wouldn't."

"You have that in common with everyone here, then," Matts points out. "That's one thing."

Rome breathes, slow and deep. He stares at Matts like he's done something surprising.

"What?" Matts asks.

Rome touches his fist to Matts's upper arm, two light taps, knuckles against the skin of his bicep. "Have you ever thought about meeting your past self? What that'd be like?"

Matts doesn't enjoy the exercise. "I'd probably want to punch him in the face."

Rome grins. "Fair. You mind doing one more lap? And then we'll get you back to the hotel so you can wait by the phone for Sydney to call."

The rest of their walk is completed in silence, but Rome's posture has slackened into something more natural. Easy.

Matts realizes he'd feel safer holding hands with Sydney here too. He wouldn't be worried for her safety. He thinks maybe he should suggest taking a weekend trip together. Matts knows she likes dancing. He'd try to dance for her if it would make her happy. Maybe they could come during Pride month? He needs to figure out when Pride month is.

Matts thinks, abstractly, about what that would be like. Drinking with Sydney. Dancing with Sydney. Getting to go home with her at the end of the night. Waking up with her in the morning.

He wants it.

All of it.

All of her.

*

"HOW'S THE ROCK star this evening?" Matts asks in lieu of saying hello when his phone rings an hour later.

"Tired," the rock star says. "Concert was great. Leaving the venue was shit."

"Protestors?"

"Protestors. Not many. But they were loud. Also, my voice is fucked, so I can't talk long."

Sydney's voice is delightfully rough. Hearing it through the phone isn't the same as hearing it pressed against his neck after a night of post-drive singing, but it still makes his chest feel oddly buoyant. The words counteract some of the charm of the tone though.

"I'm sorry. Anything I can do?"

"I could use a hug," Sydney says.

"Two weeks," Matts points out. "And then I'll hug you all you want." He's aiming for flippant, but it comes out more cautious than anything else.

"Two weeks," she agrees.

"Speaking of, I know you're only home for a couple of days, but would—and it's totally fine if you don't want to, so don't feel like you have to say yes. And you can think about it; you don't have to answer now—"

"Matts."

"Right." He breathes. "Would you want to stay with me for a night or two? Asher moved in with his girlfriend, so it would just be us. I don't have any expectations or anything. But—"

"I thought we agreed you have tenure now," Sydney says.

Matts can't formulate a response to that.

"Yes, I'd like to stay with you," she clarifies.

"Good," he manages. "Great." He clears his throat, reaching for his laptop. "Until then, do you want some cursed knowledge?"

She groans, voice going muffled for a moment. "Could you give me whatever the opposite of cursed knowledge is? Like, something that will restore my faith in humanity?"

He closes his laptop.

"Yeah, I can do that. Are you ready?"

He hears her sheets rumple as she changes position. "Ready."

"Okay. So. On April 14th, 1912, the ship *RMS Titanic* was several hundred miles off the coast of Newfoundland. Due to a combination of greed, entitlement, and a false sense of invincibility, it hit an iceberg just before midnight and quickly started to sink. It was only equipped with enough lifeboats for maybe a third of the people onboard. The crew hadn't been appropriately trained, so they didn't know the capacity of the lifeboats, meaning many of them were lowered into the water only half-full. The captain radioed for assistance and sent up distress flares, but the only ship within close proximity, the *SS California*, didn't respond. The air temperature was freezing, and the water temperature was actually below freezing. Saltwater freezes around twenty-eight degrees, and it was right at that, meaning even those who made it into the lifeboats probably wouldn't survive until morning."

"I said restore my faith, not shatter it completely," Sydney mutters.

"Shhh, be patient."

"Of course, apologies. Please proceed."

"The *RMS Carpathia* was sixty miles away. Now, the *Carpathia* was a small, slow, barebones ship. Her top speed was fourteen knots, which is, like, sixteen miles per hour, though she rarely worked her way up to that speed."

"How fast could the *Titanic* go?" Sydney asks.

"Twenty-four knots, and she was doing around twenty-two when she hit the iceberg. So, in the small, slow *Carpathia*, the operator—who wasn't even supposed to be on duty—hears the distress call on the radio, and he wakes up the captain just past midnight. Now, the captain knows that even at their top speed of fourteen knots, it would take at least four hours to reach the *Titanic*. He also knows they shouldn't be doing anything near fourteen knots because visibility is shit, and the water is full of icebergs."

"Like the one that took out the *Titanic*."

"Correct. But the captain—his name was Rostron— he said, fuck it, we're going to do our best. Rostron woke up his crew and all the passengers, and everyone got to work. They rigged all the lights they could find to illuminate their path in the water. They readied lifeboats. Passengers prepared their own staterooms with blankets and warm clothes for incoming survivors. They turned the larger community areas of the ship into triage and hospital spaces and diverted all power to the engines and the kitchens, where they boiled water for hot drinks and made soup. And, most dangerously, Captain Rostron had the engineers push the ship way faster than she was ever made to go."

Sydney makes an intrigued noise. "How fast?"

"Seventeen knots. She maintained seventeen knots, through iceberg-infested water, in the middle of the night, for three hours, arriving to rescue the *Titanic*'s survivors just as many of them in the lifeboats were succumbing to hypothermia and their injuries. Hundreds had already died, and if the *Carpathia*'s crew and passengers hadn't decided to risk their lives, pushing the little ship past her top speed, hundreds more probably would have died."

"Holy shit."

"Most stories about the *Titanic*, even the movie about the *Titanic*, all note how few survivors there were. Only seven hundred of the two-thousand-something people made it back alive. But those seven hundred only lived because a tiny steamliner's crew and passengers chose to risk their lives for the chance to save the lives of strangers sixty miles away."

Sydney makes a humming noise.

"I've always thought," Matts says, "that the rescue made for a better story than the reasons behind the ship sinking to begin with."

"No kidding."

"Is that what you needed?" he asks after several seconds of silence.

"Yes," she says, soft and warm and so intimate it hurts. "That was perfect. Thank you."

Matts doesn't know how to respond to that.

"Two weeks," he says as if either of them needs reminding.

"Two weeks," Sydney repeats.

Chapter Sixteen

MATTS PICKS SYDNEY up at the airport again.

Unlike her trip to Gunnison where she flew entirely under the radar—pun intended—here, she's deplaning first class with the rest of the band in full band-appropriate getup. Many of the good people populating the George Bush Intercontinental Airport recognize them.

There are several folks with their phones out at the baggage claim as they come down the escalator, and Rex is quickly besieged by a gaggle of teenage girls asking for photos.

A couple people try to catch Sydney's attention as well, but *her* attention is entirely caught by Matts. She tries to suppress a grin when she sees him waving at her and then remembers she doesn't have to anymore.

> *You ok with PDA at the airport, or nah?* she'd texted him as they boarded the plane.

> *PDA is my favorite,* he'd answered.

> *What if I throw myself at you?*

> *I'll catch you.*

And he does.

Sydney spares a moment to wonder if he realizes the domino effect it could have when, inevitably, someone's pictures end up online. But he gave her an invitation, and she's hardly going to turn it down.

She jumps the last few steps of the escalator, dumps her backpack off her shoulder mid-run, and crashes into him.

Matts scoops one arm under her ass, wraps his hand around her thigh, and settles her on his hip as though he's planning to keep her there for a while. The other hand ends up around the nape of her neck, fingers in her hair, pulling their faces together.

"Hey." He bumps his nose against hers. "I missed you."

And then he just…holds her there. With *one* arm.

Sydney kicks her feet. "You are completely destroying my credibility right now."

"Right. As a…sexy, stoic enigma."

"A facade I maintained until you showed up and ruined everything." It's meant to come out dramatic. Instead, it's a little too honest.

"I'm not sorry," Matts mutters against her mouth.

She's not either when he kisses her.

"Should I put you down?" Matts asks. "For your credibility?"

"I mean, it's already fucked, so—"

"Hey, Matts, if you could maybe not ravish my sister while within my sightlines, I would greatly appreciate it," Devo says behind them.

Sydney flips him off.

"If that's your way of saying we should get a room, I'm happy to oblige. I'll see y'all at the house tomorrow," Sydney says, waving over Matts's shoulder to Sky and Rex.

Sky nods toward the carousel. "You don't want to wait for your bag?"

"I've got toiletries and underwear. Matts has T-shirts, food, and guitars."

"What else could you possibly need?" Rex says

dryly.

Matts stoops to pick up her backpack and slings one strap over his shoulder without dislodging her even a little. The man is stupidly strong.

"What time are we practicing tomorrow?" Sky asks. "Morning?"

"I would prefer afternoon," Sydney says as primly as possible, considering she's still wrapped around her—whatever Matts is.

"Gross," Devo mutters.

"Respect," Sky says.

"One p.m.," Rex says.

"Deal," Sydney agrees. She rests one elbow on Matts's shoulder so she can pat his head imperiously. "Take me home, Jeeves."

"Yes, ma'am," he says.

His car is freshly detailed and immaculate, with vacuum lines on the floor mats. It smells like leather cleaner and the same glass spray that she uses on the windscreen of her motorcycle. Maybe Matts didn't clean it just for her. Maybe he cleans his car every weekend, and her arrival is just a coincidence. But Sydney gets a small thrill imagining him in his garage, wiping down the seat with the expectation that she'd be sitting in it later. She likes the idea that she matters enough that he'd prepare for her.

"I read the stuff you sent me," he says.

Sydney is abruptly no longer thinking about leather and glass cleaner.

She sent Matts a zip file of some very dry medical papers about sexual changes pre-op trans women can expect on HRT and some links to less-dry blogs and vlogs by trans women discussing experiences and preferences that align with hers.

Sydney emailed the file late one night the week before when she was post-concert high on endorphins, slightly drunk, and just brave enough to press Send. The subject line was 'So you know what you're getting into,' and the body of the email was empty. Possibly, she could have better prepared him for the contents of the attachment.

The only response she received from him referencing it was a text a few hours later:

Thanks for the sex research. I'll work on my plays.

Adorable. Devastating. Sydney actively forced herself not to think too much about it since, or at least right up until the day before, when she started second-guessing all her life choices and texted him:

You still want me to spend the night tomorrow?

He answered almost immediately: *I've already set aside another shirt for you to borrow and conveniently forget to return.*

So. Sydney was reasonably sure he at least skimmed the stuff she sent him, but she also assumed they'd have this conversation once they were back at his place, not on I-69.

Though, if they're going to have a sex conversation while driving, maybe I-69 is one of the more suitable locations. Considering.

"Oh?" she manages.

"Yeah. And then I spent some time on Reddit, found some forums, and asked some questions there too. They were helpful."

"Okay."

"And I subscribed to this one girl's OnlyFans." Matts glances sideways at Sydney as if unsure what her reaction will be.

She has no idea what her face is doing, but it can't be too terrible because he continues.

"She's actually a couple months post-op now, but the majority of her content is from the last year when she was pre-op. I've been watching her stuff, and it's been— Uh. Educational."

His ears, she realizes, are pink.

"I just figured you should know," Matts says

"That is so much more than I expected of you. Like. Way more."

"I want to be prepared. I want to make sure you enjoy anything we do."

"I can see that," Sydney says faintly. "Except now I feel like I'm *under*prepared. Do you have preferences I should know about? Things you dislike? You've done all this research to make sure it's good for me, and I'm— I have no idea how to make it good for *you*."

He looks askance at her. "That's not going to be a problem."

"Matts."

"Sydney," he says reasonably.

She kind of wants to punch him. But, like, gently. "I'm just saying. You did all this work."

"Watching a hot lady get off wasn't exactly a hardship."

Sydney takes a moment to hide behind her hands. "This conversation would be a lot less mortifying if it weren't happening in broad daylight."

"The sun is setting," Matts points out, reaching over to snag her wrist closest to him. He slides his fingers down her palm and pulls their linked hands to rest on her thigh. He's clearly gearing up to say something when her phone, tucked between her leg and the seat next to their joined hands, lights up.

> *Check ur tags on IG,* Devo advises. Before Sydney can respond, he follows it with: *Be safe. Text me by 10pm or I WILL show up at his door, and it WILL be awkward for everyone.*

She thumbs-up the second message and swipes to the Instagram app.

Sure enough, there are multiple pictures of her and Matts at the airport. In all of them, she's the only one tagged, and people are trying to determine the identity of the, as one person terms it, "giant mullet man" in the picture. There's one post near the top, though, where the most-liked comment, with over one thousand likes already, has correctly identified Matts. The next most-liked comment points out that Matts has been photographed backstage at Red Right Hand concerts, and Sydney has been photographed attending Hell Hounds games. The speculation continues, and gets more ridiculous, the further she scrolls.

"What?" he says.

"There are pictures of us on social media already.

From the airport. Most of them haven't figured out who you are yet, but a couple have, and it's only a matter of time before your IG gets flooded with comments and messages and shit."

"So?"

"So, people think we're together," she says.

His hand tightens around hers. "Are we not?"

In the ensuing silence, Matts tries to focus on the road, but he keeps cutting his eyes over to her. His hair is in his face, his top teeth are pressed into his bottom lip, and his hand is warm and a little damp around hers.

If he can be brave enough to ask, she can be brave enough to answer.

"I'd like us to be," she says.

He exhales. "Good."

"Good," she agrees.

They grin stupidly at each other for a moment before he swears, pulling his hand out of hers so he can swerve around a car that suddenly slams on their brakes in front of them.

"Maybe we should table this conversation until we're not on the highway," Sydney suggests, forearm braced against the passenger window.

"That's probably wise," he agrees.

*

SOPHOMORE YEAR OF high school, a week before school let out for the summer, Sydney found a note in her locker from Bryce Shaw.

Bryce was a junior, a football player, and firmly embedded in the popular portion of the student body. So when she unfolded the note from Bryce, asking her to meet him under the sports field bleachers during the junior/senior lunch period, which coincided with her study hall period, Sydney was suspicious.

The space under the bleachers, hidden from campus view by the concession stand, was a well-known make-out spot at the high school. There was no reason Bryce Shaw would want to meet her there aside from the usual, and the usual made no sense.

"Him and his stupid friends are planning some Carrie shit for sure," Sky advised when Sydney told her and Rex at lunch.

"You're not planning to *go*, are you?" Rex asked.

Oh, but she was.

And she did.

There wasn't a group of football players lying in wait as she expected. Only Bryce Shaw in his polo and his letterman jacket, shifting a little anxiously from foot to foot as she stalked across the parking lot to meet him, arms crossed, boots muddied, the knife Devo gave her freshman year in her pocket.

"Well?" she said.

And he shocked her when he asked if maybe they could hang out that summer.

"Why?" probably wasn't the most elegant response, but it was the only one she could come up with.

"I'd just like to," he said. And he seemed to mean it.

Sydney didn't know if *she* wanted to hang out with *him* that summer; she never thought it was within the realm of possibility. But the concept was novel enough that she agreed to give him her number, albeit with a healthy degree of caution. It wasn't until several weeks, several meetups, several long text-threads and late-night conversations later, that she stopped waiting for the other shoe to drop. She stopped waiting for him to admit it was all part of a prank or some long-game gotcha.

Bryce was sweet and funny and a little awkward. He loved science fiction, Legos, and astronomy. He was good at football, but he didn't like it, only played because it made people like him. He talked to her about his anxiety. About the stars. He talked to her about things he said he couldn't talk to anyone else about.

And she liked him.

Sydney kept waiting to feel more than that, but she also never really let herself believe that it was real. Because summer was a liminal space. They met up on horseback at the creek just past the ranch's back pasture line and a mile from Bryce's dad's land. He came to the band's practices. Swam in their pool. But he never asked her to his house or the movie theater or the diner or to drive into the city with him. Sydney knew she was a secret. She recognized the pattern easily enough. So she let him hold her hand. And she let him kiss her. But she didn't let him do anything more. And she didn't let herself get attached.

When school started again, and Bryce wouldn't so much as look at her in the hallway, when he said, "My friends wouldn't understand; won't it be easier if we just keep things the way they are?" it hurt. But it didn't hurt like it would have if she hadn't been careful. It was a hollow comfort, but it was better than heartbreak.

Sydney let it continue for a while, meeting Bryce on weekends, acting like a stranger during the week. She thought he might change his mind if she gave him a little more time. But then, on an otherwise ordinary Wednesday, one of Bryce's football friends grabbed Sydney in the hallway, one hand wrapped in her backpack strap, the other clamped with bruising force around her opposite arm. He dragged her to the men's restroom, shoved her inside, and then held the door while she rammed her shoulder against it, trying to get out.

And Bryce was there.

He didn't help hold the door. He didn't laugh when a teacher finally intervened, and she managed to stumble back into the hallway, panting and furious.

But he didn't try to stop them.

Sydney never spoke to him again.

She finds herself thinking about Bryce as she crouches to unlace her boots just inside Matts's front door. As she tosses her leather jacket over the back of his couch. As he ushers her into the bathroom to shower the last dozen hours of travel off her skin. As she pulls on the shirt he's left for her on the counter. As she looks at her reflection in the steamed mirror and tries to be objective. Tries to look at herself as Matts will see her: flushed and damp and too wide-eyed.

She's pretty. Mostly. Her hair is more curl than frizz and her skin has been shockingly cooperative despite the stress she's been under. She's proud of her body. She thinks it's beautiful most days. But that's no guarantee that Matts will like it, and while she'd love to say she doesn't care about his opinion, that couldn't be further from the truth. She wants him to be attracted to her. So much it makes her feel a little crazy.

Sydney thinks about the one time Bryce tried to slip his hand up her shirt, fingers pushing at the bottom hem of her sports bra. She caught his wrist, met his eyes, and he relocated his hand safely to the nape of her neck, kissing her, gentle and sweet in apology.

"Whenever you're ready," he said.

She was never ready. Not with him. Not really with anyone.

She's ready, now.

Sydney points to herself in the mirror. *Don't fuck this up,* she mouths at her reflection. And then, she pushes open the door to the bedroom and closes it behind her. She leans back against the door, weight on her heels, toes pointed. Sydney looks down at them so she doesn't have to look at Matts sitting on the bed.

She painted her nails the night before, a blue-black with gold flecks that look like the night sky. She thought it might give her some little measure of confidence when it came time to get naked. It isn't working.

"Hey," Matts says, pausing, hands mid-spin on a Rubik's Cube.

It's dark in his room, the only light coming from the

lamp in the corner and the streetlight bleeding through the half-closed curtains. His shadowed expression falls as he takes her in. "Are you okay?"

She is not okay.

She wants to say: *I'm terrified that I'm already in love with you, and if I show you all of myself and you find me lacking, I'm not sure if I'll survive it.*

But she can't.

Mostly because he would *hear* her.

"Peachy," she says instead.

Matts glances at the unfinished cube in his hands and then sets it aside on the nightstand.

"I did make it clear," he says. "I have zero expectations about what we do this weekend. Right? Like we can get out the guitars or watch a movie or—anything you want."

"I want *you*," she says, honest and damning. "Badly. And I want to show you how badly. I just don't know how to—" Sydney waves one hand fruitlessly before crossing her arms. "I know I gave you the impression that I was experienced, but my experience is actually pretty minimal, and I'm freaking out a little."

Matts starts to stand and then sits right back down again. "How minimal?"

"I've kissed a dozen people and hooked up with

two. Sort of."

"What does 'sort of' mean?"

"It means I've never had an orgasm in the presence of another person," she says, mostly exhaled rather than spoken. "Or been fully naked." Because that's probably something he should know.

His expression doesn't change; he just keeps looking at her. Steady. Intense.

"I would like to change both of those things," he says.

"Yeah, so I gathered. That's what's freaking me out. If all I had to worry about was getting *you* off, I'd be less worried. And obviously I want to"—she gestures between them— "with you. It's just…"

She breathes: inhale four seconds. Exhale five.

Her voice is rough when she speaks again. "Usually, I get by with bravado when I'm doing something for the first time. But this isn't something I can BS my way through."

"Okay."

Matts shifts, bracing elbows on knees and lacing fingers together, head ducked to study them, brows pinched.

"What if—" He pauses, touching his tongue to his bottom lip. "I used to do this thing when I was a kid.

Not that I think you need, like, childish coping mecha-
nisms or anything, but I still do it sometimes now as an
adult. I came up with it when I was a kid and used it a
lot more then. And it's going to sound stupid, but it also
works most of the time, so—"

"Matts."

"Right." He laughs softly. "Sorry. But sometimes,
I'll act like I've already done whatever the thing is that's
making me anxious. And I talk myself through the steps
I took to do it. Out loud. So, what if you told me what
you want us to do in the past tense. Like we've already
done it. Would that help?"

"Past tense," Sydney repeats.

"Most things aren't as scary the second time you do
them."

That's…accurate. She still isn't sure what he means
though.

"So," Matts continues, attention still on his hands.
"For example, I watched you come out of the bathroom,
wearing my shirt and nothing else, and"—he nods to the
Rubik's Cube—"I completely lost track of the sequence.
Because all I could think about was touching you. But I
didn't know if that was allowed."

"It was," she says slowly. "I wanted you to. I was
just—"

Weeks of filling up the Notes app on her phone and the spiral in her bunk with words words *words*, and now they've all run out when she needs them.

"I was nervous."

"I was too," he says, finally looking up, meeting her eyes. "Because I didn't want to fuck things up. I may have slept with other people before but no one I cared about or wanted to keep, and you're—" He looks back down, twists his hands to study his palms. "You're important to me. So, it was a first time for me too."

Sydney uses her shoulder to push off the door, not quite brave but as close as she's going to get, and moves to stand between his knees. She thinks she gets it now.

"I kissed you," she says.

Matts tips his face up, and like this, with him sitting and her standing, they're nearly eye-to-eye. He unlaces his fingers so he can settle his hands on her hips. He leans into her and only stops when their noses are practically touching.

"You kissed me," he agrees, breath against her mouth.

It's easy to close the space between them after that. Maybe it's because Matts is right, and she's tricked herself into some past-tense-related confidence; maybe it's because of the way he's looking at her. But it's easy. Like most things are with Matts.

And it's easy for Sydney to step closer until her knees butt against the mattress, easy to open her mouth under his and wrap her arms around his neck.

Matts tips his face to the side to let them breathe, then rocks their foreheads together. Her eyelashes catch against his.

"You took off my shirt," Sydney whispers into the warm pocket of air between them.

Her heartbeat is so loud in her ears she barely hears Matts's sharp intake of breath. He moves slowly, palms sliding down to cup the back of her thighs. When they slide back up, this time against skin, the fabric of her shirt collects in a well between his thumbs. Matts doesn't look at her body as it's exposed — he looks at her face, eyes dark and focused entirely on hers as his fingertips trail up her ribs until she raises her arms and her vision obscures. He stands to free her wrists from her shirt, the heat of him pressed against her. And then his hands are on her face again, two fingers in front of her ears, two behind them, his thumbs pressed, gentle but unyielding, to her cheekbones.

"You were so fucking beautiful," Matts says, hard and a little angry, as if he needs her to believe it. "And knowing no one else had seen you like that, that I was the first, made me feel—things I probably shouldn't."

"Things like what?"

"Possessive things," he grinds out.

He's restraining himself again. Sydney feels the tension in his hands and sees it in his arms and shoulders where he's ducked to keep his face close to hers. It should feel dangerous, maybe, having someone so much bigger than her looming like that. Holding her like that. But she feels safe. And she feels brave.

"I like that you're possessive," Sydney says, and her lips catch against his. "I wish you'd stop being so careful with me."

He straightens abruptly, reaching behind him to grab his shirt and pull it off in one fluid, stupidly compelling movement. He pops the button on his jeans. He doesn't look for her permission before shoving them down his thighs, before kicking off his boxers and crowding back into her space, toppling them over onto the bed. And then she has a solid expanse of naked hockey player on top of her. He's heavy in a way that feels grounding. Perfect.

But Sydney has to admit, in the face of his shadowed chest and the curve of his shoulders and what might be banked desperation in his eyes, that she loves him. She's so in love with him it feels as if her ribs have been cracked open. But the vulnerability seems less like a death sentence when he braces his elbows on either side of her head and carefully pushes hair out of her face, looking at her like she's something worth the gentleness in his hands. Matts implied before that he wanted to keep her. Sydney can almost believe it, given the way he's touching her.

Her heart is racing for an entirely different reason now. Sydney hears him swallow. She watches his throat move.

"I wanted to go slow," Matts says. "I didn't want to scare you."

"I wasn't scared. I trusted you."

"You trusted me," he repeats as though she's given him a gift.

"I did. I do."

This time, when he kisses her, he doesn't stop.

Chapter Seventeen

MATTS WAKES SYRUP-slow to sunlight on his face and the even breathing of someone sleeping beside him.

Sydney sleeping beside him.

The sun tips through the curtains they left half-open the night before, highlighting the fine hairs on Sydney's upper arms, distinct and golden between the slanted shadows painted over her. Everything feels oversaturated in the early-morning light: Her tattoos are a riot of blacks and blues, reds and yellows; the edge of her teeth, barely visible between parted chapped-pink lips, are a stark white; a dozen different shades of brown shine in the curls spilling across her pillow and partially obscuring her face. Matts watches as slow-moving dust motes circle Sydney's still form; he watches with a possessive thrill as her chest moves beneath his shirt, and with sudden clarity, it comes to him that he is well and truly fucked.

There's no uncertainty anymore.

He's in love with her.

Now, he just has to figure out how to keep his feelings in his chest and not in his mouth long enough so that maybe she'll fall for him, too, and then they can both be terrifyingly beholden to each other.

Matts shifts, sitting up in a careful forward crunch, and slowly, so slowly, pushes her hair out of her face. He strokes a finger down the soft wispy curls at the nape of her neck. He resists the urge to press his thumb to the pale bruise under the hinge of her jaw even though the animal thing in his ribcage demands it.

Matts knows that humans are most vulnerable when sleeping and evolved the capacity for recuperative, deep, sound sleep because they could. With cooperation and trust, humans developed a method to resist predation that many other species didn't.

He watches Sydney breathe, realizing her trust feels like a responsibility. He wants to be worthy of it. He wants to *show* her he's worthy of it. He wants to touch her. Maybe even more than he did before. Now, Matts knows what the weight of her feels like in his arms.

He goes to make coffee. Staying in bed is no longer an option.

When Matts returns, two mugs in hand, Sydney has roused enough to locate and put on her glasses but is still sprawled out, rumpled and ethereal in a tangle of sheets. She's muttering something about the sunlight's audacity and writing an angry letter to the solar system.

He sets Syd's mug on the bedside table as she probably can't be trusted to keep it upright yet. Also, he doesn't trust himself to touch her right now, feeling as much as he is. Wanting as much as he does.

A brush of fingers could be his downfall.

"Oh God, I love you," Sydney mutters, wiggling toward the coffee. Matts nearly trips over the rug that has been in the center of the bedroom since the day he moved into the apartment. He decides a shower is in order.

When he returns, damp, cold, and with what feels like a better grasp on his dignity, Sydney is sitting up in the bed. She still doesn't look entirely aware of her surroundings, but Matts isn't worried for the safety of his sheets anymore as she cradles the mug in her hands.

"Mmph," Sydney says as Matts moves to the closet

to find a pair of sweats.

"Good morning to you too," he says.

"I slept for nine hours," Sydney mutters, voice creaky from disuse. "I can't remember the last time I slept nine hours straight."

Her hair is a positive riot of bedhead. He wants to see her like this every morning.

"Do you need to get a topper for your bed in the tour bus?" he asks.

"I think it's more related to the company than the bed," Sydney says, completely without artifice.

She's smiling softly at him as she sips her coffee, and Matts can't help but follow the line of her throat as she swallows. A pair of moles rests just where the stretched collar of his shirt falls over her collarbone. He knows what they taste like now.

Matts looks away. "I guess I don't snore then?"

"You don't. And I feel safe here."

"You don't feel safe at home? Or when you're traveling?"

"No, I do. But I sleep lighter, usually. Small noises wake me. But last night—" Sydney gestures toward the bed. Toward him. "You took the side closest to the door. And I think subconsciously, I felt, I don't know... like I could...relax. Like you wouldn't let anything happen to me."

She's doing this on purpose, he thinks. She has to be.

"That's true." Matts does not reach for her and counts it as a personal victory.

Sydney yawns into her mug before swinging her legs off the bed and standing, one hand clutching the coffee to her chest, one fisted and stretched up toward the ceiling.

"Breakfast?" she asks.

The morning is slow—scrambling chicken-spinach eggs and buttering toast interspersed with small teasing sips of kisses before Sydney pulls him back into the bedroom. She eats her food while mostly in his lap. And then she stays there, demanding that Matts show her his electric guitar skills.

It's awkward, playing with her pressed between his chest and his guitar, but it's also sort of perfect, especially when it devolves into her trying to finger the strings while he mans the fret for a truly discordant rendition of "Layla."

Sydney's just as reluctant as he is when they have to leave, and she holds his hand in the car, singing along softly to the radio, hair in her face, smiling into the wind. When he parks at the ranch, Sydney dramatically proclaims she's lost the ability to walk, and perhaps, he should take her back home with him and provide some sexual healing. Matts makes the obvious decision to pick her up and carry her inside while she sings Marvin Gaye in his ear.

"I come bearing your lead singer and guitarist," Matts calls to the assorted people in the living room. "Where should I put her?"

"Oh, wherever there's space," Sky says, gesturing magnanimously to the couch.

Except when Matts moves to dump Sydney on the empty cushions, she tucks her face, oh so sweetly, into his neck…and sinks her teeth into his shoulder.

"*Ow*," Matts says and sits with her in his lap instead, which was probably her goal.

"What?" Devo asks.

"She fucking bit me," Matts says.

"Maybe don't sound so pleased about it," Rex suggests.

"Or look so enamored," Devo adds.

"Sorry. I don't have any control over that." Matts doesn't sound sorry. Probably because he isn't.

"Disgusting," Devo proclaims.

"Oh, you are *not* one to talk," Sydney says over Matts's shoulder. "We had to put up with your slut era.

You can handle a little light biting."

"Facts," Sky agrees. "Nothing Sydney does will ever surpass the Flamingo Incident."

"Slut era?" Matts repeats. "*Flamingo* Incident?"

"We don't need to discuss it," Devo says.

"It involves Devo's pasty ass, a sorority girl, and a large but honestly not large enough flamingo-shaped pool floaty," Rex explains.

"Stop talking, or I'll quit, and you'll have to find a real manager," Devo threatens.

They all consider the hassle that would entail and, evidently, decide silence is the best option.

"Thought so," Devo mutters.

Sydney reaches for the acoustic guitar propped against the arm of the sofa and pulls it into her lap, nearly hitting Matts in the face with the headstock. She strums a few cords.

"Hey, Deevs, speaking of managerial duties and nudity, did you hear back from the *Rolling Stone* people about the pictures they want to use?"

Sydney leans her head back to whisper into Matts's ear, "These photographers are obsessed with getting me naked."

"Same," he whispers back.

Devo sighs. "They sent the proofs. I can show them

to you later."

"Judging by your tone, you're willing to admit I have grounds for concern, then."

"Maybe," Devo says.

She picks out a lazy scale. "I have so many grounds I'm the master of an estate. I'm landed gentry with all these grounds. I'm high society."

"Yes, Syd. Fine. Jesus."

She strums for emphasis. "I dine with four and twenty families!"

"Oh, look, we made it two minutes before our first literary reference. I think that's a record."

"You recognized it."

"I've been indoctrinated against my will."

"Sorry," Matts says. "What was the literary reference?"

"Jane Austen," everyone present says.

"'*Pride and Prejudice*,'" Devo specifies.

Sydney pretends to wipe away a tear. "I'm so proud."

"I still don't get why you don't want to embrace your role as rock's new sex icon," Sky says. "I guarantee those pictures are bomb."

"I'm a sexual icon in the same way that a potato is a battery," Sydney says.

"Disagree," Matts says. "Hard disagree."

"Gross," Devo mutters.

He doesn't want to, but... "I need to go," Matts says, shifting Sydney out of his lap so he can stand. "You'll be at the game tomorrow?"

"I will."

"Good."

"Good," she agrees, grinning up at him.

"Oh, just fucking kiss already," Sky mutters.

They do.

*

MATTS'S DAD CALLS him the following morning. Nine hours before their fifth—and final, if they lose—game in the second series of their playoff run.

Other guys, they might expect a pep talk. Encouragement.

Matts has been expecting a call for a different reason.

He sits down and retrieves his Rubik's Cube before answering on speaker.

"Dad," he says.

"That girl you brought home with you," he starts because God forbid they exchange pleasantries. "Karl says she's a transexual."

Of course it was fucking Karl.

"Transgender," Matts corrects. "And Syd's a lot of things. The transgender part doesn't even make the list of top five most interesting things about her."

His dad ignores the deflection. "Son, the tattoos and the clothes I could handle, but this—"

"I'm not asking your permission," Matts interrupts. "Just so we're clear."

His dad's voice goes flinty. "Justin. It isn't right. You have to see that she, or he, or whatever—it isn't *right*."

"I get that this is a shock to you," Matts says levelly. "But I need you to understand that you're talking about the woman I love. So, if you can't be respectful, I *will* hang up on you. And we won't speak again until you can be respectful."

He practiced those sentences. He workshopped them. Tried different inflections for emphasis. He said them to himself in the mirror. In the car. Because he knew how his dad would react when he found out, and Matts wanted to be ready. He's spent most of his life fumbling through arguments, unable to get his words out the way he wanted, inelegant and embarrassed by his fumbling. He needed to be better than that for Sydney. So, he practiced. And he's proud that his voice doesn't waver.

His dad says nothing for several seconds, and then, "You love her?"

"I do."

"I thought you said you weren't together."

"We weren't when we had that conversation."

"How long?"

"Since that night in Gunnison, actually. She heard what I said to you. About how if she showed the slightest bit of interest, I'd get on my knees for her." Matts solves the cube with a last, deft twist of his fingers. "She showed interest."

He gets a vicious enjoyment from his father's heavy silence.

"You know what people are saying about you online?" he says finally.

Matts slides the cube into the GAN ROBOT. "I cannot emphasize enough that I do not care what strangers on the internet think about me or my relationship."

"It could impact your career."

"You said the same thing about staying with the Hell Hounds after Alex and Rushy came out," Matts reminds him. It was probably the biggest fight they ever had. Another one where Matts tripped over his words and ended the call wanting to punch something. Or cry.

"And then, we won the Stanley Cup, made it to the final the following year, and my contract renewal last year was three times what I was making before."

"You'll be out in the second round this year," his dad says.

It's cruel. But it's also true. He knows their odds of winning their game tonight, much less somehow crawling back from a 3–1 deficit, is unlikely.

"Because Alex and Rushy and Kuzy are injured. Our performance in the regular season was excellent. The fact that we've gotten *this* far in the playoffs without them is—" Matts stops to breathe. To focus. He won't let his dad derail the conversation into rehashing old arguments he's not prepared for. "That doesn't matter. You were wrong then for telling me to leave. And you're wrong now."

"I'm trying to protect you."

"I don't think you're hearing me. I love her."

His dad falls silent again.

"It doesn't make any sense to me," he says finally. "I don't know how you can—" He sounds helpless. "I don't understand it."

"I'm not asking you to understand," Matts says.

"Then what am I supposed to do with this?"

"Nothing. Just—" Matts's chest is suddenly tight.

"Just try to love me. And maybe try to love Syd too. You shouldn't even have to try that hard because she's—" He clears his throat. "You could try. And you can tell Karl to fuck off."

"Justin."

"I need to go."

"Justin," his dad repeats. "You know I do, right?"

"You do...what?"

"Love you." It's gruff. Unpracticed. Unexpected. Matts exhales. "I do."

"Well. Good luck tonight."

"Thanks, Dad."

He hangs up, uncertain how he's feeling.

Matts decides he doesn't have the emotional bandwidth to interrogate it.

He opens Instagram instead and goes to Sydney's profile.

Her most recent post is a close-up of her leaning into a mic stand toward the end of a concert, hair sweat-tangled around her face, eyeliner smeared. Her eyes are closed, and she's smiling, fierce and sharp around whatever lyrics she's singing. She's gorgeous.

Matts makes the mistake of looking at the comments, but before he can generate any rage about the shit-talking taking place, he realizes that Sydney has already answered several of them.

Like one from a woman who commented a bible verse and said, very passive-aggressively, *I'll pray for you.*

Oh, that's so sweet, Sydney responded. *In that case, I will dance naked under a full moon for you.*

Or the one who commented, *Doesn't matter what lies you tell yourself, your birth certificate will always say you're a boy.*

Sydney answered that one with a confused emoji and, *My birth certificate also says I'm six pounds. Things have changed.*

Or the one from some asshole with a truck as his icon: *Wonder whose dick is bigger, yours or your boyfriend's?*

What an offensive question, she responded. *Have you SEEN Matts? Obviously, him.*

Instead of telling the guy he's a fucking idiot, Matts likes Sydney's response.

And then he forces himself not to moon any longer over his girlfriend—is she his girlfriend? They didn't ever specify; he'd like to specify—because he has a PT appointment and still needs to pick up lunch before his nap. Matts scrolls back up to the picture one last time before shoving his phone in his pocket.

Hockey. He needs to focus on hockey. He can deal

with feelings later.

*

MATTS PLAYS ONE of the best games of his life.

He's on the ice for thirty-six minutes and thirteen seconds, and he pushes hard, as hard as he can, through every single one of them. Through two overtimes. Through twelve face-offs. Eight face-off wins. Six shots on goal. Two goals. One assist. One fight.

He finds lanes. He makes passes. His stick is an extension of his arm, and his skates are solid underneath him, and all he can think about when he's on the bench is his next shift. His next pass. His next goal. It's math and muscle memory. Physicality and fear. Matts uses every bit of his skill, his weight, and his height to dominate. And it works. Every time he comes off the ice, someone pats his helmet or yells compliments at him — for an interception, a breakaway goal, a poke check to a Stars forward that Jeff turns into a goal, a backward between-the-legs pass to Rome for a goal with three seconds left in the power play.

Matts plays one of the best games of his life.

And it's still not enough.

They lose 6–7.

It shouldn't come as a surprise, and it doesn't. Not

really. But hope is a dangerous thing. And he had hope, small and desperate as it was.

When Matts enters the locker room to the tight condolences of Alex and Rushy and Kuzy, wearing their suits and pained half-smiles, he feels like the worst kind of failure.

Maybe he could have done better. Maybe he could have pushed harder. It was just one point—*one* point. Maybe if he didn't lose his edge on that breakaway in the first period, or he won that face-off in the second, or if his pass to Asher were an inch closer in the third. Maybe. Maybe. Maybe.

When Matts walks into the garage, flanked by his equally quiet teammates, he finds Sydney leaning against the driver's side door of his car.

"Hey," Syd says.

He doesn't respond. He can't. She doesn't touch him. Matts wonders if she knows—if she can somehow tell that if she hugs him, he'll start crying, and he doesn't want to do that. Not now. Not here.

"I'm taking you home with me," Sydney says.

Matts needs a moment for the words to compute. "You're flying to California tomorrow morning."

"And I'm taking you home with me *tonight*. No arguments."

He obeys.

And she takes him home.

Sydney drives him in his car, no words, no music. She pulls him down the hall and into her room. He already showered at the arena, but he doesn't fight her when she bullies him into the bathroom, turns on the water, strips him with perfunctory sweetness, dropping occasional kisses to his skin as it's revealed.

The shower isn't big enough for both of them, not really. But there's enough space to stand under the nearly-too-hot spray and for Sydney to wrap herself around his back, hands linked over his belly, forehead pressed between his shoulder blades.

Matts wonders if this is intentional too. If she knew this was the only way he'd be able to cry, with the beat of water on his face to excuse the tears and his back to her so she could feel his shuddered inhales but not see the painful, embarrassing devastation on his face.

It feels ridiculous to be so upset over what is, objectively, just a game. Matts wasn't lying when he told Sydney that hockey wasn't an intrinsic piece of his identity. But his performance, the validation of winning, and the guilt of losing are a part of him, even if he doesn't want them to be.

He tried.

So fucking hard.

Sydney presses wet kisses to his slick skin, humming indistinctly, holding him with zero indication of urgency to be elsewhere until, finally, the tension in his back dissipates. Until he's able to scrub his hands over his face and inhale deep the steam-thick air.

"Hey," Sydney says into his shoulder. "Can you help me with my hair? It got all tangled, and it'll take forever to sort it out by myself."

The request is a relief.

Matts snags a wide-toothed comb from the basket hanging on the showerhead and turns in her slackened arms. She's docile under his direction, letting him push her until their former positions are swapped: her back to his chest. He has to duck a little to start at the ends of her hair and work his way up, careful not to pull too hard. He shampoos her hair while he's at it, because it needs to be done, and he wants to do it. Matts combs through it again before rinsing, then discards the comb when he conditions so he can use his fingers on the now silky, clinging curls. He's careful to cover her eyes when he tips her head back to rinse and digs his fingertips into her scalp to separate the strands, making sure all the product is gone.

"Okay," Matts says finally, wishing there was a step

after conditioning. "I think you're good."

"I'm better than good," Sydney murmurs, leaning into him with a lax drowsiness that he decides is complimentary. "I guess soft hands on the ice translate to haircare as well because that was the gentlest my hair has ever been detangled and probably the most thoroughly it's ever been washed. It was perfect. You're perfect. Thank you."

She's managing him, he realizes, giving him space to feel without scrutiny. Distracting him with a simple, manual task—one he can complete with tangible success within a few minutes. Praising him for completing it well. Filling, just a little, the empty well of failure in his chest.

She knows him.

And it feels good to be known.

*

BY MORNING, THE disappointment has turned into resignation. It still sits like a dirty, shameful thing in his gut, but it's not pressed tight against his throat like it was when he left the stadium the night before. Matts probably has Sydney to thank for that.

She woke him up just past dawn with weirdly endearing headbutts and an invitation to make omelets before she had to leave for the airport. However, his hopes of a slow, quiet morning cooking with her are dashed when they enter the kitchen and find it full of people.

Sydney's parents are at the table with Sky and Paul, Devo is frying something, and Rex is pouring milk into a bowl of cereal.

"Morning, sunshine," Devo says to Syd. "I have news. From your label. I would have told you last night but—" He nods to Matts. "You seemed occupied."

"News," Sydney repeats. She squints at Rex, Sky, and Paul who are all studiously looking at things that are not her. "News which you have clearly already shared with the rest of the class. Okay, then."

Devo winces. "They want to release 'Love You Whole' as a single. I pushed out our departure from LA next week so y'all can have two extra days at the studio."

"Oh," she says. "Fuck."

"What?" Matts doesn't know much about the music industry, but he's pretty sure that dismay, or something close to it, is not the standard artist reaction in a situation like this.

Everyone else in the room looks at him as if they know something he doesn't.

"But I'm still workshopping it," Sydney says, maybe a little desperately. "The lyrics aren't even that good."

"Maybe not," Sky agrees. "But the way you sing them is…"

"Devastating?" Paul supplies blandly. "Heart-wrenching? Poignant to the point of tragedy?"

"That," Sky agrees, pointing at him with her spoon.

"You haven't played that for me, have you?" Matts thought he's heard most of the songs they've been considering for their next album, but that's not a title he recognizes.

"Uh," Sydney says.

"Here." Rex digs his phone out of his pocket. "I've got a recording of it if you—"

"Wait," Sydney says. "Hold on."

"He's going to hear it anyway," Rex points out. "Like, you know, when it's *on the radio*."

"*What* is going on?" Matts asks.

"It's not about you," Sydney says—well, shouts. "The song. It's not about you." The framing of the statement makes it feel distinctly untrue.

"Okay?"

"*Fuck*," she says again, even more fervently.

*

THE SONG IS about him. Maybe.

Syd asked him to wait to listen to it until she and the rest of the band left with a string of slightly desperate qualifiers and reassurances that Matts didn't find reassuring at all.

"Musicians are dramatic assholes," she said. *"I was just having feelings one day, and that was the way I dealt with them. It doesn't mean anything. I swear."*

Except now, he's sitting in the empty kitchen with Devo's phone and borrowed headphones, trying not to cry again because he's already filled his crying quota for the year.

The recording quality isn't great; it's an audio file they created in the practice space. But the raw emotion in Sydney's voice as she sings is palpable, even with the poor acoustics.

The song starts loud, aggressive, a blare of guitars, a veritable stampede of drums, thrumming bass, and shouted lyrics. But the chorus goes plaintive, searching. And by the time it ends—just Sydney and her guitar; no more drums, no more bass—her singing is soft and aching and imperfect. The vocal equivalent of a sob.

Paul was right. It's pretty devastating.

*Where do I keep my love so it won't eat me
alive
Cuz right now it's pressed against my
chest
like a fucking forty-five
I'd hate you if I could,
But that's not something I control
I don't know how to love by halves,
So I'm gonna love you whole*

*Until it kills me, I'll keep calling
If you keep letting me through
Not your fault that you don't love me
The way that I love you
God, I know, I know how this ends
I just don't want it to*

*Why do you touch me like you love me
When you don't
Why do you treat me like you'll keep me
When you won't
My heart's not on my sleeve, it's bloody
in your hands
Don't want your fucking sympathy, just
understand*

Until it kills me, I'll keep calling
If you keep letting me through
Not your fault that you don't love me
The way that I love you
God I know, I know how this ends
I just don't want it to

I'd hate you if I could,
But that's not something I control
I don't know how to love by halves,
So I'm gonna love you whole

Listening to it makes Matts feel like he's swallowed glass. It's like the opposite of catharsis, so many feelings piled up on top of one another with nowhere to go.

The fact that he might have inspired it is—

"You okay?" Devo asks.

He startles and pulls the headphones down around his neck.

"Not really." Matts slides the phone across the table, then shoves the headphones after it.

Devo makes a noise that could mean anything as he collects them to put in his bag.

"She said it wasn't about us," Matts murmurs. "That it was...creative license or whatever. That our situation was just a catalyst."

"Sure," Devo agrees.

Matts exhales. "I'm asking if that's true or not."

"I can't tell you. I'm not in her head, thank God."

"If you had to guess."

Devo scrubs both hands into his hair then drags them back down his face, pressing the heels of his palms into his eyes.

"When Syd was sixteen, she had a thing with this kid at school. He was a year older than her, a year younger than me. Popular, good-looking. Nicer than most of his friends. Decent, you know?" He drops his hands from his face, looking exhausted. "I liked him, before everything."

"Ominous."

"Honestly, I think he might have been a little in love with her. But he didn't want anyone else to know that they were—whatever they were."

"Why?"

Devo gives him a look, and yeah, that's fair.

"He was her first kiss—the stupid dare when she kissed Sky doesn't count in my book. But for months, through the summer and into her junior year, they'd meet up outside school. When they were alone, he treated her right, but he wouldn't so much as look at her in the hallways. Didn't even intervene when one of his friends fucking assaulted her one day. After that, she ended things."

"What was this kid's name?" Matts asks.

"No," Devo says.

It was worth a try.

"Point is," Devo continues, "she was pissed, but she wasn't broken-hearted. Because she went into it cautious. She knew from the beginning he was keeping her a secret."

Matts thinks about sixteen-year-old Syd who already had to learn caution rather than falling head-first into love like teenagers are supposed to. He thinks about why.

"People can't hurt you if you don't give them the opportunity to," Matts says. It's a familiar philosophy.

"Right. Exactly. And it doesn't help that our biological parents had already fucked her up about being a thing that had to be hidden, you know? Before she ran away, they'd started leaving her at home when we went to church or out to eat. But *after* she ran away, they didn't fight for her at all. Which was good for Syd, obviously. But they just— A week after she left, all the pictures of her on the walls were gone. They never once asked to speak to her on the phone or asked me how she was. It was like she didn't exist to them anymore."

There are multiple people Matts would like to have a private conversation with.

"I need you to recognize," Devo says quietly, "Syd's had too much experience with a very specific kind of—I don't even know what to call it—subtle cruelty? Maybe? And listen, you're not like that. You're not keeping her a secret. That's good. But this also isn't like the Bryce situation."

"So his name was Bryce," Matts says.

"Can you focus?"

"Sorry. Why is it not like the Bryce situation?"

"You can't be this stupid," Devo says. "Because she didn't let herself fall in love with *him*."

Matts might forget to breathe. Just for a minute.

"Oh," Devo says, studying Matts's face. "Okay, you are this stupid."

"Hey," he objects, and then, just to be sure, "She loves me?"

Devo makes a strangled noise. "Of course she fucking— Did you *listen* to the song?"

"I—"

"Look, anyone can see that you're just as crazy about her as she is about you. Except her. Maybe it's the trauma or whatever. Maybe it's something else, but I'm pretty sure the pining songs are going to continue unless you give her some explicit reassurance that you're in just as deep as she is."

"She hasn't said anything," Matts argues. "She didn't— *I* was the one that asked if we were even together."

"And she won't. She's going to be all skulls and crossbones on the outside, but on the inside, she wants that Jane Austen shit. She wants shouted declarations in the rain and grand public gestures, and—she wants to be wanted. Loudly. Visibly."

"I can do that," Matts says. "Are you sure she wants that from *me* though?"

"Dude," Devo says.

"I can do that," he repeats.

She wants that Jane Austen shit, he thinks.

"I have an idea," Matts says. "But I'll need the band's help."

Devo considers him for several seconds, lips pursed. "Grand public gesture?" he hazards.

"Grand public gesture," Matts agrees.

"Are you sure you're ready for that? There's no taking it back. And you've only been together for what, a couple months?"

Matts just looks at him.

"I'll add us to a group chat without Syd." Devo sighs. "No promises they'll be down, but you can ask."

Matts nods. He shakes Devo's hand because it seems like the thing to do.

As Matts walks to his car, he pulls up Rome's contact information.

"Hey," Rome answers. "Why are you calling me like a sociopath? Just text me."

Matts ignores him. "Is Damien there?"

Rome is stymied enough that it takes him several seconds to answer. "He is. Why do you want to talk to my boyfriend?"

Matts exhales. "I need his help writing a song."

Chapter Eighteen

WHEN SHE WAS fourteen, Sydney learned how to sew.

It was to make her first of many battle jackets.

She agonized over patches, band logos, and set lists cut out of secondhand tour shirts. She spent hours comparing thread colors and learning different stitch patterns and then many more hours constructing it.

After a summer of work, the denim vest was a riot of color and logos, song titles and lyrics, glimmering with buttons and paint and enamel pins—a loud and undeniable encapsulation of *her*. She loved it. And she refused to take it off for months afterward.

It was that summer that Sydney realized how

customizable clothes could be. For a while, every piece of fabric in her closet had seen her scissors, her needles, or both.

Now, she's not quite so insistent about personalization, at least not day-to-day. But when they're on tour, she winds down in her bunk by embroidering little skulls on the cuffs of her jeans or sewing floral patches on the elbows of her jackets or adding colors to the buttonholes of her coats.

Tonight, though, Sydney has Matts's Hell Hounds jersey spread out on the bed. Red and black backgrounds a white tape name and number.

She holds fabric scissors in one hand, her sewing kit in the other, paralyzed with indecision when Devo slides past her on his way to his own bunk.

"You all right?" he asks.

"Am I ever?"

"Rephrase," he agrees. "Is there a reason you're standing in the middle of the bus holding scissors like a serial killer?"

"I'm thinking about making a statement. During the second Nashville concert. When Matts is there."

"*Are* you." He's looking at her like he knows something she doesn't.

Then again, that's his default expression most of the

time because he's an infuriating older brother, and he usually thinks he knows more than her even when he doesn't.

"A wearing-his-jersey-on-stage kind of statement?" Devo clarifies.

"I mean, not the way it is. I want to give it some pizzazz first."

"If your fans knew you used the word 'pizzazz,' they'd think you were a lot less cool."

"I probably *am* a lot less cool than they think."

"Well, it's not as funny if you admit it," he grouses, pulling himself up into his bunk. "What are you doing to the jersey?"

"I'm not sure. I'll cut off the sleeves, obviously. Maybe do pins down the sides." She reaches out to touch the *M* of the Matthews. "Gotta keep the name intact though."

"Well, yeah, obviously. Does Matts know you're planning to make a statement?"

"No. But I think it'll be a good surprise. Maybe. He's been tagging me in things. And he's said he's fine being public. He's not—"

She's thinking about Bryce.

Judging by Devo's face, so is he.

They don't talk about Bryce though. Not since the

day that Sydney came home with tear-swollen eyes, and a few hours later, Devo came home with punch-swollen knuckles.

"Anyway," she says. "I think he'll like it."

"He'll like it. He'll be insufferable about it. Which— can I just say how annoying it is, trying to be friends with someone who's grossly in love with you? Because it's annoying. *Very* annoying."

"He's not in love with me," Sydney mutters. "I'm not even sure if he's my boyfriend."

"Here's a novel idea," Devo says. "*Ask* him."

"Pass."

He taps his phone against the wall next to his bunk. "No. Here, we can act it out for you." He raises his voice. "Sky! Come be Matts for a second."

Sky, at the front of the bus, arguing with Paul over the Scrabble game they've been playing, vaults over the back of the couch and into the sleeping area.

"Hi," she says. "I'm a brick shithouse of a man with weird hair, an incredibly symmetrical face, and an ass that won't quit. What can I do for you?"

"Hi, Matts," Devo says. "I'm Sydney. Do you want to be my boyfriend?"

"That would bring me the utmost joy," she says seriously. "Like equal or greater joy to winning the

Stanley Cup. Probably greater."

"You're insufferable," Sydney tells them. "Go away. I want to call the real Matts."

Sky bows as she exits, and Devo rolls his eyes, pulling the little curtains around his bunk closed.

Sydney sets the sewing kit and scissors aside, climbs into her bunk, and pulls her own curtains closed. She traces the white *Matthews* tape as the FaceTime call rings.

"Sydney!" Eli says when the line connects. "Matts is in the bathroom; he'll be right back."

Sydney squints against the reading light reflecting off her phone screen. Eli has a green-toned rice paper mask on his face. "Do you have him doing *skincare*?"

"I've got Alex regularly using moisturizer, and Kuzy is moisturizing *and* using a vitamin C serum. I figured it was time to start working on Matts. He's just had his first-ever facial and only complained a little. He's picky about smells, so we had to find some unscented products, but now that we have, he's glowing like—I don't know. My head hurts. Something that glows."

"The sun?"

"The *sun*. Yes."

"Well, you have my thanks."

"You know, I asked him how he washed his face,

and he answered—"

"—with his body wash," Sydney finishes. "Because his face is part of his body. We've had the same conversation. But hey, at least he uses sunscreen."

"There is that. How are you? How's the band? The family. The"—Eli shudders dramatically—"horses."

"I'm excellent; the band is good. Paul has settled into tour life like the pro he is, and my parents are healthy enough. Also, I still don't understand how you kiss goats on the mouth but have an issue with horses."

"That's because goats are bouncy puppies with hooves, and horses are freaks of nature who can see ghosts. *Your* horse, in particular, looked like he wanted to eat me the whole time I was in that barn."

"Horses are herbivores," Sydney points out.

"Then why was it looking at me like it wanted to *eat* me?"

"Anyway. The horses are good too."

"How nice," Eli says in a way that seems to mean the opposite. "Oh, hey, lover boy. Your girl called."

"Sydney?" Matts says, taking the phone from Eli. "Are you okay?"

"Totally fine. I just wanted to see your pretty face."

And ask if I'm your girlfriend, she doesn't say. She'll get to that. Eventually.

Matts wrinkles his nose.

"What?"

"I'm handsome, sure, but no one in their right mind would call me pretty."

"Ah, that's probably it, then," Syd says wisely.

"What?"

"I'm not in my right mind. As at least two psychologists can attest. But I do think you're pretty."

He grins at her, soft and familiar, as he takes her into the guest bedroom and closes the door. "Why are you like this?"

"Worry about your own issues. You're the one that wants to sleep with me. How embarrassing."

His face goes serious. "Hey, no. That's not funny. Don't say self-deprecating shit like that. No one gets to talk bad about my girlfriend, not even my girlfriend."

Well, Syd thinks. *That was easy.*

"Girlfriend, huh?" She's aiming for suave. It comes out far more giggly than she would prefer.

"If that's cool," Matts says stoically.

"It's very cool. The coolest."

"Good."

"Good." She clears her throat. "Anyway."

Sydney still doesn't know how they got here. How they went from an awkward party encounter to daily phone calls and flights marked on calendars and words like "girlfriend." It doesn't feel real, even though it must be.

She's started dropping random observations about herself into conversation. Not because she's afraid she's going to scare him off, exactly, but if she is, she'd rather do it sooner than later.

Tonight, what comes out of her mouth is: "You know I can't have kids, right?"

"Yeah?" Matts says, ignoring the abruptness of the subject change. "The whole...not having a uterus kinda clued me into that."

"Points for using correct anatomical language." She yawns. "Just checking. I was talking to someone this morning who thought being on HRT made me grow one."

"That's—wow. Okay."

Sydney laughs along at the incredulity in his voice but then sobers. "Even if I could, I'm not sure I'd want to."

"Even if you could grow a uterus?"

"No. I definitely don't want a uterus. From what I've heard, they cause a lot of problems. I mean, I don't think I'd want to have kids. I could maybe be talked into adopting, but like...that's a *strong* maybe."

Matts is quiet for a moment, and the worry starts to claw its way up her throat before he says, soft and careful, "I wouldn't."

"What?"

"Not to make assumptions or anything, but if I were the hypothetical person in this scenario, talking you into adopting, I...wouldn't want to talk you into it."

"Oh." The relief is palpable. "Okay. So, no interest in kids, then?"

"None. At all."

"Well. Good."

"Good."

There's noise in the background, and Matts turns to face the door before looking back down at her. "Hey, Alex just got home with dinner. Can I call you later? I've got some exemplary cursed knowledge for you."

"I can't wait."

"I miss you," he says because he's braver than her.

"Two more weeks," she says.

"Thirteen days," he corrects.

"Thirteen days," she agrees.

*

WHEN SYDNEY GETS dressed for the Nashville concert, she takes her time. Leather pants, shitkicker boots, the jersey—cut and stitched and ironed. She chooses necklaces at random from the tangle that sits in her travel box, six standard rings, the bracelet she never takes off. She rubs coconut oil down her neck and arms and the exposed parts of her ribs to make her tattoos dark and her skin shine. Sydney lets Sky paint her face with gold on the crests of her cheekbones and eyelids, black wings of eyeliner, and gloss on her lips.

She looks good. She feels good.

The opener is wrapping up their set when Devo sticks his head in the green room and says, "Special delivery for Syd, but also, you're on in five, so don't get distracted."

It's Matts.

She knew he was here. He sent her a series of selfies from the plane, sitting next to a mom with a toddler. He let said toddler carefully place stickers all down one arm to keep the kid occupied while her exhausted mom took a nap.

> *Still don't want kids,* he texted her. *To be clear. But they're not terrible in short doses. Also, look at these kickass dinosaur stickers. They have feathers!*

He's not wearing dinosaur stickers anymore though. What Matts wears is...black. Head to toe. A too-big T-shirt with the sleeves cut off, skinny jeans ripped down the thighs to his knees, and thick-soled lace-up boots. His nails are painted black too. Her ring is in its now-customary place on his pinky. It takes Sydney a second to return her attention to his face because it gets caught first on the ring and then the tendons in the back of his hand and then his tanned forearms and the one vein in his bicep that's pressed close enough to the surface of his skin to be visible, like a faded blue watercolor stroke. Eventually, Syd does look at his face again, at the fresh-shaved sides of his hair and the curls falling in his eyes and— Is he wearing *eyeliner*?

"Holy shit," she says.

They stare at each other for a moment, and she remembers she's also wearing something unexpected.

"Jesus," he says, taking a faltering step forward. "Is that my jersey?"

Sydney does a little spin for him. "It *was* your jersey. I improved it. Do you like it?"

"I do. Are you...wearing that on stage?"

"That was the plan." Sydney doesn't want to ask, but she's run out of bravery at the moment. "Is that okay?"

"Yes," he says, and it sounds a little strangled. "Please."

She grins. Stupid and in love and feeling okay about it. "What about you! You look like you belong on stage with us." She closes the space between them so she can press her hands to his chest, go up on her toes, and say, lowering her voice conspiratorially, "Are you trying to seduce me?"

"Is it working?" he whispers back.

"I mean, yeah."

"Okay, that's enough," Devo calls. "Let's go."

"Duty calls," she says.

Matts salutes her seriously, and she salutes him back as Sky grabs her arm and pulls her away.

Sydney can tell it's going to be a good concert as she runs out onto the stage, waving. As the lights flare, and the hum of speakers and the whir of smoke machines drown out her racing heartbeat. As the crowd screams and screams and screams.

There are some concerts that are magic. When everything comes together just as it should. No technical difficulties, no mistakes, no stress, only a shared euphoria because they're here, together, and they've come so far, and they're *here*.

This is one of those nights. Sydney's overflowing with a bursting tension she can't explain. It's as if her blood is full of the music she's playing. There's something inside her she's barely restraining, but she can channel it through her hands and her fingers and her voice. And rather than destroying her or obliterating her completely, the thing inside her casts a spell on the audience. Suddenly, the thousands of people in the undulating mass can understand her, can *feel* her. It's nights like these she wants to bottle, keep on a shelf, and take down when she's older, when she can't stalk and prance and shout anymore, but the tension is still there inside her, still trying to find a way out.

If memories are all she'll have one day, she'll make them good. So, Sydney revels in the lights and the smoke and the unbridled fervor of the audience. With Matts's jersey on her back and his eyes on her, she throws her entire body into the music and sings like God might be listening.

And it's magic.

They're coming to the end of the set, only two songs and the encore left, when Sydney crouches to grab one of the water bottles littered across the stage. Rex pulls his mic off the stand and wanders toward the front, and she falls back into a sit, taking a drink, waiting for Rex to start his spiel about how honored they are to be here and what a great crowd the audience has been.

Except he doesn't. Instead, he says, "We have a

special guest tonight."

That's news to Sydney.

She pauses mid-drink to look at Sky, then Paul.

They're both grinning at her, assholes.

"And the reason Syd looks so stupid right now is because we've been keeping it a secret from her," Rex continues.

Sydney is so completely lost. She flips him off for appearances though.

The audience enjoys this.

"So," Rex says. "We're going to ask Sydney to sit this next song out. And we'd like your assistance in welcoming to the stage—Justin Matthews, center for the Houston Hell Hounds and, at least for the next five minutes, our interim lead singer and guitarist."

And then Matts walks out to raucous cheers.

He's got his guitar slung around his back and earpieces around his neck, and he's carrying a chair that he sets a few feet away from Sydney before offering her a hand.

She lets him pull her to her feet. Slowly.

"What the fuck is happening right now?" Sydney asks.

But Matts isn't looking at her. He's looking at the crowd, clearly nervous and trying to hide it, as he pulls her forward to sit and then stands behind her for a moment, hands on her shoulders, squeezing. He ducks to kiss the side of her head. Once. Twice.

"Please don't kill me for this," he says, barely audible over the anticipatory screams of the audience.

He squeezes her shoulders one last time, and then he approaches her abandoned mic stand and pauses to extend it because he's a giant.

"Hi." Matts shades his eyes with one hand. "Holy shit, the lights really are blinding. So. Hi." He waves in the general direction of the audience and gets a louder cheer in response. "I'm Matts. And Syd didn't know about this, but the band was cool enough to help me out with a surprise for her. And, uh, the surprise is that I wrote a song for Sydney."

Her heart might stop. Just for a minute. But then it starts right back up again, double-time, because she needs to stay *alive* for whatever the hell is about to happen.

Matts glances at her, then immediately away again.

"I wrote the music, but I had some help from Damien Bordeaux with the lyrics. He's a poet; he's great. But, yeah, I wrote a song for Sydney. And I'm going to steal five minutes of your concert to try and make a grand romantic gesture—if that's cool with you guys?"

Judging by the roar it produces, the audience thinks this is a very cool plan, indeed.

So does Sydney.

Rex comes up behind Matts to help him get his guitar plugged in to the house while he keeps talking. Rex winks at her from behind Matts's back.

"All right," Matts is saying, laughing a little at the crowd's exuberance. "Thanks. So, this is for Sydney. Obviously. But I'm going to sing it to y'all. Because I think if I look at her, I won't be able to do this. Okay? Okay."

He slips in his earpieces, looks to each of the band members, skipping over Sydney in her chair entirely, before playing a quick scale.

He steps back, then pauses, leaning into the mic again. "Sorry. It's called 'Eurydice.' So. Here we go."

He nods to Paul.

And they begin.

The spotlights fan away from the stage, out across the audience, up and away. Darkness settles save the green-blue backlight behind Sky and her drums, and the arena goes eerily quiet. Waiting.

The fog machines start up, and the two guitars take their sweet time building a slow, wailing riff together as the smoke coalesces around Matts's feet, as he shifts to butt his lips against the mic cage, as he exhales, long and slow, like it's a lyric.

Finally, he sings:

> *You act like you don't know*
> *That I wage a holy war*
> *Watching you sleep in my bed,*
> *Leaving your jeans on my floor*
>
> *How do I prove to you*
> *I'm not what I was before*
> *When all my words are crossed out lines*
> *scattered on the floor*
>
> *See, if I loved you less,*
> *I could talk about it more*
> *But I don't, and I can't,*
> *But I'll try this once to implore*

Rex slams into the song at the same time Sky enters with a clash of cymbals, and Matts abandons his guitar to hold the mic stand with both hands, eyes closed, voice rough and deep and perfectly imperfect as he ramps into a shout at the chorus:

Eurydice, please,
I'll get down on my fucking knees
I don't want you
I need you
Oh God,
don't leave me to drown
If you're going to hell,
Take me with you
Or I'll follow you down

He starts the next verse—something about desperation, something about being consumed—and she watches his fingers, his hands, his throat, his mouth. The feral way he's got his legs braced and his chest curved and his guitar resting on his thigh. Sydney wants to look at all of him at once, but she can't because too much is happening, and it's—it's too perfect. She wants to slow time down, to rewind and start over from the moment he walked on stage, to replay the way his breath hitches and his mouth curls in a beautiful grimace around lyrics he wrote for her. *About* her. She wants to live right here, sitting in this metal chair, forever, maybe.

And then Matts is coming off the second chorus with a rough hum, an exhale, cutting his eyes to look at her for the first time—dark and serious and more than a little wild.

She's dreaming. Or hallucinating. Or maybe she's dying. Maybe there was some freak accident during mic check, and a piece of scaffolding fell on her head, and she's in the back of an ambulance right now while the last of her remaining neurons paint a pretty fantasy for her while she gasps her final breaths.

Paul digs into a guitar solo as Matts shoves hair out of his face, then resets his hands on the strings. He reenters with both his guitar and a wordless croon, drifting up and then down into the next (final? She hopes it isn't final) verse:

> *Half agony half hope*
> *I've loved none but you*
> *I won't look back, but I'll beg*
> *because begging's what you're due*
> *Tell me what you want, tell me what to*
> *say*
> *Look what you've done to me*
> *I wouldn't have it any other way*

Matts slings his guitar to his back and wrenches the mic off the stand, then stalks to where she's sitting, and then—

Then he *kneels*.

Right in front of her. He sits back on the heels of his boots. He looks up at her.

> *Eurydice, please,*
> *I'm down on my fucking knees*
> *I don't want you*
> *I need you*
> *Oh God,*
> *don't leave me to drown*
> *If you're going to hell,*
> *Take me with you*
> *Or I'll follow you down*

And the rest of the band is wrapping up the song—Paul is doing some truly impressive work, she's pretty sure, and Sky is wailing on the drums. But Matts is on his knees in front of her in a stadium full of thousands of people, and he's breathing hard, and he's *looking* at her.

It feels like déjà vu when she stands and closes the scant space between them:

Her fingers on his face, her rings against his heated skin, there's something close to desperation in his eyes as she rubs her thumb over his bottom lip.

The crowd is in an absolute uproar even before she kneels with him, even before she tips her head and pushes forward into him, slow, inevitable, to brush their mouths together, even before his hands come up to frame her face, to pull them closer, to cling.

But after, the crowd gets even louder.

Epilogue

ONE OF THE perks of being a professional athlete is that Matts has a good portion of the summer to spend doing whatever the hell he wants. If he keeps up with his workouts and gets regular ice time, it doesn't matter where he is. Which means he can go on tour with his girlfriend.

When Matts officially joined them, Devo ceremonially presented him with a shirt that says SECURITY on it, front and back. He thinks it was supposed to be a joke, but Matts doesn't take it that way. Instead, he wears it to every concert, trailing Sydney through meetings with VIP pass holders and lurking in the background of press events and interviews.

Mostly, he sticks to the shadows and comes to loom if someone gets too handsy. It's fun. No speaking required, just glaring and flexing. He thinks when he retires from hockey, he'll find a lot of personal fulfillment in being Sydney's full-time bodyguard.

They're backstage in Indianapolis, and the last of the VIP passes are milling around with various band members. Matts is scrolling through Uber Eats options on his phone because Sydney definitely has not eaten enough, when he notices her posture change in his peripheral vision.

She's signing the record sleeve of Red Right Hand's first album for a pair of twenty-something women, but her eyes are on the man behind them, and her smile is forced.

Matts pockets his phone and steps a little closer.

When the women move away, whispering excitedly as they cling to each other, Sydney caps the pen in her hands and crosses her arms. Her eyes are hooded. Her jaw is clenched.

The guy looks nondescript, if handsome. Tall. Athletic build. Sandy hair. He's wearing a tour shirt and an awkward smile. His hands are empty.

"Sydney," the guy says. "Hi."

"Bryce," she says evenly. "Hi."

And Matts goes very, very still. Before moving closer.

"Bryce," Matts repeats, just to make sure.

Sydney and Bryce both seem surprised by that.

Sydney's eyes narrow. "I'm going to kill Devo," she mutters.

"Yeah, that's me," Bryce says. "Sorry, do I know you?"

"Justin Matthews." Matts doesn't extend his hand. "Sydney's boyfriend."

"Oh," Bryce says, glancing between them.

His eyes, inevitably, linger on Sydney. And Matts may not be able to read most facial expressions, but he recognizes this one. Matts knows he wears it himself — desire, pure and simple. It doesn't make him want to punch Bryce any less. Rather the opposite.

"Listen, Sydney," Bryce says, "I hoped I could talk to you. Apologize to you, mostly, but—"

"What *the fuck* are you doing here," Devo says, suddenly appearing beside Matts.

"Devo, hi," Bryce says, wincing. "I was just—"

"Leaving?"

"Hey," Sydney interrupts, "enough. I'm due an apology, and he says he has one. I'll hear it."

Devo raises his eyebrows, glancing at Matts. Matts isn't sure if it's in solidarity or to see if Matts is planning to punch Bryce in the face. To be fair, Matts isn't sure himself. He's still leaving it as an option. Depending.

"Okay, as much as I appreciate the protective looming," Sydney says to Matts and Devo, "can you two take a couple of steps back?"

Matts takes two steps exactly. Small ones. Judging by the minuscule amount Devo moves, he seems equally invested in doing the bare minimum to comply with her demands.

Sydney glances between them, rolls her eyes, but doesn't say anything.

"All right," she says to Bryce, who is looking more and more punchable by the second. "Go ahead."

"I'm sorry," he repeats. "I'm so sorry. I was—I cared too much about what other people thought, and I never should have treated you the way I did. And that day—" He swallows hard. "When Jack—"

He stalls out. Sydney doesn't rescue him.

"When Jack hurt you," Bryce continues, "I should have stopped him."

Jack, Matts remembers. Just in case.

"You should have," she agrees.

Bryce gazes at her now with sadness and regret.

Matts doesn't empathize with him, not exactly. But he's also uncomfortably aware that he could have been standing there himself, asking forgiveness for the biggest mistake he ever made if he'd been in Bryce's shoes and met Sydney just a few years earlier. Matts is suddenly, intensely, grateful for Eli and Alex, for Jeff and Rushy and Rome. For his past self's willingness to *listen* to them. To grow into the happiness that was waiting for him.

"Anyway," Bryce says. "I'm glad everything worked out for you. For the band. I knew from the start you guys were something special, and the fact that you're here now is just—it's cool. And I'm sorry I didn't—that I wasn't brave enough to stick around with you to be there as it happened. I'm—sorry." He exhales, clearly out of words. "I'm just sorry."

"You're forgiven," Sydney says. Like it's true. Like it's easy. "Thank you, for making the effort to apologize. I have good memories of us, you know? Now that you've apologized, and I can see you mean it, it'll be easier for me to think about the good times again. So, thank you."

Bryce looks like he wants to touch her, and Matts isn't sure what he'll do if he tries.

"That's—good." His fingers curl at his sides. "I appreciate that. I'll, um, I'll let you get back to it. Thanks for hearing me out."

"Hey, Bryce," she says. "Hug for old times' sake?"

As if he'd turn that down.

When Sydney steps into him, Bryce's hands are careful around her back, as they should be.

He inhales, face tucked close to her hair, and Matts grits his teeth until Sydney pulls away again.

When Bryce leaves, Matts follows. Sydney doesn't stop him, but Matts can feel her watching.

Bryce turns to face him, wary, once they're out of earshot. "What?"

"You," Matts says lowly, "are the stupidest fucking person I've ever met."

"I know," Bryce says. "Jesus, you think I don't know that? I was just—"

"A coward," Matts supplies.

Bryce swallows. "I know," he repeats. "I really am sorry."

"Be better," Matts says because that's all he can think of on short notice. And then he turns away from him and stalks back over to Sydney.

"Can I kiss you?" he asks. "Not because I'm a possessive asshole, but because you deserved better than that shithead, and also because I might be a little bit of a possessive asshole."

She smiles softly at him. "Both reasons are accepta-ble."

Matts kisses her. Thoroughly.

"What did you say to him?" Sydney asks when he sets her back on her feet.

"I told him he was the stupidest person I've ever met," Matts answers.

"Why?"

"Because I want to tell anyone who'll listen that you're mine. He didn't when he had the chance. And that's…stupid."

She goes up on her toes to kiss him again.

And again.

And again.

*

MATTS'S PHONE RINGS an hour later as they're walk-ing into their hotel lobby, and he braces himself because late night calls from Aaron aren't historically good news.

"Please tell me," Aaron says, "that this isn't you."

"What?" Matts asks.

"Red Right Hand's new album. Track three. 'Devo-tee.' With the stupid sex noises in the background."

Matts had been waiting for this call ever since the

song was recorded. The chorus includes a low, hitched inhale, a breathy exhale, sampled, layered, repeated, while Sydney sings on top of it about a lover, down on their knees, worshiping the object of their affection.

Matts coughs, trying to stifle his laughter.

"Please tell me," Aaron insists, "that my girlfriend's current favorite song on *your* girlfriend's newly released album, doesn't include *you*—"

Matts can't suppress the laughter anymore.

"Oh, you motherfucker," Aaron hisses. "That's just...indecent. How did you even—no. I don't want to know."

"She brought me to the recording studio. Just me and her in the booth."

"I said I didn't want to know."

"If it makes you feel better, they aren't sex noises. They're foreplay noises at best."

"I hate you."

"Yeah, okay," Matts says. "Guess I'll return the new saddle I got you for Christmas, then."

"I hate you less. Wait. Are you coming for Christmas?"

"The week before, technically, since I have a game right after Christmas Day. But yeah. Dad invited us. Yesterday, actually."

"Us," Aaron repeats.

"Us. Me *and* Sydney. By name. Extremely awkwardly. But he'd already checked to make sure her tour was finished by then and everything. He's trying."

"Well," Aaron says after several seconds of contemplative silence. "He probably got my mom to check because, as far as I know, he's still shit at computers, but that's something."

"It was me," Ellie yells from somewhere in the background. "He asked me to print out Red Right Hand's tour schedule for him, and he's got it hanging next to Matts's game schedule above his dresser now."

"Yeah," Matts agrees, swallowing around the sudden heat in his throat. "That's something."

"You seem, uh…" Aaron pauses, whispers something to Ellie before starting again. "Are you happy? Because you seem a lot happier now."

Matts looks at Sydney, draped over Sky's back, pretending to fall asleep while they wait for the elevator. She glances at him, just to check in, to make sure he's okay. She winks exaggeratedly. And then sticks her leg out to trip Devo.

He winks back while Devo pulls her, protesting loudly, into a noogie.

"I am," Matts says. "I really, really am."

Acknowledgements

A heap of thanks to my OG betas/sensitivity readers: Camila G-N, Savannah, Trent, Guy, and Claire. To my editor, who deftly handled all the em dashes, run-on sentences, and my inexplicable need to have characters "rock back on [their] heels" every other scene—the passive voice reference was for you, E. ☺ To my eternal writing cheerleaders: Chelsea, Ishita, and David. To B, the best partner an anxiety-ridden author could have. To my parents and Uncle R and Deacon (still the best dog in the world). To the climbing crew that reminds me to socialize with IRL people (and assists with bike heists, when necessary). And to Every Single online friend, IG, and BookTok reviewer, and A03 commenter who has encouraged me to keep writing my silly idealistic stories, whether fic or fiction. Thanks. I love you. Stay hydrated.

Finally, a shoutout to the Gayborhood in Dallas and the folks that make it magical. It's a real place! I lived there in grad school, and that community was entirely responsible for my being brave enough to slap a "y'all means all" sign on my office door and start openly identifying as queer to my friends, peers, and students. The

Resource Center does fantastic work, and I highly recommend checking out Gaybingo.

About the Author

E. L. Massey is a human. Probably. She lives in Denver, Colorado, with her partner, the best dog in the world (an unbiased assessment), and a frankly excessive collection of books. She spends her holidays climbing mountains and writing fan fiction, occasionally at the same time.

Email

elmasseywrites@gmail.com

Website

www.elmassey.substack.com

Instagram

www.Instagram.com/el_massey

Tumblr

www.xiaq.tumblr.com

Other NineStar books by this author

The Breakaway Series

Like Real People Do
Like You've Nothing Left to Prove
All Hail the Underdogs

Connect with NineStar Press

Website: NineStarPress.com

Facebook: NineStarPress

X: @ninestarpress

Instagram: NineStarPress

BlueSky: NineStarPress

Threads: @ninestarpress

www.ingramcontent.com/pod-product-compliance
Lightning Source LLC
LaVergne TN
LVHW010200020425
807511LV00034B/1178